P9-CCR-473

INCENSED

ALSO BY ED LIN

Ghost Month

INCENSED

ED LIN

Published by Soho Press, Inc.
853 Broadway
New York, NY 10003

Library of Congress Cataloging-in-Publication Data

Lin, Ed.
Incensed / Ed Lin.

ISBN 978-1-61695-733-9
eISBN 978-1-61695-734-6

1. Street vendors—Taiwan—Taipei—Fiction. 2. Teenage girls—Taiwan—Fiction. 3. Taipei (Taiwan)—Fiction. I. Title
PS3562.I4677 I53 2016 813'.54—dc23 016011152

Interior design by Janine Agro, Soho Press, Inc.

Printed in the United States of America

10 9 8 7 6 5 4 3 2 1

For Walter

The Perfect Man of ancient times made sure that he had it in himself before he tried to give it to others. When you're not even sure what you've got in yourself, how do you have the time to bother about what some tyrant is doing?

—ZHUANGZI (369?–286? BCE)

INCENSED

I DON'T CARE HOW much you hate your family; there are certain things that you just don't do, and you certainly don't do them during the goddamned Mid-Autumn Festival—the one time of the year where you're all supposed to pretend to love each other.

Number one, you don't lie to your family. If you don't want to say something that you know will upset them, just don't say anything. As a general rule, eat more, say less.

Number two, show gratefulness for the things your family does for you. Even if it doesn't help you all that much, when, say, your cousin tries to give you advice about your music career, say thank you and try to do something nice in return, like leaving halfway-decent clues about your whereabouts when you run away with your gangster boyfriend.

Speaking of which, number three, don't run away with your gangster boyfriend, especially when you're only sixteen and your father—my uncle—is one of the most powerful figures in the underworld of central Taiwan. He'll come after you hard.

I'm a twenty-five-year-old man, so I know these things full well. I was raised properly and I am humble at my core. My little cousin Mei-ling, however, is of the younger generation of Taiwanese. She's stubborn and ready to fight for what she believes in. She is also very cute. These are all qualities that a future singing star needs in order to make it, but they can also hurt your family, put your life in danger, and kill the people who fall in love with you.

And the Mid-Autumn Festival is supposed to be about living, not dying.

I will remember this particular holiday because it was the first time I celebrated it with my girlfriend, Nancy—a solidifying moment in our relationship. It was also the first time in a long time that I reconnected with my uncle, who last I heard had been in self-imposed exile. It was also the first and possibly last time I would see my darling little cousin Mei-ling, unless she pops up in the tabloid news.

I will sometimes wonder if I would have been better off not getting back in touch with my uncle and living the rest of my life thinking that I had no family left.

When the full moon rises, I'll put on one of Mei-ling's songs. I'll think about her, feel wistfully sad and then deeply ashamed that I couldn't do more for her. I have to believe that she is in a better place.

CHAPTER ONE

If you want to get hustled good and proper in Taipei, try to buy some freshly cut fruit at the Shilin Night Market.

The vendors are fluent in several languages when they're giving you the hard sell, poking at your face with toothpicked samples of creamy cherimoya and pretty-but-bland-tasting star fruit, but once you agree to buy something, they start filling up your bag with every fruit in stock and suddenly don't understand when you say "stop." Ask for half a kilogram of some bell-shaped wax apples and they'll cut up a whole kilogram, bag it, and then grab two dragon fruit, dice them up and drop them in as well. After giving the bag a token sweep on a tipsy scale, showing a weight of more than four kilograms, you'll be asked to pay 400 New Taiwan dollars for a bundle of stuff you mostly didn't want.

In the scheme of things, you, being a tourist, may not think that thirteen American dollars is a lot to pay for a fairly heavy bag of exotic fruit. As you stab into a sticky cube with your bamboo skewer and pop it into your mouth, maybe it will taste sweet. Maybe the dragon fruit hasn't been sprayed with saccharin. Maybe the wax apple hasn't been dipped in formaldehyde to preserve its pale flesh. But even if your lychee were lopped from a tree this morning and trucked in from a farm this afternoon, the wholesale price of fruit is less than a fifth of what they charge tourists—and that's when they're honest.

A few years back a group of Singaporeans sued Taiwan's tourism bureau after one stand charged them three times the normal price for atemoya, a grenade-shaped hybrid of the sugar apple and the cherimoya whose flavor explodes in the mouth with the taste of a slightly tart piña colada. The Singaporeans weren't aware they'd been overcharged until one of them just had to have another and went to the one honest fruit seller in Shilin Market. When the tourist saw how much cheaper it was, the atemoya hit the fan.

Now all the fruit stands have posted prices and digital scales. It's a new level of transparency that is nonetheless still subject to some old tricks—for example, the piling on of extra fruit you didn't order, or the concealed thumb under the bag on the scale.

I'd let a pickpocket get closer to me than a fruit vendor. Which is why I kept my eyes peeled and my hand on my wallet as I saw one of the latter making her way toward us.

Nancy and I were hemmed in by the rest of the crowd, so that offered a measure of protection. All of us were gathered in an open area to watch an eating contest, and Nancy and I were here in particular to see our friend Dwayne take on the competition. A Taiwan crowd is respectful of personal space, so there was enough room for the big American cameras to maneuver through the spectators.

Unfortunately, that also left enough room for the fruit vendor to wend her way over to us. Nancy and I happened to be standing next to a film crew that was shooting "B-roll," footage that would run beneath stats and sponsor logos, as they explained to us. It was the Americans the fruit vendor was after, not us. I could practically hear the woman panting as she drew closer.

I shifted my feet so that my body shielded Nancy from the inevitable fruit pitches.

"Fresh, fresh!" she yelled in English at the Americans. She was dressed in traditional farmer garb, a brightly colored short-sleeved blouse over a long-sleeved one of a different pattern. The outfit lent an aura of authenticity and nearly compensated for the craftiness in her eyes as she sized up the men. Who to hit up first? The white man dressed like a biker wearing a fisherman's vest and brandishing the boom mic? The balding black man who had just finished laying down the steel track for the camera dolly?

"Perfect for Moon Festival! Perfect for Mid-Autumn Festival!" the tiny woman declared in English, articulating both names for the same holiday. Her pronunciation was good but the rising tone through the sentences made her sound like a liar.

She stepped between the big Americans and menaced them with her toothpicked samples.

"Sweet sweet, fresh fresh!" she yelled up at the men, meeting their tight smiles.

"Don't bother them," I told her in Taiwanese. "They get their food free, as much as they want and better than what you have."

The woman violently turned her head to the right, cracking her neck. "These Americans," she hissed. "They never want to pay for anything! So cheap!"

"They're cheap because they don't want to be ripped off by you!"

"They're ripping *me* off! They're blocking customers from coming in with all this!" She pointed at the lighting rigs. "How am I supposed to do business?"

I put my hands on my hips and cocked my head at her. "Nobody's blocking you, and I already saw you selling plenty tonight. You're only upset because you haven't been able to gouge the Americans working on the TV special. Go back to flimflamming the everyday tourists."

She pointed a finger accusingly at my nose. This is an extremely rude thing to do in Taiwan. "Chen Jing-nan," she said, using my full name, "just because you spent some time in America doesn't make you one of them, okay? I've been working here at the night market longer than you've been alive! You have to respect me!" She slammed the fruit samples to the ground in disgust.

I turned my back to her. This is an extremely rude thing to do pretty much anywhere.

Her stand hasn't been here that long, so that was a lie. But it was true that I had gone to UCLA and that I had once aspired to be one of them—an American, that is. I dropped out of college and returned to Taiwan because my father was diagnosed with a late-stage cancer. My mother was killed in a car accident on her way to the airport to pick me up.

To this day, whenever I hear people being paged over an intercom, I think they're going to be told that their mother is dead.

I had no idea when I left UCLA that I would never be going back, but how could I leave Taiwan after that? I was a soon-to-be orphan who would inherit a huge family debt and my parents' business—a food stand with two faithful employees who would be jobless if I didn't keep it running.

During the grief-stricken weeks that followed my mother's sudden death, my father and I only talked about what we were going to eat next, never about his inevitable departure. He told me again and again that a person in food service should have integrity.

"You're giving people something that will become a part of their bodies and their memories," my father had said. "They should be able to trust that your food is good, your kitchen is clean, and that you've done your best."

Those have been my guiding principles in carrying on the family business, a skewer and stew stand here in the Shilin Night Market. It's a little joint with only a few tables, but I have big dreams and a modest international following. I'm sort of a local hero, honestly.

This evening the sounds of the market were amplified by the pre-Mid-Autumn Festival crowds and the excitement surrounding an American television station's taping of a stinky tofu-eating contest. I watched families walking by, wives and husbands and kids with gangly fawn legs, gawking at the American crew and their cameras. They pointed and laughed together. It looked like so much fun to be them.

I didn't have a family anymore. I sucked in the inside of my left cheek and clamped my teeth on it.

"Hey," said Nancy as she touched my arm. "Jing-nan, don't let that fruit seller get you down. She's just mean."

I looked at Nancy and I had to smile. I wasn't alone in the world as long as I was with her. I was an adult orphan and she was a twenty-two-year-old grad student who didn't talk to her single mom. The two of us weren't part of Taiwanese society's accepted narrative, that of families of two and three generations living in one house, or at the very least gathering together on a regular basis. It made sense that Nancy and I had found each other.

We'd met at Bauhaus, a CD store, when she was working there. It had the best import and bootleg sections. The store mysteriously shut down recently. I don't know if it was due to legal action or illegal action; the place had been run by a criminal with exceptionally good taste in music. Some underworld figures run scams selling fake slots in columbaria. Others sell pirated copies of limited-edition pressings of Joy

Division songs that would otherwise only be in the hands of a few collectors. Surely the latter was an honorable thing to do, if illegal. And if Bauhaus hadn't existed, I might have never met the woman that I love.

I patted Nancy's hand. "The holidays get so annoying," I said. "Even without this TV special."

"I know that Johnny would never let anything get to him," Nancy teased. Johnny was the name of the persona I put on to sell food—a happy-go-lucky guy who ropes in tourists with his fluent English. He's not a bad guy, but he's too mainstream. For example, Johnny would be willing to take money from someone wearing a Justin Bieber shirt, even pose in a pic with him. Meanwhile the inner Jing-nan would be screaming, "No, no, no! We don't need his business!" One of Johnny's best qualities, though, is his unabashed love of the band Joy Division. Extra points for that. I'm lucky that I have access to that persona when I'm behind the cash register. I'm also lucky that I have the two best workers in the world, Frankie the Cat and Dwayne.

In fact, both Nancy and I were here tonight at the stinky tofu-eating contest to support Dwayne, who didn't have a goddamn prayer against either the Japanese champ, Sadao, or the American contestant, Chompin' Charlie. Either Sadao or Charlie had won nearly every eating contest in recent years, most notably the Nathan's Famous Hot Dog Eating Contest in New York City that happens every Fourth of July. Sadao and Charlie are always the top two and the championship has flipped between them like a shuttlecock. Things get heated there, as American pride is on the line. Some idiot in the crowd was arrested at the last one because he had brought a samurai sword and vowed to use it to chop off Sadao's head.

Nancy and I pushed our way through the crowd on Jihe Road, which had been shut down for the program. The rumor was that a producer at the American-owned Realtime Sports, which normally would never have been interested in something as obscure as stinky tofu, greenlit the eating contest because he had a Taiwanese wife. It was probably a lie but the story still ran on the cover of the *Daily Pineapple*, Taiwan's most unethical newspaper, which is saying a lot. Stinky tofu was the wife's favorite dish, the story alleged, and after she had eaten her fill of it during the preproduction, the producer refused to sleep in the same bed with her.

There are many ways of preparing stinky tofu, but all result in a wet or dry fermented product with a foul, lingering smell not unlike that of a trash chute in a diaper-testing facility. If you could get past the smell, you'd find that the tofu itself tasted like a blue cheese and has the consistency of whitefish. But asking most people to ignore the smell of their food is like asking them to ignore crawling maggots.

Even Andrew Zimmern, the fat, bald American guy who bounced around the world eating roasted bugs and testicles of all animals, drew the line at stinky tofu. I didn't think that anything that went into that mouth had any hope of escape until I saw the Taiwanese news program's slow-mo clip of Zimmern regurgitating. The half-chewed stinky-tofu bite was named "Jonah" while Zimmern was bestowed with the title "The Whale."

The frivolity of today's event was nearly done in by the weather, however. The stinky-tofu-eating contest had to be held outdoors as no indoor venue would tolerate such a permeating stink. In the predawn, a low-lying cloud slid down from the mountains and formed three coils in the evaporated lake basin that now cradles Taipei. The morning cable shows claimed that the form of a dragon could be seen in the mists, and that didn't bode well for Taiwan's crazily superstitious people.

Meilidao Network's rockstar Taoist priest had said that if it was cold enough to see your breath in the air and if a shadow moved across the face of the sun, Taiwanese people weren't taking family values seriously. He was a judgmental prick and people loved him for it.

The priest got his start in showbiz on the program *Caught in the Act*, which featured spouses confronting cheating partners on camera as they exited love hotels. His simplistic and chauvinist advice to couples ("Just listen to your husband!") had found an audience, and the network had given him his own show to fully display his complete ignorance of human affairs.

Not to be outshone, a celebrity Buddhist monk at the right-wing leaning Big East TV upped the ante on the weather outlook. He had visions of a wrathful storm hitting the island on the exact day of the Mid-Autumn Festival as punishment for its people even entertaining the legalization of same-sex marriage. "Guanyin, the goddess of mercy herself, will show no pity on Taiwan!" he had declared, rattling the beads around both his wrists for emphasis. "We're sowing bad karma for future generations, if there are future generations, with all the sinful couplings going on!"

THE WEATHER TURNED OUT to be fine, if a little chilly. The contestants were seated on a mobile stage that had been trucked in. Sadao and Chompin' Charlie were placed in the middle. Everyone else was expected to be a nonfactor.

Dwayne was seated on the far left, decked out in a traditional Amis beaded sash to pay honor to his aboriginal ancestors. He was the lone Taiwanese contestant, and although I wouldn't call him fat, he was the heaviest person. Why was everyone else so skinny? Rounding out the stage were a middle-aged man from Hong Kong, a white teenage boy from Australia, a black woman from Canada who looked like a real-estate broker, and a young Spanish woman taking time off from college to food-tour the world. There had been another American man besides Chompin' Charlie, but he had vomited during a pre-match tasting, disqualifying himself from the contest.

Chompin' Charlie was wearing a red, white, and blue bandanna and a black 9/11 commemorative T-shirt of stars and stripes with the words NEVER FORGET. He should've worn the sweatshirt version. The eating champ huddled and rubbed his hairy arms red in an effort to stay warm.

Nancy shook her wet licorice hair and the ends brushed the collar of her No Age sweatshirt.

"Are you cold?" I asked her.

She turned to face me, both ears slightly jutting out from her hair like light brown bass clefs. "You're staring at me?" she asked, the beginning of a smile clenched in the left side of her mouth.

"No," I lied. "There was a bug on your face." I touched her forehead lightly. "There. It's gone."

Taiwanese are annoyingly shy in dating and relationships. We can't walk around holding hands or giving any public displays of affection. At the airports you see long-time lovers waving goodbye without a final embrace. On the other hand, we have no problem sneaking into love hotels with our partners and/or other people as long as we're sure Meilidao's camera crews aren't hiding in the bushes.

I saw Nancy blush. As much as I wished she would be less uptight in public, I knew that her learned behavior was a part of who she was, and I loved who she was.

I touched her arm and pointed to Dwayne. "Look at that guy! I've never seen him look so worried."

"Has he been practicing?" asked Nancy.

"He's been eating deep-fried stinky tofu, but I don't think he's ready for the wet kind. They changed the type at the last minute because the producer said it looked better on camera, all slimy and green."

Dwayne looked a little green himself. The night-market association wanted one representative in the contest and in an act of bravado Dwayne had put in his name, never thinking that he would be the only volunteer.

A crew of four wheeled out a giant vat behind the contestants and dished out backup plates.

"Ugh, I can smell it from here!" said Nancy. We were about twenty feet away from Dwayne. They turned on the lighting and the stage was nearly as bright as day. Dwayne looked even more green, an apprehensive Shrek at the end of the table.

All the contestants were dealing differently with being in the heart of the stink. The Spanish woman was laughing heartily. The young Australian tightened his over-the-ear headphones and rocked in his chair, his face grim. The real-estate broker breathed through her open mouth and looked slightly embarrassed in a way Canadians seem good at. The Hong Konger cracked his knuckles and stretched his arms. Charlie rolled his jaw clockwise then counterclockwise. Only Sadao sat completely still. With his shaved head he resembled a lanky Buddha contemplating nothingness.

I heard some terse announcements crackle through the crew's walkie-talkies.

A spotlight swung on to a Ryan Seacrest-wannabe at the corner of the stage, his voice booming through the PA system. "Welcome to a very special Realtime Sports presentation! Let me hear you, Chinese Taipei!" he declared.

The crowd mostly groaned at the use of Taiwan's international moniker, forced upon us by China, which still claims the island as a province. "You're in Taiwan!" yelled someone in the front.

Fake Seacrest smiled hard. Acknowledging the comment might mean no Realtime Sports broadcast deals in lucrative areas of China, including Shanghai, Hong Kong, and Macau. Instead, the man bounded downstage and began introducing the contestants, impressively pronouncing the Spanish name but blowing it on the Hong Konger's Cantonese name. He declared that Dwayne was a "Formosan native," which was less correct than "aborigine," but Dwayne himself didn't mind. After all, the guy constantly joked that someday his people were going to massacre all the "invaders" of Han Chinese descent. He didn't look so tough now, though. He raised his arm weakly to acknowledge the crowd.

"Breathe through your mouth!" Nancy yelled.

"*Jia you!*" I shouted to him. "You can do it, Dwayne!" I didn't define the "it" but winning was definitely not one of the options.

Fake Seacrest held out a plate of stinky tofu to the camera. "Let me show you the best way to eat this sucker," he said as he dramatically produced a spring-type clothespin and clipped it to his nose. "P-U!" he cried to the television audience, who would be watching the contest in dramatically edited form.

"Of course our brave challengers aren't allowed to cover up their noses," the man continued. "They can't even drink any iced beverages up here, since ice dulls the sense. This is one competitive eating contest in which winning stinks! The question is, who *will* win? The patient and inscrutable Sadao, or the lusty American, Chompin' Charlie? Or maybe one of our nobodies? Are we all ready to go?"

"Yeah!" yelled the crowd, which was far more enthusiastic than any of the contestants.

"Let's get this challenge going! Five, four, three, two . . ."

At the end of the countdown, Sadao transformed into a multi-armed bodhisattva, each hand delivering a lump of stinky tofu into his barely opened mouth. His bald head was the eye of calm in a furious hurricane of flailing limbs.

Chompin' Charlie took a plunger approach, shoving down as much food as possible with his right hand.

The two of them were set to eat more in the first thirty seconds than the rest of the contestants would in the entire five minutes allotted for the event, although the real-estate broker was struggling to make third place look competitive. The projection screen switched from oddly serene Sadao to foam-mouthed Charlie. Suddenly, it featured Dwayne, who was a portrait of pain.

"Dwayne, let's go!" I yelled. What I really meant was, "Please don't come in last."

I knew that face he was putting on. Shifty eyes, pursed lips, flared nose. I revised my thought to, "Please don't puke. Our whole country's honor is riding on you."

He managed to keep down what he had eaten—half a piece of stinky tofu. Sadao won by wolfing down forty cakes. Chompin' Charlie put away a manly thirty-two. The broker had managed to eat eleven. Everybody else ate fewer than five. Luckily, Dwayne finished second-to-last. The Spanish woman had taken one bite and spat it out. She spent the entire contest shaking her head and laughing at the others.

Sadao stood up. He stretched his arms and rubbed his biceps. He was immediately swamped by autograph seekers, so Fake Seacrest grabbed the closest contestant, the middle-aged Hong Konger, who looked as lost as a substitute teacher in a tough school.

"Where did things start to go wrong for you, fella?" Fake Seacrest asked him.

The man shook his head. "That was the worst taste I've ever had in my mouth," he said. "I've eaten brains, balls, and anuses of all kinds of animals and none of that even comes close."

Fake Seacrest chuckled and touched the man's arm. "Well, better luck next time!" A handler wrangled Sadao away from the crowd and brought him to face the camera. "Sadao," said Fake Seacrest as he bowed slightly, "yet another championship for you. What's next?"

"I am going to travel in Taiwan with my good friend Charlie. We both love everything and everybody here," said Sadao, adding, "*Xie xie, da jia*," in perfect Mandarin. The crowd cheered appreciatively.

Chompin' Charlie was signing autographs as well. Who knew competitive eaters were so popular? When they managed to get him next to Fake Seacrest, Charlie said, "Sadao beat me fair and square, but my mouth is always up for a rematch. Bring it on!"

I felt someone leaning heavily on me. I turned and stared into Dwayne's bloodshot eyes.

"This was a big mistake," he said.

"Are you all right?" asked Nancy. "I have some mints if you need them."

"I could use a few," he said. Nancy handed him the entire pack. He rattled out a handful and popped them. "I thought I could handle it but they used the foulest stinky tofu ever!"

"You looked like you were going to be sick," I said.

"I haven't ruled that out yet. Let's get out of here. The losers have no right to hang around the field after a championship game." I noticed several people looking at Dwayne with sad smiles.

"Are you sure you don't want Sadao's autograph?" I teased. He grunted and sucked down more of Nancy's mints.

We walked Nancy to the Jiantan MRT station. She was behind on a project, the orientation packet for first-year students of Taiwan National University's College of Life Science. My girlfriend was in a doctoral biotechnology program. Nancy and I did a one-arm embrace when we parted.

Dwayne slumped noticeably after Nancy was gone. Showing weakness in front of women is taboo in his culture, or in every chauvinistic culture, I guess. We pushed our way north on Dadong Road.

"Do you want to go home?" I asked Dwayne. He was a leaning tower of muscle with a top floor that reeked.

"I'm good to work the rest of the night," huffed Dwayne. His breath smelled like a scoop of mint ice cream melting on a steaming pile of shit.

We passed a stand selling the deep-fried variety of stinky tofu.

"How about we get a couple plates of that?" I asked Dwayne.

He grimaced in pain but I could tell he was suppressing a laugh. "I'm not going to eat any more of your bullshit Han Chinese food."

We turned west on Danan Road and passed Cicheng Temple. Supposedly this is where the night market originated a century ago as a series of snack stands outside the temple to feed hungry worshippers.

"Maybe it's appropriate for you to make an offering for Mazu," I suggested. "Our Heavenly Holy Mother might be able to help you out."

Dwayne soldiered on. "If I don't sit down soon, I'll be making an offering in the street," he said.

I gave him a wider berth as we continued down Danan

until we reached the corner of Daxi Road. He ducked into the best skewer and stew joint in all of Shilin Night Market, Unknown Pleasures—that's my food stand, the one I run with the help of Dwayne and Frankie the Cat, the one I inherited from my parents.

By the way, do you like the name? It's the title of the first album of my favorite band, Joy Division. I used to be stupidly obsessed with the opaque lyrics, which drove me to learn English, and of course I was as fascinated as the rest of the world by the dramatic suicide of singer Ian Curtis just as the band was about to break big.

I'm older now. Death isn't as cool as it used to be.

Unknown Pleasures used to be located one block north on Daxi, at the intersection with Dabei Road. But that area was recently declared an emergency route and all the merchants located there were evacuated. We moved to our present space, which is actually nicer and bigger, but I lost some friends, people I'd known since I was a kid, who took buyouts and decided to seek their fortunes elsewhere.

Dancing Jenny, who used to run a clothing boutique, left the country altogether. I'd heard that she was now modeling BDSM gear in Tokyo. Kuilan and her husband left their hot pot business to start a full-fledged restaurant in Beijing. My family, Dancing Jenny, and Kuilan all worked together for nearly two decades and then, boom, we were all gone from that block.

Yes, things have changed dramatically in the last two months since I became a minor national hero. That's how it is in Taiwan, though. Nothing seems to change until it suddenly does.

Now how did I become famous? Well, it's a little embarrassing, but a guy I knew from high school tried to shoot me one night while I was working. Luckily I happened to be holding *Da Pang*, or "Fatty," a big cast iron pot that had been a favorite of my grandfather. The pot deflected the bullet, the gun jammed, and my erstwhile acquaintance fled.

It had made the news and all. I did a few interviews brandishing Little Fatty, retold the tale of how I could only see the gun and not the gunman, and of feeling the sting in my hands when the bullet ricocheted. Soon, keychain replicas of Little Fatty began to pop up all over the island. Unknown Pleasures' traffic increased in a big way. People took selfies at our stand, more with Fatty, dent side out, than with me.

Everything turned out all right. Well, my classmate later killed himself, so that was a bummer, but you know what? Every time we open for business and I reach up and touch Fatty on his dedicated trophy shelf, I am glad to be alive and overworked.

I FOLLOWED DWAYNE AS he teetered into Unknown Pleasures and disappeared into its tiny, staff-only restroom. That was one good thing about the new location. I sure don't miss the communal restroom.

Frankie the Cat stood behind the main grill, chatting with another elderly mainlander man. Both were born in China and were probably in their late seventies, although Frankie could pass for a man in his fifties. His hair was still thick, combed back and impossibly black. He had to be dyeing it, right?

Frankie had joined the army when he was a gung-ho kid just entering his teens. He was an orphan who had washed up in Taiwan with the rest of the Nationalists, also known as the Kuomintang or KMT, after the Chinese civil war ended with their defeat in 1949. Later, he was a political prisoner of the KMT for more than a decade after his brother was mistakenly reported to be a Communist. Still, Frankie never showed any bitterness about his lot in life and took orders from a punk like me because my grandfather had hired him before I was even born.

I regarded Frankie's friend, who was greyer and thinner. He shared the same sad smile of someone whose life had been derailed. If this was a prison pal, was he a fellow political inmate or a legitimately hardened criminal?

The two men also wore the same bandages on their forearms.

Frankie's wrappings were a few days old. "I had some old tattoos removed," he'd said casually when I asked him if he was all right. "They're bad for your skin when you're older."

I'd just nodded but I knew that he had removed the KMT army slogans that ran down both his forearms: TAKE BACK THE MAINLAND and KILL MAO AND ZHU. He had been wearing long sleeves to cover them up as long as I had known him.

Frankie glanced at me and nodded, indicating that now was a good time to introduce me.

"Hello, sir," I said to Frankie's friend.

"Jing-nan," said Frankie as he held an open hand to the man. "This is my old service pal from the orphan brigade!"

The unit had been made up of boys whose fathers had been killed by Communists in China. They'd been among the KMT's toughest soldiers even though they were as young as twelve. The brigade itself had been orphaned years ago, just another forgotten cockamamie Cold War relic.

I gave the man an informal salute that he returned immediately. "It's an honor to meet you, uncle," I said. It was best to be deferential, even though Frankie hadn't told me his name. "Please have something to eat. Anything you want."

"No, I should be going," the man said before turning to Frankie. "It's a miracle to see you again, my friend. A real blessing from Mazu. Take care for now." The two men clasped both each other's hands and smiled like boys. Frankie's friend turned away and disappeared into the crowd on Danan Road. I saw Frankie's smile fade. His face was neutral but his eyes were sad.

"Is everything okay, Frankie?" I asked.

"I'm fine." I appreciated that he didn't try to fake a smile.

"Did that guy say something to upset you?"

"No. It's just upsetting to see him and remember those times. We were so innocent, you know? Sure, we had guns, but we were naïve. There aren't many of us left." Frankie shook his head. "I didn't introduce you properly because he changed his name. He'd probably prefer you didn't know either of them."

We were rudely interrupted by Dwayne's groans from the restroom.

"Did anything big happen while we were away, Frankie?"

"Naw, this place was dead while the contest was going on." He turned on the faucet and ran his hands under the water. "Dwayne didn't come in last, did he?"

"He almost did, but I don't think anybody noticed. It was a two-man contest."

Dwayne stepped out of the restroom, looking as fresh as a newly wilted flower.

"Well, that stinky tofu's not going to be a problem anymore," he declared.

CHAPTER TWO

NEAR CLOSING TIME SOME friends from other stalls walked by Unknown Pleasures to lightly sprinkle shit on Dwayne for performing so poorly in the eating contest.

"I was thinking about your face and I lost my appetite," was his standard reply. Dwayne could have come up with something better under normal circumstances, but he wasn't so sharp after his system cleanse. He wasn't even up for horsing around during the lulls.

At around one in the morning I left the night market. I'd scrubbed down the side grill and mopped the tiles in the front. Dwayne would take care of the main grill and Frankie, who always left last, would finish everything else. I would be screwed without those guys because honestly they worked like they were family. No days off. I could tell when one of them was feeling sick only by their excessive tea drinking, and even then, neither would ever cop to it. They never seriously complained about anything.

Maybe they felt sorry for me.

I touched Little Fatty on the way out. I don't believe in luck, superstitions, or gods, but that little pot had saved my life. I know it's an inanimate object but I will feel a great deal of affection for it until I die.

I walked down the darkened streets that only a few hours

ago were choked with people. Death. Why was I thinking about death again, much less my own death? I was alive, in love, and happy. Very happy.

I turned west on Jiantan Road, away from the night market. I continued along the boarded-up future site of the Taipei Performing Arts Center, which looked like a moon base in artist renderings. I was sure that it was going to have many important cultural events that I wouldn't have the time, money, or desire to attend.

I crossed Chengde Road and stopped at the all-night fruit stand, which had way better deals than the cheats at the night market. I bought a pineapple that had already been shorn of its headpiece and skinned. It's always good to have one in the fridge.

After I turned the corner, I saw a huge billboard and a wave of foreboding came over me. The giant ad was from a hospital. Like all hospital ads, none of the people in it seemed to require hospitalization. A three-generation family was sitting in their living room, smiling like dopes and pointing to a full moon that was perfectly centered in their apparently high-definition glass window.

THE MID-AUTUMN FESTIVAL: A TIME TO LOVE, declared the ad.

I TRUDGED ON ABOUT four blocks to Qiangang Park, which was pretty big for a neighborhood park and included an outdoor pool near the obligatory temple to Mazu. My apartment was on the second floor of a generic concrete building that had sprouted up in the 1990s. From the bedroom I had a great view of a lighted small dirt patch in a neglected section of the park. It's a decent apartment with unwarped floors and gets quite a bit of light. Plumbing's in great shape, too. I couldn't understand why the preceding tenants had all broken their leases. Not until my first weekend.

Every Friday and Saturday nights, a pack of stray dogs entered the park and the alpha fought off challengers on that dirt patch. Dogs of all sizes, shapes, colors, and hair lengths let loose with howls of laughter and pain like partying teenagers in American films. It was loud enough to rattle my windows. Nancy refused to stay over on weekends. "Those are incarnations of evil spirits!" she declared.

At about three in the morning, the alpha would pull his head back and wail a saga. He had the general shape of a German shepherd wrapped in knots of long, dirty white hair. His head fringe hung at a rakish angle over his face, covering one of his eyes. By the end of the night, he was often splattered in blood. He would lick it off and smile at the moon. I named him Willie after Willie Nelson.

I watched Willie after his victories. At first I hated him for presiding over all that noise but I came to admire the beast as a decent fellow. The dog wouldn't kill his defeated rivals, as was his right to. Not only did he forgive them, he seemed to grant them high ranks in the pack as a consolation prize.

How could Willie be an evil spirit?

The Council of Agriculture, which was responsible for rounding up strays, showed up only during the big ferret-badger rabies scare. They were supposed to vaccinate the dogs, as well. But when the guys left their truck for a dinner break, Willie led his top dogs into their cab through an open window and pissed all over the interior. The COA workers called a tow truck and took a cab home. It was all caught on security cameras.

Not only is CCTV the nation's top crime-fighting tool, it doubles as source material for cable news programs and talk shows. One news station created an animated meme of giant dogs pissing on things, including the Taipei 101 skyscraper, the face of the head of the COA, and the full moon of the Mid-Autumn Festival, turning it yellow.

So what if my bedroom was a box seat to dog mischief? It was still an improvement from my old home, the one in the benignly sleazy Wanhua District that I had grown up in. That was an illegal building that had burned down to the ground more than a month ago. Seems like a former life.

When my parents died, I had been saddled with a family debt related to my grandfather's gambling habits and a loan from a local crime boss to cover losses. The *jiaotou*, as these neighborhood bosses are known, was really paying himself back with his own money, since he ran the gambing parlor as well.

Gambling has been a fixture in Taiwan since Chinese people arrived en masse in the 17th century and it's been a hard habit to break. Organized criminal activity to support gambling and other vices took root under the Japanese colonizers; after they left at the end of World War II, Taiwanese took over.

*Jiaotou*s are local-level guys. Maybe they have a dozen guys and five blocks under their control. They were Taiwanese Taiwanese. *Benshengren*, descended from Chinese who fled China when the Ming Dynasty collapsed in 1644. They also have aboriginal blood, since nearly all the Chinese who came over were men. *Benshengren* also speak Taiwanese and only resort to Mandarin Chinese under duress.

The big gangs in Taiwan, the ones that operate on a national level, are mostly staffed with so-called mainlanders, descendants of Chinese who came over in waves after World War II and the Chinese civil war.

One may think that after seventy years there wouldn't be much difference between the two largest populations of Taiwan, or that the tension would not be noticeable on a day-to-day basis. But memories are long and the past remains present. We worship our ancestors, after all.

Some *benshengren* are still bitter about their perceived mistreatment at the hands of the mainlanders during the forty-year martial-law era. Mainlanders say *benshengren* are looking for ways to segregate themselves, which is interesting because that's what *benshengren* say about the Hakka, an ethnic minority originally from China. And don't get anyone started on whose fault it is that the indigenous people of Taiwan continue to be marginalized.

There are many issues we all have with each other and past grievances are stoked every election as the country tears itself apart.

An old friend told me once that criminal organizations offer more stability than the government, and without all the fake promises and red tape. Whenever there are natural disasters in Taiwan—earthquakes, hurricanes, or mudslides—who are the first people on the scene with food, water, blankets, and medical supplies? The gangs.

The rare times that there are stabbings, it's gangsters killing each other. The police and the community at large don't have problems with that. Gangsters by code use knives and swords. They disdain guns, which any dissolute amateur can use. No honor in using them.

Taiwan's gangsters operate outside the law, but that doesn't mean they don't have a sense of integrity for the profession.

IN FACT, AFTER THE fire that destroyed my old house, the *jiaotou* who had inherited the lender end of my family debt slashed what I owed and later wiped it away altogether. We had always gotten along on a superficial level, but I was taken aback by his newfound charity. The guy even sent me a little housewarming gift basket when I moved out of Nancy's place and into the Qiangang Park apartment. Nancy had said I didn't have to move out, but I felt weird living there, maybe because I'm old-fashioned in the sense that I believe a man should really have his own place. I was also against staying there because a rich married dude had given Nancy the apartment while she was his mistress. He was in jail now for bribing officials, otherwise I would totally be kicking his ass on principle alone.

I ENTERED MY APARTMENT and was greeted immediately by thumping from the ceiling. The people above had installed a Japanese-style floor of raised wood planks over a hollow center. The trapped air pocket acted like a layer of insulation that kept the floor cool during hot summer days and warm in the winter. The downside, borne entirely by me, was that every step my neighbors took sounded like a beat of a tom-tom drum. Apparently they were having a stomping party right now, at one-thirty in the morning. I fought back the only way I knew how. I lifted my stereo speakers to the top of my dresser, pointed them upwards and cued up a live recording of Joy Division covering "Sister Ray." It was the loudest music file I had.

I unbuttoned and peeled off my shirt, which was sweaty in the back and greasy in front. I was normally against wearing a collared shirt, but Nancy said I should look nice in case I was on television during the eating contest. I showered, snaked into a V-neck and light cotton slacks, and brushed my teeth as "Sister Ray" played on. The track was only about seven and a half minutes long, but I had it on repeat. I hoped my neighbors' hollow floor acted like a subwoofer and throbbed like a bass cabinet under their feet.

I was chuckling as I imagined their furniture jerking around from the sound waves when an insistent knock came at the front door. Oh, shit. I'd only ever blasted music at my neighbors, not confronted them in person. That would be rude. Taiwan is mostly a passive, non-confrontational place.

More knocks.

I had no idea what these neighbors looked like. Maybe it was a really big guy. Maybe he wanted to punch my lights out. I should take a weapon to the door, but something not too threatening, in case it was actually, say, an older woman. I grabbed my toothbrush in my right hand. It didn't look very threatening, but I could poke an eye out with it, if I had to.

My apartment door had a peephole that had been painted over on both ends.

"Who is it?" I called out.

"Jing-nan?" I didn't recognize the man's voice. He didn't sound big or angry.

"Yeah," I said. "Are you complaining about the noise?"

"What? No. Just open the door." I could hear his fingernails tapping impatiently.

"It's really late," I said. "Who are you and what do you want?"

"Fuck this," said the man. I heard something rattle in the lock. I dropped my toothbrush and grabbed at the chain lock. Before I could slide it into place the door swung open.

I backed up as two men intruded. The guy in front was of a medium build, about the same size as me. He wasn't happy. The man behind him stood at about six feet three, his muscles spread out over his large frame like the multiple trunks of a banyan tree. The big man had a dull look in his eyes that said, "I would lose zero sleep over your death from prolonged violence."

"Jing-nan," said the man who was my size. "Your uncle sent us, so there's nothing to worry about. Call me Whistle. This is Gao." His teeth were stained red from chewing betel nut. A ring of keys and lock picks danced around his hairy knuckles.

Contrary to what he said, I became even more apprehensive at the mention of my uncle. "My no-good brother," as my father used to refer to him. I hadn't seen him in maybe fifteen years. He had the Chen family habit of accumulating debts. He partially paid them off and then, after a brief cancer scare, he skipped town. There were rumors that he had established himself on a remote island in the Philippines, doing who knew what.

Whistle lifted an open hand to me. "Jing-nan, we have to go," he said.

"Gonna use the can," grunted Gao as he pushed his way past me.

"Where are we going?" I asked Whistle.

"We're taking you to your uncle," he said, surprised that I wasn't able to figure that out. "He has to talk to you."

"Where is he?"

"Taichung City!" said Whistle, surprised that I hadn't known that, either. Taichung, true to its name, "central Taiwan," is located above the center of the island, to the southwest from Taipei. It's about a two-hour drive.

"Couldn't I talk to him on the phone?" I said, not meaning to whine.

"Jing-nan!" Whistle chided. "He's all the family you've got! You know what time of year it is! You have to see him in person!"

I licked my lips. "Is he in trouble?"

"Of course not. Now, let's go. Put on some clothes and shoes, not sandals." I heard a loud hocking sound echo in the bathroom, followed by the toilet flushing.

I CAN'T PRETEND TO understand how families work in other cultures. I know American kids can't wait to move out of the house and that they see their grandparents only a handful of times a year. In Taiwan we live in the family house basically until we're married. You see your grandparents every day because grandma cooks for the entire family and grandpa's parked on his favorite chair by the window, reading newspapers and eating roasted melon seeds, piling the shells on an already-read section. Your aunts and uncles and their kids are probably living in another room or in an adjacent apartment where the adjoining door is never locked.

I remember in one of the *Godfather* films someone says to keep your friends close but your enemies closer. In Taiwan we keep our family even closer than our enemies.

Just hearing about my uncle brought up these feelings of familial ties and the inherent duties. He might indeed be no good but that wasn't a reason not to hear and obey him. We shared the same name, blood, and fate. It was actually strange for us not to be in touch and our reunion was timely considering the Mid-Autumn Festival.

WHISTLE AND GAO BROUGHT me to their Infiniti SUV, which was parked around the corner in the shadows. It was customized with tinted windows. I took a seat in the back. Whistle got behind the wheel and Gao heaved himself into the shotgun seat. He wasn't armed with a shotgun, though. He was armed with a handgun that he checked before stashing it somewhere under his seat.

Yep, I thought, these guys sure know my uncle.

My neighborhood is never completely quiet at night, but all I could hear inside the car was Whistle making faint slobbering sounds as he chewed gum. He was probably banned from chewing betel nut (and spitting out the juice) while inside the SUV.

I noticed that the tint seal was bubbling in a few places. I tapped my finger to a double bubble. The glass was unusually thick—more than two inches.

Bulletproof.

Just a few months ago I would have been scared out of my mind being in the company of armed criminals. A lot has changed since. I've been beat up, shot at, and I even whacked some guy in the head with the butt of a gun. It sounds like a video game but in real life, fighting is exhausting and you feel bad about the people you hurt—even the bad people. Once you experience something like that, it's easier to remain calm in times of distress.

Then again, I wasn't being kidnapped. Presumably these two guys were my uncle's henchmen, and presumably my uncle wished me well. I hadn't seen him in a long time, but I had good memories of him, despite my father's misgivings. "Younger Uncle" was how I was taught to address him, but his friends and people in the neighborhood called him "Big Eye." It was an odd little nickname, because he didn't have big eyes at all. In fact his eyes were often narrowed and shifty.

Come to think of it, he had a pretty mean-looking face. Yet my uncle was also very generous with me and laughed easily and louder than anybody else. He had given me candy and chocolate. The night before he took off, he asked me if I had what it took to be a man. I said I did, and he let me try cigarettes and beer, turning me off to smoking and drinking for years. Could that have been the plan?

I looked out the bubbly dark windows and watched streetlights and buildings whip through my dark reflection.

Way too late to call or text Nancy. I probably wasn't in danger, but I wanted to let her know where I was. I tried to write her an email to explain that I'd been called away to visit my uncle. Everything I came up with sounded like I had been abducted and like it was written under duress. In the end, I settled on: "I have gone to visit my uncle because he is having personal problems. I should be back soon but I'm not sure when. Don't worry about me. I'm fine."

I copied Dwayne. Frankie didn't trust email. He didn't like putting anything in writing because your own words could be twisted and turned against you. If I'd been a political prisoner like him, I'd probably feel the same way.

All three of them would understand. Long-lost relatives could pop in at a wedding, a funeral, or near the Mid-Autumn Festival, as it turns out. My girlfriend and friends would only be alarmed if it turned out to be the last message they ever got from me.

We circled up a ramp to the highway and passed by a roadside betel-nut stand. I watched a so-called betel-nut beauty, dressed in a hot pink halter top and matching miniskirt, standing frozen in the glass window. I thought about my first and lost love, Julia. She had been working as a betel-nut beauty, or posing as one, when she was murdered.

When I was just a kid I was so sure I was going to marry that girl. The pain of losing her for good made me a man better equipped emotionally.

The streetlights passed at a regular pace that entranced me. My eyelids constantly slid shut. Rain began to fall and I watched droplets of water shiver across the windowpane. The last things I saw before I fell asleep were blurry flashes.

I STOOD BEFORE AN offering table that was adorned with burning incense, plates of fruit, and a bunch of other sacred objects I've never understood the purpose of. Smoke from the joss sticks obscured everything beyond the table but I could feel that my old classmate Guo was near. While he was alive, I used to refer to him by his childhood nickname, Cookie Monster.

"Jing-nan?" he asked. "Is that really you?"

"Yes, it is," I said. "Where am I?"

"You're standing at one of the doorways between the world of the living and The Courts."

"What are 'The Courts'?"

"I'm being judged and punished for all the wrong I've done in my life," said Guo. He had made some mistakes in life; one of the last ones had been pointing a gun at me. "Jing-nan, the gods here are all mainlanders! And they're really loud and mean!"

"I'm sorry you're having a hard time, Cookie, er, Guo. But why are we talking?"

"I had to see you to apologize for trying to kill you," he said. With all sincerity, he added, "I'm very sorry."

"It's all right," I said.

"You have to say that you forgive me, or it doesn't count!"

"Okay, I forgive you."

"Thank you, Jing-nan. Please allow me to apologize to you 9,999 more times."

"What!"

"Ten thousand times every day for the next ten thousand years."

"I'll be dead by then, Guo."

"That doesn't matter! All of the dead are apologizing to each other as we try to work our way out of this maze."

"I forgive you to infinity," I said. "Please consider the issue closed."

"It doesn't work that way," Guo said sadly. I dimly felt my physical body sway and recognized that I was dreaming.

"Say, Guo," I said, "while I'm here, could I talk to Julia?"

I sensed fear in his response. "You want to talk to Julia? Before your parents? Jing-nan, how could you put anybody before your father and mother?"

"Well, why the hell am I talking to you, then?"

"I'm here to grovel," said Guo. "Under any other circumstance, you should be paying respects to your family. Nothing's more important!"

I WOKE UP WITH a start.

"Sorry, Jing-nan," said Whistle. "I can't control shitty drivers on the highway. Please forgive me for waking you up."

"I forgive you," I said.

I rolled back into a sleep that was as dreamless and grey as a Taipei afternoon sky.

When I woke up again our wheels were churning along a dirt road. Through the windshield I saw tall reeds on both sides stream by.

"You ever see sugarcane up close, city boy?" asked Whistle. Gao made a short grunt that suggested a small measure of amusement.

"Why are we in a sugarcane field?" I asked.

"You'll see, Jing-nan," said Whistle. Gao grunted again.

Ah, they were going to kill me after all and dump my body here. No one would ever find me in the field, at least until the next harvest.

I yanked my door handle. It thumped like a bad knee and didn't do anything else.

"Hey, calm down there!" called Whistle. "What are you trying to do? Hurt yourself? We're almost there."

"I could call the police!" I hissed. "They might not get here on time, but you two won't get away clean if you kill me!"

Gao roared with laughter, a big baritone sax blaring into a microphone. Whistle's eyes looked at me sharply in the rearview mirror.

"We're not going to kill you, Jing-nan," he said. "And the cops are already here."

Our bodies were tossed around as the SUV galloped over two ditches. After a turn the sugarcane rows opened up, revealing what looked like a sprawling campsite with six large tents in the middle of the field. What the hell was this? A circus?

We pulled up next to the smallest tent and parked.

"Let's stretch our legs, shall we?" said Whistle. I saw Gao reach down under his seat for his gun and slide it under his left armpit.

I opened my now-unlocked door and was assaulted by the sound of chugging generators. The predawn air was warm and sticky. A ghostly blue mist from the setting moon mixed with the exhaust fumes and pancake-syrup smell of raw sugarcane. I stepped on some felled stalks, which were segmented like bamboo. I felt some give under my foot and remembered chewing fresh sugarcane, feeling the juice run over my tongue as I crushed the soft pulp. I used to love destroying my teeth with it when I was young, before I discovered chocolate. Still, on a hot and humid day, there's nothing better than a frothy cup of green sugarcane juice from iced stalks cranked through a cast-iron press. I was tempted to pull down a stalk to gnaw on. I wasn't a kid anymore, though, and I wanted to present myself as a man to my uncle.

Would I recognize him?

Gao pulled up a flap on a tent and evaluated the situation, his dead eyes revealing nothing. He then gave Whistle the smallest nod and headed in.

"Your uncle's gonna be excited to see you," said Whistle. He lifted the flap and cocked his head at the entrance. I rubbed my hands on my pants and stepped in.

This was the mahjongg tent. Above the din of voices I could hear the loud clicking sounds of ivory tiles. There were thirty tables packed tightly together. Most of the patrons were men, in every manner of dress ranging from sharkskin suits to worn-thin tank tops and shorts. The women were generally dressed better than the men and seemed to be the more serious players. Everybody was smoking, as if it were an admission requirement. Two upward-blowing fans were propped up on ladders, pointed at side vents. Tripod-mounted LED lamps, bright enough for a surgeon to operate by, cut through the smoke columns.

I followed Whistle to a table all the way in the back. It was only slightly set apart from the other tables, but it was a world away. While nearly everybody else playing was boisterous and happy, the four men in black suits and white shirts at this table were stoic and grim. Their hands only moved during their turn. The smoke trails from their cigarettes dangled in the air.

My uncle hadn't aged a day but he was dressed better than I remembered. Upon recognizing him, I felt elated and concerned. He was hunched over his tiles, a hand clamping the base of a cognac tumbler to the table. The man didn't seem to notice my arrival, but within two seconds he stood up and held his hands together in a begging gesture to the other players.

"Gentlemen, if you'll forgive me, my troubled young nephew has arrived," he said in Mandarin to the other three men. "I have to attend to him now, but I hope to see all of you soon, my brothers, hopefully under circumstances that are more fortuitous for you." My uncle bowed. The three glares, heavy as loaded railcars, that were fixed on my uncle switched over to me. I was on the spot, so instinct kicked in and I bowed.

The oldest man, probably in his sixties, nodded and took out his cigarette. He blew out smoke and said nothing. Whistle walked away and my uncle followed.

"Hey, why—" I began to say.

"Shut the fuck up until we're in the car," my uncle muttered in Taiwanese and roughly pulled me along by my elbow.

We had only just exited the tent before we heard a commotion behind us. We stopped and turned around and beheld a man with a white beard that flowed over his simple farmer shirt. His slacks were rolled up to the knees, exposing unusually muscular calves and Japanese *geta* on his feet. He was of average height but his entourage of younger, bigger, and meaner men accorded him an unusual amount of personal space, as if he were radioactive.

"Big Eye," his voice boomed in menace-laden Mandarin. "Are you leaving my hospitality so soon?"

My uncle stretched his neck and gave a shit-eating grin. "I'm so sorry, Wood Duck," he said. "I have a bit of an emergency. A family issue. My young nephew has come down from Taipei and he needs my help most urgently."

Wood Duck stared at my face hard. I couldn't help but twitch.

"He looks fine to me."

Big Eye stammered. "He has dysfunction of his private parts. I have special tea to help him."

Wood Duck reached into the folds of his shirt and withdrew a small pistol. "You've been lucky over the last two days, Big Eye," he said casually. "Very lucky." The pistol lay sideways in his hand as if it were taking a nap. It was pointed at nobody and everybody.

"Yes, Wood Duck."

"Maybe we can have just one last bet before you leave. Double or nothing. What do you say?"

"Of course, Wood Duck. I would never deny you. One more game."

Big Eye began to walk back to the tent, but the old man

held up his empty hand. "We're not going to bet on cards, Big Eye. It's my right-hand man against yours. Sima against Gao!"

The man named Sima presented himself. He was the same size and build as Gao but his suit was tailored better. The insects in the surrounding field went silent.

Wood Duck reached into his shirt again and withdrew a second pistol.

"*Gan,*" Whistle swore under his breath.

"A duel, Wood Duck?" Big Eye asked cautiously. "Is that what you want?"

Wood Duck laughed out loud. "No!" he said. "I want a skills competition!"

Two young men in black T-shirts, low-ranking members of Wood Duck's clique, carried out two donut-shaped glass decanters, each with a hole in the center. I thought pieces like that only existed in liquor ads. Wood Duck watched the men pour bottles of red wine into the decanters and nodded. "Gao!" Wood Duck called. "Your choice. You're the visitor."

Gao walked up to Wood Duck without glancing at Big Eye. He looked over the two pistols in Wood Duck's open hands, picked up both and weighed them. He stuck with the one that had been in Wood Duck's left hand and replaced the other one. Wood Duck nodded and tossed the other pistol to Sima, who caught it nonchalantly in one hand.

Two women in long sparkly dresses came forth, each holding small red apples. They walked up to the two flunkies and plugged the fruit into the decanters' holes. The women slinked off to the side and lit cigarettes for each other.

Wood Duck jerked his head to a bare table that was about fifty yards away. It had probably been used to burn incense and fake money to the field gods before the gambling got underway. The decanter bearers fast-walked the fifty yards and set down the vessels side by side on the table. Wood Duck slyly produced a string of Buddhist beads and with his left hand began to count off the 108 afflictions of the material world. Big Eye registered the action. It was a tell that the old man was nervous.

"Since Gao picked the pistol," Wood Duck declared, "Sima gets the first shot. If he hits the apple and Gao hits the decanter, then Big Eye loses all his winnings. If Sima misses and Gao hits his target, Big Eye can leave with his money doubled. But if they both hit the apple, then Big Eye has to stay another night—for the sake of restoring his luck!"

There was one more possible outcome. All my years of preparing to study in America, a country where everybody was expected to speak out against the teacher, forced me to ask a question.

"What if they both hit their decanters?" I challenged.

Everybody, even the indifferent smoking women and the stoic flunkies, turned and stared at me.

Wood Duck expressed his extreme displeasure by laughing hysterically and clapping. The Buddhist beads rattled a warning. "Who is this little boy?" he exclaimed. "Of course he's from up north! Taipei people don't understand the courtesies of country folk." He pried his lips back, showed his teeth and rubbed his cheek as if I'd slapped him. "If both of them miss—which is almost impossible—then we'll have a second round! Happy now, little boy?"

I nodded. I felt Big Eye's stare sticking me with poisoned thorns.

"Now! Sima! Stand right here!" Wood Duck pointed with his right hand to a circular spot where something had been burned. His left thumb clacked away at the beads.

He should be nervous. Wood Duck stood to lose a lot of money, but more importantly, his reputation was on the line.

If he lost, how could he live this episode down? There had to be at least two hundred people here.

Wood Duck had partially protected himself by having a proxy take the shot. If Sima won, people would remember tonight as Wood Duck's triumph. If Sima missed, people would primarily remember that fucking loser Sima.

Sima threw his head back and shook his hair like he was about to launch into a guitar solo. He raised his right arm and fired. There was deafening silence.

"You idiot!" yelled Wood Duck. "You didn't even hit the decanter!"

"It's a hard shot," Sima said to his left armpit as he bowed out.

Gao didn't wait to be cued. He stepped to exactly where Sima had stood and held his pistol at waist level in his right hand. The man kept his eyes on his decanter, his left hand caressing the gun.

His swung up his right arm and fired twice. Two soft punching sounds came back. Nobody moved or said anything. Except for Whistle.

"I'll go start the car, get the AC going," he said, walking away briskly.

"Impossible!" yelled Wood Duck. He twitched his head at the taller of the two flunkies. The man ran out to the table and returned with two cored apples. Wood Duck grabbed them and stared at them hard, willing those bullet holes to close up.

"Wood Duck," Big Eye said, "let's put my additional winnings in the books. We can settle up later." He said to Gao softly, "Nice." Gao blinked.

Big Eye and Gao stepped away. I lingered, looking at Wood Duck and Sima. The slinking women had already disappeared and the other people in the clique were quickly falling away like Antarctic ice shelves in the face of global warming. Why did I stay? I liked watching losers. I have empathy these days.

Sima stood with his head bowed. Wood Duck crushed the apple in his right hand and mashed the applesauce all over Sima's face.

"Open your mouth!" Wood Duck ordered. Sima complied and Wood Duck tucked the other apple between Sima's teeth. "Stay like that until I come for you!" Wood Duck flapped his hands clean and headed back into the tent.

CHAPTER THREE

WHEN WE WERE BACK on the road leading out of the sugarcane field Big Eye tilted his head back and laughed hyena hard.

"Jing-nan," he said, slapping my knee. "So good to see you!"

"It's been so many years," I said. "How are you, *ah-jiet*?"

He slapped my knee again, harder.

"Don't start that 'younger uncle' shit! Call me 'Big Eye'! Everybody else does." He looked at me sideways with that familiar leer. There were traces of grey now in the hair above his ears and it made him charming even though you knew he was up to no good.

"I didn't expect for you to send for me," I said. "I could have just taken the high-speed rail down here." Big Eye grunted and brushed off his knees.

"I needed you here right away," he said. "Those guys wouldn't let me go without a good excuse after all the money I've won over the past two days."

I twisted in my seat, afraid to know the answer to the question I was going to ask. "Who are they?"

"Aw, just some men I know. Business contacts."

"You were gambling in a sugarcane field."

"So what? Was it a little too country for your tastes, city

boy?" His right hand dove inside his suit jacket and retrieved cigarettes and a lighter.

"Isn't gambling illegal, um, Big Eye?"

He lit up and took a long draw before blowing smoke over his shoulder and out the slit at the top of his car window. *"Illegal."* He sounded out each syllable with utter contempt. "It was just friends playing, a private gathering. Hey, little Jing-nan, you think you can judge me just because you were on TV? You think you're on some reality-show panel and you're going to vote me off?" He thumped Whistle's headrest in a rude and yet familiar way and repeated, "He thinks he can vote me off the show!"

Whistle gave a practiced and forced laugh. "Yes, that's very funny."

Gao rolled his neck to crack the bones and yawned. I tried to fight it but I had to yawn as well. I was tired and now that flying bullets were out of the picture, I rediscovered a particular bad mood that only your relatives can put you in with their impositions.

"Look, Big Eye," I said, "I just want to know that you dragged me down here for a real reason."

"I needed to see you, Jing-nan! Of course I had a legitimate need!" He scratched his neck. "My daughter—your cousin—needs your help. Mei-ling wants to go to America for college and since you went there, you could help counsel her."

"I didn't know you had a daughter!" I said. "You're married now?"

He looked at me full on, calculating something. I saw my father's face in him. "Mei-ling is sixteen," he said. "Her mother's a cheap-ass Hakka bitch and we separated a number of years ago. We share custody." He flared his nostrils and pointed at my nose. "Don't get married until you're sure in your heart that it's what you want. You promise me that."

"Your daughter was born before you left. How come I didn't know?"

"I didn't know, either, little boy!"

We slowed and then took a highway exit lit only with a single withered lamppost. A large red sign warned PRIVATE ROAD. As we began to ascend, I asked Big Eye, "You live up on a mountain?"

He laughed and rubbed my shoulder. "A brief detour first. We're going to pay our respects to Tu Di Gong. He's been so good to me ever since he warned me that I had to take that little vacation to the Philippines a few years ago."

I was tired. The restorative power of the nap on the way down to Taichung was now tapped out. I wasn't sure how much more stimuli I could take.

Just reuniting with my uncle would have been heavy enough. The illicit gambling and sharpshooting exhibition were more than icing on the cake. It was like another cake on top. It was pretty cool seeing Gao shoot both apples. No special effects, either. The entire criminal world of *heidaoren* was probably already buzzing about how Wood Duck lost face big time. My uncle and his crew were even more fearsome now. Surely after such events it was time to head home, catch up a little and cook up alibis?

The road was dark and rocky. Trees whipped by and the occasional clearing showed nothing but stars, as if we were ascending to heaven. I cleared my throat, preparing to ask Big Eye a Big Question. "Is there still something like a warrant out for your arrest?"

Both Whistle and Gao exchanged mortified looks. Big Eye gave me a big fat smile.

"Jing-nan! There was never a warrant out for me! Well, not officially. It was all a big misunderstanding. The guy they were looking for, his name was pronounced the same way, but the third character was different, just a few strokes off from mine. Can you believe that?" He clicked his tongue to emphasize that the question was rhetorical.

We rode in silence until we reached the temple to Tu Di Gong, the earth god.

OUT OF ALL THE deities worshipped on Taiwan, Tu Di Gong is probably the most informal, the most empathetic to the human world. The god you could have a beer with and bitch about life to. He would probably nod slowly, reach his hands through the sleeves of his ancient Chinese bureaucrat robe and stroke his Santa beard. "Yeah, sorry, that sucks," he would say.

You can get more than empathy out of Tu Di Gong, but you have to get in real tight with him.

You need to offer him enough sweets to say good things about you to the Jade Emperor, the ruler of heaven. You should include a generous serving of rice cakes to stick to the roof of his mouth so he can't say anything about your bad deeds. The most important offering, though, is money to the temple priests, presumably to fancy up Tu Di Gong's altar.

Then and only then will Tu Di Gong risk the abuse from his wife and the wrath of the Jade Emperor to intercept an interoffice memo in heaven and discreetly make an adjustment or two in your favor.

OUR HEADLIGHTS FELL UPON metal gates blocking access to the temple but as we rolled up, two sullen young men swung them back. As we entered, the gates closed behind us.

Big Eye tapped his nose. "Listen to me, Jing-nan. Stupid people worship Tu Di Gong only when the lunar calendar says his wife is away. That makes them part-time believers. I give thanks to him every fucking day." He slapped his hand against his thigh to emphasize his words. "That's how devout I am. That's how unselfish I am."

I shifted in my seat. "Why do you say you're unselfish?"

He raised a fist to my face and extended his index finger to point at the roof.

"You think I come here for just me? Huh? I'm here because I care about my family, what's left of it. How many years have I asked Tu Di Gong to watch out for you, my dead older brother's son and my only nephew? When you survived the shooting at the night market, did you think that was plain luck?" He solemnly touched my shoulder. "Tu Di Gong was protecting you."

We took a turn and the temple sailed into view. It wasn't that big, just a single-hall deal. The roof, with its curled corners, probably wouldn't shelter more than thirty people from the rain. As the SUV slowed to a stop, Big Eye sprang out of the vehicle. I almost pitied Big Eye for his unabashed affection for Tu Di Gong. He was a boy who believed in Santa Claus.

The rest of us exited with undisguised reluctance. It was distressing to see the skepticism of his right- and left-hand men.

I'd spent my childhood being dragged to temples. It must be in my karma. Now, I neither believe in nor fully understand the concept of karma. I blame myself, my incarnation as the young man known as Chen Jing-nan, for my present circumstances.

Well, maybe I could ask if I could stay in the SUV and rest. When he saw me last I was a boy but now I was a man. I could speak my mind, even to him, an older relative.

BIG EYE BOUNDED FROM his side of the car and put an arm around my shoulders.

"Let's go, Jing-nan!" he said, adding needlessly, "I'm excited you're here!"

I wilted as his enthusiasm bowled me over. "I am a little tired, Big Eye."

"Tired? What the hell are you talking about? You know how much sleep I get? Zero. C'mon, now. The incense will wake you up."

He guided me to the temple's entrance with Gao lagging behind us. Whistle leaned against the SUV and toyed with his phone.

"How come Whistle's not coming?" I asked.

Big Eye stifled a laugh. "Aw, Whistle? He's been on this Jesus kick." Dammit, that's what I should've said!

"He's been born again," offered Gao.

"Just once?" Big Eye coughed. "Whistle should become a Buddhist. You know how many times they get to be born again?"

"He seems serious about Jesus," said Gao. Big Eye waved a hand and grumbled.

The temple wasn't as gaudy as others I've been to. There were only two pairs of ceramic dragons and phoenixes perched on top. Two ten-foot-high wood columns at the entrance were painted over with scenes of gods, mythical creatures and a shape-shifting monkey. A pair of stone guardians, modestly human-sized, stood at either side of the door, hands on the hilts of their swords, their hollowed-out mouths in eternal grimaces.

The Tu Di Gong idol sat on a throne holding a *ruyi* in his right hand and a gold *yuanbao* in his left. The *ruyi* is a short curved scepter with a knob at one end. It resembles a backscratcher with a tassel attached to the bottom. The *yuanbao* is a metal ingot shaped like an egg with a brim around the long oval circumference. From the side it could pass for a sailor's cap or a boat. Tough guys in Chinese historical novels could break off pieces of the brim with their bare fingers to pay for trifling amounts of food and drink.

This particular Tu Di Gong idol was the unhappiest one I'd ever seen. The smile was pained, one that a now-diabetic old man would have while remembering the first time he had tasted chocolate. His fellow idols were depicted in chortles approaching Buddha's open-mouthed guffaw.

The offering table was crowded with dishes of cooked meats and candy, and planters of burning joss sticks, some already reduced to fuzzy columns of ash.

Big Eye and I stood side by side at the offering altar. Smoke from the incense gave the glistening skin of a roasted-chicken offering an Instagram-like filter. The lack of sleep weighed on me and I yawned again. My uncle pushed a finger against my arm and whispered.

"Stay awake and be respectful, Jing-nan. I've been to many Tu Di Gongs all over Taiwan. This one's the strongest." He gestured to the bare stone floor. "See? No padded cushions here. We feel the floor when we kneel down."

Alarmed, I whispered back, "*We* have to kneel?"

A Taoist priest, suspiciously young at about fifty and suspiciously clean-shaven, approached Big Eye. He also seemed too muscular to wear the robes. This guy was more ex-jock-turned-sports-announcer than withdrawn follower of the Tao.

"Dearest Big Eye," said the priest softly. "Thank you for gracing us with your presence again."

"I'm here every night, right?" Big Eye whispered back. He tipped his head at me. "My nephew, Jing-nan."

The priest put his hands together and nodded at me. "Tu Di Gong blesses you."

"Thank you, sir," I said.

He blinked. "Don't thank *me*." He handed two joss sticks to Big Eye. "Please."

Gao stepped forward, touched a lit lighter to the joss sticks and then slipped behind a thick column carved with a dragon spiraling up to heaven. Big Eye blew out the fire at the end of the joss sticks. The glowing embers that remained would slowly digest the rest of the sticks and release the poison into the air. Release the scent, rather.

Big Eye held out a stick to me. A thin curl of smoke trailed from the tip.

"Thank you, Big Eye," I said as I took it.

"Do what I do," Big Eye said. He clasped the stick in his hands and gave three forty-five-degree bows. I did the same. When I thought I was done, Big Eye grabbed my left wrist and whispered, "Do it again, Jing-nan. This time face Tu Di Gong square-on."

I obeyed and when Big Eye was satisfied he jabbed his stick into a sand-filled censer. I did the same.

"That was a nice ceremony," I said as I checked my phone.

He glared at me. "We're not done by a long shot."

Gao returned and handed him a pair of crescent wood blocks, each about the size and shape of shoes for a ten-foot-tall marionette. One side of each block was flat, the other rounded.

Big Eye got on his knees and pressed the flat sides of the blocks together. I heard my uncle take in a deep breath and hold it. He cast the blocks to the floor with a flourish and finally exhaled. One block stood on its flat end and the other teetered on its rounded side.

The priest tilted his head and evaluated the blocks.

"You should ask again," he said. "Let's have Jing-nan kneel down, too, to show how devout your family is."

Big Eye, still on his knees, gathered the blocks together

and looked at me, one eyebrow raised. I dropped to my knees and felt the floor smack back, cold, hard, and angry. I grimaced and noticed the priest's smirk.

Big Eye blew imaginary dust from the back of both hands and cast the blocks once more. The priest nodded. "All right," he said and withdrew. Big Eye remained on his knees.

"Can I get up?" I asked.

"No!" he snapped.

The priest returned and handed Big Eye a bamboo canister filled with carved wooden strips.

Big Eye shook the canister with the vigor of a mischievous toddler.

"Careful," admonished the priest. Big Eye reduced his fervor and a single stick slid out apart from the pack, centimeter by centimeter, until it clattered on the floor. Big Eye handed the canister back to the priest and snatched the stick from the floor. We stood up and Big Eye's knees cracked before he read out the characters on the stick.

"Seven. Nine. Moon. Mountain. What's that supposed to mean?"

The priest laughed and walked over to an ancient chest at the side of the temple. He opened a drawer in the seventh row and ninth column and plucked out a small scroll. The priest's crawling fingers unrolled the piece of paper. He gave it a studious read and then nodded.

"It's a good time for Mei-ling to go to Taipei. She has to visit a mountain before the Mid-Autumn Festival. Then everything will be okay. Your family's going to be just fine."

"You hear that, Jing-nan? My daughter needs a trip to the mountains."

Well, so what?

"Sure," I said.

The priest crumpled up the note and tossed it at a small brazier, meant for burning ghost bank notes. He was unconcerned that he missed. The priest bowed deeply to Tu Di Gong, then turned to confer with Big Eye and accepted an envelope with both hands.

I snatched up the crumpled fortune and flattened it in my hand. It was covered with the crazed strokes of fake characters. I knew it. This whole charade was a scam, from the lighting of incense at the beginning right through the written prophecy at the end. The drawers were filled with bullshit scribbles and the priest "read" them while saying whatever the hell he wanted to.

On our way out of the temple I showed the paper scrap to Big Eye. "I hope you didn't give the priest too much money. All the fortunes are nonsense."

"It's written in a spiritual language, Jing-nan," he said. "Only priests can decipher it." I could only shake my head. Well, his faith in Tu Di Gong had been working for him this far. Why should I care?

We walked down the temple's steps. I noticed that Gao turned and did the briefest bow, one that said, "If you really exist, please don't hurt me."

As our SUV wound down the mountain, I said to Big Eye, "How much do you trust that priest?" Big Eye drummed his fingers on his flask.

"I trust him with my life," he said. "He's one of us. He wouldn't bullshit me."

One of us. That meant *benshengren*, the long-time Taiwanese. Yams, as we sometimes call ourselves, since the island is in the shape of a yam.

Those winnings against Wood Duck must have been especially sweet. An upstart yam pulled one over on a powerful mainlander, or *waishengren*. The division between *benshengren* and *waishengren* was evident at all strata of society, even at the illicit seam.

BACK ON THE HIGHWAY, traffic slowed to a standstill. Big Eye tapped Whistle's headrest.

"What's going on?" he asked. Whistle snorted and hunched his shoulders to get closer to the windshield.

"Police barricade ahead."

Oh shit, I thought. If they searched this car, who knew what they'd find. Whistle checked his hair. Gao bent over as if tying a shoelace. Big Eye stuck out his jaw and stretched his lips. We slowed to a stop and then crawled forward to our doom.

I considered throwing open the door and bolting. Yeah, that wouldn't be suspicious. If I remained in the car and these guys were busted, I could be arrested and charged as a hooligan for just being with them. I've been in a lot of compromising situations but I couldn't go to jail. I couldn't.

"Look at you," said Big Eye as he grabbed my left shoulder. "You've gone all pale, Jing-nan. You look scared, like you're hiding something." He patted my hand. "You would have never made it with me."

"My shoe prints are back at the gambling site," I gasped. "They've got me."

Big Eye's lips ripped apart into a toothy smile. "You're talking crazy, little nephew!"

"Are we going to be okay?"

"Only if you fucking relax. *Ma de!* Want some candy to take your mind off things? You still like candy, right?"

"No thanks."

He shrugged and popped something into his mouth. In a few seconds it was apparent that it was a honey-loquat cough drop, one of those medicine-candy hybrids that has questionable merits as either. The smell was unmistakable and inescapable: menthol and Coca-Cola.

Soon enough two men wearing orange vests with National Police Agency patches on the short sleeves of their khaki uniforms stood on either side of the SUV. Whistle powered down his window. The cop swept a light across our eyes.

"Officer," said Whistle, "what seems to be the problem?"

"Who said we had a problem?" the cop spat.

Gao reached into his jacket and the cop's flashlight followed his hand.

"Hey, you! What do you think you're doing?"

Gao slowly pulled out a leather ID holder. The cop grabbed it, flipped it open, ran his thumb over the oddly cheery picture of Gao and read the text out loud. *Gao Ming-kung, Under Chief Superintendent, Taichung Police Department.*

"Sir, I'm sorry," said the cop.

Gao grabbed his ID back. "Don't sweat it. You're doing your job." He wiped his nose. "I'll bet you're looking for one of those no-good Indonesian monkey-ass punks."

The cop nodded and crossed his arms. "There was a shooting, you see. We had to take certain measures."

Gao shook his head. "We let these people into our country, out of the goodness of our hearts, and this is how they repay us." The cop nodded. "Well, officer, the good people in the Taichung Police Department and you guys will catch them all soon."

Whistle powered his window up and we were on our way.

"Listen, kid," Gao said to the roof. "About what I said, that's not how I think, but it's what those people believe. All right?"

"Yeah," I said.

"I'm an immigrant myself."

I SAT CROSS-LEGGED ON the floor of the living room of my uncle's house. My shoes were off and the woven straw of the tatami mats imprinted a pattern on my calves as I shifted. I can't sit Japanese-style, on my knees. My legs fall asleep. I like chairs, but there weren't any.

Big Eye and even the hulking Gao sat casually, comfortably drinking tea. Whistle had gone to sleep, saying he was beat from driving. It was probably six in the morning, and judging by the ease with which Big Eye and Gao operated, tea at this time was a long-established routine.

"Look at Jing-nan," Big Eye scoffed. "He sits like an out-of-shape foreigner!"

I shifted and spilled my tea. "Could you please give me a cushion?"

"If I give you a break," my uncle said, "you'll never learn to sit properly."

With that admonishment, I felt it was within my rights to be a little defiant. "I did you a favor by coming down and getting you out of a tough spot," I said. "I shouldn't have to suffer for it."

"Ha! What do you know about suffering? Look at this guy." Big Eye flapped his left elbow at Gao. "You know what he's been through? He escaped from China by himself when he was only twenty. He floated across the Taiwan Strait on a fucking door! He survived by fishing through the hole where the doorknob used to be and he drank his own piss! After he washed up in Houlong Township, the Kuomintang put him in jail! You know why?"

"They thought he was a spy?" I asked.

"They would have shot him if they thought he was a spy, Jing-nan! I'll tell you what happened. Gao said he wanted to escape from China. But the very idea that Taiwan wasn't a part of China offended the local governor of Taiwan Garrison

Command, you know, the secret police. They jailed Gao in Green Island for a decade for sedition. In 1992, Taiwan Garrison was disbanded and those guys went underground and handled dirty work for the government under subcontract. The former secret police hired the toughest guys they had originally imprisoned. Of course they had to get Gao. He was such an ass-kicker in Taichung, the regular police went on to hire him. Look at him now! He's the number-three man in law enforcement and the door he floated over on is his office door."

"It's not," said Gao. "Also, I didn't drink my own piss. I had some water and it rained a lot." He cleared his throat but he didn't have anything else to add or revise. Big Eye poured out more tea.

Damn, another hardcore guy who had done time on Green Island just like Frankie the Cat. If the prison didn't kill you, you came out a serious badass.

"This is a real man, Jing-nan," Big Eye said as a clump of steam from his refilled cup punched the air and disappeared. "Your generation never knew the tyranny of the KMT regime." He shook his head. Disappointment is a privilege older Taiwanese people hold over the young.

I wasn't ready for a lecture. If my phone weren't recharging in Whistle's room, I would have been on it. I glanced around the bare room. No clocks. The only furniture was the low table we were gathered at and a side table supporting a vase that held an ugly jade-encrusted plant. Big Eye tracked my attention.

"You like that plant?" he asked. "Do you want to take it home?"

"That's all right," I said. "I wouldn't know where to put it."

"It's awful, isn't it?"

"Maybe," I said. Gao and Big Eye chuckled.

There was a scratching sound to the left. A screen moved aside and a sullen young girl stepped in. She was dressed in a skirt and two layers of tops.

"Where have you been?" Big Eye thundered. "Do you know what time it is?"

She crossed her arms and jutted out her chin. "You haven't been here for two days, you can't be asking where I've been," she shot back, her earrings swinging. Gao coughed to cover up a laugh.

"Unbelievable," said Big Eye. He put down his teacup and added, "Mei-ling, say hi to your big cousin Jing-nan."

"Hello," I said. Now that she was finally home, maybe Big Eye would let me hit the sack. There had to be an empty guestroom in this house.

"I've read about you online." Mei-ling, who had just acted so boldly to her father, now turned to me, calculating how to inflict defeat.

"Are you packed already?" said Big Eye with a tone of admonishment.

"Of course."

"Two suitcases?"

"Just like you said."

I hid a yawn by pretending to scratch my nose. My eyes watered slightly. I wiped them dry and tried to follow the conversation because I didn't know what was going on.

Big Eye clapped his hands.

"Okay, wake up Whistle. He's going to drive you two to Taipei."

Mei-ling left the room.

"We're going to Taipei?" I asked.

Big Eye stood up and stretched. "Well, that's where you live, Jing-nan." He yawned. "Mei-ling is going to stay in Taipei in a condo I own on Xinyi Road in Da'an District. She got thrown out of private school again. There was a fight in the school courtyard and one of the asshole teachers blamed Mei-ling for it. It was a case of mistaken identity, but the headmaster didn't want to hear it."

"Girls were fighting?" I asked.

"Crazy shit, right?" he snorted. "Anyway the only real trouble Mei-ling has is her boyfriend, this no-good Indonesian fuck. The deal is, she'll stop seeing him if I let her visit Taipei for a week, so there you have it."

"Why does she want to be in Taipei?"

"Supposedly it's more sophisticated than anything we have to offer here in our tiny hamlet of nearly three million people. Anyway, I want you to keep tabs on her." Big Eye pointed at my nose. "If that piece-of-shit boyfriend—Chong is his name—shows up, you call me right away. Apart from that, if anything happens to her, I'll kill you and make it look like an accident."

He smiled but he wasn't kidding. I looked over at Gao to see if the high-ranking cop objected to Big Eye's naked threat to my life. He shrugged.

"Don't screw up, Jing-nan," said Gao.

CHAPTER FOUR

Whistle and Gao sat in the front of the SUV again while Mei-ling and I sat in the back. With my third ride in one night, my ass was taking on the shape of my seat. I almost never rode in cars. Mei-ling flipped open a compartment and pulled out a glass and a plugged crystal decanter that refracted the light from the rising sun. A jittery rainbow slid across her face. She poured herself a shot, both of her knees bouncing.

"I don't think you should be doing that," Whistle said cautiously as she threw the shot back.

Mei-ling coughed and smiled. "Too late now." Turning to me, she asked, "Are you hungry? I am."

"I could eat," I ventured, sure that this twitchy teen probably wasn't going to let me sleep.

"Whistle," she yelled, "take us to La Corona!"

"It's a little out of the way," said Whistle as he looked sheepishly at her in the rearview mirror. "In fact, I'd have to turn around to get there."

"Then stop driving the wrong way," Mei-ling snapped.

Whistle had wanted to get the food to go but Meiling insisted on staying to eat, otherwise we wouldn't get free tortilla chips. A good decision, because the chips were better than the burritos, which were packed with mung-bean sprouts and came off as soggy spring rolls with refried beans.

La Corona was hopping at eight in the morning. It's one of those places that people support only because it's open twenty-four hours a day. They brag that there isn't a lock on the door without mentioning how their food is. I guess the point is that it doesn't matter how the food is. Look at the people who came here. Hungover kids. Red-eyed and red-toothed truck drivers. No gourmets. Nobody's taking pictures of their food and posting them online.

The only difference between my breakfast burrito and Mei-ling's grilled-pork wrap was that mine allegedly included a scrambled egg. I looked around the table. Mei-ling, Whistle, and even Gao were scarfing the food down. I wasn't going to make it half way. I wasn't a snob—it's not like Unknown Pleasures had a Michelin star—but I couldn't bring myself to choke down food made from inferior ingredients.

I forked over the mess to make more room on my plate for salsa and chips. I drank some more coffee. Also not great.

I was feeling lousy for coming down to see Big Eye but honestly I would have felt worse if I hadn't. Not that Whistle and Gao would have entertained that option. If it weren't for me, Big Eye would probably still be at that gambling table and Mei-ling would have spent a third night wondering where her father was.

I looked at Mei-ling closely. She had an innocent, heart-shaped face but the same tight mouth and steely eyes as Big Eye. As I watched, she gathered up her dirty napkin and smeared it across her mouth.

"I'll be back," she told her plate and headed to the restroom.

"Say, Whistle," I asked. "What sort of guy is Chong?"

He took a swig of coffee before answering. "He's in a bad situation. He's after the wrong girl."

"You can say that again," said Gao, breaking into a smile. "Those people should just stick to their own."

Whistle cut in. "The guy's a petty criminal. He runs with this group of kids who came over from Indonesia. They shoplift and push old ladies down for their purses. Their own people are the victims, usually. You wonder why the parents don't have better control of their kids."

"The parents are too busy drinking and gambling!" said Gao. "All day, that's all they do!"

I decided not to point out that my uncle drank and gambled for days on end.

"But worst of all, Big Eye gave Chong and his buddies some work for good pay and they were completely ungrateful in the end," said Gao.

"Did Big Eye try to rip them off?" I asked.

"He's entitled to a cut," said Whistle. "And he's entitled to decide how much."

"They felt they got the short end of the stick, but without Big Eye, there wouldn't be any stick," said Gao.

"How did Mei-ling meet Chong?" I asked.

"In school," said Gao.

"In detention," Whistle added. "This was back when Mei-ling was in public school."

"She seems to find trouble," I said.

"You have no idea," said Whistle. Gao gave him a meaningful look over his slick plate.

Mei-ling came back and sat down.

"You two should go to the bathroom," she said to Gao and Whistle. "It's a long trip." Amazingly, they got up and went.

"You really shouldn't talk to people like that," I said.

"So what? They work for us. They're not our family."

"Do you talk to Chong the same way?" Her face went stiff. "After all, he's not family, either."

"It's none of your business, Jing-nan!"

"It is. Your dad told me to keep an eye on you. Part of the deal if you get to visit Taipei is that you give this guy up."

She looked at me for the first time with sincerity. "I did already, so don't worry about it," she sniffed.

"Is he going to come after you?"

"No."

"Good."

"I don't care about him, anyway. I was with him just to piss off Big Eye. He hates new immigrants as much as he hates gays and lesbians."

"But he has a lot of love for you, his only daughter."

"Hah!"

Whistle and Gao came back and stood at the table.

"Anything else, Mei-ling?" asked Whistle.

"Let's get going, already. Jing-nan was wondering what was taking you guys so long!" They both gave me dirty looks. I shook my head but they didn't buy it.

MEI-LING CURLED UP AND fell asleep right after we piled back into the car. I started to drift off, too, but her snoring prevented the door between wakefulness and dreamland from closing entirely.

"Tired?" asked Gao.

"Naw," said Whistle.

That was the end of the conversation. These guys did what they were told and they were efficient. I wondered what other jobs they did and what else they wouldn't talk about.

A couple hours later, I felt a warm patch of sun on my face. I opened my eyes and sat up. I could tell by the ugly construction barriers that formed the median that we were on Xinyi Road, a major artery of downtown Taipei that sliced through Da'an District. Xinyi connected Chiang Kai-shek Memorial

Hall to the Taipei 101 skyscraper. We drove toward that gleaming spire that symbolized not only Taipei but the future of Taiwan itself. The past with its memories of colonization, defeat, dead dreams, and oppressive martial law rose up behind us, always close.

The Memorial Hall grounds, which also include the National Opera House and the National Concert Hall in addition to ponds and gardens, covered almost as much area as fifty American football fields. My dad used to say that no fair and honest man would have conscientiously allowed something that big to be built in his honor.

TRAFFIC WAS BAD ON Xinyi. Whistle cursed as some madman in a van cut us off. I crouched to look out the windshield. The van ahead of us looked like it had been through the Chinese civil war, a driving patchwork of welded metal sheets. A sign in the rear window declared, in English, its opposition to the legalization of same-sex marriage: MADE BY MOMMY AND DADDY.

I looked over to Mei-ling. She was awake and glaring at the sign.

"This is Taipei," she said. "I thought people here were more open-minded in the city."

"What do you care, Mei-ling?" I said. "You're not gay."

She crossed her arms. "Some people are."

"Let other people worry about it. You've got enough problems."

"Who are you to criticize what I say and think? You're not that great!"

I was about to tear into her when I heard Gao cough. I looked up and saw him gesture discreetly with his left hand. Let it go, it said.

I'm not experienced in talking to young people, even

though I once was one myself, but I do know you're supposed to let babies get their way. Once they started crying, it was almost impossible to make them stop. All I could do was sigh and look away. I've noticed that Whistle and Gao were already well-versed in this tactic.

Mei-ling took out her phone in a dramatic gesture and fiddled with it.

"Turn on the Bluetooth, Whistle," she ordered.

Some awful sounds began to throb out of the SUV's speaker system, synthesized dance music with layered vocals so devoid of character they could all belong to the same robot. The lyrics seemed to be about finding someone to kiss.

I yawned. Music of this ilk was popular now and was destroying the finest young minds of East Asia. Mei-ling bounced to the beat.

"What do you guys think?" she squealed.

"It's good," offered Gao.

"Yeah," said Whistle. "Even better than the other one you played." Mei-ling gave a measured smile and turned to me.

"And what do you think, Jing-nan? I know you're a big music fan."

"How do you know that?"

"Big Eye told me. He said you never stopped listening to Black Sabbath."

"Yeah, that was when I was young. My tastes changed as I matured. I've moved on from Sabbath and metal in general."

"Tell me what you think of this song!"

"It's not my kind of music at all."

"You don't like girl singers, huh?"

"It's not that." I shifted in my seat and turned to face her fully, so there would be no misunderstandings. "I really hate this genre. It's nothing but a bag of bones. There's no meat. The keyboards are so cheesy. Worst of all, the lyrics are completely vapid. Now that you're in Taipei, you can stop listening to crap like this. I can give you some real music."

Mei-ling turned red and her pursed lips resembled the anus of a tied-up balloon.

"You think this is crap, huh?"

I can be well-humored about almost anything except someone questioning my informed taste in music. "Yeah. It sucks!"

"If it sucks, then why did it win a song contest?"

"Because shit like this is popular, that's why."

"You think it's 'shit' now, huh?"

"It is shit, and if these two guys," I pointed to Whistle and then Gao, "were honest, they'd say the same."

Mei-ling slapped her car seat and stopped the music. "It's *my* song, Jing-nan. I did it all by myself on my computer. That's me singing, too."

I immediately felt like a monster. It was my first day with a cousin I didn't know I had and already I had shattered her dreams. I knew how it felt to be put down by older people but I never thought I would be one of those older people. I should say something constructive. Something moderately positive. Something you'd expect from your older cousin.

I cleared my throat and ran a finger on the inside seam of my jeans. "That song's not so bad for something you did all by yourself," I said.

Mei-ling searched my face for an artery to bite. "You said it was *shit*!"

"I won't lie to you, Mei-ling. I really do hate it. But if you're serious about your music, you shouldn't care what critics say. You should just pursue it and to hell with what other people say. If you think it's great, then it is great."

She shifted. "You think so?"

"Of course. Every successful artist has had to overcome

adversity. If it were easy, then everybody would be a star. When you make it, you can throw all my words back in my face. You should probably do that now."

She let out a heavy sigh. No one had ever been honest with her about her music before.

"Did you really win a contest?"

She nodded. "It was online."

"What was the prize?"

"They played my song in their podcast."

What a lousy prize, I thought, but I said, "That's great."

Somewhat placated, she decided to busy herself with her tablet.

I sat back and debated offering her my phone to listen to Joy Division. She wasn't ready for something that intense yet. I would have to start her off gently, maybe with late New Order stuff. Our ride continued creeping east on Xinyi.

"At the next light, make a right!" Mei-ling called out. "There's a store that sells a microphone I want."

"It's open now?" asked Whistle.

"It opened at nine and it's nine-thirty now."

"Well, then I guess it's open, but we really shouldn't take too long."

"It's not going to take long at all," she said. "I do need to borrow some money, though."

"How much?"

"Five thousand NTs." That had better be a decent microphone at more than 150 American bucks. Whistle passed his wallet back to her and she counted out the bills, folded them into her hands and gave the wallet back. After we made the turn, we went down two blocks to the entrance of a side alley.

Alleys in Taipei are narrow roads that have a Japanese look to them. Supposedly the roads in Tokyo are confusing and narrow to confound any potential invaders. I think the

Japanese colonizers brought that concept to Taipei, which they renamed Taihoku, when they redesigned and planned out the city. When the Japanese left after fifty years of rule in 1945, the Republic of China administration tried to remove everything overtly Japanese, but renamed the roads and alleys instead of carving out new ones.

"Where?" Whistle asked as he drove along the curb.

"This should be good," Mei-ling said. She popped the door open.

"Do you want Jing-nan to go with you?"

She rolled her eyes and let her mouth fall open. "I don't need my biggest critic as an escort."

"Mei-ling needs to do this herself," I said. She slammed her door and smirked at me through the cloudy window. "This girl's a handful."

Whistle reached back and slapped my leg hard.

"Dammit!" I said.

"What's wrong with you, telling her her song sucks?" he said.

"Someone had to tell her," I said.

"I've known her all her life," Whistle said. "She's practically my little girl, too."

"Then you should be honest with her."

"There are ways to be honest without making discouraging remarks!"

"I know, I know, I went too far."

"Jing-nan," said Gao, "Whistle's sore because he has some money invested in Mei-ling."

"Money?" I said.

Whistle sighed. "Big Eye wouldn't pay for the online-song contest. So I spotted her the money."

"It was a lot," Gao interjected.

"A lot of these entrance-fee contests are a scam."

"I know," said Whistle. "But, hey, she won."

"Everyone who pays the fee wins."

"He paid for a photo session, too," said Gao.

"What photos?"

"The contest required headshots and full-body shots," said Whistle. "We went to one of Taichung's best studios."

"Some of those pictures . . ." started Gao.

"Hey!" said Whistle.

"Some of those pictures, what?" I asked.

Gao sniffed. "Inappropriate."

"She's a girl," explained Whistle. "She has to look sexy."

"Whistle," I said, "this contest is sounding sleazier by the minute."

"It doesn't matter! She won!" said Whistle as Gao chuckled.

We sat in resigned silence in the car until Mei-ling swung open the door and plopped back in her seat.

"Do you know anything about microphones, Jing-nan?" she asked.

"No," I said, "but show it to me, anyway."

The box felt solid, but after scanning the specifications, I sounded the alarm.

"Hey, this thing's made in China!"

"What's wrong with that? You hate China?"

"I hate the cheap crap they make."

"This is the highest-rated PC microphone," she said before slyly adding, "in this price range."

"You need a better one?" asked Whistle.

"No. This should be good enough."

I'm still being too negative, I thought. "You know more about these things than I do, so if you say it's a good microphone, I'm sure it is."

"Don't patronize me, Jing-nan!"

We looped through another small road to get back to the traffic jam in Xinyi. A bright spot caught my eye. When I turned I saw a single bright flame flicker in a burner in a back-alley temple to the Mother of Heaven, one of Mazu's manifestations. An extended family of about a dozen people was bent at the waist before her, heads low.

Mazu was a goddess whose legend is based on a young girl, a fisherman's daughter, who lived nearly two thousand years ago in China. This young girl could go into trances and rescue people from sinking boats and guide home the lost. Unfortunately she died young, but apparently ascended to heaven immediately and has been worshipped ever since.

When people crossed the strait for a new life, they built temples to Mazu in Taiwan out of gratitude for their safe arrival. Mazu's powers transitioned as her worshippers moved inland. She could make it rain to assure plentiful crops, divert an approaching hurricane, and comfort earthquake victims. Some of her followers still brag that Mazu appeared in the sky and opened her skirt to catch and deflect American bombs during World War II.

My parents believed Mazu could do anything. I was made to bow before her temple throne for the sake of my health and my fortune. I looked at her face behind the beaded veil of her headdress. I saw that her gaze was focused above and beyond us, trying to find people with more status and money to give to the temple.

CHAPTER FIVE

Big Eye owned a condo in a tall, tapered building that had no windows on the first five floors. It looked like a Taiwanese space shuttle with booster jets attached to the left and right sides.

Whistle took us up the short drive to the entrance door. Gao raised a hand.

"All of you wait here. I have to make sure the apartment is clean first."

When he was gone, I said, "I can't imagine that guy scrubbing toilets and mopping floors."

"You have no idea what he means," said Mei-ling before bursting with laughter. "He wants to make sure there's nothing incriminating in the apartment where Big Eye brings his women! Right, Whistle?"

Whistle made a low rumbling sound and stared ahead. Mei-ling slapped his headrest. "Stop making that sound! It's annoying." She turned on the car radio with her phone and dialed up a death-metal song.

"This is your kind of music, isn't it, Jing-nan?"

"Not quite," I said. "I like to understand what the singer's saying."

She turned up the volume. "Is that better?"

"No, it's not better at all. Feel free to change the station."

Mei-ling did some mock head-banging. I tried to grab her phone but she switched it to her far hand and made it dance in the air, out of my reach.

"Whistle!" I yelled, "can you turn the radio off?"

"Can't. She put it on override."

Mei-ling stuck out her tongue and threw up the devil horn hand sign.

This was what I was going to have to put up with for the next week. This crazy little demoness and her awful music. Well, it was only a week and she was my cousin, after all. As I watched her continue her antics, something did crack through my thick shell of fatigue and I smiled. She sure wasn't afraid to look stupid. I'm glad she wasn't afraid. Too many kids these days are all about playing it safe and quiet to get into the best schools and then get the best jobs. I'd probably really lose my mind if Mei-ling were meek and sedentary.

Gao came back with a canvas bag about the size of a laptop and shoved it under his seat. He stood outside next to the open door and lit a cigarette. After two quick puffs he tossed it aside and slapped the roof. "Whistle, let's get Mei-ling's bags up there."

Mei-ling finally killed the music.

The apartment didn't look as good as the building's exterior. The size was obnoxious, half of the eighteenth floor, and the furnishings were stylish to the point of not being functional. But the window in the living room was the main problem. It showed too much of the ugly city environs outside. Some people say the pollution is from China, brought in by the cold front from the northwest, weather warfare meant to break the Taiwanese will for independence. I say the city looks better with the smog. From this high up in the air it looks like used cotton swabs are floating by. That still beats seeing the city for what it is: blocks of squat illegal houses peeking out from behind the office towers of Xinyi Road. Rows of sideways-parked mopeds and motorcycles looking like the exposed gills of poisoned bugs on their backs. All over, single-eyed air-conditioning fans stared out blankly from behind dirty slats.

Mei-ling walked up to the window and touched her fingers to the glass.

"Don't you love this city? It's so exciting to be here!" She squashed her face against the window and looked hard to her left. "I can see Taipei 101!"

"If you think all this is great," I said sarcastically, "you're going to think your first beer is amazing."

"I already know how to handle liquor, Jing-nan! Didn't you see me do a shot on the ride up? Let's go back down to the car and see if you can do one!" She glanced at Whistle who curtly shook his head.

"Oh, I get it," I said. "You took that shot to show off. That's a lousy reason to drink."

"What's a good reason to drink? To relax? To get a buzz? Are those good *adult* reasons to drink?"

"Working full time is a good reason to drink." Man, that was weak. It was annoying that she was challenging me, but even more distressing was that I didn't have good answers. "At your age, drinking will stunt your growth and brain development." I spoke like it knew it was true.

Mei-ling made a dismissive hand flourish cribbed from Big Eye.

Gao stepped toward the door. "Well, that's it, then. Back to Taichung, Whistle?"

"Wait!" said Mei-ling. "Let's go to Din Tai Fung!"

I suddenly perked up. It had been a while since I've had soup dumplings and that restaurant made the best. I knew they opened at ten and now would be a great time to go—no line! We could easily grab a table for four.

I noticed crestfallen faces on Whistle and Gao, the saddest I'd seen on either. How could Mei-ling not see that these guys were pretty anxious to finally be cut loose?

"You and I can go, Mei-ling," I said. "You don't want to detain Whistle and Gao any longer, right? They've both had really long nights."

"Didn't you want to go, Whistle?" Mei-ling asked. "You've never been to the original location. It's right down the street!"

The two men dithered like boys about to be assigned tasks.

"Mei-ling," I said, "they probably have something else to attend to. Do you want them to get into trouble with Big Eye because of you?"

"They're supposed to look after me. How are they going to get into trouble?"

"You're in Taipei now. I'm looking after you." I looked at Whistle and Gao. They were relieved. How could they let a teenager wield so much power over them?

I texted Nancy to see if she was up for soup dumplings. Who wouldn't be? She said she'd meet us there in twenty minutes.

ALTHOUGH THE RESTAURANT WAS on the same street, it was five major blocks from the apartment and each block was about 500 meters long. Mei-ling's shades covered half her face and the skirt she changed into barely covered her thighs. She made sure to lag behind in case some age-appropriate boys (who were supposed to be in school at this time, anyway) wanted to sidle up to her, the latest online pop sensation.

"Too embarrassed to walk next to me, huh?" I called over my shoulder.

"I'm not embarrassed. I just want people to see me completely."

"No one knows who you are, Mei-ling."

"Tell that to the thousands of people who voted for me," she said.

Annoyed, I retaliated by picking up the pace. Everybody these days wants a bit of fame. Andy Warhol said that everyone was famous for fifteen minutes but in this fast-paced age it must be down to five or maybe even one. Maybe Mei-ling would get her time to shine, but when those sixty seconds were over, it was going to be ugly. I knew that Whistle and Gao wouldn't be able to handle it but I hoped that Big Eye or Mei-ling's mom could.

I had never met her mother and I had no idea who she was.

"Mei-ling, tell me about your mother."

"What's there to tell? You know she's Hakka."

"That doesn't tell me much."

"Your parents are dead, right?"

"Yeah."

"Is that why you want to know about my mother? Because you don't have one anymore?"

Confucius was right to hate children.

"No, Mei-ling. I'm just trying to understand *you* better. You're a troublemaker in school and yet you want to be a famous singer. Is your mom a singer?"

"She has a beautiful voice, but she never pursued it professionally. She should have, though. When my mom was younger she could have been a model, even after she had me. She's tall and has these big cheekbones. We have mountain-people blood. Big Eye saw her on a bus and he chased after it until she got off because he didn't have the money to get on. You know that he was away for a while and she had to work and raise me at the same time. It wasn't easy for her. I wasn't always a good kid."

I thumped my chest to cover my involuntary coughs.

"We had to scrimp and save but she was raised that way. Her parents worked seven days a week and they sing, too. The Hakka life is work hard, play hard, but showbiz isn't a part of it."

"Do you get along with her?"

Mei-ling wiped her eyes. "I actually get along with Big Eye better. He tries to tell me what not to do. She tries to tell me what to do. There are a lot more options with the former."

I didn't know much about Hakkas except that their language sounded like Cantonese. The stereotype was that they were really cheap but that idea was probably propagated by other Chinese who tried to take advantage of them, and nobody took advantage of Hakkas. If Hakkas are anything, they are tough as nails. Historically they worked backbreaking jobs from sunup to sundown. Hakka women did the same physical tasks as the men.

Most of the early Chinese settlers lived in Taiwan's lowlands by the shore but the Hakka were driven into the mountains, where they established the camphor and logging industries. The Hakka villages bordered—some say overlapped—areas claimed by different aboriginal tribes, who were already being marginalized. The Hakka depended on the protection of the Lords of the Three Mountains to keep the savages at bay. In time, of course, the two communities were bound by intermarriage and they both found common struggles in the coming centuries against other Chinese immigrants, the Japanese, and an authoritarian government that wouldn't recognize the legitimacy of Hakka culture and language.

When I saw someone like Mei-ling, I had to wonder if she was what her ancestors had in mind for the sacrifices they made for later generations.

"You're looking at me funny," she said, lifting her shades. "Stop it."

"I can't help it," I said. "You're acting ridiculous."

"How much farther is this place? We should've taken a cab!"

"Don't you want to give your adoring public a chance to see you up close?"

Three boys, aged between fourteen and eighteen, walked by. The youngest happened to glance at Mei-ling and she smiled too hard at him. An apologetic look came over his face and he dashed to hide behind his two brothers, who continued walking with their eyes fixed to Taipei 101's ghostly outline against the oily sky.

When they were too far to hear, Mei-ling said, "What's wrong with that boy? Is he gay?"

"He may or may not be," I said. "He's not local, though. He and his family are on vacation here, from Japan, I'll bet. The parents look Japanese."

"Where are the parents?"

"We're just passing them now."

"How do you know that's them?

"The mother's holding the youngest boy's coat."

Mei-ling nodded and gave me a half-smile that was tempered with a newfound respect. "That was very observant of you."

"If you watch people closely, you'll know how to sell to them."

I FELT TRIUMPHANT AS we crossed the street to Din Tai Fung. No crowd waiting on the sidewalk, just Nancy in tapered slacks and a collared charcoal shirt. It was one of her professional looks and a departure from her standby indie-rock style.

"I'm meeting one of the sponsors of the foreign students orientation today," she said as a disclaimer. Mei-ling latched on like a younger sister.

"You're very pretty. What are you doing with this troll?"

Nancy didn't miss a beat. "I have to serve him because in a former life I was a farmer and he was my water buffalo."

Mei-ling gave a genuine laugh. I liked that she liked Nancy right away.

"You don't look so bad for not sleeping last night," Nancy told me.

"I dozed in the car coming back," I said. I answered her raised eyebrows with a knowing look. *More on this situation later.*

"I've been so busy getting ready for these new students, I haven't been sleeping enough, either." She gave Mei-ling an encouraging look. "After you spend some time here, you'll see that nobody sleeps in Taipei. We just work all the time."

"I like it already," said Mei-ling. "I want to work hard on my singing."

I had told Nancy on the phone that Mei-ling was going to start high school in Taipei in the fall, but I hadn't mentioned the teen's star aspirations, so this was a surprise.

"You're a singer?" Nancy asked. "What do you sing?"

"I sing everything. Michael Jackson, Britney Spears, Jess Lee."

"I'll bet you're really good," said Nancy with a smile. I couldn't help crossing my eyes.

"Thank you," said Mei-ling. Turning to me, she said, "Your girlfriend is very nice and pretty. You should marry her, Jing-nan, because you can't do any better."

"Maybe you can sing at the wedding," I said. Mei-ling slapped my arm and Nancy kicked my leg both at the same time. We all laughed and then turned to the menu. I don't know why Nancy and I bothered to. We always got the same things.

"It's Mei-ling's first time here," I said. "Why don't we let her order?"

"I don't like soup dumplings," she said, dismissing the signature dish.

I shifted in my seat. "That's the most popular thing here," I said. "Din Tai Fung is famous worldwide for them."

"All their food is good, though, isn't it?"

"Oh, yes," said Nancy.

"Well, let's order them anyway," said Mei-ling. "Maybe their soup dumplings will blow my conception about them."

"Seriously," I said. "These soup dumplings are the best food outside of the night markets."

Nancy and I watched Mei-ling tick off items on the order slip, silently regretting that she selected shrimp fried rice and left empty boxes by the spicy cucumbers and pea shoots.

"Let me see that," I said. I added the two vegetable appetizers to our order. A waitress took our slip and scanned it. With a small nod she left.

"This is one of Jing-nan's old haunts," Nancy told Mei-ling. "He started coming here when he was your age."

"Younger," I said as I poured tea for everybody, my own cup last.

I couldn't remember the first time my parents brought me here, but I do remember coming here with my childhood sweetheart. I hate that term. It's clichéd and even worse it undermines the seriousness of the relationship. "Childhood sweetheart" sounds like something you grow out of or maybe even laugh about one day. But I will never laugh about it nor will I ever really feel completely at ease while eating here.

Yes, Din Tai Fung was definitely an old haunt and I remained haunted by it.

"My cousin's not looking too happy," said Mei-ling. "He's annoyed because he didn't like the way I ordered."

Nancy looked at me with her gentle eyes. "Jing-nan has a lot on his mind," she said. "If you had a business you'd probably worry a lot, too. Right now he's comparing the customers and the tickets for each table."

"Is that right, Jing-nan?" asked Mei-ling.

"I can't help it," I said. "The prices and the typical wait here would never fly at the Shilin Night Market. Where I play, it's got to be good, fast, and cheap. Here, they're only good. So I beat them on two out of three counts."

Mei-ling sat up. "I've never been to the Shilin Night Market!"

"Do you want to go to his stand?" asked Nancy. "I'm sure Jing-nan would love to take you tonight."

My lips peeled back, revealing my clenched teeth. "I think Mei-ling has to rest tonight," I said. "She must be bushed."

"I feel fine," she said. "I wanna go! When are you going?"

"Honestly, I wasn't counting on having an extra person on hand. You might be in the way."

"I won't be! I'll be good! Let me come!"

A woman dropped off the spicy cucumbers, stacked stumps of jade in garlic sauce as thick as gauze. Even though I hadn't used my chopsticks yet, I did the Taiwanese thing by reversing them and using the handle ends to transfer a few cucumbers to Mei-ling's plate. It's a polite way of forcing food upon someone without involving a saliva transfer.

"That's enough," she said.

"They're very good," said Nancy.

Mei-ling chewed one thoroughly. "I like them," she said. "Not too spicy." A swirled dome of pea shoots with a shallow moat of garlic sauce arrived at the table. "Why did you order so many vegetables?"

"Because we're not at McDonald's." I dumped a healthy portion of pea shoots on her plate.

"If I eat all these vegetables, I get to go with you to the night market."

I wiped the handles of my chopsticks against my napkin. "I'm responsible for you, so you have to promise me that you won't go off with some boys or drink or take drugs. You understand?"

She frowned and kicked me lightly under the table. "You sound like my dad! Do you think I shouldn't get pregnant tonight, too?"

"No, I'm all right with you getting pregnant. Nancy will help you raise the child."

"Crazy talk," said Nancy with her mouth full.

"I have to be at the night market until almost one in the morning. You're probably going to run out of things to do there way before then. How are you going to get back to your apartment?"

"I'll just take the train back."

"You know how to ride the train by yourself?"

She crossed her eyes and stuck out her teeth. "Duh, I no know how to do anything, duh!"

When my cousin excused herself "to go piss," I told Nancy about my gangster uncle, the gambling den in the sugarcane field, the shootout, and the crazy temple. She told me that she had joined a protest group that was going to storm a government building and occupy the space.

We were each surprised the other wasn't.

When we hit the street the full weight of my exhaustion fell upon me. I staggered to the MRT subway system while Nancy escorted Mei-ling back to her apartment. From there Nancy would walk south through Da'an Park to the university and go on plotting revolution.

I MET MEI-LING AT 3:30 in the afternoon just outside the northern exit of the MRT at Jiantan Station.

"You're on time!" I exclaimed.

"Why wouldn't I be? Did you get enough sleep?"

"A few hours are all I need. Did you sleep, too?"

"I stayed up and read about the student movement. I appreciate Nancy's activism."

"I appreciate that you changed into something less flammable. Anyway, you can never go wrong with jeans and a T-shirt."

She did that Big Eye hand dismissal. "I changed for me, not you."

Mei-ling and I walked briskly through the early hours of the night market as vendors were unloading their goods and setting up signage.

"This is like watching a circus set up," she said. "Only there aren't any animals."

"Just wait for the people to show up. They're all beasts. I have to tame them a little and take their money."

We entered Cixian Temple, where the vendors prayed each night before the market opened.

"You know who that is?" I asked, pointing to the goddess seated behind a table overlain with offerings of lit joss sticks, flowers, and baskets of fruit.

"Of course I do," said Mei-ling. "It's Mazu."

The indifferent eyes of the idol of the Empress of Heaven stared at us through her beaded veil.

I bought a pack of incense sticks from a shady-looking guy at a booth in the temple. The tattoos went above his inner elbow and under his rolled-up sleeve. Half these guys who work at the temple look like criminals, or *heidaoren*, because they are. They're not at the temple to cultivate their karma. They're here to handle the menial work of collecting tax-free money for their outfit. After all, almost every neighborhood temple is owned by criminals.

Don't think they don't take the gods and goddesses

seriously, however. This is Taiwan. Everybody's superstitious. Nobody blindly believes in any deity yet nobody wants to incur their wrath. Even the most cold-hearted, willing-to-sell-his-own-mother-for-money thug wouldn't release intestinal gas until leaving the temple, or at least getting a respectable distance away from the offering table.

Personally, I wouldn't give a dime to this enterprise. But my hands were tied. The temple had been complaining that the night-market merchants weren't being supportive enough and suggested that everybody at least burn some incense every night. As a strictly pragmatic matter, I agreed that it made the temple and by extension the entire night market look more legit to the tourists. Cixian Temple is cited in all the guidebooks as the origin of the night market, so people like to start there.

Sometimes it's a pain in the ass to maintain history for the sake of tourism. I'll go along with it, though, because I like having money.

I handed several lit joss sticks to Mei-ling.

"Bow three times to Mazu," I told her.

"I know what to do," she said as she proved it. As I paid my respects to the Mother Ancestor, another one of Mazu's many aspects, I heard Mei-ling mutter, "This whole thing is stupid, anyway."

My hands shook as I planted my sticks in the ash-strewn urn.

"Don't ever call it stupid," I warned her. "If people find comfort in something without hurting anyone, it's not stupid. How would you like it if I told you your singing's stupid?"

"You've already told me my singing's stupid."

"And it was a hurtful and wrong thing to say, right?"

She slapped my arm. "You're so annoying!" she said, her mouth curling into a playful frown. "I can't believe I came to the night market with you."

"If you think I'm bad, you should meet the guys I work with."

DWAYNE'S BLOOD-SPLATTERED ARMS WORKED like hairy pistons as he cut up organs destined for skewers. As Mei-ling and I approached Unknown Pleasures he glanced up and immediately adjusted his body language to bulk up his arms.

"Dwayne, this is my cousin, Mei-ling," I said and made a point to emphasize every word of, "She is sixteen years old." It was a warning for him to watch his language, but Mei-ling was the one I should have warned.

"Hello, Dwayne," she said. "Are you a mountain person?"

I tensed up at the use of the phrase as Dwayne put down his knives and crossed his arms. At best, "mountain person" was outdated. At worst, it was plain racist.

But I knew Dwayne. A pretty girl who was related to his employer could never offend him. "Please call me an 'original inhabitant,'" he said with gleaming eyes. "Many people prefer that term. We didn't all live in the mountains."

"Oh, sure," she said. "I'm sorry."

Dwayne made sounds like he was cooing to a baby. "Don't worry. It's all just words, anyway." He rubbed his nose roughly with the back of his right hand.

Frankie the Cat, subtle as ever, appeared out of nowhere and presented himself to Mei-ling before I had a chance to. "I'm Frankie," he said. "You must be Big Eye's kid."

"Yes, he's my dad."

Frankie face softened. He gazed across the years. "The last time I saw you, you must have been about a year old."

"But this is my first time in Taipei."

Frankie nodded. "Yes, I believe it is."

I was dumbstruck. "Hey, Frankie."

"Yeah?"

"You've met my cousin before?"

"Yeah."

"When did you meet her?"

"I was down in Taichung briefly with some old acquaintances."

"Why didn't you tell me I had a cousin?"

"It wasn't my business to tell you. It wasn't my business to know, either, but I couldn't help that. Now you know, so I guess Big Eye's back in touch with you."

He turned and went back to his station. Sometimes I forget how attuned Frankie is to the *heidaoren* and all their misdeeds. As a political prisoner on Green Island, he was treated the same as the flat-out criminals—like shit. By the time Frankie was released, he had brothers for life who would kill for him.

"He knows my dad," Mei-ling said slowly.

"Frankie knows a lot of things." I wondered what else he was holding close to his vest.

"Well, what are we gonna do now?"

"Mei-ling," I said. "I have to help set up. If you walk around, you won't get lost, will you?"

"She's a big girl," said Dwayne. "She'll be fine."

"There's not too much going on right now," Frankie called out. "Be another hour before things start swinging."

Mei-ling shifted her weight to her right leg. "Do you want me to help with anything?" she asked.

"I'm just going to make about a thousand skewers," I said. "It's pretty boring work."

"I want to try it! I've never really cooked anything."

"I don't know about this. You could cut yourself."

"Let her give it a shot, Jing-nan," said Dwayne. "Are you afraid she'll be better at it than you?"

"I'm afraid she'll stab her finger, get an infection and then lose her entire arm after gangrene sets in," I said. Everybody laughed. "All right, young lady, if you want to try this, wash your hands first at the sink. Use lots of soap."

When she was done, I gave her a stack of bamboo skewers and a bowl of pig intestines.

"Frankie's already done the hard part," I said. "He's cut them down and washed them out thoroughly. Dwayne's sliced and marinated them." I reached in and grabbed a strip dripping with sauce. "You want to take these, squeeze them off but not all the way. Roll 'em up like a sock and then stick it through with this."

I was distracted by narrating what I was doing, as the process was intuitive to me after all this time. Talking about it was making me consciously think about what I was doing. A skier wouldn't say out loud what muscles were doing what while slaloming. When I scratched myself by accident, I played off the pain with a flourish of my fingers. "Yep, the skewers are nice and sharp!"

Mei-ling cringed. "Your fingers must be tough from this job. I would be bleeding if I did that."

"Then don't. So, put four on a skewer and you're done," I concluded. "Pretty basic stuff."

"Why four? There's room for more."

"It's a dirty trick," said Dwayne. "He always wants the skewers to have four chunks each because he wants people to buy two in order to get that lucky number." The word for "eight" in Mandarin sounds like "wealth," so the superstitious Taiwanese buy things in eights, and get phone numbers and license plates that include as many eights as possible. It also helps me that four is considered an unlucky number.

"You should put five on a skewer," said Mei-ling. "They'll fit and that's a lucky number, too."

Frankie called out over his plastic tub of organs, "Why sell five when you can sell eight?"

Mei-ling nodded as she stabbed another rolled-up intestine. "I think I'm starting to understand the night-market culture," she said. "You're all a bunch of scammers!"

IT WAS FUN SHOWING Mei-ling what to do. Her presence added a soft note to the usual roughhouse idiocy that Dwayne and I could degenerate into.

Foot traffic picked up around 5:30 and I stood at the front of Unknown Pleasures, surveying the crowd and listening carefully. I heard a group of men speaking English, of the English-accent variety. I stepped out into the crowd and spied a group of four middle-aged white guys, a little out of shape but cheerful.

They had no idea what to do with their money, so naturally they needed my help.

"You lot!" I called to them, using the expression for the plural third person that I learned from the chorus of The Clash song "Magnificent Seven." "Come over here!"

The men burst out laughing—a common reaction to hearing fluent English spoken—and ambled over. A guy with wispy dried-garlic-root hair wearing a Hawaiian shirt was the first to reach me.

"Haw haw," he laughed in a decidedly American way. "You fell for Bob's fake accent. Thought we were British, right?"

"I did," I said. "You got me."

"We don't want the wrong people to know we're Americans!"

Bob came up and rubbed his pink sea-anemone mouth. "We can tell you're not the wrong sort of people. Did I really fool you?"

I nodded and smiled. If I played along, they'd buy more. "Yes, I fell for it completely. It was perfect."

The other two guys gathered around. They looked like retired cops—walking around with guarded casualness. A surprisingly high number of American tourists are ex-police. I guess the word was out among them that Taipei was a great vacation place that was seemingly crime-free. What they don't know won't hurt them.

"Wait a second, hold on now," said Bob. "Are you an American? Your English is just a little too good."

I crossed my arms and smiled. "I went to college in the States," I said, not mentioning that I never finished. "You're Bob, right? Please call me Johnny." I shook hands with him. He had to buy something from me now. You can't not buy something from someone whose name you know. I made sure to introduce myself to each of them.

"What have we got here?" the ex-cop named Jeff said to himself as he cast a critical eye upon my award-winning skewers. "How about that one? What the heck is it?"

"You don't want that one," I said. "I think you better go with something safer. It's too Taiwanese for you." That would challenge their manhoods.

"Jeff is tougher than he looks," said Bob. "This man's seen murder victims."

I raised an eyebrow and threw out a challenge. "Well, Jeff, do you think you can handle pig uterus? If that's too much for you, the chicken uterus is just to the left."

Jeff sucked in his lips and opened his eyes wide. "I'm not even sure what the uterus does," he said with a nervous smile. "How about, you know, a straight-up beef or chicken thing?"

I reached over the counter and touched his shoulder. "I've got you covered, Jeff. We've got satay-style chicken and beef." I called out in Taiwanese for Mei-ling to bring over the goods from the main grill in the back that was manned by Dwayne.

All four men immediately evaluated Mei-ling's teenage cleavage as she transferred a tray of skewers to the front grill.

"I didn't know," said Bob, "that Taiwanese women were so alluring."

I shrugged. "I don't think of her like that," I said. "For one thing, she's my cousin, and she's sixteen." Three of the men shoved their hands in their shorts pockets while Jeff let out a low whistle. I didn't know what the age of consent was in the US but it sure wasn't sixteen, which was Taiwan's. "Say hello to the customers, Mei-ling," I said in English.

"Hello," she said. Like most Taiwanese, she sounded nice and innocent when she spoke English. I pointed out the intestine skewers to the men.

"Mei-ling made these herself. It's only her first day but I think she did a pretty good job. Should I add these to your order?"

"Oh, yeah, we want to support Mei-ling," said Bob.

"Sure thing," said Jeff. I loaded them up with skewers and even threw in a small bag of sausages. Mei-ling thanked each of the men. They looked at her wistfully as they left.

"I should have told them I was a singer," Mei-ling said. "They would have bought my songs!"

"They wouldn't get your kind of music," I said.

She pouted. "They would've bought it just because I'm cute. I could tell."

I couldn't argue with her. They had gone for her hideously asymmetrical (by my standards) skewers, which I'm sure they wouldn't have the guts to eat. They would eat the sausages, at least—they had a familiar form factor.

Some Australian women came by and were also charmed with Mei-ling. "Cute as a button," they called her, which I thought was odd since all the buttons I had ever seen were rather utilitarian and plain.

I should have hired a girl sooner. Maybe Dwayne and

Frankie and I hadn't been able to squeeze all the New Taiwan dollars that Unknown Pleasures was capable of yielding. I could crunch the numbers and see if it was cost-effective to keep her for a month or so. I'd have to pay her, after all.

Maybe I could even get a karaoke system and let her sing her songs a little bit.

No, scratch that. She would drive people away.

As the hours went by I could tell we were picking up substantially more cash than the typical night. Mei-ling seemed to enjoy learning the ropes, how to read people and draw them in. Too bad her English wasn't so great. I think part of the problem is that the English language is overt and specific in a way that Taiwanese find offensive. The Taiwanese language, like Mandarin, is by comparison vague and indirect. Speaking it in a familiar way with a stranger gives you an assholic quality.

"*Ma de*, this is the place!"

The foul mouth belonged to a short and enthusiastic high school student, his shirt untucked. He had brought a dozen boys and girls to Unknown Pleasures. I smiled. It was always a short kid who led the packs. Why?

"Hey guys, welcome to my venerable stand!" I called out.

The little leader nearly fell over. "You! You're the guy who got shot!"

"If you all buy something, I'll show you the bullet wound."

"You didn't actually get shot, Jing-nan!" yelled Mei-ling.

"Who said I did?" I lifted Fatty from its shelf and hefted the pot over my head. "This is the brave little soldier who took a bullet for me! When you're all done eating, take a picture with Fatty!"

The kids lit up and lined up. I caught Mei-ling's exaggerated look of disgust at my sales technique. Maybe she didn't have it in her to do this.

CHAPTER SIX

An opportune time came for my bathroom break. I posted Mei-ling in the front; Dwayne and Frankie said they'd keep a lookout.

A few young women were waiting to get into our restroom. It's our private restroom, yes, but a group of attractive women attracts both men and women. For such an attraction I was willing to self-sacrifice and trudge all the way to the common restroom halfway across the night market.

The bathrooms in the pavilion were poorly marked, sparing many souls from their horrors. They were cleaner since the Singaporean tourists sued the tourist bureau but still not up to Taipei's usual standards. Some people blame the foreign tourists but I suspect the cleaning company just plain sucks. I checked myself in an unsplattered quadrant of the mirror and flashed my warmest smile. That was a face that could sell two hundred skewers an hour.

I left the bathroom and almost immediately a hand crashed into my left shoulder.

"Jing-nan!" It was the new captain of the local precinct, the one just outside the northern border of the night market. He had the squat head of a panda and the same baggy eyes. But his face was unfriendly and his voice downright mean.

"Hello, Captain Huang," I said. He was about my height

but his shoulders were half a foot wider. Those shoulders pressed in on me as we walked, threatening to smear me across the front fenders of a row of parked mopeds.

My fame from the shooting incident came with not a small amount of embarrassment for the cops. Loose policing was blamed by the media for the attempt on my life and the assailant's clean getaway. The old captain resigned shortly thereafter. Captain Huang was appointed last week and had paid me a personal visit at Unknown Pleasures. It was a courtesy call minus the courtesy and he wouldn't even accept a free skewer. If a cop won't take free food, then something is seriously wrong.

"That girl you got at your shitty booth," he started. "She's quite a looker." An evil gleam came over his sad eyes.

"She's my cousin," I said.

"Oh, I know. She's Big Eye's big girl, isn't she?" He examined my surprise and added, "Didn't know I knew about your uncle and his buddies, huh?"

"Say, Captain Huang, would you mind not walking so close to me? I bruise easily."

He grabbed my left arm and braced it at the elbow in a way that was just painful enough. We walked two more paces and I could feel where his grip was loose. If I cranked my arm clockwise half a turn, I could free my arm. If I went the full turn I could grab his wrist, pull his arm behind his back and have him on his knees.

The things I've learned from wrestling with Dwayne during the lulls.

I decided to allow Captain Huang to continue believing he had me restrained. For one thing it would be bad to antagonize a cop, much less a captain. After all, the local precinct already had it in for me for making them look bad. For another thing, the captain would never forgive a public humiliation and he'd find a way to shut down Unknown Pleasures. My good business sense prevailed but my impulses couldn't be restrained entirely. I made some token gestures to free my arm.

Captian Huang responded by tightening his grip, a crucial strategic mistake, by the way. "Stay with me, Jing-nan," he growled.

In exasperation, I turned to him. "Why are you treating me like a criminal?"

He couldn't suppress a laugh. "You are a criminal! You and your whole crooked family! Just wait. I'm going to get enough on you to shut down your rinky-dink cover operation and put the whole Chen clan in jail."

I stopped walking, bringing the both of us to a halt. "I'm sorry that you personally didn't have a chance to play hero to save me and that your predecessor ended up getting sacked because he didn't, either."

"You're not sorry. You're not innocent, either! Everyone running a stand here has something in their past. You're nothing but a bunch of carnival barkers."

I looked at him hard. "I've never done anything wrong."

The captain pushed back his hat, revealing a forehead scarred with acne. He must have had it rough in high school. "What about Big Eye? How innocent is he?" The captain finally let go of my arm to poke a thumb into my left breast, centimeters away from the nipple. "Did you know that a couple years back this farmer plowing his field outside Taichung accidentally dug up two charred bodies?"

"It was all over the news."

"Why did Big Eye kill those guys?"

"Was it Big Eye? I thought the case was still unsolved." I felt smug because I was sure that my uncle, as bad as he was, hadn't killed anybody. Big Eye didn't have it in him. At heart, the guy was a comedian. Big Eye's pal Gao was a hell of shot, but I was sure my uncle only used him for protection. Cops don't go around murdering people.

Captain Huang twisted his hand and pointed at my nose. "I know all about you people. You went down to Taichung for that big summit meeting with Big Eye and Wood Duck and some other *jiaotou*s. Think I don't know about that, either, huh? You think I don't know about all the properties in Taipei that Big Eye owns? You think I don't know that his daughter is living in one of them?"

One talent I have learned in all the self-promotion that I do is to realize when it's useless to talk to somebody. They've already made their mind up and they won't consider anything I say. I usually leave them and fish elsewhere. In this case, I didn't want to have the captain tag along all the way to Unknown Pleasures. Dwayne would punch him in the face and end up in jail.

Dwayne is a fighter. In all my roughhousing with him, I've learned that simply doing nothing usually confounds an opponent. I relaxed my arms at my sides and stared directly at Captain Huang, keeping my face blank. At first he had both hands up like a praying mantis, ready to counter any sudden move from me. The captain was baffled when none came. His eyes narrowed and his mouth twisted into a bait worm waiting to be cut up and hooked.

"Think you're funny or something?" he asked. "Just wait. Everybody thinks you're some big hero. I know the real story." He straightened up, turned sideways, and disappeared into the crowd.

WHEN I GOT BACK to Unknown Pleasures I saw Mei-ling sitting in a corner seat, turned to the wall, while Dwayne handled the orders.

I sat next to my cousin as she brought up a wad of tissues and dabbed her eyes.

"What happened?" I asked.

She hid her hands under the table. "Some policemen came by and said I wasn't permitted to work here and you could lose your license."

"Aw, shit," I said out loud.

Her shoulders slumped to her knees. "I'm sorry, Jing-nan. I think I got you in trouble."

"You didn't do anything wrong. Those people are out to get me and you just got in the way." I patted her hand. "Well, maybe now would be a good time for you to walk through the night market. Have some fun. Motherfuck these guys."

She smiled. "Wow, I didn't know my cousin cursed like a truck driver!"

"Your dad was the one who taught me. You should have been there to hear the things he said in front of me when I was a kid." I smiled and reached into my wallet. I forced a NT$1,000 note onto her. About thirty American dollars. You could feed a family of four for two days with that. "Get a nice dress or something. The clothes stalls all have unique things. Call me if someone tries to overcharge you."

Young people recover quickly, especially when they have money. We didn't see her for a few hours. When she came back she had two boys in tow, skinny shirkers wearing glasses. They looked smart but I pegged them as destined for dead-end office jobs.

"Who are your friends, Mei-ling?" I asked.

The slightly taller boy spoke up first. "She said her name was Shu-hui!" He turned to his companion. "Told ya she was lying!"

"I'm sorry, boys," Mei-ling said. "But a woman has to protect herself. You could be ruffians for all I really know." She smiled sweetly.

"Are you going to be here tomorrow night?" asked the

shorter boy. His hopeful, plum-tomato face showed signs he was preparing himself for disappointment.

"Probably not," she said. "But please drop by my artist page and stay in touch." She handed business cards to both of them and I saw their eyes pop open.

"Can I get one of those, too?" I asked Mei-ling.

"I don't have many left," she said quickly. I reached over and grabbed the wrist of the smaller kid and turned it.

The card featured a full-color picture of a naked Mei-ling stretched across a couch, her legs strategically posed and the index fingers of each hand covering her nipples.

I grabbed the cards back from the boys.

"Time for you to go!" I declared.

The taller boy frowned. "Too late! I already memorized the web address!"

I took a step toward him and both of them scrammed. "Mei-ling, are you trying to break into the porn industry?"

She jutted out her bottom jaw and bent her neck like a vulture. "I am not naked! I'm still covered up!"

"Is that picture from the session that Whistle paid for? No wonder you won that online contest!"

Foiled and found out, Mei-ling now bared her front teeth like a rat making a last stand. "Hold that pose," I said, snapping a picture of her with my camera. "I'm going to upload this so people can see what you really look like."

"Why are you trying to ruin my career?"

I dangled the card in front of her. "What does this have to do with singing? You're just trying to sell skin!"

"If that's what it takes, I'll do it." She screwed her face hard.

"Yeah? What would Big Eye say if he saw this picture?"

She blinked. "No, don't. Please. Whistle will be in a lot of trouble."

I sure didn't want to ensnare that guy in this bullshit. He was already preyed upon by Mei-ling. "Look. You've seen enough action for tonight. It's almost ten o'clock and it's time for you to go home."

"It's still early," she said. "Whistle and Gao would let me stay out later!"

"The difference between them and me is I don't work for you."

DWAYNE AND FRANKIE TOOK over the stand. If my presence weren't so key for roping in the tourists, I would leave early every night.

Mei-ling and I walked south and entered the Jiantian station. "Mei-ling, how much do you have left on your EasyCard?"

She looked at me apologetically. "I don't have one. I bought a single-journey ticket to come here. Was that wrong?"

"It's cheaper to use a card. Please tell me you still have a valid student ID. We can get a student EasyCard."

Mei-ling twisted the clasp to her bag and it puckered open. "I have it somewhere. They wanted me to come back to school so they could confiscate it, but I never did." She cackled.

"You sound like Big Eye when you do that."

She produced her ID and held it over her head in victory. "Of course I do. He taught me the value in being smug."

The woman at the booth solemnly issued Mei-ling a SmartCard and reminded her she wasn't supposed to let anyone else use it. The pass was a handy thing. Not only did it work in the metros and the buses, it could also be used to pay for things at 7-11 and Friendly Mart.

I broke out my wallet and added more money to her card at a machine. "Now you're a real Taipei person," I told her as I handed the card to her. "Don't embarrass us."

The train came quickly and was mostly empty. I took a seat but Mei-ling continued to stand, mesmerized by the video ads. We shot south over the Keelung River and I watched her steady herself by grabbing a strap by the plastic handle. Mei-ling might be all right in Taipei, I thought. Her arms were spider-leg skinny. She needed to eat more. Everybody needed to eat more, especially at my night-market stand.

I watched Mei-ling sway with Taipei's city lights blinking by in the background. I had to admit that she did look like a singing star. Too-skinny actually worked for her, and her skin glowed. As the train plunged underground, Mei-ling dropped into the seat next to me. She'd already seen every commercial twice.

"You need something to read for the train," I said.

"I have a book on my phone, but I think it's rude to read since I'm with you."

"You're so polite."

"I don't need a chaperone, you know. Taipei isn't that dangerous."

"I'm trying to protect Taipei from you!"

She stepped on my foot. "What are we going to do tomorrow?"

"How about we go to the National Palace Museum?"

She wrinkled her nose. "Sounds like a school trip."

"It's an interesting place. I never wanted to go when I was young but once I was there, I didn't want to leave." She didn't look convinced. "It's a lot more than just the jades that look like fatty pork and cabbage."

She laughed at the mention of the museum's most famous pieces. "I can't remember the last time I was at a museum," she said. "The last few times they wouldn't let me go on field trips because I was a discipline problem."

"For both our sakes, be good while you're here. You and

your dad have issues, but you and I have a clean slate. Let's keep it that way. Promise not to hand out any more of those cards while you're here."

She clasped her hands together and smiled sweetly. "Anything you say, big cousin, because you know best!" I smiled because it was funny and I could tell that she was still going to do whatever the hell she wanted to.

At the Da'an Park station we stepped out of the air-conditioned car and the cool humidity of the night closed over us like a hood. I noticed Mei-ling shivering.

"I hope you packed a jacket," I told her.

"I have a few," she said, rubbing her bare arms.

"You don't have enough fat. That's why you can't take the cold."

"If I'm not skinny, people won't love me."

"That's a healthy way to think," I muttered.

We waited to cross Xinyi Road. Small flocks of overloaded mopeds zipped by. A souped-up sports car and a delivery truck raced to beat the light. The truck went through the red while the sports car rolled to a stop. As we crossed we heard bass beats emanating from the car's speakers.

"That's what I want more than anything," Mei-ling said. "To make music that people play and feel good about, whether they're on a dance floor or driving around."

"Music's more than that to me," I said.

"What's more important than feeling good?"

I had to admit that I was stumped. It was enjoyable to listen to music I liked. Was that all there was to it? Wasn't there something intellectual to it, too? Maybe some guys named Johnny at the record labels, both major and independent, were laughing at how they were selling songs to suckers.

"Mei-ling, I really hope you do make music that makes people feel good."

"I already do! Read the comments on my music page. You know where to go, you've got my cards."

I had a flash-forward to Big Eye going through Mei-ling's suitcases upon her return to Taichung and finding the pictures of a naked little girl. If he thought I had anything to do with it, surely he would thrash me to the extent that any man is allowed to on a nephew. "Mei-ling, about those cards—I think you should throw them away altogether."

"I want to mail them out to radio and TV stations! They're not dirty. I want people to come to my page!" She stared at me defiantly.

"What the hell would your father say if he saw them?"

She hunched up her shoulders. "I don't care what he would say. I've seen porn on his computer!"

What a family. My family. I was throwing in the towel. "I can't control what you do with your cards. Just don't do it when you're around me."

She nodded. I decided to try to be around her as much as possible.

We went up a side street to her apartment building. A group of twentysomething guys spilled out of a Friendly Mart. Obviously they were on their way to a club. One guy with spiky hair stared at Mei-ling.

"She's too young for you," I said pointedly.

"Sorry," he said.

I watched as they turned the corner.

"He was just looking," said Mei-ling. "What's wrong with looking?"

"Looking is how it all starts."

In the lobby I told her to have a good night and watched her board the elevator. As I left the building, I wondered how I could keep this energetic teen out of trouble. Maybe she should use this time for a job or a productive internship. If she could learn discipline, she could get things back on track in the spring semester.

When I stomped down into the train station, I noticed a Japanese food stand doing pretty good business. The main attractions were the hot entrees. I looked over the racks of plates ready to be snapped into bento boxes. Breaded and fried chicken and pork cutlets were matched up with mounds of rice or glistening tangles of *yakisoba*, pan-fried noodles. I was impressed with the evenness of the dark-amber crust on the cutlets, a sign that the oil was very hot and the temperature painstakingly maintained throughout the cooking process. Feeling the panko crisps breaking down on my tongue would be sublime.

Some people say that panko are just breadcrumbs, but they are pure magic. First of all, they are slivers of special Japanese bread cooked by a live electric current, not heat. This method creates a light and fluffy bread with no crust. The crumbs made from this bread are crumbs from heaven. When used as a deep-fry coating, they retain less oil than conventional breadcrumbs. I liked the way those cutlets looked—browned by a benevolent sun god.

The little things in food service are actually as important as the big things, and this tiny stand had it covered. I noticed small pleated-paper portion cups of hot mustard whose horseradish kick would cut through the grease and meld the starch with the yielding strands of meat. If this condiment isn't offered with your fried cutlet, you are not getting a complete experience.

"May I help you?" asked the counterman. I looked up. I hadn't realized that it was now my turn. The man was about my age and clean-cut. We locked eyes. I recognized instantly the lonely look of fraught-filled proprietorship. Likewise he knew right away I was minutely evaluating his technique.

"Well done," I said. "I mean it."

As I entered my building, I saw a shadow cross the street headed directly for me.

I stood in the entranceway and allowed the street door to swing shut behind me. I switched the plastic bag to my left hand and unlocked the building door with a measure of resignation. I wouldn't have time to get in and secure the door behind me. The lock was cranky from the interior side.

"Hey!" I yelled out. "Are you coming in or what?"

I was taken aback when a young man wearing a BMX jacket opened the street door and entered, a helmet under his left arm. I saw some Chinese DNA in his face, maybe a quarter's worth. He was dark-skinned and had broad shoulders that would serve a lover or a fighter. The man looked me over, determined and yet uncertain. I showed him that my palms were empty as my bag slid to my left wrist.

This had to be Mei-ling's boyfriend. He looked like the kind of guy a father wouldn't trust with his daughter.

"Are you Chong by any chance?" I asked him.

"Yeah," he said in lousy Mandarin. "Are you Jing-nan, the cousin?"

"That's me," I said.

"Is she upstairs?"

"Mei-ling?"

"Yeah, Mei-ling. Who the fuck else would I be talking about?"

"Calm down."

He leaned his head back and glared at me. "Don't tell me to calm down! I just rode my motorcycle all the way from Taichung!"

I sighed and opened the building door wider. "Come upstairs with me."

"What's in the bag?"

"Food."

He stepped forward, grabbed thc bag and searched for himself. "Two bento boxes. She's upstairs, right?"

"Nobody's upstairs, Chong. When we get up there, it's just gonna be you and me."

"Then why two bentos?"

"Research." I planted my feet. "I had to try both the pork and the chicken cutlets. I have a stand at the night market and I have to know what the competition is up to. Are you hungry? You can have one."

He was indeed hungry. Actually, Chong was starving. He scarfed down the pork so violently I wondered if he had access to hot meals on a regular basis.

"That's some good shit, huh?" I asked him. He nodded. That was the extent of his appreciation but I felt compelled to go on anyway. "I could tell it would be by the presentation and how wary the guy in charge was. He was on top of everything. Chong, have you ever been to one of those crappy sidewalk joints where you know right off the bat they don't care? The dude running the place has his face buried in the paper or is asleep against the wall?"

"That sounds a little like my family business," said Chong. "It claims to be an Indonesian restaurant but it's really just home cooking."

I brought out a pair of Kirins from the fridge. We popped them open. "We have something in common," I said. "We're both food professionals."

He growled. "I don't work there," he spat. "I'm not feeding racist Taiwanese assholes who fucked over my family and friends."

"Fucked you over? We let you into the country."

Chong slapped the table twice. "To work all the shitty jobs

no Taiwanese wanted! My father worked his ass off in illegal construction, until the scaffold he was working on collapsed. My aunts still work as housekeepers. Their employers treat them like shit because if they complain, they'll be fired and deported." He took a big swig of beer and swallowed hard. "My father sleeps against the wall in the restaurant. It's too painful for him to sleep lying down because those injuries never healed properly." He tapped the side of the bottle. "I want to cry when I see him limp."

I nodded. "I'm sorry to hear about your dad."

Chong drained his beer. "He doesn't need *you* to feel sorry for him. Doesn't need anybody to feel sorry for him."

I picked up my chopsticks and lifted the last piece of chicken cutlet. I gingerly dipped the flat bottom in the thick brown *katsu* sauce, then dragged the long edge along a squib of hot mustard. I popped it in my mouth. The horseradish in the mustard opened up my passages and I inhaled through them, highlighting the cool and sweet taste of the *katsu* sauce on my tongue. The flavors stabilized in my mouth and I began to chew. The still-firm breading broke up like shattered corn flakes as the juicy chicken flesh succumbed to my teeth. Five millimeters of chicken fat and skin underneath the coating was exactly the right thickness to add to the mouthfeel without compromising the taste profile.

I chewed thoroughly and swallowed. Why is this chef in a subway stand, I wondered. More importantly, why was Chong here in my apartment and why was he comfortable enough to get up and grab a second beer on his own from my fridge without even asking?

"Chong," I said. "Why did you come up here? Are you looking to cause trouble?"

He tossed his bottle cap into my sink and shrugged. "I came here for my girl. That's all I want."

"You think you're just going to take her back to Taichung? How is Big Eye going to feel about it?"

He cradled his beer. "I don't give a fuck. That guy is a big snake! All the Indonesian boys of Taichung used to be united. We had different sets, you know, cliques, but we all got along. Then Big Eye got us beefing against each other, giving each other lumps. I don't know how he did it, but he did it!"

"I'll admit that Big Eye isn't a nice guy. But isn't that even more reason not to date his daughter?"

He took in a slow, noisy breath. "You can't help who your parents are," he said. "You also can't help who you fall in love with."

"I'll be honest with you, Chong. Mei-ling doesn't care about you. She talks about being a singer but she doesn't talk about you. Don't chase after someone who doesn't value you."

I heard his shoes jog against the floor. "I bought her a nice microphone for her birthday. She uses it all the time!"

I rubbed my hands together. She probably didn't even have his cheap-ass microphone anymore. "Apart from the singing, Mei-ling has to graduate from high school. She has to hang out with a new crowd. You don't want to hold her back, do you?"

He looked over his knuckles. They were worn out like he'd been punching holes in walls for years. "No," he said softly.

"Take it from me. Let her go for now. If it's meant to be, you'll hear from her again soon enough."

"She never even said goodbye. My boys told me they saw her leave today."

"I thought you two had broken up."

"She didn't mean it," he told himself.

"You can sleep on my couch, but in the morning, you have to go back to Taichung."

He stood up and crossed his arms over his head. "I'm gonna go now."

"Are you sure? It's really late."

Chong looked at me funny. "Why do you talk like you care about me?"

A picture was becoming clearer in my mind. Chong may be a low-level criminal, but he was aware of kindness and how to be kind. I don't think Mei-ling was the same way. In fact, I'll bet their relationship was perennially one-sided and that Chong spent most of it nodding and keeping his mouth shut.

"I'm worried about you, Chong," I said. To tell the whole truth, I was worried about my own well-being, too. Big Eye would not be pleased if he found out I'd had any contact with Chong, much less fed him and allowed him to stay over.

Chong walked over to my kitchen sink, ran water over his hands and splashed his face. "Don't worry about me," he called.

Could he drive so soon after two beers, though? A lot of these kids have trouble driving while completely sober. "You're good to drive on your motorcycle?"

He laughed as his face dripped. "I could ride that thing with my eyes closed and my hands behind my back!"

Ride right off a cliff, I thought.

If I wasn't going to see him again, I wanted to know something, man-to-man. "Did you really think the bento box was good?"

"It was great!"

Gimme a break. He had eaten it all without tasting a single bite.

CHAPTER SEVEN

I HAD A SCARY dream that involved a trail of flaming footsteps in a sugarcane field at night that were dying out faster than I could catch up to them. Any other details fled from my memory as soon as I looked at the time on my ringing phone. Ten-something in the morning.

I hit a button and growled, "Why the hell are you waking me up so early, Mei-ling?"

"It's not that early," she said. I heard the television in the background. "I've already been up a few hours."

"I had a visitor last night. You know anything about it?"

"Who was it?"

"Your ex-boyfriend, Chong. Or is he still your boyfriend?"

She sighed so heavily I could feel her breath. "I ended it with him weeks ago! He doesn't mean anything to me."

"He was waiting for me at my house."

"It's not hard to find out where you live, Mr. Shooting Victim Who Exploits Himself." I heard her chuckle to herself. "What do you want to do today?"

"Let's start with lunch in a few hours."

"Lunch? I want to eat now, Jing-nan! I'm hungry!" She spoke through a yawn. "Let's go to Fu Fu Dou Jiang! I've read about it!"

"Aw, fuck that place," I said. "Wait, I'm sorry, I shouldn't be using that sort of language with my little cousin."

She snickered. "I know curses you don't even know, older cousin. Anyway, what's wrong with Fu Fu?"

"It takes an hour to get through the line and they charge too much for their *youtiao* and *doujiang*."

Youtiao are foot-long deep-fried sticks of dough stuck together in pairs. They live up to their literal name, "oil stick." Oversimplified English signs call *youtiao* "crullers." The oil stick is airy and almost as hard as a dried loofah. They detonate with each bite, sending crumbs and flakes everywhere. *Doujiang*, meanwhile, is thick soy milk served up warm in a bowl and sweetened to taste with white sugar.

I thought about the hot crispy *youtiao* floating across a mouthful of creamy, syrupy *doujiang* and I swung my feet from the bed to the floor.

"We're going to Yong He Soy Milk King," I told Mei-ling.

I heard her hair brush the mouthpiece as she switched the phone to her other ear. "Let me look up the rating online."

"Don't look it up," I said. "I know the place and it's good." I didn't want to give her a chance to see the no-frills decor and paper plates. Yeah, the Soy Milk King doesn't photograph well and young people don't look so cool in selfies taken there so they don't post them; Mei-ling wouldn't get how great the place was by Googling. I told her to meet me there in fifteen minutes. It was practically across the street from her apartment, just south of the Da'an MRT station. It's good to live so close to someplace worth getting up to eat at.

Mei-ling stood outside of Soy Milk King. Her arms were crossed and her head was down, although I could see her mouth twisted to the side.

"This place is SPP, Jing-nan," she said to her shirt.

SPP is shorthand for *song piao piao*. No class.

"I know it's not very pretty," I said. "But for a restaurant, only the food matters. Please, just try it for me." I touched her arm. She dragged her leaden feet inside.

We picked up plates of *youtiao* and freshly made stuffed *shaobing*, a dense sesame-seeded pan-fried bread packed with eggs and veggies. Unstuffed *shaobing* was also available but why would you get that? I was surprised by the number of tourists chowing down. Loud Chinese tourists. I grumbled about the lack of seats and how one of my favorite places was being invaded. Sure, I can be a hypocrite when I want to. I know my livelihood depends on tourists, but I need my safe spaces. Look at this! Nowhere to sit. Well, good for Soy Milk King.

Mei-ling looked around, frowning. I nudged her with an elbow.

"This place is so good there's not even a free seat," I joked.

"If you can't sit and eat, it doesn't matter how good it is."

Two seats opened up at a table near the back and we squeezed in with the Chinese people. They were city folk from Shanghai, judging by the slurred-sounding Mandarin they spoke. They were loud as hell and really good at ignoring people who weren't a part of their group. They had been told not to smoke numerous times, so one ingenious man, the leader of the table, held his cigarette under the table between puffs. He didn't have access to his hands so he talked with his broad shoulders. Every sentence out of him was peppered with curses and he misted the air with *doujiang*.

"This fucking bumpkin showed up at the office with two baskets on a carrying pole. He opens one basket and it's full of chicken and duck eggs. He says, 'You said it was bad to put all your eggs in one basket, so I brought you another so now you have two baskets!'" The three other people roared with laughter and the table shifted and our *doujiang* spilled out of the bowls. Mei-ling and I didn't mind much. The man was captivating.

He was probably in his early sixties and had the jaded eyes of someone who had survived the Cultural Revolution. The man's hair was a marble swirl of grey, white, and black. Unlike his friends, he hadn't been swindled into buying a Taipei 101 shirt, or at least if he had he wasn't wearing it. In fact he was dressed in a long-sleeve T-shirt that he possibly had slept in. His body was free of jewelry. The only indications that this man had money were the Japanese cigarettes that he snuffed out half-smoked. He lit another one before continuing.

"So then the guy opens up the other basket and it's full of smallish tomb artifacts. Little dolls, some jade. He said that he dug these up while drilling a new well a few years back and maybe these were worth something. I've been around, as you all know, and I've come across some clever fakes. These were the real deal and the man really had no idea what he had."

Middle-aged Chinese women had their elbows on the table while the men twisted in their seats to get a better view. Even the staff behind the counter held off on chopping chives so they wouldn't miss a word. The best old Chinese stories are about war and killing. The most gripping modern Chinese stories are about making a killing.

"I told him I would credit him a thousand yuan for every piece he could bring in but he said those were all he had. He gave all he found to the head of the village and the artifacts were split evenly amongst all the families."

Everything paused as the Chinese man made a token attempt to duck under the table to take a drag on his Mevius stick. The storyteller held in his smoke while surveying the audience. He seemed to look at me and winked. With a dramatic exhaling of smoke through both nostrils, the Chinese man resumed the story.

"I said to myself, this guy is the worst kind of idiot. The honest kind!" He took advantage of a burst of laughter and ate a chive omelet in two bites before going on. "Well, he was happy with what he got and later I showed the pieces to my partner. He knows people who used to smuggle artifacts out of the country. Now they make more money keeping it in the country, selling to collectors, but back then, there weren't Chinese millionaires.

"My partner told me the jade was from the Han Dynasty and he could probably get millions of yuan for them but he would need time to sneak them out of China. I let him have them and about a month later he took off for Canada for good. I don't even know what city. He claimed political persecution. My ass. He should be persecuted for being a thief!

"I was ripped off by a pal while the guy I was trying to rip off was completely honest with me. So I made things right by hiring the bumpkin to clean my offices. He does a good job, too!"

He squeezed off his cigarette and reached for his Mevius pack. For some reason he focused on me again.

"Hey, my friend, have a cigarette," he said to me.

"No, thank you," I said.

"Hey, you're not a part of my group, are you? You're a *taibazi*, eh? Too good to take a smoke off me, huh?"

Taibazi is one term that Chinese people use to put down Taiwanese people. It's meant to be applied to people who want to declare independence from China, but the slur insults all Taiwanese as it means "Taiwanese dicks." He sure didn't know me well enough to call me a dick in jest.

I could get mad and call him something, maybe *gongfei*, "commie bandit." Mainlanders brought the term to Taiwan when the civil war ended and it lives on to describe the atrocious behavior of Chinese tourists.

Then he would have to come back at me with something terrible. After all, his crew was watching. He couldn't be shown up by some Taiwanese punk like me wearing a New Order shirt from the *Low-Life* era. Maybe he'd call me a worse name, like "brokeback," a *duanbei,* a faggot—a term that came from the film *Brokeback Mountain*. The film was never officially shown in China, but everyone had seen it on bootleg DVD.

Then things would have gotten really ugly.

Instead, I allowed my inner night-market persona to surface. Johnny could handle this. Every confrontation was an opportunity. I matched the Chinese man's big smile.

"Well, now that you're in Taiwan, you're a *taibazi*, too!" He laughed and then his friends joined in. "You might as well get used to our food now before we declare independence." I handed him a card for Unknown Pleasures. "Map's on the back."

He ran his right index finger along the edge and raised his eyebrows. He could tell it wasn't printed in China because the corners were precise but smooth. Chinese cards are designed for paper cuts.

"How does your food compare with Soy Milk King?" he asked.

"Let's put it this way," I said. "I only come here to tell people about my place."

Someone from behind the counter charged over at us. As the guy who lifted out the *youtiao* from the hot oil, he was in charge of the kitchen since his skill made the business. In fact, he was the Soy Milk King himself. He looked to be in his mid-thirties. His face was smooth and soft as a silent-film star's. His retro glasses frames and animated expression completed the look.

"Are you trying to do business here?" His Royal Highness accused me.

You could smoke, yell, and probably even piss on the floor and it would only warrant a minor rebuke. Hand out a business card and you threatened the sovereignty of the restaurant.

The Chinese guy held up his free hand. "We're old friends," he said. "And look, he just got engaged! You should congratulate him!"

The King wasn't buying it. "Don't come here anymore!" he said, pointing to me and then shifting his finger to Mei-ling. "Neither of you!"

My heart sank. Or maybe I was feeling the grease seeping through my arteries. It would really suck being barred from this place. I licked my lips. Well, it was good to the last drop.

Then the Chinese guy did something unexpected. He dropped all the friendly play and his smile faded. "Don't be like that, friend," he said to the King. "I bring a lot of people through here. You don't want to be mean to people I like. How would you like me to bring my groups to that other place, aw, what's the name?"

"Fu Fu," Mei-ling offered.

"Fu Fu!" declared the Chinese guy, saying it with conviction as if it were a Taoist deity who kept *youtiao* crispy. "I'm going to take my groups to Fu Fu instead. What do you think of that?"

The King crumpled a little. "Okay," he said in a restrained growl.

The Chinese guy nodded and said, "Okay."

Dismissed, the King walked back to the fryer, his head held high.

"God, what a prick!" the Chinese guy cracked.

"He can hear you!" exclaimed Mei-ling.

"I hope he does!"

I had to speak up for a decent chef. "You have to admit he fries a mean oil stick."

He crossed his arms and nodded enthusiastically, using his full neck in the way Chinese people do. "He does, doesn't he?"

I hadn't tried a cigarette since middle school, but I clapped the Chinese guy on the shoulder. "I'll take that cigarette now," I said.

He laughed heartily and obliged. What a great guy!

As he was lighting me up, he said under his breath, "That's one sexy bitch you got there."

"She's sixteen," I said through my chokes. I wasn't going to tell him her name or our family relation. No need to bring him into my confidence.

"Age of consent in Taiwan," he said coolly. It was a litmus test he had applied many times before. "Ah, this is my card. Sorry about the shape it's in, but it's the last one." He handed me a card that said his name was Li Jishen and his occupation was "Best Taiwan Province Tour Guide."

Mr. Li hooked an index finger into his mouth to pick the back of his teeth. He dislodged something and I heard him swallow it as he rose to his feet. "Maybe I'll see you soon, Jing-nan."

After we left Soy Milk King, Mei-ling was anxious to go out and do stuff. I casually asked her if she wanted to visit the offices in Taipei 101—a part of the landmark skyscraper the tourists never got to see—and she fell for it.

Taipei 101 was barely a decade old but it had already become a symbol of the city, as iconic as the Eiffel Tower but loaded with an upscale shopping mall and two million square feet in office space. The food court has a number of comforts the night market didn't offer—there are chairs and tables, and you can pay with credit cards. But the food itself? If you're willing to sacrifice quality for convenience, well, you should learn to hold your tongue because there was nothing actually worth tasting here.

And I was very good at holding my tongue. In fact, I had a hidden agenda for our little visit to Taipei 101. On my way to breakfast, I had messaged my old classmate Peggy Lee, who worked for her family. I asked her if she would take on my little niece as an intern as a favor to me.

Peggy and I had gone to high school together, although we were never really friends back then. She's the youngest generation of a well-connected and sickeningly wealthy mainlander family. I certainly didn't fit in with her style- and status-focused crew. Still, we have a common history and know, or knew, the same people, including my late girlfriend, of whom Peggy was unabashedly jealous. Yes, Peggy had liked me, but that was a long time ago and I'm sure she doesn't feel that way anymore.

While Mei-ling and I were sitting in Soy Milk King and Mr. Li was regaling his table, Peggy had messaged back that she would welcome my dear little cousin as a temporary intern. Could I bring her by soon?

I replied, ONE HOUR.

WE WALKED INTO TAIPEI 101's entrance at Xinyi Road and stood in the cavernous lobby. It was like a church of capitalism. The endless windows strangely seemed to allow in more sunlight than was typically available in Taipei at noon. Tourist groups from all over the world marched off to the left for the multilevel mall and "food."

Mei-ling stood on her toes and took in the bigness of it all. "Maybe we should go shopping right now!" she squealed.

"I want you to meet someone first," I said. "Peggy Lee. She's an old classmate." Mei-ling nodded. "You're going to be her intern."

Her eyes flashed. "What! You mean I would work here?"

"I have to keep you out of trouble and you can't work with me anymore. Besides, you'll have more fun here. It's like a hundred times classier than the night market."

I could already see it in her eyes. Mei-ling was lulled by the spectacle of the skyscraper's expansive interior. Yes, this was as big as her ambition.

I saw the stars flicker in her eyes before she blinked. "What would I be doing?"

"Peggy runs a hedge fund. I'm sure she'll find something. Are you good with numbers?"

"No."

"Decent at typing?"

"No."

"How's your business English?"

"Bad."

I crossed my arms and looked into her eyes. Mei-ling wasn't lying about any of it.

"Well, just pretend to be capable," I warned her.

THE HEDGE-FUND OFFICE WAS on the 88th floor behind double doors that opened automatically. A secretary was perched behind his desk, arms folded. He watched us with his cat eyes.

"Well, hello," he challenged.

"Hi," I said. "We're here to see Peggy."

"Peggy?"

"Peggy Lee. I'm her old classmate, Jing-nan."

"Jing-nan, is it? Hmmm, Ms. Lee doesn't have you in her calendar at this time." He suddenly touched his earpiece and looked to his left at an unseen terror. "Yes. Yes. Of course." He raised his arms in defense, his eyes widened in fear. "She'll be right out," he stammered. I heard a door slam shut followed by footsteps heavy enough to crush nuts.

Peggy barreled around a corner. She was dressed in a black pantsuit and black platform shoes. A panther walking upright. Her hair was cut into short, purposely messy fringes. Her eyes were cunning but not altogether devoid of humanity.

There was a time when I disliked her strongly and that time ended not too long ago. Now I considered her a friend whom I didn't entirely trust.

She put her arms up when she saw me, sending metal bracelets rattling down to her sharp elbows.

"Jing-nan!" she said. "I was so glad to hear from you!" Peggy petted my shoulders.

"Hi, Peggy," I said, touching her left arm.

"And you must be Mei-ling!" Peggy held out a hand to my niece.

"Hello, Ms. Lee," she said as she shook hands.

The receptionist was standing, looking shocked. He'd never seen Peggy act so nice, probably.

"Are you hungry?" asked Peggy. "Do you want something from the kitchen? We have fresh ramen and some really great curry beef jerky."

"We just ate," I said.

She guided us past the guardrail of a pool that held koi older than our parents' generation. For luck, of course.

"Those are the biggest fish I've ever seen!" declared Mei-ling.

"I took care of them when I was a kid," said Peggy. "They were the rejects from my grandfather's pool. He didn't think they had the right markings to compete in the koi shows.

Look at them now. Meanwhile, all the prize-winning fish died long ago."

Peggy waved her hand above the water and a fish that was mostly orange rose to the surface and wiggled. I saw a pattern on the top of its head.

"I think I see a lion's face on that one," I said.

"I call him the Lion King. I feel like we have a psychic connection."

The fish, which was obviously hoping for food, turned to me and judged me to be lacking as well. It yawned repeatedly and swam away.

We left the fish and continued down the corridor. After seeing the fish, all the wall art we passed by was a letdown. We came upon a framed unrolled scroll of a landscape of mountains, mists, and rivers. Commentaries on the art in the handwriting of several different princes were a testament to the antiquity and provenance of the scroll, which seemed to end with an abrupt rip.

"Where's the rest of it?" I asked as we stood just outside her office.

Peggy leaned back and petted the back of her head. "The rest decomposed. The tomb in China that it was recovered from became partly flooded. Sucks, doesn't it?" She cranked open her door and jerked her head at the entrance. I walked in, followed by Mei-ling.

"Your desk seems bigger," I said.

"Everything's bigger," said Peggy. "It's a whole new office. Didn't you notice?" She kicked the door closed behind her with her right heel.

"The last one wasn't too small, either," I said.

Mei-ling, entranced, walked to the window at the far wall. The clouds looked like cotton balls smudged with facial oil, and close enough to pick up and throw in the trash. The city below was a Lego toyset that only included off-white, grey, and black blocks. Altogether the view was somber and yet empowering to the beholder. "Look at this view," said Mei-ling. "I wouldn't get anything done if I worked here."

"That's the wrong way to talk to a potential employer," said Peggy as she yanked open a drawer. "Sit down, you guys. Let's get acquainted, Mei-ling. You want a drink?"

"Some water will be all right," said Mei-ling as we took our seats in soft-cushioned client chairs.

"Water's boring. How about an aloe drink? Or some scotch?"

"She's sixteen, Peggy," I said.

Peggy tilted her head and held out her hands, framing Mei-ling with her index fingers and thumbs. "She looks eighteen. You've drunk before, right?"

Mei-ling nodded.

"You're not drinking today," I said. "This is supposed to be an interview."

Peggy came around to the front of the desk and sat on the edge. With a wink she asked Mei-ling, "Will you work hard?" The girl nodded. Peggy slapped her knee. "Good enough for me. Can you start now?"

I felt a great burden lift from my shoulders. I was going to have my afternoon free!

Mei-ling turned to me with one eyebrow raised.

"She can start now," I said.

"But I'm not dressed properly for an office," Mei-ling blurted.

"Who's going to see you behind a desk?" said Peggy as she stood and stretched. "This is going to be a great day!" She undid the two buttons on her jacket and fanned herself with the lapels. "Now, where did I . . ." Her hands shot to her pants pockets and flapped around. She fished something out of her right pocket and held it out to Mei-ling. A flash-memory drive shaped like a salmon nigiri. The top half of it was pink with thin white parallel lines while the bottom was white and bumpy like rice. It would be convincing if a metal USB port weren't sticking out.

"Cute, isn't it?" she asked Mei-ling.

Mei-ling smiled and swung her legs. "Yes, it's very cute. Is this a present for me?"

"It's more than just a present, because it's something useful," said Peggy. "Go to the office next door and use the PC. You don't need a login. There's an Excel spreadsheet on this sushi drive. I want you to update the closing prices of the stocks and funds on it." My cousin picked up the drive gingerly. "You've used Excel before, right, Mei-ling?"

"I used a little bit of it in school," she said. It was more likely that she only saw a Microsoft commercial.

Peggy smiled like a truant officer the kids couldn't bullshit. "Then get to it. It's pretty intuitive. You promised you'd work hard so show me."

CHAPTER EIGHT

I MET UP WITH Nancy at the benches near Taida's western entrance on Xinsheng Road. With wide walkways and monumental palm trees, the campus always reminded me of my school-orientation visit to Universal Studios in Los Angeles.

Nancy had been making protest signs. She was dressed to get dirty in an old smock over thin jeans. Paint and glitter were splattered on her smock and her neck. I recognized the faded green sleeves hanging off her shoulders as belonging to a Flaming Lips shirt. She was done with the Lips now. I never liked the band. Dipping the entire shirt in bleach and obliterating the band photo would be a service to humanity.

"I'm glad you were able to tear yourself away," I said as I gave her a sideways hug. It was the only public display of affection along the entire entrance path apart from a foreign couple holding hands. "You're doing something important. Our country is counting on you."

Nancy crossed her right leg and picked off some paint splatter near her ankles. "You could join us, you know," she said. "You don't have to be an activist to care about Taiwan."

"Someone has to feed the revolution." I pointed at the smock and said, "I like your new dress. It's really you."

She kicked me with her crossed leg. "Most people wouldn't wear smocks today, because they're white," she said, picking at the straps. White is the traditional color of mourning and a white smock would be akin to a shroud. Wearing it could only foreshadow a period of mourning for you and your family. You'd have to be superstitious to feel that way but that applies to the entire population of Taiwan. "Apparently the lady at Drunken Moon Lake has been showing up again."

I crossed my arms and sighed. Taida, like Taipei in general, is supposedly haunted by a host of ghosts. An elevator somewhere on campus always stops on a certain floor at midnight because a worker was killed there. If a student walks through Fu Si-nian memorial garden in a manner disrespectful to the late former president of Taida, she or he will fail classes that semester. Then there is the Ghost of Drunken Moon Lake.

There are a few different stories about a female student from decades ago (boyfriend broke up with her, boyfriend was going to break up with her, boyfriend was gay and going to break up with her) who jumped into the lake and drowned. Supposedly, when the moon is full or when something bad is imminent, a young woman in white can be seen pacing in the pagoda on the lake's tiny island or floating around the perimeter of the lake. She may approach an unsuspecting person and ask, "What time is it?" before fading into a mist.

"Did you see the ghost?" I asked Nancy. She opened her eyes wide and crossed herself. "What are you doing, Nancy? You're not Christian."

"I'm not, but don't use that word! Call her a 'lady.'" Nancy cleared her throat. "I don't believe in any of that supernatural stuff. Not really. On the other hand, I don't want to invite trouble. It's so close to the Mid-Autumn Festival."

I leaned back and laughed. Once upon a time when I was just a stupid kid, I believed that in order for our society to move forward, Taiwanese would have to give up all their crazy superstitious beliefs. Nobody in the world tends to more deities than we do. There are pantheons of Taoist, Buddhist, and folk goddesses and gods, all with their birthday celebrations and entourages. We flock to temples and pay cash donations to appease the divines for guidance and comfort. There are even dog deities. Dogs. I like some dogs, even my local pack leader, Willie, but they lick their own assholes. Maybe there's a deep meaning-of-life lesson in that action, but those animals don't belong on altars.

What a waste of time, effort, and money it was to worship, the young me had thought.

Now, however, I know that burning incense, throwing down divining wood blocks, or asking a fortune teller's approval on life decisions such as home purchases or marriages is just a matter of setting one's mind at ease, finding comfort in the moderate hell of indecision in the greater hell that life can be.

After all, there's always some wiggle room. Your fate isn't really set by your *bazi*, the eight characters of the time, day, month, and year of your birth. People argue with diviners like haggling over goods at a market. If a goddess or god doesn't grant your wish, then say to blazes with them and move on to the next one with a better fruit offering this time. Feel free to hop among the Taoist, Buddhist, Christian, Muslim, and animistic beliefs until you get to the spirit who will give you want you want.

I HANDED A HAM-AND-CHEESE sandwich and a box of cold chrysanthemum tea to Nancy. This wasn't just any sandwich, mind you. It was from a bakery that roasts the ham slowly for twenty-four hours and tops it with shavings from sharp cheddar cheese aged more than two years. They slice both right in front of you and lay it upon their own rye bread, which has a hint of cinnamon. The top piece of bread is coated with a spicy, seeded mustard that tickles the tongue. I like those sandwiches so much I'd eaten mine on the sidewalk upon exiting the store.

I told Nancy about the internship I'd hooked up for my cousin.

"Is Mei-ling going to be safe with Peggy?"

I sipped some tea and swished it around my mouth to dislodge a mustard seed stuck between my molars. "Of course she is! Peggy's not going to eat her."

Nancy jabbed me with her right elbow. "You're so annoying! I meant that Peggy is going to make her work long hours. Maybe too long."

"I hope so. The office work will give Mei-ling the discipline she craves so badly."

"But she wants to be a singer."

My tea box bottomed out. I shoved the straw back inside and crumpled the paper box. "The sooner that dream is crushed, the better," I said. "If you heard what I heard, you'd know what I'm talking about."

"Not all famous people were so great when they started out."

"Nobody who ever made it was that bad at the beginning!"

"Jing-nan, don't you see that you're treating her the same way her father treats her? If you encouraged her to pursue her dream, maybe she wouldn't become famous but she'd definitely stop acting out in school."

Nancy had really hit on something there. I looked down at my feet. I was being a jerk to Mei-ling. Who was I, really, to say she had no talent? I didn't like popular music but clearly there was an audience for it.

"You're right, Nancy."

She stood up and brushed her smock down flat. "Of course I'm right. I'm going to take this food back to the meeting room."

"You're sure you can't hang out with me some more?"

"I told you! I'm in charge of the Taida mobilization. If I slack off, everyone else will, too!"

I stood up and we hugged again before she left.

Damn, if Bauhaus, the CD store, were still open, I would go there now. Nancy told me the space is a Starbucks now.

I wondered what the *heidaoren* who had owned Bauhaus was doing these days. I guess there was some poetic justice in the fact that illegal music downloading had driven out of business a store that sold bootleg CDs, but Bauhaus certainly served a demand while it was around.

Organized crime isn't always an evil thing in Taiwan. Sure, they handle a lot of illegal dumping and they cheap out on construction. But they also had installed cable television throughout the island while the government sat on its hands, unsure of how to coordinate through different jurisdictions. The gangs simply rolled out the wire and threaded it through where they could. People had been dying for cable back then. The government didn't give us what we wanted, but the *heidaoren* did. Good for them!

Whoever can make things happen, we Taiwanese back them one hundred percent.

Speaking of people who make things happen, my phone rang and I answered right away when I saw that it was Big Eye.

Dispensing with pleasantries, he asked, "Is Mei-ling with you?"

"No. She's at her internship." I was walking north on Xinsheng Road, which would eventually take me to the jutting western border of Da'an Forest Park. I always seemed to gravitate to that park when I didn't know what to do with myself.

"Internship?" Big Eye asked, articulating each syllable. "I thought she was maybe going to work at your food stall." I heard him swig a drink and give a satisfied exhale.

"She worked there one night but I found her a better job." I crossed the street and found myself on the perimeter of the park. I passed a group of Chinese visitors arguing about where to go next.

"She's not answering her phone," Big Eye said. "She must be really busy."

"Her boss probably confiscated her cell phone."

"Oh," he said, sounding impressed. "Must be a good boss. What is she doing? And where?"

"Mei-ling is doing office stuff at Lee & Associates in Taipei 101. It's a hedge fund run by an old classmate of mine. The Lees are a pretty prominent mainlander family." The wind rose cinematically and the trees at the perimeter of the park swayed, making a white noise that masked the voices of the Chinese tourists.

"The boss probably took Mei-ling's phone so she couldn't tip someone off on what stocks to buy."

"I didn't even think about that," I said.

Big Eye cackled. "I know all the angles, Jing-nan! You think I'm stupid because I didn't go to school?"

"Big Eye, you're smarter than I'll ever be," I admitted. "I would never lie to you about anything."

Over the line I heard ice clinking and then a slight delay before he spoke. "I know, I know," Big Eye said. "That's why I trust you with my daughter."

He sounded like he was in a good mood. Maybe he was buzzed. This was a good chance to talk about Mei-ling's dreams. Meanwhile, the trees began bucking like water buffalo stuck in mud. A storm was upon us.

"Say, Big Eye, I was wondering if you ever thought about getting Mei-ling some singing lessons."

"Why?" The way he asked made it sound like a threat.

"She wants to be a singer. If you encouraged her, then maybe . . ."

"If I encouraged her, I would be prolonging her delusion and wasting my money. You've no doubt been tortured by one of her songs by now. She sucks."

"She might behave better in school if you helped her pursue her dream."

"Did she tell you this?" A crack of lightning broke the sky. Grey sheets of cool rain swept down. My arms became drenched as I used my free hand to cover my phone. I wasn't going to allow this conversation to be disconnected by a sudden storm.

"Actually," I said, "my girlfriend suggested that maybe what Mei-ling needs is encouragement." I peered across the street, searching for refuge. The Chinese tourists had gone into turtle formation, interlocking their opened umbrellas into plates of a gigantic shell. My eyes were drawn to the windows of a Friendly Mart that glowed in the rain like an electric bug zapper. I jogged to the corner and across the street.

"Don't listen to your girlfriend." Big Eye sounded like he'd tasted something sour. "Girls all stick together. Don't you know this by now, Jing-nan? I thought you were a man!"

Some people blame Confucian values for Taiwanese chauvinism. Others blame residual Japanese culture. Maybe it's both. It doesn't really matter. It's fucked up.

"This is not a man versus woman battle," I told Big Eye. "I'm worried about my little cousin. Your daughter is a sixteen-year-old girl. Shouldn't you support her interests?"

I entered the Friendly Mart. I was assaulted by lights bright enough for an autopsy theater, unnervingly clean floors, and optimized product placement dictated by corporate headquarters. The complete antithesis of the beautiful chaos of the night market. I stood near the soup station and looked over the sausages and skewers. Up close they looked like the fake rubber food in restaurant display windows.

"Listen, Jing-nan," said Big Eye. "I give her everything she needs and more—iPads, iPhones, Galaxies. *Gan!* I bought her a galaxy of gadgets and she still won't give up the singing!"

"Maybe one reason Mei-ling won't give it up is because you're pressuring her to give it up."

"If someone's shooting heroin, do you encourage them to do more drugs to get them to quit?"

"Singing isn't illegal."

I heard the tinkling sounds that ice cubes make in a glass after a last gulp. "The way she sings, it should be," he muttered. "Well, the most important thing is that I finally got her away from Chong. You haven't heard any sign of him, have you?"

I felt my mouth go dry. Did Big Eye know?

"Well, he came to my apartment last night," I said. "He wanted to see Mei-ling, but I convinced him to go back to Taichung."

"I heard Chong was in Taipei. He had to clear it with Black Sea so he could enter their turf. He had said it was about a girl. Black Sea thought Chong and his darkie friends might be trying to set up a branch of their gang in Taipei."

I couldn't imagine why Black Sea, the biggest criminal organization in Taiwan, would be concerned about a single person of interest in their turf. After all, not only did they have politicians in their pockets, some Black Sea members *were* politicians. I guess they couldn't let anything slip and from Chong's point of view, it was best for him to ask for permission to enter first.

Chong. He hadn't turned out to be the gangster I'd expected. I would call him a nice guy. Naïve, even. Certainly not someone who deserved to be slurred.

"Big Eye, you don't have to call Indonesian people 'darkies.'"

"You're right. I don't."

I became aware that a Friendly Mart employee was giving me the evil eye. I held the phone against my chest and said, "I'm just waiting for the rain to stop. Do I have to buy something?"

He jerked his head at me. "My mother's from Indonesia," he spat. "Does that make me a 'darkie'?"

"I wasn't talking about you," I said weakly.

"Yes, you were!" He pointed to the rain outside. "Now get the fuck out of my darkie store!"

"Hold on," I said.

The second Friendly Mart employee abandoned his post at the checkout and came at me wielding a mop. It was clear that they didn't care for any repeat business from me and the situation was quickly developing into a two-on-one thumping. I only knew how to grapple one-on-one.

I held up a hand. "I'm going."

I jogged back into the rain and slipped down two doors to stand under the awning of a pharmacy. The deluge splashed against the tarp, sending mists of water across my face. I brought the phone up to my ear and heard Big Eye laughing.

"What's so funny?" I asked.

"God, Jing-nan, you sounded like a scared little girl! If someone told me to leave their store, I'd put my hands in my pockets and tell them to make me! Do you ever stand your ground on anything, little boy?"

"I'm standing my ground on Mei-ling. Give her a chance."

"Ah," he said in a drawn out exhale. "You know what? I don't care, in the end. If you think it's going to help keep her behavior in line, that's all I want." Thunder suddenly cracked so loud I even heard it in the ear I had pressed to the phone. No, wait. That sound was Big Eye leisurely cracking melon seed shells with his teeth. He tried to hack out a seed that had gone down the wrong way and it felt like he was spitting on me.

CLOSE TO ELEVEN THAT night, a victorious Peggy and defeated Mei-ling arrived at Unknown Pleasures. I slid over to let them sit with me at a table.

"How did today go?" I asked Mei-ling.

"It went just fantastic!" Peggy gushed. Suddenly, a look of concern came over her face. "You have a restroom here, don't you?"

"Right here," I said. "I wouldn't let my good ole classmate use the common bathroom."

"I'm sure it's sparkling," she said as she dropped her saddlebag of a purse into Mei-ling's lap and patted my cousin's shoulder meaningfully. You'd better not let anything happen to this bag, the gesture said.

Mei-ling watched Peggy strut off with disdain. "She's a functioning alcoholic," she stated.

"She's a workaholic, too," I said. "That's one good quality."

Mei-ling stared hard at me, trying to turn me to stone. "How could you leave me with her?"

My hands formed a prayer position. "Do you know how many people would die for an internship with the Lee family? You can learn how money really works there."

"I know how money really works. I've seen how Big Eye moves his little cash piles around."

Frankie walked over and slid a plate of skewers between us. I admired the glistening char on the chicken intestines, which were perfectly folded into a string of continuous Ws.

You may not think it matters much if your skewer is neat or not. You'd be extremely wrong, too. When someone has trained enough to precisely fashion each skewer, she or he is likely also fastidious about the freshness of the food and the cleanliness of the preparation area.

Frankly, it's easy to learn how to skewer folded intestines. After some practice, nearly anybody can do it. Mei-ling herself was becoming halfway decent at it on her first night. After a week at it, the knowledge is embedded in your fingers. You could make thousands of perfect skewers while in a subconscious state, thinking of the time when you and your high-school sweetheart were going to conquer the world.

Other things in a kitchen are much more linear. They don't get any easier with experience or repetition. No matter how many times you scrape grill grates clean, once you know how, you can't do it any faster. Likewise, the only way to be more efficient at mopping a floor is by cutting corners.

If those intestines you've ordered are looking as sloppy as a victim in a cheap slasher film, put them down. Seeing the state of the kitchen that served it is probably more horrifying than that movie.

I picked up a skewer and spun it slowly in my hand. The black char and meat browning were even on both sides.

"Even if I weren't hungry," I said, "I wouldn't be able to resist this."

Mei-ling continued to sulk but she picked up a skewer and looked it over. "It is beautiful," she said.

"Perfect," I said with my mouth full. Mei-ling dug in and her mood improved. As soon as I could I told her, "I've got some good news for you. I talked to Big Eye today."

"What's good? Is he dying?"

"Don't say that so close to the Mid-Autumn Festival!" I chided her. She rolled her eyes and kept eating. Actually, it was bad year-round to speak of the death of one's parents, even if they were already dead. "Listen, Mei-ling, he's going to pay for you to take singing lessons, as long as you agree to behave."

"Fuck that," she yelled in English.

"Hey, watch the language, Mei-ling," said Dwayne. "This is a family establishment. If you want to curse, keep it down."

Mei-ling went silent, but it wasn't because of Dwayne.

"*Gan!*" said Peggy as she returned to the table. "You guys are talking so loud!"

Dwayne rubbed his nose with his thumb. "I'm going to allow that one to curse because she's experienced life," he declared.

"Hey stud, get me a cup of soda and ice but just fill it halfway!" Peggy called to him. Dwayne abandoned Frankie and bounded across the stream of tourists for the fruit-shake stand. "Oopsie, I didn't mean to send him on an errand, Jing-nan. Why don't you have drinks here? They have good profit margins."

"They do, but then you have to load them in, store the syrup and seltzer tanks, store the cups and lids and straws, have an ice maker, and deal with the additional litter. On top of that, people feel entitled to ask for refills." I waved the idea away with my bare skewer. "We just stick to what we're good at and make money that way."

"You're such a good businessman," said Peggy. "How come you're not the one working for my family?"

"You've already got the brightest and best of our clan," I said. "Please have a skewer."

"I'm on a diet," said Peggy. "I never eat solids for dinner."

Dwayne returned with a plastic cup partially filled with Coke. She touched his elbow. "Ah, that's the stuff. Thank you, big boy." Dwayne went back behind the counter.

Was he blushing?

Peggy produced a flask from her purse and tipped it into the cup. Mei-ling looked at me directly and raised her eyebrows.

"I'm glad you're staying hydrated, Peggy," I said.

"I make sure to," she said. "It's an easy thing to overlook when you work as hard as I do. Whoops, I mean we do!" Peggy hugged Mei-ling with one arm.

"This is actually pretty late for Mei-ling to be working," I said pointedly.

"Well, I need her on the late side. She can come in later tomorrow, but Mei-ling has to be with me through the market openings in the US. She was so good today. It was a first day that will go down in history." Peggy took a generous swig from her cup and patted her chest.

Big Eye would love Peggy, I thought.

Mei-ling stood up and gave a huge fake yawn that would work on stage but be too big for film.

"I should be going to bed," she said.

"What time do you want Mei-ling in tomorrow?" I asked.

"Oh, you know," said Peggy. "Anytime is fine."

"Seriously. What time?"

"Two is fine."

I also stood up.

"What," cried Peggy, "you're going, too, Jing-nan? How can you leave your old classmate?"

"I'll be back. I'm just making sure the best intern in the world gets home all right."

Peggy toasted me with her cup.

I ENDURED A SHORT MRT ride of Mei-ling's bitching about how the hedge fund's database was completely out of date, how the computers ran operating systems from two generations ago, and how Peggy had spent the entire day texting or on instant messenger.

Mei-ling had to reconfigure the network so she didn't have to walk to the other side of the office, a half-mile jog apparently, to pick up her printouts. The poor girl also figured out a way to make the spreadsheets update with closing stock prices automatically instead of keying each one in.

She was much better at computers than I had suspected. I guess you learn a lot when writing and editing original compositions (I hesitate to call them "songs") on a computer.

I suffered some more humble-bragging about Mei-ling's technological prowess as we got off the train and walked to her building. But by the time we got to the lobby, I couldn't take it any more and blurted out, "But did you learn anything today?"

She searched the floor for an answer. "I did," she admitted.

"Then that's a good thing. Stuff you learn in business will serve you well no matter what you end up doing. If you're a singer, you'll have more control over your career if you're comfortable with numbers and money." Mei-ling looked away. "Like I mentioned, I convinced Big Eye to let you take singing lessons."

"I don't want his help!" she said as her arms pushed weakly against my chest. "Or yours!"

"Hey, now. I'm not your enemy." She rested her head against my chest and I patted her back. Please don't cry, I thought. "Mei-ling, your father and I are your family and we're worried about you. We want you to stop your reckless behavior. You want to be a singer, that's fine. But you have to finish high school. I hooked you up with Peggy because I wanted you to see what an empowered woman is like. Sure, she may be a little crazy, but everyone has problems. I have problems. You have problems. All we can do is help each other, all right?"

Mei-ling jerked herself away from me and scowled. "I only want help from people who believed in me from the beginning, Jing-nan." With that she strutted to the elevator.

She did learn a lot today. Mei-ling had Peggy's crush-the-world stomp down perfectly.

CHAPTER NINE

In the morning, Mei-ling said she was too tired to meet for a late breakfast or early lunch. She had stayed up watching music videos and chatting with people who had favorited her songs online. She needed a few more hours of sleep. I warned her not to be late for Peggy and she warned me not to be late for Frankie and Dwayne.

I turned on the television and saw that there was some emergency at the Legislative Yuan, Taiwan's Congress. Oh, wait, today was the day of Nancy's protest! A bunch of crazy students and their kooky allies had climbed over the barricades and forced their way into the building.

Taiwan Action Eye, the most shameless of the nation's cable stations, had snuck in a reporter with a wireless lapel cam. There was a shrill quality to his voice but the man knew how to walk steadily so that the images didn't rollercoaster.

"Our nation's young people have daringly risked bodily harm to scale the walls of one of our most sacred institutions to make a statement!" the reporter screeched. "Who said that the new generation was complacent? Why did that one politician mock young people as 'Boys and girls who are in self-imposed exile in the land of texting and streaming Internet'? In fact, dear viewers, that politician who uttered those insulting words, Kung San-cheng, was last seen running with his staff for the parking garage when the students began to breach the perimeter!"

The camera panned through the hallway as the reporter made his way to the main auditorium. He glanced back at the camera and frowned before continuing. "Unfortunately, due to a glitch, footage of Mr. Kung wasn't able to be recorded. I promise you, though, that we will accurately depict his desperate flight in an animated reenactment when I return to the studio."

He came upon a student who was wrapping a bandage around her left hand. "Excuse me, miss!" called the reporter. "How did you get hurt? Did a policeman beat you?"

"No," she said, giggling. "I got a papercut while I was handing out flyers." The student slouched and tried to hide behind her bangs.

"May I see a flyer, miss?"

The reporter held up the piece of paper in an awkward way that was convenient for viewers to see. It read, "Taiwan is a small island but a giant nation." The writing was an indirect call for formal independence from China, which is what the student takeover was peripherally about. There were other grievances, too. Taiwan's ruling party, the KMT, was trying to ram through a bill to open our markets to Chinese imports. The KMT said the bill would shore up Taiwan's economy and lower the overall cost of food and raw materials. Critics said the bill would destroy jobs, crush small businesses and make Taiwan even more dependent on China's economy.

The flyer shook in the reporter's trembling hand. He was obligated to make some disparaging remarks about it, as the cable station belonged to a woman who ranked highly in the KMT. The editorial voice of Taiwan Action Eye was a steady drumbeat of ruling party dogma. We don't have the unbiased media that the US enjoys.

Taiwan Action Eye's stalwart reporter cleared his throat as he prepared to forcefully confront the introverted student. "It is obvious to me, miss, that this occupation of a government building is a misguided action." He tossed her flyer away. "Tell me something. Why are you opposed to creating more jobs in Taiwan?"

She stiffened and some of the hair fell away from her face. "Hey, are you a reporter or something?" The camera focused on her chin, drifted downward for a breast shot of her knit top and then came back up to catch a concerned expression on her face.

"No, miss, I'm a student, just like you. Are you trying to distract me with your body because you can't defend your position?"

She clenched her jaw as she took the bait. "The only jobs the bill would create are more positions at Friendly Mart. The skilled jobs would move to China. And stop looking at me like you're some kind of pervert!"

"You think people who work at Friendly Mart are perverts? Aren't you illegally trespassing because you don't have a boyfriend and you're stupid?" Friendly Mart was a main advertiser for Taiwan Action Eye and sponsored the Breakfast Break roundtable discussion on Sunday mornings.

The student rolled up her flyers and jabbed them the reporter's face. The camera jumped with each thrust. "You're the one who's stupid. If you don't like the protest, then why don't you get out of here?"

The reporter remained defiant. "You should get out of here! You're acting like an old homeless woman!"

The student stormed off. The reporter wheeled around and continued down the hallway in search of another victim.

"I'd like to caution our viewers that they are watching this live and some inappropriate language could come up from time to time," he said. In other words, "Stay tuned for more!"

As he approached the auditorium's open doors, my heart stopped.

There was Nancy, handing out bagged pastries to other protestors.

"What do we have here? Free food!" the reporter said. He tapped Nancy's arm. "Where did you get the money to pay for this?"

"The food was all donated by mom-and-pop bakeries opposed to the bill," she said. "The people support us." She tucked some loose hairs behind her right ear. My girlfriend looked like a naïve and pretty woman who was open to talking. Another perfect cam target.

"The food is a bribe, then, isn't it?" he asked cautiously.

"A bribe?"

"Of course. Students don't have much money and they're hungry. That's why they're here."

"Not everyone here is a student."

"Show me someone who isn't."

Nancy shrugged. "Right here," she said, pointing to her left. The camera panned and my heart stopped again. It was Frankie.

Frankie flicked his lighter and put the flame in the reporter's face. The camera took a step back.

"Watch it!" the reporter warned Frankie. "You should be in the park feeding birds, you senile old man."

The camera swerved back to Nancy, lingering over her chest.

"Now," the reporter continued, "a pretty girl like you shouldn't be doing something like this."

Nancy's surprised face turned out to be the last stable image he managed to capture. The camera jerked down, transmitting jittery images of the floor and the reporter's stumbling feet.

"Senile old man, huh?" I heard Frankie growl.

"Leave me alone!" cried the reporter.

There was a loud bang and the ugly carpet background gave way to tile.

"You're the one who's senile." Frankie's voice was calm yet furious. "Only somebody mentally unstable would drink from the toilet."

"No!"

A stall door banged open and a toilet bowl came into view. The water seemed to be discolored.

At this climactic point, the camera slipped and transmission was cut off.

After five seconds of a black screen, Taiwan Action Eye's male anchor appeared on the screen. "Thanks for your report, J.D. We hope you're doing all right." He smiled straight into the camera. "We're going to replay the last fifteen minutes of J.D.'s story because it was the consummate 'live action' report you want to see and see again.

"But first! Taiwan Action Eye brings you some breaking news! The two famous eating champions, Japanese Sadao and the American Chompin' Charlie, have announced that they support homosexual marriage in Taiwan and that they are in a homosexual relationship!"

The station ran footage of Sadao and Charlie at a sausage-eating contest in Germany.

"It's no wonder that both of those homosexuals are so good at eating meat! Again, Sadao and Chompin' Charlie are homosexuals and they support unnatural marriage in Taiwan! And now, Taiwan Action Eye replays our video captured by J.D. in the student occupation of the Legislative Yuan."

I turned off the TV and washed my hands and face. Nancy

was right. I should have been at the occupation. If I had helped to take a stand or at least support my girlfriend, I would have gotten to see the reporter drink from the toilet.

I called Nancy but it went to voicemail. "Nancy, I just saw you and Frankie on TV," I said. "I'm proud of you for standing up to that reporter. If the students need more food, send someone to Unknown Pleasures and I can pack up some skewers or containers of stew."

I hung up the phone and shook my head. That poor reporter had picked the wrong old man to provoke and had learned the hard way what Frankie the Cat could dish out. Frankie was strong and spry as hell. He had that special trait that only elderly Asian men have. At some point, their aging process bottoms out and they begin to grow younger.

Frankie is a former flag-waver who had learned the price of having a perceived political position. He never expressed opinions on political candidates. I don't even know if he voted. For him to be at a protest was nothing short of remarkable.

On my way in to work, I noticed that the stage for the stinky-tofu eating contest was still standing in the central area of the night market. The Americans hadn't bothered to dismantle it and take it away. Some kids sat on the platform edge, kicking their dangling legs, but the vendors had to take their handcarts around it, another minor public nuisance left standing in Taipei for a forgotten purpose.

Frankie was early at the stall, as I knew he'd be. He sat on a plastic stool, a shallow plastic pool at his feet and a large bucket at his side. His hands moved like two coordinated cormorants diving into the pool and surfacing with entrails. Frankie washed off the entrails with a hose, snipped them down to size with scissors that he kept concealed somewhere in his clothes, hosed down the entrails again and dropped them into the bucket. It was mesmerizing to watch him work.

"Jing-nan," he said without looking up. "I didn't expect you here until later."

I looked him over for signs of struggle, scratches on his face or hands, but saw nothing. "Frankie, I thought climbing over a few police barricades would slow you down."

He turned to me and opened his mouth completely before speaking. "Ha! I've been working here since before you were born!" He shrugged as his fingers danced through dirty innards. "Nothing could stop me from getting here."

I sat on an upside-down bucket and leaned toward him. "Frankie, I saw you on TV. You were at that occupation inside the Legislative Yuan. The cops had the building surrounded. There was no way out. How did you escape?"

He sighed at me and then looked down, pretending he needed to watch his hands work.

"Is Nancy all right?" I asked. "My calls don't get through to her."

"Too many phones, not enough towers," he said. "All the students plus the media. Nancy will be fine as long as she stays with the group."

"What were you doing at the protest, Frankie?"

"I was an innocent bystander."

"You're not innocent. I saw what you did to that reporter."

He patted his mouth with the back of a bloody hand and said, "You didn't see anything. The camera was out of commission."

DWAYNE, BY CONTRAST, WAS uncharacteristically late by about half an hour.

"Stupid protestors and stupid police blocking the streets," he grumbled. He tore off his gloves and chucked them into his motorcycle helmet. "I can only hope that this is the beginning of the end. All you Han Chinese start fighting amongst yourselves. Then all the survivors crawl onto boats and float back across the strait to where you come from. Good riddance!"

I couldn't help but laugh. It's cute when Dwayne gets so over-the-top about the demise of the historical oppressors of his people. I know he's joking. Less funny is when Taiwanese officials call aboriginals "lazy," "backwards," or worse. Donald Trump would have serious competition here for making gaffes.

"Dwayne," I said. "Who would run the island if all us 'Han Chinese' were gone?"

He posed as if he were being awarded a medal and thumped his chest. "We would! We'd put nature first again and heal the land after all the pollution and violence that you people brought here."

"What do you mean 'we'? The aboriginal tribes fought each other before anybody from China set foot on Taiwan."

He pointed an accusing finger at my nose. "You people killed us on a genocidal scale! We only killed each other for specific purposes."

"Like headhunting."

"Damn right!"

"You couldn't hunt heads for your life, Dwayne."

He growled and grabbed me around my waist. The guy had thirty kilograms on me, easily. He tried to spin me like a top but I managed to bring my knee up and wedge my way out. I anticipated landing on my left foot and softened the brunt of the impact by bending my knee.

"Do you two idiots have any idea," Frankie said to his hands, "how hard it is to get a stretcher through the night market?"

"Aw, it's just our little ritual," said Dwayne.

It was true that our improvised wrestling matches were a part of the nightly routine at Unknown Pleasures. Grappling with Dwayne was like washing my hands. I couldn't go through a night without it.

Our antics had begun at a time when the food stand wasn't doing so well. It was outdated and the deaths of my parents scared away the superstitious locals who thought they'd die or be cursed if they ate our food. Meanwhile the tourists were turned off by the "weird" food choices set by my grandfather and the off-putting menu, which was only in Chinese and Japanese.

I took charge after my father died. I didn't change the menu so much as emphasize the foreigner-friendly items. Visitors generally didn't want to eat organs on skewers but they loved offal when it was socked into a casing and grilled. I put the sausages front and center and made sure to brush them with oil regularly so they glistened. I installed hanging lamps over them expressly for this purpose. I wanted all the elements to be visible through the sausage skin—to make them look more "homemade"—so I instructed Dwayne to ease up on chopping the herbs and to use a coarser grind on the pepper. I installed a chopping block to the left of the sausages and told Frankie to stand behind it every ten minutes or so and cut up a sausage link. To the right of the sausages I installed a grill with show-off flames.

I also translated most of the items on the menu into English. You don't want to translate all of it—tourists love a mystery.

The biggest change I made was within myself. After being in America for two years, I learned how to sell an idea by osmosis. Tourists come to Taiwan because they want to buy stuff but they also want you to sell it to them. I created an alter ego because I knew my moderately introverted nature would never be able to greet strangers and chat them up. That wasn't me at all. But Johnny could do that. He loved people and he loved their money even more. He could go up to anybody and ask how they liked Taipei before steering them ever so gently, only using a touch on the shoulder, to see the quality of the sausages Frankie was slicing.

"Please try a bite," Johnny would say. Once the meat was in their mouth, the deal, and a corresponding glassine baggie of sausage, was as good as sealed.

I also gave the business an English name: "Unknown Pleasures."

Results were immediate. The old-school stall operators decried me as a pimp for actively recruiting customers, but Johnny cried all the way to the cash register. The first night we were back in the black—figuratively and literally, as the decor was a blatant rip-off of Joy Division's bleak album cover—Dwayne celebrated the event by pinning one of my arms behind my back and nearly strangling me. I had saved the stall but more importantly I had saved his job. Every night since, my ass has been up for grabs.

When I look back to the early days, it's hard for me to remember just how desperate we were. I don't know if I could make such drastic and prescient choices now. People loved us and more importantly rated us highly online, so we have a bit of a cushion to rest on. After all, is anybody else in Taipei going to open a food stand with a Joy Division theme?

I continue to change things, little things that can make us look marginally better. For instance, I asked Dwayne to use more red peppers instead of green ones in the sausages. Red looks better on Instagram through any of the special-effects filters.

A newer ritual I added was more sedate than squaring off with Dwayne and called for precision.

"No horsing around right now," I warned him as I laid out the wooden skewers. They were light but sharp enough to pierce a hand right through the palm.

All three of us got down to our culinary knitting, folding flesh and piercing it through the center with the skewers. This was our religion. This was our life. Sure, I lured in tourists, but if the food didn't look or taste right, there would be consequences—food blogs dissing Unknown Pleasures, or negative reviews on our Facebook page.

The Facebook fan page is new. I try to keep it populated with pictures and other content. I had originally hoped to have a staff picture, but both Frankie and Dwayne refused to let me post their pictures. It actually works out for the better. I put up pictures of me with attractive young visitors.

Marketing note to myself: Get more famous people to come by!

I put my thoughts aside. The three of us filled the first tray with twenty skewers in no time. Dwayne spread out his hands, picked up the first eight, and laid them out on the main grill. These would be used for the offering.

When the skewers were half-cooked, he laid them across an ornate rectangular plate and carried them to the corner below a small altar. He lit a stick of incense and bowed as a scarlet-faced Lord Guan idol glared down at him, one hand on the long staff of his moonblade, holding the weapon upright, and the other hand held over his heart.

Like many deities, Lord Guan is based on an actual person, a hero from China's Three Kingdoms period nearly two thousand years ago. He was a fugitive from justice. While on the run, he obtained a potion from one of those wandering Taoist immortals who pop up every now and then, particularly on mountain paths. Lord Guan washed his face with the potion and it became red like the Kool-Aid Man. Lord Guan never smiled like the Kool-Aid Man, though.

People who run small businesses worship Lord Guan to ward off criminals, because Lord Guan is known for his sense of honor and for punishing the amoral. I'm not sure why Dwayne worships him, though. Lord Guan is a god of the Han Chinese colonizers. But like most Taiwanese, Dwayne believes in all gods, goddesses, and charms. That fool was even crossing himself for a while after seeing *The Godfather* on television.

Dwayne finished bowing before Lord Guan and backed away, leaving the skewers there for the god to "eat." There aren't any official guidelines on how long it takes a supreme being to consume offerings. In the old days, food would sit out and putrefy, the rotting smells covered up by incense. Now, the divine meal time doesn't even last an hour.

Lord Guan should be able to polish the skewers off pretty quickly. After all, he had help. Dwayne had tucked in a few other idols around Lord Guan's feet. I didn't know them all. The statues of three old men grouped together I recognized as the Three Immortals, who represented fortune (the one holding a baby), prosperity (the guy in traditional scholar robes), and longevity (the one holding a peach). Why the three were close, I had no idea. Maybe they had a co-branding deal to maximize offerings. Apart from them I only recognized Mazu, by her beaded veil. For a joke, I once squeezed a little Hello Kitty doll into the altar, and that really pissed off Dwayne, who was scared of no man but terrified of divine judgment.

Me, I didn't take temples seriously, so how could I put any credence in our little shelf of idols? I could, however, recognize the menagerie as one more thing for tourists to take pictures of and to linger over. Marketing note to myself:

Make a video of Dwayne offering skewers before the altar. I looked them over and noticed a few were uneven. That could look sloppy online in a cropped close-up.

I approached the offering plate and Dwayne nearly ripped my arm off.

"Don't!" was all he said.

"Calm down, man," I said in a soothing voice. I straightened out the skewers to make them all parallel. "Now don't they look better?"

Dwayne held one hand over his heart, subconsciously imitating Lord Guan's idol. "If you had eaten one or played another prank . . ." he started.

"I don't do that anymore," I said. "I have nothing but respect for Lord Guan's many accomplishments and this particular idol's many Facebook and Twitter appearances."

Dwayne shook his head at me. "Just wait until the afterlife, when you meet Lord Guan face-to-face," he muttered. "We'll see how snarky you are, then."

"Are you going to spend the afterlife with Han Chinese, Dwayne?"

"Ha, the gods don't see race or creed, and the fires of Hell burn everyone equally to a crisp!"

An idea struck me.

"Dwayne, we should have an altar to some of your Amis gods," I said. "It would really stand out in the night market. Even more people would come here just to take pictures."

Dwayne scoffed. "Amis gods are no good," he said, returning to skewering. "They didn't stop you people from invading and destroying our lives."

"Lord Guan couldn't stop the mainlanders from taking over Taiwan," I said.

"Listen to the kid, Frankie," said Dwayne. "He doesn't know that heaven is fickle and always favors the strong."

"Hmm," said Frankie, his mouth curling into its characteristically enigmatic smile.

AN HOUR OR SO later, I fell into a discussion of Joy Division with a group of young Kiwis in Taipei for a programming confab. New Zealanders are among the biggest fans of the band as Joy Division's songs went Top 10 there. I was older and had a bigger music collection than any of those kids, and in the unspoken rules of fandom, that made me the authority figure.

"Have you ever heard the early New Order demos with the drummer Stephen Morris singing?" I slyly asked. "This was before the band had settled on Bernard to replace Ian as the singer."

The tallest kid shook his dreadlocks. "How do they sound?"

"Terrible!" I continued talking as I snapped up skewers with my tongs and distributed them in equal portions to five different bags. "They were recorded live and you could tell he was struggling with drumming and singing at the same time. The man's a machine. Just let him drum, already."

A young woman with two silver studs in her nose looked askance at me. "How did *you* hear those demos, Johnny? You're not old enough to have been there."

I held up the tongs like I had a point to make. In reality I was pausing to see which sausages were on the verge of becoming overcooked. "A friend of the band had remastered and uploaded all these studio outtakes and live recordings."

"What's the site?" Dreadlocks asked as I targeted five prime-for-moving sausages with my tongs.

"It's gone now. Joy Division's record company shut it down." I sighed as I shook each bag to settle them, then handed them out. "That's why the music industry's hurting so badly now.

They just don't get the way it works. They didn't know that people downloading bootlegs already own everything that was officially put out. If they had any brains . . ."

My phone rang in my pocket. I could feel that it was the beat to "Love Will Tear Us Apart," the end of the introductory passage with the crash of the drums before the keyboards kick in.

"Whoa!" the kids said in recognition and admiration.

That ringtone meant that the caller was Nancy.

I clamped the phone between my left shoulder and ear. Instantly I switched from English to Taiwanese.

"Nancy!" I said, dragging out the pronunciation of her name. "I saw you on TV at the protest! I couldn't get through to you—are you all right?" I showed an index finger and then cupped all five fingers to indicate to the Kiwi kids to pay a mere NT$100 each. A bargain for them but, more importantly, still a profit for me. I heard people yelling at her end.

"Jing-nan! I'm so angry!" said Nancy. "Do you know what those so-called student leaders did? They struck out the demand for marriage equality from the platform. I walked out with half the group! I had convinced my bandmates to get together to play our song about gay marriage at the occupation. Now that's not going to happen."

Boar Pour More, Nancy's on-again, off-again band, was as volatile as the lurching post-punk music they played. Nancy herself was a bedrock-solid drummer whose beat could stamp metal sheets.

"Gan!" I said as I folded money from the Kiwis into my pockets. "These student leaders are already thinking about their political careers."

"I should have known by the way they were taking video of themselves, giving speeches on the floor. The worst thing is that Sadao and Chompin' Charlie were going to stop by the occupation to give moral support. All the marriage-equality people have now warned them to stay away."

Sadao and Chompin' Charlie. Unknown Pleasures' Facebook page could use a few pictures with them.

"Nancy, what are Sadao and Charlie going to do instead?"

"I just talked to Sadao. He wants us, that is, Boar Pour More, to find somewhere else for everyone to hang out and make some noise for marriage equality. I tried calling around to a few clubs but nobody has enough space for us."

"How many people have you got?"

"About two hundred people, at least."

"Where is Sadao now?"

"He and Charlie are in a cab. They're just driving around, seeing the city, waiting for us to find a place." One can actually meander in a cab in Taipei. The rides are notoriously cheap.

"I have an idea," I said. "Bring everybody here."

"To Unknown Pleasures?"

"Bring Sadao and Charlie to Unknown Pleasures because I want to take pictures of them here, and bring everybody else to the center of Shilin Night Market. The Americans left the stage up from the eating contest. You guys could have your little rally and concert there."

"Are you sure it's going to be all right?"

I thought about little unofficial rules all us vendors abided by, about not having overt political messages, not using amplified sound, and giving ample notice for activities that may disrupt others. I also thought about the homophobic remarks from the old guard and hicks who ran some of the less-interesting stalls.

If anybody had a problem with a gay-friendly crowd of two hundred-odd people, they wouldn't as long as it was a hungry crowd.

"There's no problem," I said.

"Okay," Nancy said to me. I heard her yell out to her crew, "Jing-nan says there's a space at the Shilin Night Market. Let's go there!"

"Fuck that place," some woman yelled back. "It's too touristy!" I recognized the voice as belonging to Hazel, Boar Pour More's singer.

I couldn't help but smile. Listen, Hazel, you have no idea what a good thing that is.

Not too long after, Nancy brought Sadao and Chompin' Charlie to Unknown Pleasures with about a dozen star-struck students in tow. "Sadao, this is my boyfriend, Jing-nan. This was all his idea."

I was about to bow to him but Sadao reached out and shook my hand. He had a tight grip.

"It's a pleasure to meet you," I said.

"Thank you for thinking this up." He took his hand back and Charlie came up and gave me a hug.

"People in Taipei have been great," he told me.

I smiled and patted him on the back a few times.

Sadao recognized Dwayne from the eating contest and the two shook hands. I couldn't help but be amazed that a guy who was much smaller and skinnier than Dwayne could eat so much so fast. Sadao spoke some rudimentary Mandarin to Dwayne, who reciprocated. Jealousy flashed in Chompin' Charlie's eyes.

Frankie told Sadao in Japanese that we were honored to have him at our stand. Sadao asked if he could light an incense stick to Lord Guan at our altar. He pointed at the god's stern smile.

"I'm a big fan of his through the video games," Sadao told me in English, the lingua franca among Asians from different countries. "I have every version of Romance of the Three Kingdoms on every platform."

"I'm into them, too," said Charlie. "We fight over who gets to play as Guan Yu." The disrespectful use of Lord Guan's civilian name near the altar caused Dwayne to stretch his arms over his head to mask his discomfort.

"I haven't tried the video games," I said. "I don't have time."

"Aw, they're so good," said Charlie.

"Sadao and Charlie," I asked, "would you mind if I make a video of you guys planting joss sticks?"

"That's fine," said Charlie.

"Okay with me," said Sadao.

Dwayne showed them both how to bow and plant the joss sticks the proper way, or at least the way that he had adopted.

Both eating champions were more than happy to pose for pictures, but the pitchman in me pushed things too far in the end. "Sadao, can I get a picture of you and Charlie with skewers clenched in your teeth?"

He shook his head slowly. "That's a bit much, Jing-nan."

I couldn't complain—he had already done plenty for my business. I left Unknown Pleasures in the care of Frankie and Dwayne. Nancy, Sadao, Charlie, and I went to the stage so we could figure out how to put on a show. The students had already dispersed in search of food.

We couldn't do much about the lack of lighting. The jeans and purses store, Junk in Your Trunk, agreed to lend me one of their outdoor spotlights for the stage. Beefy King, Home of the Shilin Sirloin Steak, contributed their PA system on the condition that its sign could hang on the stage monitor, visible to the audience. One microphone and one loudspeaker would have to do.

While we were still setting up we began to hear a commotion approaching the stage. The breakaway protestors were arriving. A number of them had dyed their hair in rainbow colors. The night-market patrons stopped and took notice of the influx.

"Wow, Nancy," I said. "I think there are more than two hundred people coming."

"I put up some notices online about the show here, but I didn't know if anybody saw it."

Sadao held up his phone. "I texted everybody I know in Taipei to come and bring their friends."

WHEN SADAO HIT THE stage he took dramatic steps to the microphone at the center and then stood silently. He waited for the applause to die down and when it didn't he held up his hands for silence.

First he said thank you in four different languages. Then he spoke in Japanese for about two minutes. Taiwanese students in the know shouted encouragement.

Then in English he said, "For me and my love, we are not allowed to marry in my home country. It's hard sometimes to go on, knowing that you're not allowed to exist as a couple. Both Chompin' Charlie and I hope that things can be different in Taiwan. I'm very happy for Taiwan Pride. It's so big! It makes me proud! You know what it's like, being told you shouldn't exist. China says Taiwan is a part of China. But in reality, Taiwan is not China. That is why we also support the defeat of the trade bill. Thank you."

The crowd, which now stood at about four hundred people, cheered. For an improvised gathering, it was pretty damned impressive.

Sadao then introduced Boar Pour More as "Taiwan's original Pussy Riot." I wasn't sure that the comparison was apt. Nancy's band did indeed have three women like the Russian art-activist group, but Boar Pour More had actual songs, some of them rockin'.

But there would be no rockin' tonight. They had planned an unplugged performance in the Legislative Yuan's cavernous chamber, where the acoustics would have been perfect. Unfortunately, in the open air and with no amplification, the two acoustic guitars with Nancy's tambourine were in danger of being drowned out by Boar Pour More's singer, Hazel. The right thing would have been to put the microphone in a place equidistant from the three members. But Hazel was too much of a post-post-punk diva. She had to have it on a stand, right by her mouth, even if it made the group sound like crap overall. Hazel sang flat, probably because she couldn't hear her own guitar, and the only other thing the audience could hear, from time to time, was Nancy's tambourine ringing, an incidental sound like the bells of a lost reindeer.

Surprisingly the crowd tried to hang in there. In fact, there wasn't enough space on the side I was standing on. Some woman was working her elbow into my gut, trying to get by me. I turned to her, ready to give her my dirtiest look, when I saw that it was Mei-ling and she was laughing at me.

"Jesus, Jing-nan, you get so uptight!" she yelled.

"What are you doing here so early, my young cousin?"

She tilted her head as if she were doing me a favor by explaining herself to me. "Peggy had some dinner function so she released me early. I read on the LGBT bulletin board that Sadao was hosting a show here and that some musical acts were needed."

"Well, there's only one group on tonight that I know of."

"That's perfect, then. I can get up there and sing after these guys."

"Says who?"

Mei-ling fiddled with her phone and showed me a message from Sadao himself on the TaiPride board: "Please come and bring your music, Mei-ling! The *kawaii* guy who runs Unknown Pleasures can hook you up!"

I'll be honest. I was a little unnerved that a gay man called me "cute." I should feel complimented. Even Nancy never told me I was cute.

"Mei-ling, what were you doing on TaiPride?" I asked.

"You can't make dance music without knowing what is going on in the gay community." Her face suddenly darkened. "Why do you want to know, Jing-nan? Do you have a problem with queers?"

"I was just curious!" I said. "I don't have problems with anybody!"

"Hah!" Mei-ling crossed her arms and legs. "So how much longer are they going to play?"

"I don't know."

"I like Nancy a lot, okay, but they sound awful."

"I know. They're really a lot better than this."

"Can't you do something about it?"

"Nope. They just don't have the equipment. No amps, guitars, or real drums." I cut myself off as I looked Mei-ling over. "Hey, are you going to sing *a cappella* or something?"

"I have my backing tracks on my phone. Just run it through the PA and I'll sing through the microphone."

I hid my hands in my armpits. Hadn't this audience suffered enough? Why did anyone here deserve listening to a shitty set from Boar Pour More followed by something even worse? "I wish I could hook you up, Mei-ling, but I don't have a cord to connect your phone to the amplifier."

She reached into her back pocket and produced the exact cord needed. "I carry this with me," she said.

"For what?" I said as I unwound the cord.

"If I happen to go to Ximending, someone might want to jam with me." Ximending is a neighborhood known for its youth culture. Bands set up on sidewalks with portable amplifiers and play to passersby. It's known for shopping malls, clubs, cinemas and for love hotels that accommodate local teenage prostitution. It's always crowded with people looking for a good time.

"Promise that you're not going to Ximending, not without me," I warned her. "Or else you're not going on tonight."

She stomped her foot. "Okay, okay!"

I looked her over. What could this skinny little girl do on stage? I had to admit, though, she couldn't do worse than the disgraceful Boar Pour More reunion.

As the band bowed and mercifully ended their set, Sadao took up the microphone. "Please, let's have a big round of applause for my favorite band in the whole world, Boar Pour More."

The audience applauded at a volume that was marginally more than mere courtesy. "So good, so good," he added in English, Mandarin, and Japanese. Mei-ling stepped up to the stage and approached Sadao. He cupped his hand over the microphone as she shyly introduced herself to him. They spoke briefly and he began to nod and bow. She bowed back awkwardly.

I went to the amplifier and set up Mei-ling's phone.

She jogged over to me and said, "When I give you the signal, hit the play button, Jing-nan."

"Got it," I said.

As Boar Pour More packed up and left the stage, Sadao turned to the crowd and clapped his hands. "Now, we have something special from a new artist. She calls herself Orchids! Thank you!" He slid the mic back into the stand and stepped off the side of the stage.

Orchids? Well, whatever. Mei-ling would be off the stage soon. The audience members already had enough pain in their lives.

I saw Mei-ling standing near the back of the platform. She turned to me and when I saw her eyes, they seemed to glow a little and I didn't recognize her. Orchids nodded and I hit the play button.

I knew the sampled beat right away. It was the same song of hers that I suffered through in the car. It sounded better outdoors.

Mei-ling put her arms to the sides and slinked to the microphone like an aroused cobra. Where did she learn to do that? I didn't recognize the creature that my cousin had become. She threw her head back and snapped it forward just in time to sing.

She wasn't the greatest singer, but she was better than how Boar Pour More's Hazel had come across, and that was all that mattered. What Orchids was doing wasn't so much singing verses, but voicing snippets, including, "Do you love me?" and "Are we in love?" Banal for sure, but when phrased properly, as Mei-ling was doing, the words had more meaning.

Now I knew what was so wrong with her song demos. They weren't produced properly. The synthesized treatment of her voice was completely wrong. You did that for performers who couldn't sing but looked good in videos. It was dawning on me that Mei-ling did indeed have some ability.

During an instrumental break, she put her forearms together and slowly opened them, revealing her face. The crowd mimicked her movements.

"Open your mind! Open your mind!" she sang as the song came to a close. I clapped and realized that I should be recording her on video. Her next song started up and I fumbled with my phone to focus on her performance.

The second song was the same fare, the other bookend, but that was all right, especially for a dance crowd. "Do you love me?" was now "Don't you miss me?" The chorus sampled the drum fills from Echo & The Bunnymen's "Monkeys," unlicensed, I was sure.

I nodded in time with the music and parted imaginary curtains with my free hand as Mei-ling was doing. "Look at me! Look at me!" she sang as the song closed with the dying echoes of a snare drum.

The crowd cheered as she said apologetically, "That's all I have. Please go to Orchidsmusicnow.com and check out the songs. Thank you!" She bowed. I applauded her as a new fan.

Sadao came back on the mic. "Oh, wow, Orchids. That was something! Excellent! Excellent!" The audience applauded wildly. Chompin' Charlie jumped on stage and ran to embrace Sadao and kissed him intensely. Sadao looked a little embarrassed as Charlie grabbed the mic and yelled, "Thank you, Taipei! We love you!" They both bowed and then rushed off the stage.

I turned and saw Nancy standing with their lead guitar player, whose name I can never remember. I made my way over. My girlfriend cradled her tambourine and shook her head.

"We broke up again," said Nancy. "Hazel says she's resuming her solo career."

"That's too bad, but maybe it was for the best," I said. The guitarist and I briefly nodded to each other.

"How did we do?" asked Nancy. The ends of her mouth were turned down. "Were we bad?"

"Bad? Naw, it wasn't bad," I said. "The mix was off. If you had had time for a sound check, it would have been great."

The guitarist looked me square in the eye. "You're lying," she said. "We fucking sucked out loud! Nobody could hear our goddamned instruments over Hazel's singing!"

I looked at her and then at Nancy, and ended up dropping my eyes to the ground. "Well, I wouldn't go that far."

The guitarist turned to Nancy. "Don't marry this one," she said as she rattled her guitar case for emphasis. "He's a liar and he can't even remember your friends' names." With that, she turned and stomped off into the night.

"Hey," I called after her, "maybe it's the guitar playing that's the problem!" She flipped me off the British way, with two fingers, and I gained some respect for her.

I rubbed Nancy's shoulders as she observed the groups of people taking pictures with Mei-ling.

"I'm not asking you to marry me right now or anytime soon," I said. "But I don't think you can count on a rock guitarist for matrimonial advice."

Nancy shuddered. "You should see some of the people she's been with."

"Still, though, she's not a bad guitar player. It was just a bad setup for Boar Pour More."

Nancy leaned against my hands. "Anyway," she said, "I don't think anybody remembers our set now. Your little cousin was great! Why did you say she couldn't sing?"

"She's a lot better on stage. You see, the problem with her song demos is that . . ."

Mei-ling suddenly appeared between Nancy and me.

I started my apology with, "Mei-ling, you were really . . ."

"Quick!" Mei-ling interjected. "Please walk with me, these people won't leave me alone!" About a dozen giggling kids, mostly girls, followed her. I swept myself in front of the kids, blocking them off while Nancy locked arms with Mei-ling. I'm sure she was telling my cousin all sorts of complimentary things, judging by the pitch of her voice. And Mei-ling deserved to hear them. Her ego must have been starved to hear feedback from someone who had gigged like Nancy.

When I caught up to them, Mei-ling showed me what Sadao had texted to her: "If you want to play shows in Japan, please let me know. I love your songs. Do you want to go to a club tonight?"

"Wow," I said. "Um, are you going to hang out with Sadao?"

"No, I'd rather be with my cousin and his awesome girlfriend!"

I'd been too busy to eat and now that the adrenaline was wearing off, I was feeling hungry. "Do you want to try 'little bun inside big bun'? We're sort of heading toward them."

"I've never tried that. Let's go!"

I looked back and saw that we weren't putting much distance between us and the younger kids. "I guess your fans are going to try some, too."

We entered the indoor area of the night market and walked down the perennially broken escalator. The kids followed us, to the delight of the stall owner.

The kids wouldn't let us pay for the double buns. They wouldn't even let us wait for them to be prepared. Two girls asked us what we wanted and then got in line. One of the boys seemed a little older. Grad student, I guessed. His hair was in a perm and resembled a pack of dry ramen out of the wrapper. Probably didn't get out much. He seemed thrilled just to be hanging out with us.

The "little bun" is a little fried pastry, filled with something either sweet or savory. When you order, a woman who looks as stern as a temple guardian statue places your little bun on a cutting board and smashes it up with a metal mallet. She then scrapes the pieces onto a soft flour pancake. The pancake is then rolled up, forming the "big bun." It's definitely heavy on the carbs, but hey, it's fun to eat.

Pictures of celebrities adorned the bottom of the sign for the little-bun-inside-big-bun stall. President Ma Ying-jeou himself, rocking a rubbery Devo hairdo, flashed a toothy grimace while shaking hands with the owner, a thin man with dark skin. Judging by how much less hair the owner had now and the confidence in President Ma's eyes, the picture must have been from Ma's first campaign, the 2008 election, and not the contentious 2012 drive before his re-election.

Another picture featured the owner with one arm around the waist of Yao Yao, a young singer known for her baby face and large breasts. Yao Yao brandished a double bun in one hand and gave a peace sign with the other.

The last picture was with an exhausted-looking Jackie Chan. I've never seen him look so old. Jackie wasn't smiling and he also didn't seem aware that his picture was being taken or that the owner was trying to hand him a freshly wrapped double bun.

In every picture Mallet Woman stood in the background, small and forlorn. You hear about images of long-dead classmates that show up in group pictures taken at graduations and reunions. She looked like one of those ghosts.

Mallet Woman was sullen and silent in real life but she let her tool do the talking. Pow! Pow! Pow! The poor little buns had no chance. You could feel each angry strike through your feet.

"That woman's a wrecking ball!" said Nancy.

"Don't steal money from her," said Mei-ling.

"I wonder if she only uses one lucky mallet," I said.

"She's got more than one," said Nancy. "She's got that one with a rounded head and one under the counter with a square head."

I watched and felt the mallet crash down. Guilty! Guilty! Guilty! She didn't really need to make such a racket but it was a great marketing gimmick. How could you not look at what was going on?

The kids brought over our food. I had gone with the

red-bean filling. Mei-ling destroyed her curry pork one and Nancy took measured bites of her taro-root double bun.

Mei-ling's new fans were too shy to talk to her. Ramen Head was eating with shaking hands. I asked Mei-ling an interview-style question to help break the ice. "How did you come up with the name 'Orchids,' Mei-ling?"

"I thought of a vagina," she said. The girls in the group giggled. "It's like a flower, a receptacle with petals, stamen."

"As an artist"—and I almost cringed when I said the word—"why do you have to sexualize your work?"

Mei-ling tilted her head and stared up at the ceiling. "We are sexual animals. That's how we reproduce and it's how we have fun. Hiding it is trying to deny who we are."

I noticed a skinny young man wearing a Doraemon T-shirt sidling up to Nancy. "Great show," he told her. "I'm a big fan of Boar Pour More."

"Did you really like it?" asked Nancy as she nervously tightened the outer wrap of her double bun.

"Of course! I mean, you guys don't specifically sing about being gay, but your music helped give me the courage to come out of the closet." He scratched his ear. "I was very inspired to hear that your guitarist was a lesbian. I'm sorry, but I can't remember her name."

"See?" I said to Nancy. "Tell your guitarist I'm not the only one who can't remember!"

ON OUR WAY OUT of the night market I insisted on seeing Mei-ling back to her apartment. Nancy hopped in a cab to meet like-minded students at a cafe. There was online chatter about breaking off from the main activist group, which had showed its hand at being intrinsically self-promotional, and forming a new coalition to focus on the two main issues: trade pact and marriage equality.

Mei-ling slumped her shoulders as we entered the MRT. "Really?" she asked. "Every night, you're going to personally make sure I go home?"

"Yes," I said. "You're my little cousin and while Taipei is a safe city, it's not completely crime-free."

"I can understand if it's after midnight, but it's not even ten P.M., Jing-nan," she said. "If I can handle putting on a show in front of hundreds of people, I think I can get myself home."

"I am acting under orders from Big Eye," I said. "If anything goes wrong, I suffer the consequences."

Mei-ling slapped my arm. "How do you know I won't go out again after you're gone?" she asked.

"Somebody from the building would probably follow you," I said.

"Why are both of you men so afraid of what a little girl can do?" she complained to her phone as her thumbs worked the on-screen keyboard. Young people are so rude, talking to one person while texting another. It's disrespectful to both.

"I'm afraid of Big Eye, not you. I don't know what his deal is with you, but honestly I think he wants you to be happy in the long run. Why else would he give a shit about you finishing high school?"

She shrugged and twisted the ball of her foot into the ground.

"It might not feel like love but he cares about you."

Mei-ling glanced at the lobby attendant. "He doesn't love anybody," she said. "Not even himself."

I have no problem lying so long as it makes someone feel better. But I couldn't make stuff up about a man to his own daughter.

"He's not as bad as you think he is," I offered in a tone that I hoped was measurably positive.

Mei-ling scoffed. "You say that because you're a boy. He treats you differently than he does me." Her face was still in her phone.

"Okay, maybe that's true, but you don't have to keep treating me like an enemy. You're not staying in Taipei that long, so let's commit to being friendly, and we can start by maybe having you look at me when you talk."

She sighed and put her hands and the phone behind her back.

"Can we ride the Maokong gondola this weekend?" she asked. "I've heard it has some amazing views. Big Eye said I should visit some mountains and we both know you always do what my daddy wants you to."

I didn't tell her that it was originally a temple fortune that said she should visit mountains. The gondola wasn't much more than just a fancy ski lift for tea tourists. "I know Big Eye wants you to see the mountains, but are you sure you want to go? It's not very hip." With a conspiratorial tone, I added, "We can just tell him you went."

The gondola route zipped up and across mountains on an aerial lift system on the east rim of Taipei. It wasn't a linear path. After a stop at the Taipei Zoo, the gondola line made a right turn and stopped at a temple before a final stop at several teahouses and farms. It had been a while since I'd been to the top, but I remember that there were stairs to go even higher. Supposedly, the higher you went, the better the quality of the tea.

"I want to check it out," said Mei-ling. "We don't have things like gondolas in the country and I've never been on one."

"We'll ride to the top this weekend and have a tea toast to congratulate you on your performance tonight."

"If the view really is nice, maybe I'll be inspired to write a new song."

"I think you should title it, 'My Cousin Is So Great.'"

"Sounds catchy," she said, giving the same fake smile American girls give their rivals by the lockers before homeroom in every Hollywood film.

CHAPTER TEN

LATE THAT NIGHT, NANCY and I met up at my place and wrestled in bed a while. After, she asked me why I seemed distracted.

"I'm worried about Mei-ling," I said. "Not because she wants to sing but because she really is talented."

Nancy pulled on her sleep outfit, my old T-shirt of The Cure (a band she liked more than I did), went to the kitchen and brought back two cans of Taiwan Beer (a brand she liked more than I did).

"She's good," Nancy said as she popped open her can. "It was a little depressing watching her sing. It made me feel old!"

"Music's for young people," I said. "Most people our age tune out and listen to the same albums." I took a swig of Taiwan Beer. "This beer is not so great, you know?"

"You need to drink it more often. Anyway, you're right. After college, people have less time for music. Less time for movies, too."

"Probably because they have real jobs. Not like us!"

"You have a real job! You have your own business!"

"Is it my business? I didn't start it. I still don't know what the secret marinade is made of. Dwayne won't tell me. Also, I have no idea where Frankie gets the meat from or how much he pays."

I would be so screwed without those two guys. Dwayne and Frankie are two huge reasons why Unknown Pleasures works so well. In fact, at some point we may have to expand and hire more people. My grandfather had no idea what he was starting when he opened his dinky one-man stall. He and my grandmother had walked north into Taipei on bare feet from the fields of central Taiwan to find their fortune in the big city, as the family story goes.

I took another swig of Taiwan Beer. Still not great. "I would never allow this brand to sponsor any of Mei-ling's concerts."

"She needs a good manager. Most of them are pretty crooked."

"Big Eye probably knows people in the music business."

"People like Big Eye are the reason why the entertainment industry is so crooked!"

"Yeah, you're right. Maybe that's why he doesn't want his daughter mixed up in it."

Nancy polished off her beer and wiped her mouth with the back of her hand. "If you had a daughter, and she wanted to be a singer, would you let her?"

"Do you mean our daughter?"

"I'm not asking that!" she said, laughing.

"Did you know I already have a daughter? I left her back in the States!"

Nancy screamed and pushed me down on the mattress. I was dimly aware of a can of beer sloshing across the floor.

IN THE HUMID MID-MORNING, Nancy's phone thumped with "Sailin' On" by Bad Brains. She likes to use samples from hardcore punk for her text message alerts. She figures texts are more urgent than phone calls, which she keeps tied to the default ringtone. How boring.

The occupation of the Legislative Yuan had ended with a whimper and the last stragglers had filed out around daybreak. The student leaders had broken yet another promise when they had closed-door meetings with representatives of the two major political parties. All dealings were supposed to be in a public forum and streamed online. The students were accused of selling out to the highest bidder.

Nancy's friends wanted to meet up again and talk about what went wrong. She took a quick shower and pulled on jeans with her hair still wet.

"Are you sure you don't want to come, Jing-nan?"

"I wouldn't know what to say."

"You could just come and listen."

"I'll pay more attention to politics when the next election comes up. I promise."

"Democracy is now. It's always happening and you have to take part in it."

"Would you stand in front of a Chinese tank, Nancy?"

"Why not? It's been done before and nothing happened."

She kissed the top of my head on the way out. I heard the door close and her keys rattle in the lock.

Then I heard her scream shatter the morning.

I ran to the door naked and threw it open. The first thing I saw was a splotch of what looked like blood on the hallway floor near Nancy's feet. Then I noticed Big Eye, slouching against the wall and chewing betel nut. He was wearing light blue cotton slacks and a white linen shirt that was unbuttoned too far down for my taste. Whistle and Gao stood behind Big Eye on the ascending stairwell. Both were wearing black shirts and looked as imposing as human-sized chess pieces that wouldn't wait their turn to move.

Big Eye regarded Nancy with open amusement. "You never seen anyone spit betel nut before, little girl?" He smiled, showing off the red juice glistening on his teeth. Then he turned to me. "At least I don't have my dick hanging out in public. Is that a part of Taipei life, nephew?"

I covered up and said, "Nancy, this is my uncle, Big Eye, and his two best friends, Whistle and Gao." They followed me back into the apartment, where I pulled on shorts and a shirt and got Big Eye a cup to spit into. No need to antagonize the neighbors with a splotchy hallway. Gao began to walk around my apartment, stopping at each window to look for rooftop snipers. Whistle sat on the couch, where he could keep an eye on the door.

Nancy started to excuse herself but my uncle cut her off.

"Just a moment, miss. Have you seen Chong around? Meiling's darkie ex-boyfriend?"

She recoiled at Big Eye's crude language.

"I'm looking for him. Take a look at this picture."

"I haven't seen him. I also have to add that 'darkie' is offensive to me."

Big Eye gave a small smile. "Why's it offensive to *you*? You ain't one."

"If you don't treat people respectfully, don't expect respect from other people. Have a good day, everybody." She glared at me as she left.

"Big Eye, are you trying to get me into trouble?"

He waved away my question as if it were secondhand smoke. "Women get more passionate when they're mad. You should thank me. Anyway, have you seen Chong around?"

"No, I haven't. Why are you looking for him?"

"Everybody's looking for him. His friends and his family. Chong disappeared. I figured he must have come back to Taipei to be with Mei-ling."

I tried to focus on Big Eye but the continued vigilance of

Whistle and Gao was freaking me out. "He knows where I live and he hasn't been here," I said.

Big Eye spat into the cup and watched the betel-nut juice swirl around. "That little monkey better stay the hell away from my little girl," he warned the cup. "If you see him, you call me! Get it?"

"Of course," I said. "Look, don't call him a monkey. Really, you're going way too far, Big Eye."

My uncle ground his teeth. Apparently that was also the signal to leave. Gao swung my front door open and the three men stepped out.

"Have you tried Mei-ling yet?" I asked Big Eye.

"She wouldn't tell me the truth. Anyway, I have extra guys watching the building." He glanced at his hands. "Mind if I keep the cup?"

It was one of the few microwave-safe cups I owned but it was probably already ruined.

"It's all yours," I said as I walked to the door, ready to close and lock it.

"Wait, where the fuck are you going, nephew?"

"Back to sleep?"

"C'mon, let's go pick up Mei-ling together and take her to work. I want to see what her illustrious internship is like."

The guy barely gave me enough time to put on my shoes.

WE CAUGHT MEI-LING STILL asleep and she moaned like a beached whale about being woken up. She denied that she had seen Chong and went back to complaining. Big Eye barked that she would never get anywhere being lazy and after he searched the bathroom for Chong, he demanded that Mei-ling shower and dress.

Whistle paced at the front door while Gao walked along the walls, pausing at the windows to scan for threats. I heard

Mei-ling throw things around in her bedroom before she stomped out in a red blouse, black slacks, and bare feet.

"It's still way too early for me to go in," she whined as she looked over her extensive shoe collection.

Big Eye brushed aside her complaints. "You'll impress your boss," he said.

"Nothing impresses her! Ask Jing-nan!"

"The boss is a little crazy," I offered.

"I'll bet she is," said Big Eye. "Crazy with money! I've done some research online. The Lee family has money all over Taipei—and abroad." He pointed at Whistle. "They have a goddamned villa in Switzerland near Roman Polanski's!"

Whistle frowned and wiped his nose. "What's a 'villa'?" he asked.

"Don't you know anything? It's a mansion on a mountain. They look like cookie houses." Big Eye made a sound like an angry swan and spat into his cup. "That's what I should have done. Invested in property abroad. Fucking mainlanders like the Lees always know what to do with their money."

"It's a headache," said Whistle. "You lose fifteen percent when you launder it and then . . ." He looked at me and narrowed his eyes. "There are other things to consider," he said slowly.

Big Eye had already moved on, searching the ceiling as he expressed more admiration for Peggy's family. "It's all about who you know. The Lees were always in the right place at the right time. Buying old factories and knocking them down before they were rezoned into residential blocks. They had fruit futures when there was a disastrous banana crop. Hey, Jing-nan, you ever trade futures?"

"No," I said. "But I wish I could have traded my future for someone else's." My answer hadn't registered with him.

"You put your ass on the line when you trade 'em. You

could lose everything." He moved to stand behind Mei-ling. "Get some shoes on and let's go."

"I'm not sure which ones I want yet."

"You're not walking the runway at a fashion show. Put on those."

"They're brown!"

"Then put on the black ones!"

"Don't tell me how to dress!"

"You're spoiled!" Big Eye thundered. "When I was your age, I had one pair of broken sandals to wear. I still have the scar on my ankle from that cheap-ass buckle."

Mei-ling remained defiant. "Yeah? Show me your scar!" Big Eye's jaw tightened and he shoved his hands into his pockets.

"That's your Hakka side," he said. "Stubborn and argumentative. You're only good at wasting time. Let's go!" He stormed out the door.

When he was gone, Mei-ling pulled on the black shoes Big Eye had pointed to earlier and marched out as angrily as her father. Gao's face was stoic as he followed but Whistle looked at me and shrugged. Just another day of family drama.

PEGGY LEE HAD TO come down to the lobby area of Taipei 101 to personally sign us all in.

"There's some bullshit elevated-threat warning today," she said, turning to Mei-ling. "Hell of a day for your father and his entourage to show up."

At the security desk, the man with parted lacquered hair gestured to his monitor and Peggy draped herself over the counter to get a better look. Big Eye took the opportunity to lean back and examine the backside of her pantsuit. He nodded his approval and then spat red juice into his cup.

"Is this all right with you?" the man asked Peggy.

She caught Big Eye leering and frowned. "That's fine," she told the guard.

"You can't bring up any more guests until he leaves."

"I understand."

The guard stood up and pointed at Big Eye's cup.

"Sir, you have to throw that into the garbage can over there. You can freshen up in the restroom."

Big Eye smiled. "I don't need a restroom." He spat the betel nut into the cup and dropped it into the can. Big Eye unwrapped a stick of gum and said to the guard, "You're doing a great job, you know? I feel safer with you around."

ON THE ELEVATOR RIDE up, Big Eye turned to Peggy and said, "It's my juvenile record, right?"

"You stole money from a temple that helps single mothers," she said. "Very classy."

Big Eye's nostrils flared. "That place never helped nobody! It was run by crooks!" He recovered himself. "Anyway, all charges were dropped against me. It shouldn't be on my record anymore."

Mei-ling stood in the corner, turned to one of the walls. Whistle and Gao flanked her. I stood between Peggy and the only passenger I didn't know, a middle-aged man with headphones clamped over his ears who silently tapped his foot.

"How did you know it was run by crooks?" Peggy asked. She has a knack for cultivating discomfort in social situations.

"Because I used to work there," said Big Eye as he gave a triumphant smile. "I was the altar boy! I went to the cops to tell them about the scam and, of course, the police chief was getting his cut from the so-called priests. The one blemish on my record is from me trying to be a goody-goody. That was a lesson. All the stuff I *should* have been locked up for since . . ."

The elevator stopped at our floor before Big Eye could provide an overview of his misdeeds. He had wanted to present himself as a savvy and sophisticated operator to Peggy but he blew it by gaping like a country bumpkin as the ornate double doors to Lee & Associates swung open.

"Oh, boy!" he couldn't help saying.

A man with square glasses and a long nose at the reception desk stood up and called, "Ms. Lee, is everything all right?" How many different secretaries did she have?

"Everything's great, Kenny," she said. "This is Mei-ling's family. Well, her father and his friends." Kenny nodded and settled back down like a good dog. Peggy said to us, "Let's go to my office."

Whistle and Gao made sure to stand on either side of Big Eye. They let their guard down a bit, but in all fairness there was no room for a potential danger. Could there have been a scuba diver with a harpoon gun in the giant pond?

Big Eye lingered at the guardrail, wiping his forehead repeatedly. The koi slowly churned near the surface like a giant gold, black, and orange knot lazily untying and tying itself.

"Look at these fuckin' fish," he whispered in wonder.

"Like 'em?" Peggy asked. "Look at that one. I call her Mazu because her spots look like the goddess's beaded veil. She tries to talk to me when I come up close." She took a step to the pond and Mazu wriggled over and worked her bellowing mouth and gills. "See?"

"Just looks like it expects food," I said.

Peggy punched my arm. "That's my fish," she said. "And it loves me."

Big Eye cleared his throat. "Ms. Lee, you let my daughter do real work, right? She's not doing something stupid like feeding the fish every day, is she?"

Peggy turned back to the pond. She produced a microfiber cloth from a jacket pocket and wiped the brass guardrail.

"I feed them," she said.

PEGGY OFFERED US DRINKS in her office. Not even Big Eye was willing to do a shot at ten in the morning. She shrugged, dropped into her chair and spiked her Starbucks coffee with something from her flask.

"What do you want?" she asked Big Eye. "I assume you came here for a reason."

He cleared his throat and showed her Chong's picture. "Have you seen this bastard around here at all? He's Mei-ling's idiot ex-boyfriend."

Peggy held the photo and turned it forty-five degrees to the right. She regarded it with interest before turning to Mei-ling. "Not bad for a starter," she said. "I agree with your father, though. You can do much better. Is he part aborigine?"

"Worse!" growled Big Eye. "He's one of those quarter-Chinese from Indonesia."

"I see," said Peggy. She handed the photo back to Big Eye. She took a big gulp of coffee and pursed her lips as she swallowed. "So that's the problem."

"Yes, it was a problem," said Big Eye. "Mei-ling did the smart thing by ending it with Chong, but now he's gone missing. I think he's in Taipei trying to meet up with my daughter."

Peggy turned her desk stapler on its side and played with its teeth. "Have you heard from Chong, Mei-ling?" Mei-ling shook her head. "No calls, texts, or emails?" Mei-ling shook her head again.

"She would probably lie about it!" said Big Eye.

"She's not lying," said Peggy. "I know because she looks a little sad about it."

I could smell that coffee from here and I sure could've

used a virgin cup. I felt a yawn coming on and turned it into a full-body stretch. "Well, now that that's all settled," I said, "maybe we should all be on our way and let Mei-ling work."

"Just a minute, Jing-nan," said Big Eye. "I just wanted to ask Ms. Lee something while you were here."

"What've you got?" asked Peggy, her eyes narrowing.

"A few months ago, your family's company forced Jing-nan and a lot of other vendors in the night market to move or get shut down. What are you going to do with that street?"

"We're not sure yet," was Peggy's calculated reply. Despite her penchant for boozing it up at any and all times, she was always sharp. I watched her hands come together, left and right fingers taking turns caressing each other. "And we didn't force anybody. We incentivized them with cash and better facilities. Some people took the money. Some, like Jing-nan, opted for a bigger stall elsewhere." She turned to me. "Are you happy, Jing-nan?"

"Sure, for now."

"Were people upset they had to move?"

"Honestly, Big Eye, some people took the money and ran with no regrets."

My uncle still had his doubts. "You and your family are up to something, Ms. Lee. You're probably trying to get it rezoned again so you can build a condominium there, huh?" Peggy shrugged and drank more coffee.

Mei-ling, out of concern that her internship was in jeopardy, spoke up. "Big Eye, I think—"

"Hey, be quiet! I'm trying to find out what exactly this company is about. I can't figure out anything on your website. Everything seems like double-speak!"

Peggy slid open her middle drawer and took out a pencil. She began to doodle on her coffee cup.

Peggy was always an accomplished artist. In high school, she'd once slipped into my desk a picture of me hanging from a noose with Iggy Pop's *The Idiot* playing on a nearby stereo. That was how Ian Curtis had checked out of this life. My offense was that I had chosen to date someone else instead of her. Still, I had to admire her craft. She had captured my face, if not my heart.

"If you were a client, Little Eye," she said sleepily, "you would have a password to access the material areas of the site." Peggy hadn't looked up. I stepped back to see what Peggy was drawing. Big Eye was in for the caricature treatment. He was on his hands and knees, eating from a dog bowl. "Unfortunately, we're not accepting new money at this time."

Big Eye assumed the posture of the embarrassed Taiwanese man: head slumped forward and shaking, hands on the hips, and legs together. Peggy had cowed him in a way Wood Duck hadn't. She was younger, richer, and more powerful than Big Eye and he had nothing on her. Both Whistle and Gao were wearing pained expressions.

After a few seconds, Big Eye cleared his throat and pointed at Mei-ling. "Look at that woman. I want you to be as strong as her someday. She doesn't give in to pressure!"

Mei-ling swayed slightly. "I shouldn't listen to you, then? Is that what you want?"

"Don't start getting wise!" he growled, but after his humiliation by Peggy, it came off as toothless. Big Eye flattened his shirt above his stomach. "We're going now, Ms. Lee. We have to take Jing-nan back home. You work hard, Mei-ling."

Peggy stood up and waved to us. "Thank you for coming by. I'm glad to have Mei-ling as my intern. She's very bright."

There would be no handshake but Big Eye didn't necessarily want one. He responded with a Japanese bow, the informal one that only went fifteen degrees down, and yet it was heavy with admiration.

"See you later, Peggy," I said as Big Eye, Whistle, and Gao waited for me to lead the way out of her office.

"Bye for now, Jing-nan." Mei-ling stood up and in a practiced move picked up a folder from the inbox on Peggy's desk.

When we were outside Peggy's door, Big Eye tapped my shoulder.

"Let's go see those fish again," he said.

CHAPTER ELEVEN

I FINALLY GOT BACK to my apartment and showered. Gao had offered to come up with me, to make sure that everything was safe, but I refused. After all, could there be a bigger threat in my apartment than Gao?

I pulled on a T-shirt that looked like it was completely black but when the light hit from an angle it lit up the black print of the tattoo on the cover of The Velvet Underground's *White Light/White Heat.* Maybe the shirt wasn't officially licensed but it was so cool. Nancy had had the prescience to buy it for my birthday. It was always a hit with the tourists in the garish lights of the night market. The only problem was that the Americans always wanted to touch the tattoo print, and that would make me uncomfortable even if it weren't close to my crotch.

I rarely listen to music while I commute, unless I need a serious pick-me-up. For one thing, I never have that far to go. For another thing, I've already memorized every thump and howl of my favorite albums. The Velvet Underground? Entire discography of four proper studio albums covered along with the two posthumous outtakes collections. Joy Division? You bet, and include the bootlegs, too.

I stood on the MRT platform and waited for the southbound train to the day market. I was going to buy some fresh lemongrass for tonight's chicken skewers. I tapped my foot in time to my perfect recall of the title track from *White Light/ White Heat,* which is the noisiest VU album. With the glamorous Andy Warhol and Nico gone from the band's camp, Lou Reed, John Cale, Sterling Morrison, and Mo Tucker could realize the full ugliness of their vision, most notoriously in the seventeen-and-a-half-minute long semi-improvised and bass-guitar-free squall "Sister Ray." Seems like just yesterday when I was blasting Joy Division's cover of it at my upstairs neighbor.

As a train going in the wrong direction pulled into the station, I shifted gears and contemplated "Here She Comes Now," the quiet but dissonant two-minute wisp of a song that closes side one of the album. It's the most gentle and vulnerable moment of the band's life, strung through with John Cale's tense viola. Lou Reed was never better. I don't hate any of Reed's solo albums—well, maybe *Mistrial*—but they all suffered to some degree without Cale around to keep his ego in check.

As the train I was waiting for pulled in I wondered if I had thought of the song because the title could be referring to its arrival.

These are the sorts of thoughts one is free to have when one doesn't have a proper job. I boarded the train, grabbed a handrail and looked down at my jeans and black Doc Martens. The jeans were Japanese selvage and years of constant grease splatter had made them waterproof—a bonus when a sudden rainstorm is always right around the corner. My shoes also benefited from work-related oil coatings—they always looked like they were just polished.

The train slid down from elevated tracks and as we submerged, the interior lights threw a reverse-image of myself onto the opposite window. Reverse Me looked cool. He looked like he should be in a band. You'd never think the guy worked in a night market. Maybe he was in a band that played at The Wall on a regular basis. The Wall was known as the CBGB's of Taipei before the actual CBGB's in New York closed down. Now that people are forgetting what CBGB's was, The Wall is known as the cool club that books cool bands. Camera Obscura, Deerhoof, Slowdive, and other overrated hip bands play there.

We pulled into my stop and the doors opened, splitting Reverse Me in half. I strutted out of the car. The rock star was headed to the day market.

I overtook a slow-moving group of uniformed high-school girls on the platform and thought about Mei-ling. My cousin had a job that was more academically challenging than mine and she was nearly a decade younger and technically a high-school dropout.

I felt a little down about it until I caught another glimpse of myself in the polished metal of the escalator up and smiled.

My work look was a lot cooler than hers.

HOURS LATER, MEI-LING WALKED into Unknown Pleasures, seemingly on tiptoes.

"Have a chicken-and-lemongrass skewer," I said as I held out a plate of them. "It's the special tonight."

She hoisted one up and bit in. "Wow, this vegetable really tastes a little lemony."

"I picked up a bunch of fresh stalks today. A little bit of chili pepper and oil makes the citrus taste pop out."

Mei-ling finished the skewer and winged it into the trash. "Do you think I could do another show?" she asked.

"You mean here at the night market?" I asked.

"Yeah. If it's not too big a deal to wheel out the stage again."

"What, the stage is gone?" One of the symptoms of Taipei-itis is becoming numb to the constant buildups and teardowns of major structures. Another is forgetting what had been there previously.

Dwayne sat down roughly against me. "They took it away late this afternoon," he said. "One of the platforms had broken in half. Bunch of idiot kids was screwing around."

"It's rude to shove, Dwayne," I said.

He responded by leaning even harder against me. "You Han Chinese taught us how to shove people around." He cupped my left bicep. "It's a part of your culture, isn't it?"

I felt Mei-ling's legs swing under the table. "Dwayne is funny," she said.

"He's only funny-looking," I said. "But about the stage, Mei-ling, if it's gone, it's not coming back. How about a sidewalk show in Ximending?"

She wrinkled her face. "At this point it would be a step down for me. I would love to play a club there, though."

"You have to be eighteen to get into clubs. But listen, you know The Clash used to busk on the sidewalk for change, before they made it and even after."

"Who are The Clash?"

"Aw, man!" said Dwayne. "Even I know who The Clash are! I think you're better than them, though."

Mei-ling inhaled sharply. "Really! You think so?"

"Mei-ling," I said, "don't let yourself be flattered so easily."

She punched my arm. "You only say bad things about my music!"

"I said the production wasn't right on your demos."

Dwayne stood up and rubbed his mouth. "That still sounds pretty negative, Jing-nan."

Now that she had backup, Mei-ling challenged me. "You

see? Now you want me to play in the street like a beggar! I know there are clubs there I can get in to. I'm not too young for some of them." She paused. "Why are you looking at me like that?"

"You *are* young," I said. "Your nearly naked pictures on your card and your site are wrong."

Mei-ling pulled up the collar of her shirt and shifted in her seat. "I can't help it if you think like a pervert. We're related, you know?"

"That is the only reason why I spend more than five seconds listening to you." I thought a little more and drummed my fingers. "We're going to ride the Maokong gondola Saturday. The gondola cars and platforms are decorated with Hello Kitty characters. I should take pictures of you with that in the background. I think it's more appropriate for your marketing angle than the soft porn."

Mei-ling hunched over the table as she considered my suggestion.

"That would be a new image," she said. "Do you really think it would be better?"

"It would be more commercial," I said. "That makes it better. You want to make a living from music, right?"

She nodded anxiously.

I am wary of too much tooling in the making of an artist, but a little commercial consideration is necessary. Talent will only get you so far. The Clash's manager dressed them in fatigues with stenciled slogans and their militant image became almost as important as their music. Joy Division may never have landed a record contract if they hadn't nearly forced their way on to Tony Wilson's television show.

Mei-ling definitely needed an image rebranding. The sexy look was too creepy, didn't fit her music, and, worst of all, it wasn't who she really was.

"It's settled," I said. "We'll go up to Maokong and then maybe go to Ximending if there's time. But maybe since we'll be in Maokong, we should take the time to hike the trails and check out the mountain scenery."

"I came from the country," said Mei-ling. "I'd rather stay in the city as much as possible."

"Taichung isn't the country."

"It's a hick town and there's nothing to do at night. It's not like here in Taipei."

I leaned back and crossed my arms. "I wouldn't know!" I said. "Look at how I spend my nights!"

I SAW MEI-LING TO her door and then I swung by the *katsu* place in the subway again. I'm accustomed to the fast pace of change in Taipei, but even I was in for a surprise.

The stall was renamed "Transmission." Could it have possibly been named after the Joy Division song? The question was settled when I saw the nebula motif—directly copied from the original seven-inch single sleeve—on the signage and walls.

I was hurt and confused. I walked up to the counter in a daze, my mouth dry and my hands sweaty.

"Hello," said the owner. "How are you today?"

"Why are you called 'Transmission' now?" I was blinking involuntarily. This bastard was ripping off my Joy Division theme!

"You like it? It's a new name, but we still serve the same great food."

"Joy Division fan, are you?"

"I've never really listened to them, and I don't really get into music, but I've always liked the visual aspect of the band, the artwork on the releases. I saw the 'Transmission' single online and I thought it looked like a *katsu* in space. Funny, isn't it? Thanks to the redesign I get to have conversations like this." He smiled warmly.

Why didn't this guy who was allegedly in the food industry know me and my business from the news? My business was a direct tribute to Joy Division. It was done out of love. This guy just copied the artwork. Granted, the nebula did indeed resemble a *katsu*, but still, the whole deal stank. Also, if you "don't really get into music," please go straight to hell!

If I started to tell him that I was a huge Joy Division fan and that I had named my business "Unknown Pleasures" because I loved the songs, I was afraid that I would begin to yell and wouldn't be able to stop. Instead, I wiped my hands on my pants and ordered a chicken *katsu* to stay. I wanted to see someone tell him he was ripping off an internationally known night-market stall. I'd feel vindicated.

"So that's one chicken *katsu*," he said. "Anything to drink?"

"Oh, no."

"Just a few minutes. Say, I like that T-shirt. It's got a hidden design in it. Where's it from?"

"It's The Velvet Underground," I said.

"Never heard of the store."

"They were a band," I said, unable to stop myself from chuckling at him. He didn't pick up on it.

"Have a seat there. What's your name?"

"Johnny."

"Johnny. My name's Kenny." Nice original fake name, Kenny. Doesn't sound like "Johnny" at all.

"Thanks, man."

I slid into a booth, my robe of sarcasm catching a little on the edges of the pressed-wood seat. I watched Kenny duck behind the curtain and listened to him bang around. The fryer came alive, sounding like a heavy rainstorm.

I THOUGHT ABOUT A night not too long ago when Nancy and I had argued about going on a bike trip along the Keelung River. She had wanted to go and I hadn't. I was feeling angry and vaguely righteous, yet also inarticulate.

We had retreated to opposite sides of my couch. I could have sat there all night and not said a word. I played the cold, stoic boyfriend and kept my head turned away. I knew that if I looked at her I would want to hold her.

I became conscious of my breathing. I tried to slow it down and take as few breaths as possible. I felt Nancy shift on the couch and tried to put it out of my mind. I wanted to pretend I was alone.

It was a tiring exercise to ignore somebody. Maybe I wasn't getting enough oxygen. We could have fallen asleep and woken up bloated with our unresolved conflict. The situation required divine intervention.

Out of the clear night sky, thunder cracked as loud as airborne planes meeting head-on. We both jumped for each other. As we fell to our sides we laughed and then I started crying.

"I'm sorry," was all I could say. We slid to the floor and then slid into each other while the rain gods spat on my apartment and took turns licking the windows.

I had been in a negative frame of mind then, as I was now. I should stop feeling hyper-resentful now to Kenny because there was no point to it, really.

THE *KATSU* GUY PUT a tray in front of me as I shifted in my seat. The angry shell that I had formed around myself shattered.

"I didn't mean to startle you," he said, "but I've been calling you, Johnny. It's best to eat it when it's crispy."

"Thank you, Kenny," I said. He gave a brief nod and walked away.

Spotting a bottle of lemon aloe drink on my tray, I called to him, "Excuse me, I didn't order a drink."

"That's on the house," he said. "The aloe will coat and protect your mouth while you're eating the hot food."

"I couldn't—" I started.

He cut me off with, "It was a promotional case from the beverage distributor. Just try it."

I twisted the cap and let the colloidal drink blub into my mouth. It was a pleasantly watery gelatin, the perfect complement to the *katsu*, especially after the hot mustard was applied. The freshly fried *katsu* was even better than what I had sampled before. The chicken cutlet was expertly fried yet again. The oil was at just the right temperature. The batter included the perfect blend of flour and seasoning so that the hard panko crust stuck to the supple meat like tasty scabs.

And the cutlet itself! How could it feel so tender but also offer enough resistance to provide a satisfying bite? Did he steam the cutlets before breading them? Maybe they were fresh and never frozen?

The viscous *katsu* sauce, a little more tangy than I remembered from my previous takeout order, was definitely a homemade recipe, as I could identify most of the ingredients. Cane sugar, soy sauce, onions, and tomatoes for sure. Pureed pear instead of the usual applesauce? Also, he didn't use cornstarch as a thickener. No skimping here.

I applied a touch of hot mustard. The sense of smell is stronger than taste so a whiff of the stuff is sometimes sufficient.

I looked over at the man with renewed admiration. He was talking to a woman with a key ring in her hand, a sign that she owned one of the businesses nearby and had just locked her rolldown gate. She was a country girl in the big city. Skinny, dressed in too-tight clothes, not a clue what to do with her long hair. She started and ended her sentences with flirty, dragged-out "ahs."

"Kenny-ah! Why do you stay open so late?"

"This is around the time drunk people come in and eat."

"Ah, people go to the night market to eat!"

"Some of them get lost in the subway and end up eating here."

"Why do you want to cook for drunk people?"

"I don't." The disappointment in his voice was as thick as the *katsu* sauce and far less sweet.

"You should have a night-market stand, at least. You'd have more customers."

"Maybe not."

"Ah, definitely!"

"Well, this is all I can afford. I borrowed as much money as I could."

"Oh," she said. "So that's the problem."

Kenny began to rub the back of his neck with his right hand. Nervous tic. He looked like he wanted to yank himself off stage. "At least I had the skills to do the redesign myself."

"You painted those things? You should be an artist!"

I heard his feet shuffle. "I studied art in college but this is what I'm doing for now."

I finished up my meal. I couldn't believe that cooking wasn't his true passion. Kenny was born with a gift. If I had a Japanese restaurant I'd hire him in a second. But I didn't and cooking wasn't what he wanted to do, anyway.

I rescued him from the awkward conversation by standing up. He swooped down and grabbed my tray.

"Thank you very much," I said.

"It's my pleasure," he said with a smile that pained us both.

It was almost one in the morning but Nancy was on a mission. She typed on her laptop as she lay stomach-down across the entire couch—the only position she could write essays in, she claimed. I was relegated to a cushion on the floor. If I'd known she was in "political activism" mode, I wouldn't have stopped by.

She didn't want me to touch or even talk to her. I watched a television show, on mute, that featured fan-submitted footage. UFOs, ghosts, talking dogs, you name it. The camera broke away often to a panel of celebrities to clumsily riff off what they just saw. They never said too much. Mostly they would mug a bit after a scary video and the live audience would whoop it up like trained seals.

The actor Chen Han-dian was one of the celebs and I didn't care to hear what he had to say. I didn't like him. I didn't like his face. I think it was his eyes. They popped out a little bit. I watched him blink. I knew why I didn't like him. He reminded me of my old classmate with googly eyes—Cookie Monster. He wanted to be friends but I never allowed that to happen and then he'd tried to shoot me. Too bad. My annoyance at Chen Han-dian shifted to my old classmate and then to the only other person in the room.

"Nancy, are you going to be at this all night?" I asked. She flashed me a sour look and adjusted the angle of her laptop screen, as if that could tune me out.

"I am," she said. "Just like I said on the phone. You came over, anyway. You said you would help."

I had a vague memory of saying something similar to that. "What do you need help with?"

"I'm looking for primary reasons why we don't want the trade pact with China. Something that sounds good in English."

I twisted on the floor. "Where are you going to post this essay?" I asked her.

"I'm not sure yet," she said.

"You're going to do this anonymously, right?"

She cracked her knuckles. "Don't worry. I'm going to put your name on this." Nancy gave a tight smile. "I'm also going to put in directions to Unknown Pleasures and say that you want the KMT supporters to go to hell."

"I don't want anybody to go to hell," I said. "Well, not until after they buy my food." In a serious tone I asked, "How much have you written?"

"About a thousand words, but mostly it's background on trade across the Taiwan Strait."

"God, could anything be more boring?"

Nancy tapped her foot against my jaw. "Don't you care about the future of Taiwan? Every day China is plotting how to capture the island, and our government is going to help them any way they can."

I pressed the nail of my index finger into the bottom of her big toe. "Are you going to spend the rest of your life here?" I asked.

She moved her foot away. "I might live abroad a little bit," she said defensively.

"Why would you want to leave?"

"I want to see other places in the world. Why did you want to leave?"

"I wanted to leave and never come back." I lay down flat and added, "Now I'm stuck here with you."

Nancy snapped her fingers. "Hey! Maybe you should finish your college degree!"

I bit my lip. The truth was, I had thought about it, but there were two major hurdles, one psychological and one financial. At UCLA, I'd had a pretty good scholarship for international students but it had expired long ago.

My most ambitious plans these days were the nightly

offerings at Unknown Pleasures. Now, it isn't an easy thing to draw up a menu at a night market. It requires creativity and flexibility. Your kitchen is literally steps away from something potentially more interesting.

One night I saw that another skewer stand was advertising a Jeremy Lin three-pointer skewer that included chunks of beef, chicken and chicken gizzard. I one-upped them by creating a Jeremy Lin and Kobe Bryant double skewer that included a folded pork intestine that connected the two. Wait, was it a cow intestine? In any case, it had been a great night, better than Lin and Bryant ever had playing together, that's for sure. Creating something like that was the product of years of on-the-job learning no one could ever teach in school.

"I don't need to finish my college degree," I boasted. "Have you seen Unknown Pleasures' online reviews? Thousands and almost all of them five stars!"

Nancy hit a few keystrokes and I heard her laptop chime as she saved a file. "You used to hate being there," she said. Succinct and so true.

"It used to be more of a burden. I'm a minor celebrity now."

"Celebrity," Nancy said as if her mouth were coated with expired cough medicine. "That means you've sold out."

"I said 'minor celebrity'—I still know where my roots are."

"With your lofty status, you could come out to the protest and raise our profile."

"That's not for me," I said. "I work full-time. Besides, when you get arrested, you're going to need me to bail you out."

Nancy rolled on her side and her hair flopped over half her face. She tapped her fingers on the wrist rests of the laptop. "I guess that's true. I doubt they can arrest all of us, though."

I hooked an arm around her right leg. “If I were a cop, I’d pick you out and spank you in front of everyone.” I tickled her foot, but she managed to free it and buried it under a cushion.

“I have to work, Jing-nan!” she grunted.

I fell asleep on the floor to her furtive typing.

CHAPTER TWELVE

THERE ARE LEGENDS ABOUT nearly every temple in Taipei tied to whatever deities are housed within. For example, there is the Zhinan Temple located on the Maokong gondola line. Supposedly Lü Dongbin, the main deity of this Taoist temple, has such unrestrained lust for women that any male-female couple that visits the temple is doomed to break up due to spiritual interference.

I don't believe in things like that but Nancy and I are not going to visit that temple anytime soon. It's so out of the way and there are so many other temples for us to visit, if we were into seeing them. The fact is that most people who go to temples are under some duress. They have some money/health/love problems that require divine intervention. Happy people at temples are tourists. I pray that we never find ourselves in such a dire situation that we have to pray at a temple.

Fortunately, my young cousin Mei-ling had no need to consult supreme beings. After all, she had me to help guide her life and career, for the next week or so, anyway.

Mei-ling and I took the MRT line all the way east. On the elevated tracks we went over an old *juancun* that was slated for demolition. *Juancun*s, sometimes not much more than multi-level concrete bunkers, were built as temporary housing for soldiers who retreated to Taiwan at the end of the Chinese civil war in 1949. When the counterattack to retake the mainland was put on hold, these mainlanders had no marketable skills to allow them to participate in Taiwan's economy, which was growing like mold in a humid climate.

As the island rapidly industrialized from the 1950s to the 1970s, factories went from making umbrellas that reeked of chemicals to consumer electronics good enough for Americans. We learned all about the "Taiwan Miracle" in school, but not much about how society itself changed as it grew richer nor about those left behind.

The aging mainlanders did what they could to get by, running rickety beef-noodle soup stands or driving cabs. As they died off or moved out, their rooms were taken over by working-class *benshengren*, yams new to the city. More recently, artist types moved in and squatted. The walls continued to crumble but you couldn't beat the rent, which was nearly free, apart from communal costs for water, electricity, and gas.

Now this strange alliance of elderly mainlanders, barefooted yams and freaky artists were fighting the city, which had recently declared that the residents were living in an illegally constructed apartment complex. Never mind that the government itself had originally built it.

Each tenant owed back taxes of NT$40 million. It sounded bad even in US dollars—about $1.3 million. The city generously offered to forgive the debt of those who moved out immediately. Some took the bait. Most stayed.

KILL US OR LEAVE US ALONE! read a defiant bilingual banner, strategically placed for the viewing pleasure of MRT riders.

About a year ago the courts had ruled that the *juancun* had to go, but then the judge was busted for taking bribes from developers, so this story still had some time to play out.

Nobody really wins issues in Taiwan. Whatever hot topic

has people up in arms is eventually forgotten when something new crops up. Remember how it was so controversial when China wanted to give two giant pandas as a gift to Taiwan? Those opposed were so vehement, you'd think the pandas were ticking bombs. They pointed at them and declared that the animals were evilly named "Tuan Tuan" and "Yuan Yuan" because "tuan yuan" means "reunion" in Mandarin. The Chinese want Taiwan to return to the motherland! Oh no!

After a policy change a few years later, we accepted the pandas and it was "pandamania." They had a baby and everyone was so in love with the cub that little Yi Ya was given Taiwanese citizenship. The fight was never finished. No closure was granted. Some people still sneer at the pandas, but they're here now, so what can you do? Aborigines probably felt that way when the first people from China floated over to Taiwan a thousand years ago. Taiwanese felt that way when Qing Dynasty officials treated the island like a booty bag to be raided. Then came the Japanese and then the mainlanders. Taiwan's history is a long tale of waiting games. Waiting for people you don't get along with to leave and then realizing one day they've become a part of you.

MEI-LING TOOK OUT HER headphones and watched the grey tail of the *juancun* disappear around a bend, a sick dragon from another time.

"That's the place they're knocking down to build a science park, right?" she asked. It made me a little sad to hear her say that. Like a lot of things in Taipei, the *juancun* was ugly, but it did mean something to people.

"That's one of the rumors," I said.

"How did you feel about Peggy making you move from your old spot in the night market?"

"Oh, that. Well, at first, I was mad. I had expected my

old classmate to treat me better. After I cooled off, I realized that she was being decent about it, offering better spaces or buyouts. In the end, the outcome had winners on both sides, as opposed to that standoff down there."

"There's an art collective based in one of the *juancun* suites there. They produce music and shoot videos."

"Are they good?"

She burst out laughing. "They're popular, but they're no good!"

Ah, she was learning. This young one showed much promise.

WE GOT TO THE base of Yuanshan early enough so there was no line to wait in. There was, however, the long desolate walk from the MRT stop to the gondola station.

"The Taipei Zoo used to be here?" asked Mei-ling as we passed by empty buildings with animals painted on the side. I saw remnants of the movers' last meals: empty wrappers, stubbed-out cigarettes, bottles and cans.

"I'm not sure but it looks like these were administrative offices," I said. "You can't keep animals in an office."

She hugged herself and shivered. "You should see some of the people at Peggy's office. Their desks are so messy, they bug me to help them find things. This one woman had some old *congyoubing* between loose papers. It was cold, stiff, and oily, but she picked it up and ate it!"

"Ugh," I said involuntarily. *Congyoubing*, a scallion pancake, has to be eaten within three minutes of being lifted from the pan and sliced into wedges. It has to be hot enough for the crispy outer layers to pull away from the steaming center seams. Eaten cold, it's worse than leftover pizza. There's no chewy cheese topping to correct the slimy mouthfeel. Just grassy, greasy bits of minced scallion.

A smirk pulled Mei-ling's face to the side.

"I told her not to eat it. She said, 'I grew up so poor, this would have fed my whole family.'"

"That's so Taiwanese," I said. "Trying to do something now to fix things in the past. She should have given it to someone who's poor now!"

Mei-ling laughed. "You're funny today, Jing-nan," she said.

We were almost at the gondola station.

Soon, we would disembark and the ride would be over. Before we knew it, it would be time for Mei-ling to leave Taipei and go back to Taichung. Who knew when I could see her again. I could already see that I was going to miss her. She wasn't going to stay in touch with her ancient cousin. It's not cool at that age. Yet I wanted her to know she could always drop me a line if she was in a spot.

"You're my cousin, Mei-ling," I began. "You can trust me. What I mean is that we can share things that Big Eye doesn't have to know about."

"Why are you saying this?" she asked cautiously.

"If you have some problem after you go back to Taichung, you can call or email me and I can try to help you out. I'll keep it confidential."

She gave a nod that was slightly more than a token gesture. "That's good to know, Jing-nan. Thank you."

I smiled inside and out. As we stepped into the gondola station, I felt like I was really connecting with my young cousin.

At the first tier of escalators she jumped ahead of me and I chased her. It killed my legs. I felt like an old man when I had to grab the handles but giddiness kept me going.

She was waiting for me at the very top.

"Are you trying to prove that I'm out of shape?" I panted.

She lifted her chin. "I thought you were going to catch me right away! I was wrong!"

The walkway ahead was divided by stanchions into two

lines, regular and one, intriguingly, for "Eyes of Maokong." Both were the same price, NT$50 each way.

We walked to the front and two gangly men in Taipei Rapid Transit Corp. uniforms took notice of us. One swung a car around and the other popped the hatch open. They had the right body type to do the necessary reaching.

"Not yet, guys," I said. "We want to take a few photographs. Could you hold the gondola still so she can stand next to Hello Kitty?"

The taller one adjusted his cap. "We can't hold a car still," he said. "It will disrupt the line."

"There's no one behind us."

"I'm sorry, we can't do that." To prove his point, he shut the door and let the cable carry away the car.

"Let them," said the slightly shorter one. His eyes said that he had plans for Mei-ling.

"It's for an album cover," I said.

"It's for *my* album," added Mei-ling.

The taller one pulled off his cap completely and ran his hand through his hair before replacing it. "Who are you?" asked the shorter one.

"We're not ready to launch yet, so we're keeping everything a little secret," I said. "Taking a picture will only take a few seconds. Would you guys mind?"

Both of them leapt at the next car coming in and held it still. "Here ya go!" said the shorter one.

I told Mei-ling to stand next to Hello Kitty. I'd crop out the two workers later. After a few shots the workers let the car go and I checked the pictures on my phone.

"That's a real good one," I said. Mei-ling had her hands behind her back, looking equally innocent and mischievous. The two workers stood above and behind me to review the pictures as well. "I guess the kitty is a little blurry," I said, "but maybe that represents the transition away from mere cuteness."

Mei-ling slapped my arm. "Jing-nan, you read too much into things! An album cover doesn't mean anything!"

"You have no idea, Mei-ling," I muttered.

"Mei-ling!" said the shorter one. "Is that your real name or your stage name?"

"Stage name," I said. "Nobody's named 'Mei-ling' anymore!"

I spied another gondola car coming in. I could see why it was marked as "Eyes of Maokong." It had a see-through bottom.

"Thanks for everything, guys," I said, "but I think we'll go up in this car."

"Should be nice," said the taller one. "It's cool to see things in the rain." The shorter one seemed sad because Mei-ling was fiddling on her phone and he had no idea what to say to get her attention.

"It's raining?" I asked.

"Just started."

We stepped into the car and the taller one secured the door. The aerial line tugged us upward.

"You could've thanked the guys," I said. "One of them liked you."

She continued to look into her phone. "You don't know anything about boys," she said.

Our feet grazed the forest as we slid up the mountain. The shorter guy was right. It was remarkable seeing the clumps of trees swaying like living coral. The raindrops pelleted us as the surrounding mountains melted. Mei-ling was lost in her phone.

"Check out the view," I said to her. "This is really cool!"

"Oh, I get it," she said in a withering voice. "You've never seen nature before."

I stood up and jumped on the floor, making the gondola car shake hard. She screamed.

"Oh, I get it," I said. "You've lived a soft life."

"Stop it!"

"C'mon, I just did it once."

"It's not funny!"

"I'm sorry, Mei-ling. Please, will you just look down through the floor? You've never seen such a view."

She gave a glance too fast to even cheat on a test. "Great, great, I love it."

At the first stop, the Taipei Zoo South Station, a woman in her late sixties wearing a purple blouse and a white man in his thirties wearing a tight tracksuit stepped into our car.

"We both got out a stop too early," the man said in Mandarin, the kind people speak in northern China with an emphasis on the "R" sound. "Zhinan Temple is the next one."

"I didn't mind," said the woman with glee. "It gave me a chance to chitchat with a foreigner. Doesn't he speak great? He's German but he's been living in China for business."

"I moved here a year ago," the man added.

"I hope you like it here," I said.

"It's much better for me in Taiwan than in China, that's for sure." He took in a breath, and weighed what he was about to say. "Well, in China, it's getting better for gays but there's still this stigma attached to it. Taiwan is more open."

His sexuality was news to the woman. She went into a light catatonic state.

"I'm glad for you," Mei-ling told the man.

"Thank you," he said, glancing at me.

I straightened up. "Hey," I said. "I'm not gay."

He smiled and gestured at my clothes. "I didn't think you were!"

"Why are you going to the temple?" asked Mei-ling.

"I really enjoy Lü Dongbin's poetry," said the man. "He's right up there with the best. I wanted to pay my respects." After seeing the blank stares from me and Mei-ling he added, "As Lü Yán, when he was a mere mortal, he wrote poetry. Some of the best during the Tang Dynasty."

"As an immortal, though, he's a drunk and a womanizer," I said.

"Yes, yes, that's right." He rubbed his knees. "There are legends and stories."

"Are you seeing someone?" asked Mei-ling.

"Hey, Mei-ling—that's too personal to ask!" I said.

"It's okay," said the man. "No, I'm not seeing anyone anymore." He sighed and looked down without seeing the forest below. Both of our gondola mates were now sad and silent. Of course they were going to a temple.

At the temple stop Mei-ling made to follow them out.

"We have one more stop, Mei-ling," I said.

She looked confused. "We do?"

"Yeah, one more."

We waved goodbye to the man. The woman was practically sprinting away.

"I thought the temple was the last stop," said Mei-ling. "Shouldn't a temple be a the top of the mountain?"

"This is Taipei," I said. "Nothing is sensibly built."

We swung out at the last stop on the gondola. The rain had stopped but the ground was wet. We came upon a small day market and a few teahouses. The mountain path looked like the flight of stairs in *The Exorcist* that the priest tumbles down.

"Mei-ling," I said, "how about we have some drinks and

snacks at the café here before we head up to the tea plantations to get something for your dad? I can't let you go back to Taichung empty-handed."

She looked around, seemingly distressed at what she saw. "So there's no temple at all at this stop?" she asked.

"There might be some small altars around but the only temple is one stop back. I didn't know you were into temples."

She shrugged. "I'm a spiritual person."

We walked up the steps to the café's patio, which offered a view of the forest below. To the right the stretch of Taipei's buildings looked like a pie crust on a green plate with Taipei 101 as stubby toothpick.

We shared a plate of waffles topped with whipped cream, chocolate syrup, and sprinkles. I had a cup of hot Guanyin tea, which was named after the Buddhist deity, the goddess of mercy. Mei-ling sucked up a green-tea smoothie that was also topped with whipped cream.

We didn't talk much and spent our time together looking to the horizon, lost in our own thoughts. I wondered what life would have been like if I had finished college at UCLA and was now living in the US. I would probably be married and bored right now. But instead, I'd come back, met Nancy and grew a lot. I wasn't a stubborn, idealistic kid anymore.

I was, however, sitting with a stubborn, idealistic kid. We all have to go through that phase, don't we? We all need goals, no matter how unrealistic they are. Eventually we wise up and become more accepting, both of other people and ourselves.

I looked at Mei-ling as the spotted sunlight slid down her face. What were her limitations? She really could be a pop star. I could see it. On paper she was an at-risk youth with a criminal ex-boyfriend and a father in organized crime.

That's the script for a reality show, not a singer. Parts of my life story were lousy, but at least my childhood was fairly decent—downright sheltered compared with what Mei-ling has been through.

Yet she was a typical teenager, too. She could only enjoy the view for so long before whipping out her phone.

Her behavior shouldn't bother me. When I was her age, I must have looked like a budding terrorist in my long trench coat and glowering face. I really did think I was Ian Curtis, didn't I? Well, the public Ian Curtis, anyway. I read his wife's book about him much later. He wrote the lyrics to some of post-punk's most poignant anti-love songs and yet in private life he was a controlling, misogynist jerk. Throw hypocrisy in there, too. He forbade his wife from wearing makeup, afraid that other men would find her too attractive, but he took up with a mistress.

A stray dog that got by on tourist generosity padded by and gave us a sad glance. He looked pathetic in his wet coat. I shook my head and he seemed to understand. He lay down on his side on a flat stone tile as the sun came out fully from the clouds. He sighed, but I could tell by the underside of his jowls that he was smiling.

"Jing-nan, why did you have to tell that guy you weren't gay?" Mei-ling blurted out.

I shrugged. "Just in case he had ideas about me."

"Why do straight men think that gays want to fuck them?"

"Calm down, Mei-ling."

"You're a homophobic jerk, Jing-nan."

"If you want to find a reason to hate me, I can't stop you. Dammit, I thought we were just starting to really get along!"

"You're a lot more like Big Eye than you think."

"You're even more like him. You're his kid."

"I'm not like him *at all*. I never will be."

She was right about me and the German guy. I'd been afraid he might like me. I had to walk this conversation back a few paces. I would stoop to concur.

"Okay," I said, "you're not like Big Eye and you're not going to be like him. You're right, that was very homophobic of me to act that way to the German guy."

"You're not like Big Eye because you admit it when you're wrong," Mei-ling said, softening. "Overall, I'd say you've been really nice to me."

"You're one of the few family members I have and the Mid-Autumn Festival is coming up. We should always be close."

Mei-ling stood up. "I have to go to the restroom," she announced and headed to the café's interior.

I knew that probably meant she had to have a private phone call to bitch about me.

"I'll be here waiting for you," I called after her. I took a small bite of the waffle. It was awful. They should name themselves Awful Waffle. They tried that oldest trick of food retail by covering up substandard ingredients (the batter in this case) with an overload of condiments (chocolate syrup, whipped cream, and sprinkles). It was cheap and sweet. Hey, maybe that was a better name for the place.

Mei-ling returned, giving me a glance not unlike the dog's.

"The café's bathroom is out of order," she said, not breaking her stride. "I have to use the one in the station."

"Good luck," I said as I took a sip of tea to clean out my mouth. Maybe Guanyin tea was named after the goddess of mercy because it forgave whatever caused the bad taste in one's mouth. Was it made from a high-quality batch? It seemed all right.

I pushed back my chair and stretched my legs. Get ready to do some climbing, I said to them. It's been a while since I've walked up a mountain path.

I watched a plane in the distance drift to the west, its back glistening in the sunlight. It'd also been a while since I was on a plane. Maybe I'd never be on one again.

The thought made me uncomfortable so I picked up my phone. I had an email from Dwayne, writing on behalf of Frankie, who wanted to know if it would be all right if he came to work a little late on a day the week after next. Frankie didn't give a reason but, really, he didn't even need to ask.

"Anything he wants," I wrote back. The guy's never even taken a day off. He wasn't even asking for one now. If he needed to disappear for a few hours, then good for him.

Speaking of disappearing, Mei-ling sure was taking her sweet time.

I took another bite of the waffle. I was so progressive I was willing to challenge my previously held beliefs, including, "This waffle sucks." And the next time I met someone who was gay, I wouldn't assume that he was into me.

Ugh. The waffle was still bad. Maybe a little worse.

Another dose of tea refreshed my mouth. I looked at Mei-ling's smoothie. More than half of it was left. I tried some. She had to pay some penalty for taking so long.

The smoothie wasn't bad. That didn't mean it was good, though. You can get away with subpar items that are served cold. Ground ice makes taste buds fold up and the tongue can only taste sweetness correctly. You probably wouldn't recognize lousy ice cream until it begins to melt.

I should have expected mediocrity so close to the gondola station. As I watched more customers shuffle in, I realized that the café didn't need to rely on building a customer base. New people would always show up. This crummy joint was only a place to take a load off before heading higher.

Damn you, Mei-ling, let's go! Wait, maybe I shouldn't be

so harsh. Maybe she has diarrhea. Maybe she's getting her period.

I refreshed my email inbox. Spam from a Chinese company that offered price quotes on bulk sales of plastic resins.

I went to Joyous Dividends, a Joy Division fan site and my browser's home page. Even though the band came to an abrupt end in May 1980, not a month went by in which previously unreleased studio outtakes and live bootlegs weren't uncovered and shared. Some are fake, though. One band thought they could publicize themselves by posting one of their tracks as an unreleased pre-synthesizer Joy Division track. I thought it was crap when I heard it and wasn't surprised that the surviving band members had ostensibly kept the track hidden. When it was revealed as a marketing tactic, the fake band received death threats from around the world. Things turned even uglier when the band blamed their manager and posted his home address and cell number.

The Joyous Dividends administrator, who usually stayed out of the proceedings, wisely deleted the post but not before it was seen by thousands of people. The administrator also posted a note that Joy Division fans should see the stunt for what it was and laugh it off. After all, Joy Division, while active, wasn't the humorless and somber experience that the music's legacy has become. The band in its heyday was notorious for the pranks the members pulled on each other and on unfortunate members of bands touring with them. Urine-in-the-ashtrays and maggots-on-the-bus-seats sort of stuff.

There was a rumor, never denied, that the administrator of Joyous Dividends was Joy Division/New Order bassist Peter Hook and that the site was his way to sneak his personal recordings out to the fans.

A new recording this week was a digitally remastered

version of a live recording of "24 Hours" that was previously only released on the vinyl and cassette editions of the compilation album *Still*. Supposedly it was left off the CD release because of time constraints. But why was the track included on the vinyl and cassette versions even though it wasn't listed on the sleeve? The mysteries never ended.

I took in the view of Taipei as I listened to the latest find. The studio version of "24 Hours" is Joy Division at their most turbulent musically, with charging drums, thunderous bass and dark power chords. Ian's ominous voice floats wraithlike above it all. The song is so fast and energetic that heavy-metal bands cover it. This live version also had the nervous energy that comes from working off a crowd.

It sounded great but I couldn't tell how much better the remaster was over the vinyl through my crummy headphones. Maybe it would sound even better through my PC headphones at home. If I ever got home.

Damn you, Mei-ling.

I stood up and stretched. I had to go to the bathroom myself now.

I WENT FIRST TO Maokong Station's men's room. It was spotless. This wasn't always the case. *The Daily Pineapple* did an exposé on the awful condition of public restrooms in general, calling them a "national disgrace" that tourists from all over the world would see.

I washed up and walked over to the women's room.

A paper "Out of Order" sign was taped to the door. Judging by the discoloration of the cellophane tape, the sign had been up for at least a week.

I walked through the station in disbelief, hoping to find Mei-ling, somehow knowing that I wouldn't.

I looked over the two different roads that led down the

mountain. If she had gone down either one I would have seen her from my table on the patio.

I walked over to the two women assisting passengers disembarking from the gondolas and waited until they were free. Like the two men who helped us at the bottom of the Maokong line, these women were both tall, lanky, and young. One wore a black bob. The other had pink hair pinned into a bun.

"If you want a ride down," said Pink Bun, "you have to stand in line there." She gestured to the roped-off area to her left where nobody was waiting. It was too early for people to head back down.

"I want to know if you remember a young girl, about sixteen years old, going down by herself," I said. "Maybe about half an hour ago."

"I remember her," said the woman with black hair. "She was in a hurry."

"Gan," I muttered as I obediently walked to the boarding area. Noting my compliance, Pink Bun held a car steady for me. After I was aboard she slammed the door shut and locked it. I swung out above the now-serene and fully lit forest. The sun looked like a spat-out piece of lemon candy stuck to the hazy sky. I was mildly aware of the beautiful scenery. My distress blocked me from fully registering it.

Mei-ling had ditched me at the top of the fucking mountain. Was this her idea of a joke? When I found her smiling at the bottom, I might have to go a little Big Eye on her.

"Fuck!" I said again, yelling it in English this time. Of course she wasn't answering her phone. She was probably looking at this display and laughing. I left her a few hang-up messages.

As my ride approached the last station, I saw that the two young men were busier than before but handling the job with aplomb. A line of people waiting to board now wound all the way back to the escalators.

I couldn't see Mei-ling, though. Should I make a complete fool of myself by riding down the escalators to the ground level? Would I definitely find her there or was she hiding somewhere at this station, watching me and laughing her ass off?

The guy who had the crush on Mei-ling unlocked and opened my door. "You came down yourself?" he asked, sounding disappointed and confused.

I stepped out of the car. "You didn't see Mei-ling come down earlier?"

"The girl?" he asked. "I didn't see her."

"Are you sure?"

His face reddened and the color rippled down his neck. "I'm sure. I've been looking out for her."

I waited for him to load the car with more people and when he was done I grabbed his hand. "She slipped away from me and I think she might be in trouble." She probably wasn't in trouble but I wanted his full attention.

His eyes widened and he sucked in his lips. "Let's go look at the security-camera footage," he said, leading me to an office door.

"Hey, Tai-ming!" yelled his co-worker. "What's up?"

"It's about the girl," Tai-ming yelled back. They must have been close friends because that was explanation enough.

I FELT LIKE WE were in the cockpit of a time machine with several monitors showing us where we'd been and where we were going. Tai-ming cracked his knuckles and flipped the center monitor to playback. He reversed the recording of the top station, breaking the narrative flow of the passengers. People in the center monitor walked backwards, hopping into the gondola cars and riding them.

“There she is,” Tai-ming said, pointing out to Mei-ling’s form stepping out and walking backwards while looking side-to-side. “She got on at the top station.”

“I know that,” I said. “She was asking about the temple, so maybe she got out there. Can you check?” He wiped the sides of his nose with the back of his right hand.

“Let’s take a look,” he said. There she was, hopping backwards into the car at the temple station and then hopping out as the recording was played forward. We both watched Mei-ling walk off the top of the screen.

I would have gladly taken her to the temple. Now that I think about it, she did mention it a few times. Why had she left me behind to go there alone?

“Thanks,” I said. “I’m going up there now to get her.”

Tai-ming touched my shoulder. “Wait. There’s a camera outside the station. We can see what direction she walked to. Maybe she didn’t go straight into the temple.”

Yeah, I thought bitterly, maybe she went to the bathroom there.

A few horizontal lines slid across the screen. The outside camera seemed to be an older model. A motorcycle slid to the curb backwards and a young woman, undoubtedly Mei-ling, hopped off and walked backward off the bottom of the screen.

Uh oh.

Tai-ming’s panicked fingers clicked a few switches.

The recording played forward showed Mei-ling doing a quick-step to the motorcycle. The driver handed her a helmet and took off before she had it fully strapped to her head. Was she laughing?

The driver was wearing a helmet but I knew who it was. Chong.

He’d arranged to meet Mei-ling up here by the temple and

steal her away, knowing that if he tried to meet her at her building he'd be cut to pieces.

Gan. Big Eye was going to kill me.

"She took off on that motorcycle," said Tai-ming, putting his finger to the glass in case I had never seen a motorcycle before.

"I notice," I said slowly, "that there's no way to see the license plate."

"Oh, yeah, our cameras aren't that detailed, especially not the older ones. Usually the only trouble we have are assaults. Busloads of the faithful come up and different groups have their rivalries."

I couldn't go to the police. One more strike against Mei-ling would probably land her on the hooligan database for life. Then she could kiss her high-school diploma bye-bye.

Chong! I thought we'd reached an understanding. He had been plotting against me the entire time. I even fed the guy and let him drink my beer. What a fool I was.

Mei-ling had me conned, as well, saying she didn't care for Chong anymore. I of all people should know that young love dies hard.

"Do you know the guy who owns the motorcycle?" asked Tai-ming. His tone suggested he was fishing. I gave him what he wanted to know.

"That's her ex-boyfriend," I said. "I'm sorry, make that current boyfriend."

He nodded like an idiot and stood up. Our ride in the time machine was over.

I touched his arm and said thanks.

CHAPTER THIRTEEN

MAYBE, I THOUGHT, MAYBE it was just a little joyride for the day. A romp at the love hotel. Mei-ling might turn up at the night market, sheepish and apologetic. Hell, I would even settle for a smug, defiant, and drunk teen as long as she came back.

C'mon, girl. I did make fun of you but really I've been trying to help you. I don't deserve to be treated like this and I certainly don't deserve Big Eye coming down on my ass.

I could feel hope dying in my chest with every passing hour I stood in front of Unknown Pleasures. Dwayne playfully twisted my arm behind my back but all I did was sigh. He released me immediately.

"Hey, Jing-nan, what's going on?"

"I have a problem. A big one."

"Big one, eh?" He said under his breath, "Is Nancy pregnant?"

"*Gan!* No! It's Mei-ling!"

"Mei-ling's pregnant? I'll kill the guy!"

"She ran away," I howled. "With her ex-boyfriend!"

Frankie raised an eyebrow. He was too far to hear, but maybe he was reading our lips. I wouldn't count anything out with him.

Near the end of the night and in the depths of my despair,

Frankie came up to me and touched my left hand lightly. "You're not upset about me taking time off?" he asked, already knowing that wasn't the case.

"No, not at all," I said.

"I'll bet you're wondering why."

"It's none of my business, Frankie."

"I want to tell you, Jing-nan," he said. "I'm going to burn incense for Chiang Kai-shek."

I was speechless. The Generalissimo had presided over the martial law era that saw Frankie wrongfully arrested and jailed.

Frankie, as a teen, had met Generalissimo Chiang while serving in the orphans' brigade. Frankie drew admiration from the old soldier by showing off his arm tattoos. The ones that he had only recently removed.

"Why, Frankie?" It was none of my business but my curiosity had gotten the better of me.

"I had a dream," he said.

Dwayne took a seat, put his elbows on the table and held his head up with both hands like a little kid. Frankie didn't tell stories much and when he did they were awesome.

"The Generalissimo came to me and saluted. I saluted back. Then he bent his head forward in a small bow and when he straightened up again, his face was wet with tears. He apologized for my jail sentence and said that he was suffering for all the injustices he knew about but didn't stop. I said that I didn't believe he was sorry. The Generalissimo got down on all fours and banged his head against a stone until he bled. What could I do? I tried to help him up but he refused to get off his hands and knees. I said out loud that this was the strangest dream I ever had. He looked up at me and said it wasn't a dream. When I protested, he said that he remembered me as a kid with the arm tattoos and that one stroke was missing from the character for 'country.'"

Frankie paused to unwrap a stick of gum and put it in his mouth. Neither Dwayne nor I could breathe.

"I checked my arm when I woke up," Frankie said. "The ink is almost completely gone now but I could see that a stroke was missing in that character. I'd never noticed before."

"*Gan!*" said Dwayne.

"You must've known, on a subconscious level," I said. "You've been hiding it from yourself."

Frankie leaned over to me. "Jing-nan, did you know on some level that Chong wasn't going to give up on Mei-ling?"

"He had me completely fooled," I said.

"Who had you fooled?"

I whirled around to see Captain Huang, holding a half-eaten fried pork chop in his left hand while pointing at me with his left index finger. "You're not easily tricked, are you, Jing-nan? In fact, you're the one who's usually trying to pull a fast one." He wasn't happy and looked like he was losing sleep. His normally baggy eyes now exceeded the carry-on limit.

I smiled and nodded. The captain had called me "Jing-nan," but only Johnny was here now. "I thought you'd be here earlier for dinner, Captain," I said. "I still have some chicken-anus skewers. I understand they're your favorite."

Captain Huang sucked his teeth noisily. "I just came by to tell you that I caught Big Eye's daughter's music act," he said. "I knew about the show and I was considering pulling the plug, since you didn't have a permit. But Orchids was really good. Me and all the boys were into it."

"How did you know the show was going to happen?" I asked.

"I saw it pop up on TaiPride."

"Why is everybody going to that site?"

He casually tossed the remains of the pork chop on an otherwise clean table. He was trying to push my buttons, trying to get me to overreact so he'd have an excuse for giving me lumps. "I do research online to keep abreast of potential disturbances. It's a convenient place to see when and where unsavory types are gathering. Well, I'll see you later, Jingnan." The captain pointed at the pork chop and the small skid mark it had made. "How about we clean that up?" he said and walked away.

"What a total asshole," muttered Dwayne, articulating my thoughts perfectly. Frankie said nothing but made some knives shriek against the sharpening stone.

I brushed aside the encounter and cleaned off Captain Huang's pork chop from the table. I put all thoughts about Mei-ling on the backburner along with the chicken gizzards.

When I heard the sounds of the brooms sweeping out closing stands I imagined I could hear her footsteps in them. I left Unknown Pleasures earlier than I usually did, as if I were escorting Mei-ling home again.

"I SHOULD'VE KNOWN," I wailed to Nancy. "That little bastard Chong!" She was lying in my bed, typing away at her laptop yet again.

"You have to tell Big Eye," she said for the seventh time.

"I will if she's not back by the morning," I said, also for the seventh time.

"You should tell him now. The more time Mei-ling and Chong have, the farther away they can get." A chime rang out as she saved her file. "Wait, I understand now. You want them to get away. You want to see the girl get away from her controlling father and get to be with her boyfriend from the wrong side of the tracks. That's very romantic of you, Jing-nan."

Was that true? After all, I wasn't ideologically opposed to Mei-ling and Chong being together.

Then I thought about where that left me with Big Eye. He couldn't flat out kill me, could he? I was his nephew, after all! What would he do to Chong and Mei-ling when he found them? I was sure he would find them, too. Chong would get the *worst* of it, I'm sure. A broken arm? Both legs?

"What should I do?" I asked Nancy, sure that the distress was plain on my face.

"Call Big Eye now. Tell him what happened. Maybe he won't be mad."

"NOW, LET ME MAKE sure I understand this properly," Big Eye said on the phone. He was one of those guys who became joyfully detail-oriented when seized by anger. "Chong picked up my daughter on his motorcycle at the Zhinan Temple and you're telling me about it now, nearly twelve hours later."

"I thought she might come back," I said weakly.

"She's not answering her phone?"

"She isn't."

"Listen, my little nephew. We have to talk in person. Get your ass on the high-speed rail to Taichung. Leave right fucking now and you'll make the eleven P.M. train. I'll see you at the station."

"Big Eye, that doesn't make any sense. Taichung would be the last place they would go. Don't you want to start looking here?"

His words were pleasantly marinated in menace and he ended the call with, "I'm going to make some phone calls immediately but in the meantime, get on that goddamned train and I'll see you very soon."

"He wants to see me in person, Nancy," I said.

"He probably just wants to gouge your eyes out."

"Nancy, this isn't funny. My cousin could be in serious danger."

She crossed her arms. "I'm sure she's fine. It sounds like Chong really loves her. Big Eye is what you should be worried about. Until he gets a hold of her, he might . . . slap you around a little bit."

I stepped into my left shoe. "Slapping. I can handle slapping."

THE HIGH-SPEED RAIL STATION was actually in Wuri District, a suburb outside of Taichung's city proper. It was very appropriate that I was bringing my worries to Wuri.

Outside my window I saw lit shades in lopsided buildings teeming together and then whizzing by. Sometimes there were long and bleak stretches of rice paddies reflecting the night sky. Seeing this representation of the universe made me feel small, insignificant, and helpless. It didn't matter in the grand scheme of things who I was, the things I cared about, the people I loved. The sky would be dark at night and light in the morning.

Then I had something of an epiphany. If the universe was indifferent to each person, it was all the more important to be who you wanted to be, do the things you cared about and be with the people you love because you had to live your life in a way that mattered to you.

I found myself more accepting of recent events. Nancy was absolutely right. I supported Mei-ling completely if she wanted to be with Chong, even if it meant living on the run for the rest of their lives. I couldn't stop someone from being with the one they loved and neither could Big Eye. Maybe it was up to me to stand up to Big Eye and tell him to back off and leave them alone or he was going to lose his daughter forever.

The train was silent and brutally efficient at bringing me to my uncle. It was only an hour station to station. I wasn't exactly sure what to say to Big Eye, but as Mei-ling's big cousin, I had to have her back. I could step up and have a man-to-man talk with her father. I wasn't a boy anymore.

They picked me up at the station in the bulletproof SUV—Whistle, Gao, and Big Eye. I thought we were headed to the house but then we took a detour down a dark alley. Nobody said anything.

We rolled to a stop near the end.

Big Eye pulled at his pants near the knees.

"I don't know how to say this to you, Jing-nan," he said. I was watching his hands. Those rings could really hurt my face.

"I'm sorry," I started. "I'm sorry that I couldn't stop Mei-ling from being with the guy she loved, but you can't either."

Big Eye snorted. "What the hell are you talking about, Jing-nan? There's nothing to be sorry about. No. We're beyond that." He tapped Whistle on the shoulder and the radio came up. A talk show with a rich and famous adherent to the I-Kuan Tao religion was taking questions about his faith. "You shouldn't expect to become rich," someone on the radio said, "but if it is in your fate, you will be."

Gao stepped out of the vehicle and held the door open.

"Give your phone to Gao," said Big Eye. I did as I was told. I guess he wanted to go through my history to see if I was lying. I had nothing to hide. Gao closed the door and walked into the shadows.

Big Eye gave me a tight one-arm hug and pulled me over to his face.

"Listen, Jing-nan," he whispered in my left ear as the rich man on the radio continued talking, "Chong is gone."

"I know he was missing for a while, but apparently he came out of hiding and took Mei-ling."

Big Eye gave a wry smile and loosened his grip on me. "Chong didn't take anything or anybody because he is dead. He's been dead."

I shifted in my seat. There was only one reason why he would know.

"He came to see me a few days ago." Despite his former expressions of disgust and racial hatred for the young man, Big Eye seemed genuinely shaken as he explained. "He said that he had tried to put Mei-ling out of his mind after seeing you. Couldn't do it. He said he wanted to be a man about it so he came straight to me and said he wanted to be with my daughter. I said no. Chong lost his temper. Things spun out of control. He called me a 'Big Brokeback.' How the fuck could he have thought that he could talk like that to me? The kid ended up dying."

Big Eye patted me and moved away. The radio blabbed on as we sat in silence.

My uncle was a murderer. The realization cut across all my memories of him. The hands that had fed me candy when I was a child had blood all over them. I had never thought that he was capable of such horrors. I think I could accept gambling, prostitution, and even loansharking if he joked about his misdeeds and shrugged. But killing? No.

Captain Huang had mentioned those bodies found in a sugarcane field in Taichung and I'd been so sure there was no way Big Eye was involved. How naïve of me. Not just about that one crime but about my entire relationship with my uncle.

I wished now that I had never reconnected with him. When Whistle and Gao first came for me I should have run down the fire escape and hid in the alley.

Then I wouldn't have met Mei-ling. Wait, who the hell picked her up on the motorcycle? Big Eye was wondering the same thing right from the get-go. *Gan*, maybe she was in a lot of trouble!

My thoughts then turned back to Chong. That poor guy. Why did he think he could reason with a shark? My uncle had killed him. That confused kid who'd sat in my kitchen for fifteen minutes or so was now gone forever. What did Big Eye do? Shoot him?

Big Eye snorted and reached into his jacket. I jumped.

He smirked as he produced a flask and offered it to me. I shook my head and he took a long pull. Big Eye was troubled by the murder. I could see that. He'd probably just lost his temper and got carried away.

Wait, what was I thinking? I was trying to rationalize how my uncle killed somebody.

I wasn't ready to talk to Big Eye yet, so I returned to listening to the I-Kuan Tao celebrity on the radio.

"It's the true heavenly way," the man declared. "I've been involved with different religions in the past. This is the first one that makes sense and has compassion."

Without a pause, a chipper female doctor's voice came on the air to deliver a commercial for hair-transplant surgery, saying a middle-aged man could look and feel young again and do well in online dating. Listening to this stupidity helped me find my mettle.

I turned to Big Eye. "You made a big deal about Chong disappearing. That was a cover story. You knew exactly where he was." My uncle swished his flask thoughtfully and said nothing. "Are you absolutely sure that he's dead? Is it possible that he recovered and met up with Mei-ling?"

Big Eye tapped my nose with the edge of his flask. "You

think I don't know what dead looks like, little Jing-nan? Chong's already on his next incarnation."

"Where's his body?" I asked, my voice shredding and betraying me.

Big Eye snapped the flask shut and put it away. "That doesn't matter, Jing-nan. Let's worry about who the fuck *did* pick up my little girl."

"Did Chong and his boys ever work for you?"

He tapped his fingernails against the flask. "We might have contracted some low-level stuff to them," he said.

"He told me you made the Indonesians fight one another."

"I didn't do shit! What do you think poor people do when money starts showing up? Divvy it up evenly?" Big Eye put away his flask and closed his eyes. "I have to think."

THE LAST TRAINS BACK to Taipei, high-speed or conventional, were long gone. I'd have to wait until the morning for a ride back. Whistle and Gao were needed to attend to some unspecified matter, so they dropped off Big Eye and me at the house for the night. Big Eye set me up in a small room crowded with vintage kendo practice swords decorating the wall.

The futon was a traditional one, stuffed with cotton and lacking modern adjustments for comfort, such as springs. The two pillows were filled with buckwheat chaff. The towel-like summer blanket was probably also traditionally Japanese.

Do you know people who are so obsessed with a culture that they have appointed themselves as the guardians of its traditions against change? Big Eye didn't want to be a contemporary Japanese. He wanted to be who the Japanese were a century ago, those of the powerful, blindly ambitious Great Empire of Japan who drove their own people into poverty as the military overreached. I can understand his obsession. If

I lived in a century-old Japanese-style house, I'd have to be pretty psyched for that era, too.

I disrobed and put on a set of static-free cotton pajamas I found in a drawer. I dropped into the futon and rubbed my eyes. When my focus came back I noticed that the kendo swords were all pointing at me, accusing me of losing Mei-ling and causing Chong's death.

I turned on my side and closed my eyes.

Who picked up Mei-ling? The ghost of Chong? Another boyfriend she had had on the side?

What was it like growing up in this house with this father? One thing was for sure. A man fascinated by Imperial Japan was bound to be a disciplinarian. A harsh one.

I opened my eyes and examined the blade of the nearest wooden sword. It had a multitude of nicks and dents.

I imagined Mei-ling training with this sword, knocking back Big Eye's attacks while waiting for an opportunity to strike back.

Ah, that's what this disappearing act was. Mei-ling had deliberately planned her daring escape in Taipei. She knew what she was going to do long before the trip began.

It made me feel a little depressed and I wasn't sure why. Really, the failed relationship between my uncle and my cousin wasn't any of my business. Yet these two people were all the family I had left in the world. You don't get to choose your family but there's something in not having that choice. We were destined to share our lives together. I thought about Big Eye making me laugh when I was a kid. Was he already a murderer back then?

IN THE MORNING I met Big Eye at the dining table. He looked like he hadn't slept. He stared at cross sections of kiwi fruit on his plate. The seedy eyes stared back as he put his elbows up on the table. I had been prepared to either stare him down or avoid him altogether. But I wasn't ready to see Big Eye looking so defeated and pathetic.

"I shouldn't have been so hard on her," he spoke into his right fist. "Maybe she didn't need to finish high school. I wanted what I thought was best for her. I didn't care what she thought." He grabbed his phone and frantically typed away, checking his email, voice mails, and texts. "No wonder she couldn't stand me."

"You didn't do anything wrong," I said, which is an odd thing to say to a killer. "Maybe she'll come back soon."

He nodded and drank a full glass of spiked orange juice before speaking. "She's not coming back voluntarily. Mei-ling has to be found. And when I find her, I'm going to put a fucking bullet in her head."

I TOOK THE HIGH-SPEED rail back to Taipei. I accidentally sat in a reserved seat when I had an ordinary ticket. The rightful passengers were cool about it. Young man and a young woman. Maybe they were brother and sister. Maybe they were a couple. Taiwanese are so reserved in their manners in public it was hard to tell unless they were carrying a baby. And even then . . .

I slinked down a car to an open seat in a coach car and rubbed my hands. I went over what Big Eye said was going to happen.

It was going to be a two-pronged approach. He, Whistle, and Gao were going to use their own "channels" to try to find Mei-ling. He told me that I should check out the places that she had expressed interest in, such as the arts group in the *juancun* and Ximending. Just how the hell I was supposed to cover the entirety of one of the most fashionable neighborhoods in Taipei was beyond me, but I was willing to give it a shot. How could I not?

I had had big plans for this girl. I leaned against the window and closed my eyes. Mei-ling, you and I had made plans!

I could see the digital release of her EP and then maybe a little tour and music contract. She could have gone far but I guess the attraction to a life on the lam away from her dad was too strong. I hated to think that she was in over her head.

Was it some guy Mei-ling's age? Or was it an older guy like in *Lolita*? Maybe one of those weirdos holed up in that *juancun*.

I STOOD OUTSIDE THE *juancun*. It looked more charming and less rundown up close. The complex reminded me of the toaster-shaped illegal house I grew up in. The toaster house had lived up to its name by burning down. Although I lost nearly everything I owned, the disaster also freed me from living with the memories of my late parents and grandfather.

I entered the courtyard and came upon groups of grandfathers playing mahjongg at concrete tables. Younger people of both sexes were building what looked like a parade float that featured a straw effigy in a paper suit with the President's name on it. Three young men in tank tops, apparently the lookouts, broke off from the group and confronted me.

"Can I help you?" asked the leader, a guy with spiky hair with Beats headphones hugging his neck. He was friendly but wary. The second guy held a camera phone on me. The third seemed to stand there for moral support.

"My name is Chen Jing-nan. I'm looking for a friend of mine, a young girl named Mei-ling," I said. "I think she might have come here. Here's a picture of her." I held up my camera.

Beats squinted as he gave a cursory look at the camera. "That doesn't look like anybody here," he said, curling his bottom lip. "Are you a cop?"

I looked down at my dusty shoes, greased jeans and threadbare shirt that featured the tomb-theme artwork of *Closer*, Joy Division's second album. I was going to wear that shirt until it dried up and fell off my back like a dead leaf. "Do I look like a cop?" I asked.

Beats nodded. Really?

"Search him," he said and motioned to the third guy. I put my hands up and turned to the second guy's camera.

"Whoa!" I said. "Aren't you being a little extreme here? Do you guys have guns or something?"

Beats spoke up. "We've all had death threats here. The local police precinct has been harassing us, too. People have left dog carcasses in our courtyard as warnings, so, no, we're not being extreme." He pulled his right ear. "And, no, we don't have guns."

I looked down and noticed that their feet were in neutral stances but ready to fly into action. As the third guy approached me, I knew that I had to let him pat me down if I was going to have a shot at looking for Mei-ling on the premises.

"Sorry," the third guy said in English as he crouched and ran his hands down my thighs. After he checked my ankles, waistband and the small of my back, he called out to Beats, "I recognize this guy now. I thought his name sounded familiar—he's Jing-nan, the hero of Shilin Night Market. He's clean, too."

"Wait," the second guy said to me, "you were the one who deflected that bullet?"

"That's me," I said, playing to the camera that he still held up. Something touched my left side and I flinched. It was Beats. He was patting me hard on the back.

"*Gan!*" he said. "You're the first celebrity to visit!"

Now that I had the full approval of the gatekeepers, other people freely approached.

"Jing-nan," said Beats, "I don't know who you're looking for but, seriously, it's been months since anyone new has come in." He cleared his throat. "Actually, we've been losing more people than we'd like to."

"You know my name," I said to Beats, "so what's yours?"

He shook his head. "None of us are telling outsiders our names. We have to protect ourselves and our families."

An elderly man at a mahjongg table pulled off his baseball cap and fanned his face.

"What does it matter?" he yelled. "The government already knows who we are! Sooner or later they're going to knock this place down. You might as well have some fun, not waste time building an effigy of the President to burn."

"That's not for a parade?" I asked Beats.

He nodded grimly. "We're going to set it on fire and stream the video online to show how the government is taking away our freedoms."

The elderly man spoke up again. "Start a fire for what? People are just going to think you're irresponsible! You want to make trouble, why don't you join up with those idiot students who occupied the Legislative Yuan? Don't do it here where we all have to live."

"Well, it doesn't really concern you, so don't worry about it," was Beats's weak reply.

"I'm glad I didn't spend my youth doing useless things," said the man. "I was in the army. I had fun and those memories are still great!"

As the old soldier's companions laughed out loud, Beats could only shake his head.

When I was at UCLA, I'd discovered that many people had the wrong idea about how Confucianism worked. Americans thought that younger generations of East Asians were completely deferential to older generations. That's not true at all.

We can challenge the thinking of our parents' generation. Just not verbally.

The effigy burning would go on. So would the mahjongg game.

"WHY ARE YOU SO sure that it wasn't Chong who whisked away Mei-ling?" asked Nancy. We were walking through Ximending a little after noon. The place was dead. It wouldn't begin to come to life until the late afternoon when the middle- and high-school kids started crawling in. The young people drove business in the area, especially the rich kids treating less-fortunate members of their entourages to food, movies, or other entertainment.

"First of all," I said, "nobody 'whisked away' my little cousin. She was at least a part of the plan, if not the mastermind of it. And second, I know for sure it wasn't Chong."

We stopped walking. "Tell me how you know."

I looked into her eyes and held her hand.

"Oh my god! Big Eye didn't!"

I opened my eyes wider. She punched my arm.

"*Gan,*" I groaned.

"Jing-nan! You have to tell the police he killed Chong!"

"That's a good one, Nancy. 'Tell the police.' First of all, I don't have any evidence. Secondly, I don't even know how he did it. And third, it could complicate the safe return of Mei-ling. Anyway, Big Eye's right-hand man is a cop—the big guy—so you could say 'the police' already know about it."

I wanted to continue walking but Nancy remained rooted. "Why did Big Eye kill that boy?"

"Well, I had nothing personal against him, but Chong was no angel, you know?" I rationalized. "He and his buddies had done jobs for Big Eye. They weren't boosting their community and actually they contributed to the negative perception that the country has about immigrants. I hate to say it, but Chong knew he was playing a dangerous game."

"Your beloved uncle is now a murderer," Nancy said through clenched teeth.

"He may have killed before." I quickly revised that to, "He probably has."

She grabbed the insides of her elbows and put her head down. "What a nice family you come from, Jing-nan."

"I've never asked you much about your family. Are they so much better?" I really had no idea.

Nancy lifted her head slightly and looked away from me, across the street. "They sure aren't criminals."

I could have brought up her old sugar daddy, the former semiconductor executive who was now doing time for bribery. The guy who gave her the fancy apartment and souped-up sports car. I wondered if he would try to reclaim them both when he was released.

I didn't want to say anything to hurt Nancy, though. She was clearly in shock after finding out about Chong, at least as much as I was. But there was another young life at stake.

I put my arms around Nancy's strained shoulders and said, "Big Eye and his whole crew are awful people. I know that. But the important thing now is to find Mei-ling as soon as possible because she might be in trouble."

Nancy nodded. "Yes," she said. "She's not in a good place."

We began walking again and soon came upon the triangular plaza between Hanzhong Street and a side lane of Emei Street. This was the prime stage in Ximending for a band to set up on the sidewalk and play.

When I was a kid, right here at this intersection was where I saw bands from all over the world playing everything from Mandopop to American country to reggae. As a self-righteous and all-knowing young jerk, I stood there and scowled even if I liked the music. I had to maintain my cool, after all.

Not so long ago I stood at this triangle and watched a band of middle-aged men covering the Moody Blues. The singer would have looked like my father if he had only stopped smiling. During the long instrumental breaks in "Nights in White Satin," he continued to stand front and center, waving his hands in the air and staring up at the stars.

One wouldn't think that a bunch of old farts in suits trotting out the songs of the ancients would play well to smoking teenagers but the audience was fully engaged. Boys with their ties pulled loose and shirttails out. Girls with their skirts rolled up at the waist. Me in my long London Fog trench coat with the belt and belt loops ripped out and "HATE" scrawled on the back, just like Ian Curtis. I stood in the Doc Martens boots I was still breaking in.

Julia had stood at my side. When I think about her, I think about her looking like she did that night. Pupils big, dark and mysterious as black holes, a small smile on her face, dark red lipstick that she would rub off before going home. She pulled her hair back over her ears and wiggled them slightly.

"Okay," I said. "You win."

"I knew I could make you smile!" she said, as she punched my arm. "You don't have to frown to impress me."

"I'm doing it for me."

"I know you're happy inside, though, and that you like this music more than you think."

"Why?"

"I see your head moving with the music."

"Ha, that's my head nodding because it's putting me to sleep!" I crossed my arms. I knew the band was playing the full album version—almost eight minutes long—rather than the edited version that was released as a single. I nudged closer and took her hand. This is a daring thing to do in public but the crowds provided us cover.

"Are you scared?" Julia asked.

"No way, baby."

"Your hand is sweaty."

I twisted to the side until I felt my shoulder bones crack. "I'm really hot in this coat."

She squeezed my hand. "Yes, you are."

"This is odd, isn't it?" I asked her. "Of any music we could be hearing tonight, it would be this."

Julia laughed. "What would you rather hear? Maybe the Sex Pistols would be better?"

"No, they wouldn't be."

"At least this music is kind of sexy."

I let go of her hand, pulled out the key to the love hotel and pressed it to her side. "Well, if you think it's so sexy, why don't you offer your virginity to that stud who's singing?"

She stepped on my foot, right on a blister right between the big and second toes. These damned new Doc Martens!

"Oh, fuck!" I yelled out in English, making the audience gasp. The singer was a pro, though. He improvised a long cooing sound and the crowd was lulled back into his fuzzy world.

"What's wrong?" asked Julia.

I wiggled my toes. The sock felt wet. "You popped my blister," I said through clenched teeth. "I think I have to sit down."

"Maybe we should go to the room now," she said casually. I nodded and we walked away.

I couldn't help limping. "This fucking blister's right where the shoe creases. How the hell am I supposed to walk?"

Julia slid under my right elbow and helped me walk. "Think of it this way. It's only fair that I popped your blister because you're going to pop my cherry." We both laughed and shuffled our way to the love hotel.

"You know," I said, "when we're old, you're going to have to help me into bed. Men's bodies fall apart faster."

"That's a long time from now," she said. "We're going to have the rest of our lives together."

"Dammit. I think the hotel's a walkup."

"No elevator?"

"No."

She supported me as we staggered up five flights of stairs. I wobbled like a drunk. I looked down at her face and when our eyes met I knew that we would be together forever.

NANCY ASKED, "ARE YOU hungry, Jing-nan?"

"No, not really."

"Why do you keep staring at that McDonald's?"

"It wasn't there before. Something else was."

"What do you expect?" she said as she snapped open her purse and began to rummage inside. "Nothing stays the same, especially not in this neighborhood. Gum?" I shook my head and she popped into her mouth a block of Japanese gum, a brand that is more artificial color and flavor than sugar.

"Those are so bad for you," I said.

Nancy waved my words away. "They taste good and chewing helps me think. Hmm. Now why was Mei-ling so interested in Ximending?" she asked herself.

We continued down the street and found ourselves approaching The Red House.

The octagon building was built by the Japanese more than a century ago, yet it looked futuristic and edible. A gigantic layered red-velvet cake with white icing.

It's one of those places I visited on a field trip years ago but haven't been inside since. Tourists love it, particularly the combination of Eastern and Western elements in the architecture. Which is which, I couldn't tell you.

Its former lives included stints as a public market, an opera house, and a movie theater. Now it was a city-owned teahouse and tourist shop in the main rotunda with a series of artist shops in the cruciform wing attached to the octagon.

Nancy and I were compelled to enter the building.

Two bored young women behind the counter of the teahouse acted like the government employees they were, chatting away and chasing off potential customers with scowls.

"Excuse me," I asked the meaner-looking one. "Have you seen this girl recently?" I held up my phone, the display screen facing her.

She jutted out her chin. "Maybe," she said, rubbing her nose. Her fingers had an inordinate number of rings on them and a tattoo along the index finger.

"Could you keep an eye out for her?" asked Nancy.

"No, I can't," said Mean Girl. The other employee giggled. "Want to order something?"

"That's funny," I said. "You two don't seem the type to take orders."

Other Girl said, "What's that supposed to mean?"

Nancy and I walked away.

"What a bunch of awful kids," said Nancy.

"I used to hate customers when I was young," I said, looking over the teahouse's empty tables. "This is a bust. I can't imagine young people coming here to this government-run dive and I really doubt Mei-ling had any interest in this place."

We found ourselves standing in front of several bars that were hidden from the main streets by The Red House itself. A few of them proudly flew the rainbow flag.

"Whoa!" I said. "Is there a gay pride parade coming up?"

"Those flags aren't up for a parade, Jing-nan," said Nancy. "These are gay bars. Lesbian and transgender, too. Hey, you seem a little jumpy there."

"I'm not jumpy."

Nancy smiled. "Tell me about your first gay experience, Jing-nan."

"I've never done anything, but one time this guy tried to pick me up at the Eslite bookstore." It's a flagship bookstore open twenty-four hours a day, a mandatory stop for tourists.

Nancy laughed and the gum shot out of her mouth onto the sidewalk. "Oh, shit." She worked a tissue out of her purse and promptly picked it up. "Wait, so how did you know this guy was trying to pick you up, Jing-nan?"

"I was looking for Peter Hook's memoir of the Joy Division days. I wanted it in hardcover because I knew I'd be rereading it a lot. I would have worn out the spine of a paperback. I found the book and I had to start reading it right away. I couldn't even sit down. I was leaning against a bookrack and this guy sidled up to me and started reading over my shoulder.

"I thought it was a little odd but I was so into the book, I couldn't look away. It seemed like he was really into the book, too. After a few pages, I closed the book because I wanted to head to the cashier. Then the guy said to me, 'Should we finish reading it in bed?'"

Nancy smiled. "What did you say?"

"I was honest. I said, 'I never read in bed.' Then I walked away."

"You know that Eslite is a big cruising scene, especially after midnight."

"I had no idea! I thought 228 Peace Memorial Park was for cruising." The park commemorated the victims of Taiwan's most infamous massacre, which began on February 28, 1947. It was still a sore point between mainlanders and yams, but it was created with the idea that all of Taiwan could come together and learn from the experience so that it never happened again. At the very least quite a number of people were coming together in the park's restrooms.

"The guy selection is much more refined at Eslite," said Nancy. "They don't have the rough edges that park encounters have."

"Makes sense," I said as I watched a man in a black food service uniform moving chairs and wiping off tables at a bar/restaurant named Magic Wand.

Even though I knew Mei-ling wasn't a lesbian, she had been active on TaiPride and also interested in Ximending. She had to have known about these queer bars.

"I'm going to ask that guy for help."

Nancy unwrapped a new stick of Japanese gum and looked at me mischievously. "What are you going to do if he hits on you, Jing-nan?"

"The first thing I'm going to say is, 'That's my girlfriend over there and I have sex all the time with her.'" She opened her mouth slightly and made snapping noises with her gum.

I put my hands in my pockets and walked over to Magic Wand.

The man was bigger than I'd thought. He was built like Dwayne with a trimmer waist. "Hello," I said to the man. "I was wondering if you could help me."

He folded up the towel he had been wiping tables with. "I'd be glad to help," he said. "What's going on?"

"By any chance, have you seen this girl?" I held up my phone.

"Hey, come in closer," said the man. "You're too far away." I took two steps forward. "I don't think I've seen her. Has she run away?"

"Yeah."

"It's a real shame. There used to be a drop-in center here with counselors, a library, and HIV testing. But it closed. If it were still open, I would say check there."

"She had help in running away," I said. "From a guy."

"That's a little different." He took two chairs from a tabletop, flipped them, and set them down. He sat in one and invited me to sit in the other. "Was it an older man?"

"I don't know," I said as I lowered myself into the seat.

"The runaways I see are gay youth leaving home—often because they're kicked out."

I held up a hand. "She's not a lesbian."

"Are you sure?"

"Yeah, she had a boyfriend."

He smiled sadly at me. "That doesn't mean she's not gay, and besides, why are you looking for her here?"

"Well, I know she'd been looking at the TaiPride site, but only because she's interested in music."

The man nodded and gave me a little smile. He still thought Mei-ling was a lesbian. "I wish I could help you more. I actually feel relieved whenever I see a runaway because it means they didn't fall into the clutches of pimps."

"Do you think my friend could be in the hands of a pimp?"

He raised an eyebrow. "She's your sister, isn't she?"

"She's my cousin. Her name's Mei-ling."

"What's your name?"

"Jing-nan." I shook his hand automatically and held on as I asked him his to show how sincerely I appreciated his help.

"Omi." It sounded like an aboriginal name but I wasn't crass enough to ask if it was. "Jing-nan, if you email me the picture I can post it and ask the community to keep a lookout for her."

"She had a boyfriend."

"And she's not with him." Omi leaned back and crossed

his right leg. "I've got a question for you, Jing-nan. Why haven't you gone to the police? Because you're afraid your family will be embarrassed when it becomes public knowledge." He nodded to confirm that he was right.

As forthcoming as I intended to be with Omi, I couldn't just start telling him about her murdering father and all the associated ugliness in my family. I put my hands up. "Couldn't fool you, Omi," I said.

"Don't get me wrong," said Omi. "I appreciate what you're doing because when I ran away, nobody came looking for me."

I emailed Mei-ling's picture to him. Maybe she'd see herself online, feel guilty, and text me.

CHAPTER FOURTEEN

We continued down one of Ximending's main streets, Zhonghua Road. Like most places in Wanhua District, recent years of renovation still haven't offset decades of neglect. The familiar rusty brick facades, outdated and flaking billboard ads, and mismatched window frames made me a little nostalgic for my old illegal residence in Wanhua, the toaster house. As we walked, Nancy seemed as enraptured as I was.

"There used to be red-envelope clubs on this street," she said. "This was before Zhonghua Road was widened and repaved, of course. It was a lot smaller in the nineties."

"You're too young to know about red-envelope clubs," I said. "I'm too young, too!"

I'd never actually been to one. I only knew about them from bad seventies gangster films. Fairly often there'd be some scene where a middle-aged woman on stage would be singing old sappy Chinese songs as the audience of lonely old mainlander men mouthed along. Then some young punks would burst in and try to gun down the gangster who owned the red-envelope club. If they didn't get him, it was the beginning of the film because he'd be out for revenge. If they did get him, then the film was almost over because the club owner was the elusive bad guy all along.

The clubs got their names from the red envelopes of money

the old mainlander men would hand over to tip the singers. The men, most of whom were old soldiers, had nothing else to do with their money and the singers would be obligated to talk and maybe dance with them.

"Some clubs are still here," said Nancy. "There's one." She pointed out a red sign above the walk-up entrance to the Empress of China. We walked up to the battered steel frame of the entrance door.

I was about to remark to Nancy how crappy it looked when a woman's voice called out from the intercom. "Hey, you two! Come on up here!"

I looked around but I couldn't see the hidden camera.

"You're open?" asked Nancy.

"We're always open!" The buzzer went off and Nancy pushed the door open.

"We don't know what we're walking into," I said.

"There's nothing to be scared of!" declared the voice. "Special early-bird price is only one hundred NT—it's usually three hundred NT!"

I wanted to say that it still didn't seem worth it, but I didn't want to be overheard. At the same time, though, maybe someone here would know if a young singer were going around Ximending looking for a gig. Mei-ling could have been lured in the same way as we were.

Nancy pushed the door open. "Here we go," she said with some apprehension. She must've been thinking the same as me.

The flights of stairs turned tighter than a whelk shell and the handrails were bolted on too low for me to conveniently hold. I had to put my hands on the walls between faded framed pictures of singers, all women pouting with their bloody lips.

Nancy clambered ahead of me and didn't pause to admire the empresses of the past.

"Seems a little campy, huh?" I called up at her.

"We'll see," she said. The first and second floor exits were walled off. At the third floor a woman in a shiny red *qipao* was leaning against the door frame, sipping a Diet Coke through a straw. Her body was frozen at twenty. Her face was about forty.

"Well, hello, there, young people," she said. "You climbed up here so quickly!" She looked me over thoroughly without a hint of shame. "He'll do," she said, patting Nancy's shoulder. "For now."

The woman walked into the club and we followed.

"Don't we need to pay for admission, miss?" I asked.

"It's so gauche to speak of money before a show!" She put her lips to her straw and the soda can responded with a death rattle. "Don't worry. You'll get the check before you leave."

The room was wallpapered in metallic red roses and black velvet. Half the floor was empty. A dozen two-seater tables were crowded near the stage. Three men sat alone at three different tables, spaced out to maximize the distance from one another. There was some movement behind the heavy red-velvet stage curtains.

The woman brought us to a table in the front and to the left. "You kids are just in time for the end of intermission." She jerked out the chairs and we sat down.

"Chiang Kai-shek sat at this very table in 1951," the woman said as she lightly traced her finger along the edge nearest me. "The Generalissimo brought his entourage and closed the club to the public. A German shepherd dog sat on either side of him. Chiang requested that our youngest girl sing 'Forever Suzhou.' She sang it in the Ningbo dialect, Chiang's dialect, and by the end of the song, his face was in his hands and he was crying. He gave her a red envelope from his gloved hands. Instead of money, it contained a gold necklace."

Nancy shifted in her seat. "Chiang was asking her to be his mistress," she said.

"I honestly don't think so," said the woman. "I think he was so moved that to give mere bills wouldn't suffice. He gave her the most valuable thing he had on his person."

"What was he doing with a gold necklace in his pocket?" I asked.

"Everywhere the Generalissimo went people voluntarily donated money and other goods," said the woman. "When he inspected a market, his soldiers would come out with armloads of fruit and freshly killed chickens. When he inspected a factory, he'd drive out in a new car. When he inspected a jewelry store . . ." She paused to crimp her empty soda can. "Well, the Generalissimo could not be denied." The woman patted the backs of our chairs and began to walk away.

"Could you tell me something?" I asked the woman.

"After," she called back without breaking her stride.

Nancy touched my shoulder. "Do you think you're sitting in Chiang's chair, or am I?"

"Let me check," I said as I covered my face and pretended to sob. She slapped my hands.

"Have some respect!" she said, laughing.

The lights dimmed and an off-center spotlight lit up. A singer who was probably about sixty but holding up great sauntered out from the wings in a long black dress that complimented her dark universe of dyed hair. Synthesized strings began to play from speakers in every corner of the room.

The singer waved her microphone like a magic wand as she waited for the music to build to a crescendo and wash over her.

I know you've been lying
About who you really are
I've followed you so faithfully
From here to who knows where
Someday you're going to miss me
Someday you'll be truly sorry
I'll be free from all your lying
Free from every worry

There were only five of us in the audience but we gave her rousing applause as she bowed demurely and stepped down from the stage as the lights came back up. One of the men seemed to know her personally. He stood up and handed her a rose and a red envelope. The man, who had a full head of white hair, leaned into her ear. She nodded and sat with him.

We heard a sharp snap behind us and we turned. The hostess was back, holding a new can of Diet Coke.

"What do you kids think of the show so far?' she asked, licking a finger.

"It's great," I said.

"Just like I remembered," said Nancy.

The hostess raised an eyebrow as she shucked the wrapper and stuck the straw into the can. "You've been here before?" the hostess asked. "When?"

"It's been years," said Nancy. "My mother sang here, sometimes. She sang in Taiwanese. It was exotic to the mainlanders."

"How interesting," said the hostess. "And before my time. I bought this place after a bank foreclosed on it three years ago."

"Why would you want to own a place like this?" asked Nancy.

The woman glanced at the singer, who was done milking

the first man and moving on to the second. The hostess pulled out a chair and joined our table.

"I didn't plan to own a club," she said. "I was going to renovate this whole place and turn it into an office. But I sort of fell in love with it. It's a step back in time. I felt like I had been here in a former life. More importantly, this place is breaking even—for now." She sipped soda and looked us over. "I like you two. You're not like these rabble-rousing students, venting their sexual frustrations by starting up a ruckus."

Nancy twitched and I put a hand on her shoulder. "Have you hired any new singers?" I asked the proprietor.

She drank more soda and looked to the far left. "The opposite. I've had to let some long-timers go. Sometimes I have special guests hit the stage, but not often and certainly not regularly."

"Have you seen this girl?" I asked, holding up my phone.

"No, I haven't."

"She's a singer," offered Nancy.

"I wouldn't have hired her," said the hostess. "No red-envelope club would. Our customers prefer older singers. Nobody under thirty would cut it. Ladyboys do better than young women."

Nancy stood up. "Thanks for your help," she said as she opened her purse.

"Oh, there's no charge for you two," said the hostess. "But tell your friends about this place and if you could, please tip the singer."

ON OUR WAY DOWNSTAIRS I said, "I didn't know your mom was a singer."

Nancy paused and let a foot dangle over the next step. "She wasn't very good, but the old soldiers liked the way she moved."

"Is her picture on the walls here?"

Nancy glanced at me and then continued downward. "No. I looked."

"You used to come here and see her."

"I used to come here to find her. You know, when I thought there was going to be my mother and food at home and then got tired of waiting for both. She'd buy me something from a sidewalk stand and I'd watch her for a few songs from the wings."

This must have been after Nancy's dad had left.

She slowed her pace. "It looks ramshackle now, but this place used to be nice. More tables."

"Do you feel lousy being back here?" I asked.

"I don't know what I feel," said Nancy. "Not happy, that's for sure." The staircase thumped like a hollow wooden heart.

I knew the rest of the story. Her mom met a boyfriend here who began to help provide for the household. Nancy was sent out to the movie theater fairly often. Of course the guy had a wife and family. Nancy pointed to this period as the reason she became a mistress herself while she was in college.

I also know that it had been years since Nancy and her mom had spoken. There was a screaming match along the lines of: "You did the same thing!" and "I did it so you wouldn't have to but you went ahead with it, anyway!"

We got to the street and walked along in silence for a block.

"I think I know why you don't like food from carts or the night markets," I said.

She shrugged. "I love your food," she said. "It doesn't taste like a consolation meal. It tastes like it comes from a country where people genuinely love each other."

"Could you please write that in an online review? Seriously, it's the best compliment I've ever heard for Unknown Pleasures."

"I don't want to go through the trouble of creating an account and everything." She twisted her mouth into a smirk and then her face slipped into a thoughtful position. "Shouldn't we be checking Mei-ling's computer? We might be able to find something in her browser history, or by hacking into her online accounts."

"I think Big Eye has that covered. I'm sure he knows people who are looking into her social media."

"Are you sure? You'd better call him to check."

I called Big Eye, who said, "I don't know anything about computers. I was never good at anything electronic."

"Have you tried to log into Mei-ling's laptop?"

"I think Whistle and Gao are looking it over."

"Would you mind if I tried?" I couldn't hide the annoyance in my voice. Didn't he know that kids lived their real lives online?

"If you think it will help, then do it. Stop by Mei-ling's apartment. I'm sure my boys will let you in."

NANCY LEFT FOR ANOTHER organizing meeting and I went to Mei-ling's apartment alone. Two *jiaotou*-looking guys stood in the lobby, dressed in colorful shirts, shorts, and flip-flops. The typical tattoos of dragons, tigers, and girls ran down their arms and calves. I saw them check me out as I stepped into the elevator. It took forever for the doors to close.

I rang Mei-ling's buzzer. Whistle answered and hustled me in. The apartment reeked of cigarette smoke.

He greeted me by patting my left shoulder blade. I almost didn't recognize him. The slightly stooped posture was new and he had bags under his eyes. I knew he cared about Mei-ling, maybe more than her father. "Big Eye said you were coming. Are you good at computers and hard drives? I only know locks and Gao can do GPS stuff, but . . ."

I cleared my throat. "I'm not an expert but I'll give it a shot."

Mei-ling's laptop was already sitting on the coffee table. I lifted the lid and powered it up. It was a nice machine, the latest Acer. It beeped and an error message popped up. Operating system not found.

"We didn't get too far," said Whistle.

I nodded. So Mei-ling had had a trick up her sleeve. I was surprised that I sort of knew what to do. Our high school computer teacher had disabled the classroom laptops the same way to keep us from downloading pirated movies.

"There has to be a DVD-ROM or an external hard drive to boot up this thing," I declared to Whistle. "Once we have the system software running, we can search the hard drive." Nothing registered on his face. I turned around and saw Gao, who had silently moved into the room.

"We don't know what you're talking about," said Gao.

"Did she have any computer-related belongings?" I asked.

"We've been through her laptop bag and her dresser, but maybe you should go look through her things, too," Whistle said. They escorted me to the bedroom and kept a close eye on my movement in general and my hands in particular. Big Eye apparently didn't trust me to tell him everything. He probably wanted to know exactly what I did and what I discovered.

The locked drawers, originally installed by Big Eye, had been pried open and all the contents had been dumped out on the floor. I exhaled.

"Looks like you guys were pretty thorough," I said.

"You know Big Eye wants a thorough job done," said Gao. "It's his daughter, so this situation is no joke."

I got down on my hands and knees and went through the detritus of a teenage girl. I had to give her credit for not being a typical schoolgirl. There were signs that she possessed depth. She had books of poetry by Tang Dynasty writers and by e.e. cummings. Small ribbons that congratulated her for wins in math and Chinese competitions were stuck in as bookmarks. Such accolades didn't mean much to her, but it was interesting that someone who was apparently academically gifted was also so poorly behaved. I was also intrigued by a small medal for excellence in computer programming stashed among the coins in a change purse.

I picked up a folded piece of paper that looked like a secret note and opened it up to reveal a cutout chain of women holding hands.

There was nothing here that would serve as a startup drive. There were no DVD-ROMs or even CD-ROMs. No external drives. Not even a crappy little flash drive. Dammit, maybe she had it with her, or had chucked it down the garbage chute. You can't test out password combinations when you can't even boot up the computer.

There had to be a way around this. Maybe I could put the laptop into dummy mode and access its drive by linking it to another computer.

I stood up and spied the round base of her desk lamp. I seized it and lifted it up. Nothing there. Whistle cracked up.

"We looked under there, too! Looks suspicious, right?" It was a little dim in the corner so I flicked the light on. Nothing happened.

"We unplugged it," said Whistle. "Just go under the desk." I dropped back down and picked up the cord and plugged it in. I fumbled a little bit and hit my head against the desk drawer.

"Dammit!" I yelled, maybe too loud.

Both Whistle and Gao chuckled.

"Jing-nan, you're no good at this," said Whistle. "It's a good thing you're self-employed."

I turned on the light and ran my fingers along the baseboard of the wall. "I'm trying to see if she stashed something here," I said. Both Gao and Whistle closed in on me. The wall was clean. I then searched the door casing without any luck. "Looks like there's nothing here," I said.

"We've already been through the entire house, every square centimeter," said Whistle. "If there was a secret compartment in the furniture or the walls, we would have found it."

I shrugged. "It might be a lost cause. She might be carrying the missing drive in her purse. But would you guys mind if I took the laptop with me to hook up to another computer and work on it a little? I have some ideas."

Whistle and Gao glanced at each other.

"If it's all the same to you, Jing-nan," said Whistle, "how about we keep the laptop. If you want to try something, bring the other computer here and we'll try together."

Together. C'mon, I thought, these guys don't know the difference between an Ethernet and a Thunderbolt cable. "All right," I said. "Well, I'll be going for now."

"Bye, Jing-nan," said Whistle. Gao looked directly at me and nodded gravely.

"We'll find her," I said.

I waited until I was on the MRT before I checked my right pants pocket. I had found a little flash drive wristband that had been tied to the lamp's power cord. To your average older gangster it looked like a tie to loop up the extra slack in the line. I'll bet it held a bunch of Mei-ling's secrets.

I wasn't too worried about not getting the laptop. Most of her stuff was probably stored in the cloud, anyway.

Why did I hide my discovery from Gao, Whistle, and ultimately Big Eye? I felt protective of my little cousin. Yes, she was doing something incredibly stupid, but she didn't deserve to be extradited into Big Eye's custody.

It was a good thing she was free. I mainly wanted to find her to make sure she was all right and to stay in touch with my little cousin. It's an awful thing not to have a sense of family in your life.

I TOYED WITH THE wristband and eyed an open USB port on my PC.

Maybe Mei-ling had a final surprise for me and this device would deliver a virus or two to my hard drive. It was also possible that it was blank. According to factory markings on the wristband's port, it had a capacity of only four gigabytes.

I fired up my PC, opened the wristband and plugged it into the USB port.

A folder appeared on my desktop. Even before I opened it, I copied the folder to my hard drive, just in case the original deleted itself with unauthorized use.

I was a little nervous so I triple-clicked the folder to open it when a simple double-click would have done the job. What was I going to find? Nude pictures of my cousin? Viruses galore to destroy my computer?

A window opened and I examined the icons in it. Ah, Mei-ling, you maniac! You were using a Linux operating system. No wonder you could fit it on a wristband.

Unlike conventional operating systems, Linux is maintained by volunteers and free to download and use. Conventional operating systems cost money to update and have a lot more bells and whistles that require more memory.

Most people have never heard of these so-called open-source applications like Linux but most are compatible with the corresponding product put out by Microsoft and Google. For example, I was able to open a document that Mei-ling had created using Linux-based OpenOffice by using Microsoft Word. The document popped up and I shook my head.

What an amateur move. She'd listed her various logins and passwords for a number of sites. Every guideline in identity security says not to write such a list. Now I held the keys to the kingdom. I could change Mei-ling's passwords to everything and lock her out of her own life. No. It would be better for me to log in and keep track of what Mei-ling was doing.

I logged in as Mei-ling in an aspiring musicians' forum and checked in on the latest topics she commented in. Obviously it was not her favorite site as she hadn't commented there regularly in about a year. It was easy to see why. The comments were rife with spam ads for cheap music equipment and studios.

Another forum she used was Students Helping Students. People posted their math problems and other users solved them. I wasn't surprised that Mei-ling was good at math but I didn't know she felt compelled to help others. It looked like she started commenting a few months ago, after she was kicked out of her latest high school in Taichung. Maybe posting in this forum helped make her feel secure about her academic ability.

Then there was the lesbian forum. Mei-ling had a few tentative questions in the last month.

"How do you know if you're a lesbian?" she had naïvely asked in her first post.

"Only you would know if you're attracted to girls," replied one user.

"It's like ice cream," said someone else. "Just start licking. Want to try some? You'll like it."

I ran my hands through my hair. How could I have been so stupid and callous? Anybody could have seen that Meiling was a lesbian. How could I not even detect the edge in her voice when she was calling out my homophobia? I think

I was blinded because I just wanted her to be my little cousin. Something uncomplicated.

My hand shot to my mouth. Maybe the motorcycle driver was a woman who had seduced her online!

Nearly all of Mei-ling's comments had multiple replies from users soliciting sex. To be fair, that seemed to be the standard reply to all comments, particularly to the angry, homophobic posts that popped up once in a while.

"Dykes suck cock in hell!" Mao888 had written.

AnyBayBee had replied with, "You can suck my pussy here!"

I sorted the forum so that I only saw Mei-ling's posts or replies. Then I sorted by date. She hadn't logged in since the night before she'd disappeared. That made sense if she were already hooked up with someone from the forum.

However, her last few posts had seemed innocuous, relatively speaking.

Her very last note was, "What is the difference between a clitoral orgasm and a vaginal orgasm? I was with a boy for a while and I don't think I ever felt either LOL!"

Her second-to-last post was, "Is it true that A-mei was forbidden by Singapore to perform a song about lesbian love? I would never compromise my art for money. #ameisellout"

Most intriguing was a post from a week ago, even before she had reached Taipei. "Should I stay at home with a fucking homophobic father or run away and try to make it on my own?"

My throat ran dry after I read that. That called for a bottle of Kirin. As I sucked down the beer, I wondered what Big Eye would do if he knew about this post. Shit. Maybe he'd be so mad, he'd tell everybody in his search party to shoot her on sight.

I thumped the bottom of the bottle on my desk. Damn

you, Mei-ling! Why didn't you tell me you wanted to run away? Well, maybe you knew I'd go to your dad. I'm sorry that I didn't prove myself to be trustworthy.

All I could do now was keep this new information away from Big Eye and hope that I'd be able to get in contact with her somehow and make sure she was safe—and maybe happier than before.

On Monday morning I went to see Peggy Lee at her office in Taipei 101 to update her about the situation and see if she had any ideas. Mei-ling's disappearance was something I had to tell Peggy in person, otherwise it would sound like bullshit.

Peggy looked a bit like a business-casual Catwoman in her grey pantsuit. She stood before one of her giant office windows, leaning her right shoulder directly against the glass.

I sat in an awful ergonomic chair that she had placed next to her desk. I think the chair choice was strategic. Both clients and peers would always feel off-balance and vulnerable.

"You realize," said Peggy, "that Mei-ling was here for only a few days. I'll admit she was good but now she's left me in a lurch." She paused to crack the bones in her right wrist. "What is up with you Chens leaving me in the lurch?"

"Peggy, please be serious," I said. "My cousin is missing and could be in danger."

She pulled herself away from the window and sat against the edge of her desk. "Mei-ling is probably just fine. She's smart as a whip. From what you told me about her escape, I can only express admiration. I mean, seriously, who else could plan out something like that and execute it? She was wrong about what level the temple was at and she improvised a real-time fix. That took balls and brains!"

"I'll admit that it was pretty daring," I said. "I think,

though, she was seduced by an older lesbian, someone she only knew from the Internet."

Peggy slipped around her desk, dropped into her chair and dramatically dropped her jaw. "Mei-ling is a lesbian?"

"Yes."

She put her hands flat against her chest. "Wow, I had no idea. You see, usually lesbians are really into me. I could have done it with another woman at this convention a few months ago."

I shifted in my seat. "Why didn't you, Peggy?"

She laughed out loud. "Honestly, I didn't know what we could do together. Drinking and talking with her already felt like as far as we could go. Jing-nan, did you ever . . ."

"No!" I said.

"Two guys makes more sense to me than two girls. At least you can stick each other, y'know?"

"Peggy, let's get back on track here. Do you remember anyone coming to see Mei-ling, or any phone calls she might have had?"

"Nobody came to see her, that's for sure. Especially not that guy that Big Eye was totally hating on, Mei-ling's ex-boyfriend. Did he ever turn up?"

"I think it's still an active case."

"Well, anyway, Mei-ling didn't have any phone calls, either, not from her cell. I purposely put the interns in a room where it's impossible to get reception. The intern office phone is directly connected to my headset so I can hear everything that's said. Mei-ling only made business calls."

"She meet anyone for lunch?"

"My intern's lunch break is with me. I order out and she gets to eat with me in my office. Isn't that a treat?"

"Free lunch with the boss, wow, what a deal," I said, unable to wring out the sarcasm in my voice.

"I'm not that bad to hang out with, Jing-nan! A lot of people find me to be great company."

Her desk emitted a soft tone. She picked up a wishbone-thin headset and with one hand slipped it over her ears.

"Yes," said Peggy. "Gimme a minute." She set the headset aside. "Jing-nan, you'll have to excuse me. I have an interview with someone looking for a trader position."

I struggled my way out of the seat. "Thanks for taking the time to see me."

"Hey, Jing-nan! Let's play a trick. On your way to the lobby, put on a face like I just chewed you out. I want to see if I can shatter her confidence before we even start."

"That's mean, Peggy."

She shrugged. "If that's enough to rattle them, then they can take a hike," she said. "Let them go work in the night market." She caught herself. "I'm sorry, I don't mean that what you do is completely worthless."

"That's all right," I said. "I know what you mean." Her apology was more hurtful than the actual insult. I didn't have to fake a hurt look on the way out.

DURING A BREAK IN the action at work, I used my phone to log in as Mei-ling at the lesbian board. I felt like a creep pretending to be a teenage lesbian online until I saw that Mei-ling had a direct message. I tingled as I clicked on it. This could be a major clue.

"Nice try, Jing-nan," it read. "I've fallen from my perch and I'm in a place you can't go." The user name was "fuck-offjingnan," and I breathed a sigh of relief after reading it. She was all right, at least to the degree that she could still abuse me.

"Perch" was a curious word to use. Was she a bird now? Did "perch" have a special meaning to lesbians or teenage girls?

I did a search for "perch" and "lesbians."

The Perch was a bar—for lesbians! Was Mei-ling purposely trying to tell me where she was? A criminal on the run who wanted to be caught?

Dwayne reached over and closed my mouth.

"What are you reading that is so shocking?" he asked. I told him about Mei-ling's online accounts and what I'd found. He rubbed his mouth.

"You'd better tell Big Eye," he said. "You should have told him earlier about these chat boards, man."

"I want to find Mei-ling but I'm not so sure I want to help him find her," I said. "My main mission is to make sure she's all right and to help her any way I can going forward."

Dwayne shook his head and tried to strangle a laugh. "She don't need help from you. Shit, you can barely help yourself. Big Eye has the connections to spot her on nearly any street corner."

I found myself sticking up for her abilities. "Mei-ling isn't dumb. She knows exactly the extent of Big Eye's reach."

Dwayne jabbed an index finger into the back of my left hand. "Well, what can you do at this point by yourself?"

I shrugged with my right shoulder. "I was thinking of heading to that lesbian bar to look for her."

"Yeah, great idea. You'll get real far. The Perch probably doesn't even allow men on the main floors." He rubbed the glistening short hairs on his head with his right hand. "I know what you *could* do," he said, dangling his words like necklace beads.

"I am not getting Nancy involved," I said. "Not after last time. *Gan!*"

Dwayne crossed his arms. "Seriously, Jing-nan, get a woman to help you. If you show up, you're gonna get your ass kicked."

I fixed my feet and pointed an accusing finger at his nose. "Listen, Dwayne. Straight people shouldn't have preconceived notions about lesbians and gays. We are all the same. If I show up at a lesbian bar and ask people for help, of course they'll help!"

CHAPTER FIFTEEN

THE BARS AROUND THE Red House in Ximending are primarily geared to gay men. Lesbian hot spots are more spread out in the city, primarily in the Shida neighborhood in the southern part of the Da'an District, according to my online research.

Shida gets its name from an abbreviation of Shifan Daxue, itself an abbreviation of the formal name of the local college, National Taiwan Normal University.

People around Shida are generally well-educated and tolerant. It's a college neighborhood, after all, and it welcomes people of different sexual orientations, alternative lifestyles and even foreigners.

The president of Clean Taipei, a powerful neighborhood association, was married with kids but felt the need to declare at a gay-pride event that she loved women more than men. If same-sex marriage were legal, she would have married for love.

I am well-acquainted with the neighborhood because of what the Shida Night Market has been through. It was once a bustling affair, not as big as the Shilin Night Market, but certainly a major competitor. A few years ago, developers began to buy up land around the night market and lobbied to rezone blocks to residential from commercial. The Taipei government removed Shida Night Market from city-produced tourist maps, a move that both hurt business and fulfilled the developers' allegations that the market was on its last legs. Inspectors from the Taipei Department of Health descended and shut down businesses, citing the flimsiest of excuses, including decades-old signage that was now deemed "inappropriate" because they were too big or too small or too colorful.

The writing was on the wall when the government shut down Phoenix Noodles, an eighty-year-old stew stall. The guy who operated it was known to all as "Old Uncle" and he was a complete asshole. He was grumpy as hell and apparently ancient enough to have been the original proprietor. When I think of him, all I can see is a shock of white hair and furrowed white eyebrows.

Phoenix Noodles was nearly a block long and featured a giant horizontal honeycomb of ingredients on display in wooden and metal canisters—some on ice, others over a fire. Fish-meal balls in liquid. Curls of dried fungus ready to unfurl. Chopped-up meats. His broths, varying from spicy to mild to sour, were hidden in vats under the counter.

Old Uncle stood behind the honeycomb, gathering up ingredients with extra-long chopsticks he wielded in his oddly youthful hand. He openly judged customers by what they chose. Ingredients he considered incompatible would earn his sighs and headshakes as he threw your stew together. It might still taste incredible to you, but to him it represented a missed opportunity to unblock *qi* and improve blood flow in your system.

Nobody could put a stew together like him. If you told Old Uncle that you were sick and what your symptoms were, he would look you in the eye and then grunt when he had you all figured out. His delight showed only in the flourish with which he threw together your meal.

A few years ago I had a stubborn wheeze that wouldn't leave my lungs. Nothing worked. I told Old Uncle about it. As he whipped up a stew for me, he frowned when I tried to peer through the honeycomb to get a look at his broth baths.

"Even if you saw them, you wouldn't understand!" he snapped.

He placed a steaming black stew with an iridescent surface in my hands. It threatened to overflow from the flimsy plastic bowl.

"You have to drink that in two minutes!" he ordered. I slurped it down, my throat alternately feeling burning and cooling sensations. I put the empty bowl on his shelf and felt a balloon swell up in my chest. I staggered to a drain at the side of the road and coughed out lumps of green phlegm. After two days I felt fully cured.

No one knows for sure why Old Uncle's stand was named Phoenix Noodles. The phoenix is a female element, the yin to the yang of the dragon, a male element. One rumor held that Old Uncle named his business after a sorceress from whom he had gleaned his recipes. Another story held that Old Uncle was a hermaphrodite.

One thing was certain. The space where Phoenix Noodles had stood was cursed. After the health inspectors shut down Old Uncle for "false claims," even though he never promised anyone anything, he packed up his most crucial ingredients and drove away on a cart led by a water buffalo. Old Uncle muttered the whole time, occasionally gesturing back at the market.

When an excavator came in to dig a foundation for a condominium, the operator lost control and the boom spun in a circle. The claw bucket at the end killed five people, including the developer who had been on hand for the groundbreaking ceremony. The following week, a potential bidder dropped dead of a heart attack while on a preliminary tour of the ground.

That spot still sat empty behind a wall of wooden boards painted with happy children who were "Ready to Build the New Shida."

Across the street from this forsaken ground was Shida's upscale lesbian bar, The Perch.

IF A YOUNG, ATTRACTIVE woman were on the prowl for the same, she would definitely go drinking at The Perch. It was exclusive but also rated tops for hookups by the users of lipstulips.com.

The stairs up to The Perch from the street were carpeted. I arrived there around nine at night and it was already buzzing. The first-floor bar was dramatically lit with spotlights. Slowly rotating prisms broke the light into rainbow shards that slid across the floor and up the walls. On first glance it was a paradise for straight guys because there were five men among thirty-odd women. But this was all I would get to see of The Perch. The second floor was for lesbians only. The rumored third floor was a big orgy with rubber-band masks.

The bartender poured six shots and drank three rounds with a customer. They were mirror images of each other, apart from their dress: Taipei thin and Taipei pale. That is, bone thin and bone pale. Short spiky black hair. The customer was wearing a black vest over a white blouse. The bartender's designer tank top was strategically torn and repaired with safety pins, too symmetrically to be punk.

When I thought their interaction was winding down, I made my way to the counter.

"Hi there!" I called out. Both women turned to me and frowned. I fumbled with my phone until I came up with Meiling's picture. "I'm looking for my cousin and I think she might have been here this past weekend. Have you seen her? Either of you?"

Both women glanced at my phone and then stared at me. The bartender said, "Are you a cop?"

Again? "Does asking questions make me a cop?"

"He didn't say no," said the customer.

"No," I said. "I am absolutely not a cop. Never have been. Never will be."

"Why are you so defensive?" asked the customer.

"I'm not being defensive! She's only sixteen and I'm freaking out because I don't know where she is, all right?"

"Maybe you're her ex-boyfriend," said the bartender.

"I am not!" I said.

"He's definitely straight," the bartender said out of the side of her mouth.

"I can tell," said the customer.

"This is my cousin," I said in exasperation. "She could be in a lot of trouble."

The bartender turned her back on me and became a busy octopus.

"I'm not lying," I said to the customer.

"Do you know how many creeps come in looking to catch some girl-on-girl action? Or the homophobic cops who snoop around for parents trying to 'rescue' their adult daughters?"

"I have no idea."

"I'm sure you don't." The bartender came back to me with a pint glass filled with some potion. "So you're not a cop, huh?" she said. "Then drink this."

"Have you seen her?"

"Maybe I have and maybe I haven't. We'll talk after you drink."

"I'm not drinking that!"

"Don't drink on duty, do you?" said the customer. I grunted and reached for the glass. The bartender held up a hand.

"That's three hundred NT," she said.

"What!" I said. This drink of unknown contents was ten bucks American.

"Tip is included."

I counted out three Sun Yat-sen bills and flattened them on the bar like a losing hand.

"Thank you."

I picked up the glass and contemplated the reflection of my swollen head against the swirling dark brown contents.

Well, she couldn't poison me, could she?

"Drink up," said the customer.

"Jia you," said the bartender.

I tipped back the glass for a mouthful. It started sour and ended salty. A liquefied preserved plum would probably taste like this. I felt the roof of my mouth tingling slightly.

"There's blood in this, right?" I asked. The bartender laughed and tapped her fingers on the counter.

"I'll tell you when you're done," she said. "I'll tell you anything after."

Mei-ling, if you're not in serious trouble when I find you, I'm going to kill you.

I worked the drink down. When I was finished I snorted involuntarily twice before I could speak. I looked the bartender in the eyes and said, "Tell me."

"It was mostly plum wine with a big shot of this." She brandished a fat glass bottle that held what looked like a thick coil of rope in ghoulishly yellow liquid. I blinked and the rope's braids become small scales. She had spiked the drink with snake wine.

"Ma de!" I gasped. Both the bartender and customer laughed hard and rubbed my arm.

"You'll be all right," said the bartender. "I actually gave you a discount. This stuff's expensive!"

"You're the first man I've seen drink it," the customer added.

Snake wine includes the entire animal. As the body slowly decomposes, rotting fragments of the meat, organs, blood, and even poison add "essence" into the wine.

There is the stupid Chinese idea that imbibing the snake cells increases sexual performance. More than two thousand years ago, some idiot folded his hands into his sleeves, hunkered down and examined a snake in his path. Hey, he thought. This thing sort of looks like my penis, but it's longer and more dynamic. If I eat it, then surely my cock will inherit such attributes! Of course, nobody nowadays believes in such things, certainly nobody in this bar. That wine sits on the shelf as a dare.

"God," I said to the bartender. "Can I get a Coke? I have to get this taste out of my mouth."

Now that she had had her little laugh, the woman served me with newly sympathetic eyes. "Sure," she said. "It's on the house."

I gulped down hard and the soda pricked the roof of my mouth. I glanced at the two of them and saw that apart from winning their sympathy, they finally believed that my cousin was really missing.

"I did see that girl," said the bartender.

"When?" I asked.

"Saturday night," she said. "She asked me who handled the booking at the club and I told her we didn't do events. People come here to hook up, not watch a show."

I noticed the customer tilting her head and frowning like she had lost her keys.

"Was she with anybody?" I asked the bartender.

"I'm not sure," said the bartender. "I saw someone follow her out, though."

"A man?"

"A woman."

"What did she look like?"

"Femme. Longish hair. Maybe thirty."

"Thirty!" I said. "That's twice as old as my cousin!"

The bartender shrugged. "I'm not sure they were together, but anyway, what's the big deal?" She turned to the customer. "Right, Pei Pei?"

Pei Pei was still frowning. She opened her mouth and clenched her bottom lip in her teeth.

"Are you all right?" I asked her.

"I saw your cousin and that woman on Saturday night," she said. "Not in here, but down the block. They were arguing about something."

"How are you sure it was Saturday night?"

"I was coming to The Perch from . . . a different way." Pei Pei cleared her throat. "Anyway, the three of us had to clear off the sidewalk at the same time because a car was coming out of the elevator of a below-ground garage. I saw her face clearly in the signal light."

"What did the older woman look like?"

Pei Pei shrugged. "Femme in her thirties, like Daphne said. Honestly, I found your cousin more interesting."

"What were they arguing about?"

"I think your cousin wanted to go back into The Perch, but the other woman was saying they had to do something else."

"What do you think that was?"

Pei Pei shrugged. "I have no idea."

I sat up high in my chair and crossed my arms. "Pei Pei and Daphne, I want to ask you both something. My cousin definitely is a lesbian, right?"

They both burst out laughing.

I WALKED TO WHERE Pei Pei said she'd seen Mei-ling. A now-dim bulb on the side of the building indicated the location of the underground garage. There was nothing else to see. I stood there watching people walk by, narrating their lives to each other.

So Mei-ling was a lesbian for certain. Or maybe just half. She had had a boyfriend, one she was having sex with, after all. At my orientation program at UCLA an upperclassman informed us that all people were part-straight and part-gay. Nobody was one hundred percent of either.

I had never been attracted to another man. Or was I lying to myself? A bus passed by with an advertisement that featured Jay Chou, the actor/singer guy who was known everywhere. He was such a famous Taiwanese he even did American movies. I could recognize his face as physically attractive, even if it held a vacant expression. I watched him zoom off and pursed my lips.

I felt something in the pit of my stomach. It wasn't lust, though. As my bloodstream slowly absorbed the snake wine, hunger raked its fangs across the inside of my rib cage.

Back at home, I had chopped garlic, some long-grain rice, ham, and eggs in the fridge and at least two cans of pineapple chunks in the cupboard. That was enough to whip up a batch of fried rice. But I wouldn't be able to make it home without keeling over. In fact, thinking about cooking was making me even hungrier.

I decided to pull an old trick. I ducked into a 7-Eleven on the corner and picked up more soda to fill my stomach for the time being. On my way out, I coughed into my elbow, unleashing a muffled belch, and wondered where the fuck my cousin was tonight and what she was doing.

I HAD BEGUN TO resent the student activism. The movement had kidnapped Nancy for another night. They'd already occupied a government building, blocked off major streets and even held an outdoor concert. What could they possibly do next?

I worked open my cranky kitchen window to let out the fried-rice smell that collected near the ceiling like gloom. I pulled the retractable mosquito screen across the window frame. Cool night air rolled in over me and I shivered.

The dogs were gathered in the park making yipping sounds. Willie was facing off with a new challenger, a smallish mutt that had to have some koala DNA. It was Monday night. This was a bonus fight on an unscheduled night.

Willie patiently endured the unfair fight. He leered at his puny opponent, not bothering to dodge its many feints. The little guy soon realized that the white dog wasn't taking the fight seriously and jumped on the alpha's face.

Enraged, Willie knocked down the challenger and pinned him to the ground with his left paw. The little dog thrashed but its neck remained exposed. As the pack closed in, anxious for a kill, Willie the white dog lowered his ears and growled.

Everybody was calling for blood. Even the loser seemed to scream that the white dog didn't have the balls to do it.

Willie hunkered down and curled his lips. I, along with the rest of the dogs, expected to see an extremely bloody end to the conflict. Instead, the alpha muscled his way out of the pack and walked out of the park. His steps were resolute without seeming stiff.

They all watched the white dog leave. Its bright white fur remained visible for blocks. The forlorn loser stood up, shook off the dirt and then lay down on its side.

WITH MY SEARCH FOR Mei-ling shut down, it was back to Unknown Pleasures as usual on Tuesday night. Back into Johnny mode. Fun and exciting food mode. "Hey, guys, put that on Instagram!" mode. I began to get that hollow feeling again.

Early on, after seven P.M., a shadow fell upon me. Literally. It was Li Ji-shen, the Chinese tour guide that I had met in the *youtiao* place. He stood over me and swayed slightly.

"Hey look, *taibazi*! I'm here! I made it to your joint!" It was all right for him to call me a dick now. We were friends and we had at least one story between us.

"Mr. Li," I said, "you should have brought one of your tour groups with you."

He grabbed my shoulder, jamming his thumb in my clavicle. Men like him felt the need to be a little rough when being friendly. They didn't want to come off as sissies!

Mr. Li looked back, held up a red flag and waved it. "I did bring them! They're behind me, caught up with buying pineapple cakes." I heard the Chinese people before I saw them. Mr. Li had brought at least thirty people. No, wait. Actually about fifty people. The group of retirees seemed to be multiplying as they advanced. Both Dwayne and Frankie came out from around the counter to observe. Dwayne let out a long whistle. No wonder the Communists overwhelmed the KMT in the Chinese Civil War—they had the ability to replicate spontaneously.

Dwayne scrambled back to his station while Frankie shuffled away, lit a cigarette and pretended to ignore the tour guide.

Mr. Li put his hand back on my shoulder. "So," he said in a slow drawl, "I'm sure you appreciate me bringing all these people over."

"I sure do. Thank you very much. I think they'll really like my food."

He tilted his head back and smiled. "I was thinking that there should be some compensation."

"I always give a discount to big groups," I said. Mr. Li withdrew his hand and crossed his arms. I knew what he was driving at, but I wanted him to say first how much of a kickback he had in mind. It gave me more bargaining power.

"I was thinking about *my* compensation. Sorry I didn't make that clear. I'm thinking that for this group, and for future groups, you could contribute to my, uh, education." He said "education" in a way that one would deliciously deliver a bad pun.

The NT$1,000 bill featured a bunch of little kids in a classroom, their hands on a globe. One thousand NTs was about thirty US bucks. That wasn't so bad, considering it was about fifty cents a head. I was a businessman, though. I had a deep-seated need to make a not-so-bad deal better.

"Here's what I had in mind, Mr. Li. I think I'll just give you a ticket to see a ball game." The face of the NT$500 bill presented a bunch of Little Leaguers in mid-jump after victory. We locked eyes briefly before he broke away.

"*Taibazi*! How you mistreat your fellow countryman! We're brothers, don't you know?"

I shook my head. "I'm an only child," I said, "and an orphan."

"How you do me wrong!" He turned away and put an open hand behind his back, the crablike fingers running upside-down in the air. I shoved five NT$100 bills into his palm just as the advance guard of his Chinese tourists swarmed into Unknown Pleasures.

"Very scary artwork!" said a woman shivering in a coat

that was too thin. Chinese tourists underdressed because they thought Taiwan was always hot.

"Black mountains, what does it mean?" asked a man, peering at my painted wall through glasses with iridescent grease marks.

Even if I wanted to speak up and say that the jagged lines were radio waves from a pulsar on the cover of Joy Division's first album, I would maybe get only a single word in.

"It's Taoist," Mr. Li boomed. "It's the theme of endless mountains in the dark that one can overcome!"

"Oh, oh, oh," said the Chinese masses. Mr. Li turned to me and gave me a conspiratorial grin that faded quickly. He leaned into me and said, "When Taiwan is finally reunited with the motherland, I'll remember your little insult."

"That might be a while," I said.

"We'll see, Jing-nan, we'll see. You think you know it all, don't you? You even tried to lie to me about that girl you were with. She's not sixteen. She's eighteen."

My hearing cut out in my left ear as blood rushed into my head. Ever get the feeling that you're not going to like the answer to a question but you go ahead and ask it anyway? "Why do you think she's eighteen?"

Mr. Li beamed, proud that he had something over me. "Wouldn't you like to know!"

I caught a movement over Mr. Li's shoulder. It was Dwayne waving to Frankie and me. I knew Dwayne wanted help. The Chinese tourists yelled at each other joyously and pressed right up against the counter of Unknown Pleasures, fingers on the glass. Dwayne would have to withstand this assault by himself because I needed to hear more about my cousin before I could tend to my business.

"Mr. Li, please tell me how you know?" I asked nicely.

He played with the collar of his shirt. "I like you, Jing-nan.

Let me give you some advice. Every man loves sex. It's in our blood. But that doesn't mean you need to be seen with the girls in public. Y'know what I mean?"

"Where did you see the girl?" I asked numbly.

"At the hotel I'm staying at—the Eastern Princess. I slipped some money to the overnight guy at the front desk for some entertainment for some of the men. He opened up a suite and two girls came in for a lez show." Mr. Li popped a peanut candy into his mouth. He continued talking through his chewing. "We were told there would be no penetration right off the bat and that was fine. There are some really old guys in the group. They can't process much beyond tits, anyway. Me, I remember everything about a girl, and I definitely remembered one girl's face."

"Did you talk to her?"

"Not much. After the show, I gave her money and said thank you, of course."

"How do you know she's eighteen?" I asked again. Don't tell me that you had sex with her, because I'd have to stab you right now and repeatedly.

He frowned. "Whenever you have things like that in a hotel, they're always at least eighteen," he said with both open palms thrust to me. "Just to make sure everything's legal. Don't you know that?"

I straightened up. "That girl is my cousin Mei-ling," I said. "She really is only sixteen." I was floating outside of myself.

Mr. Li cocked his head and whistled, sending peanut shards bouncing off my chest. Misogyny, judgment, and guilt all came together in his thoughts and words. "Oh, fuck, I'm sorry for your family. It was a semi-decent show but I promise I won't watch it again."

"Eastern Princess, huh?" I asked.

"That's right."

I began to walk away from Unknown Pleasures.

"Hey, Jing-nan!" cried Dwayne. "You're leaving on one of the busiest nights ever? One of the few times that we could actually use your help?"

"I have to do something!" I yelled. Way to go, Jing-nan. Great explanation.

"What!" yelled Dwayne.

I heard Frankie bark in response. "C'mon, Dwayne, we can handle this together!"

I RACED UP THE escalator at the Jiantan MRT stop. I paced the platform, my heart and head pounding. What to do?

Eastern Princess is a recently built hotel in the Xinyi District meant to cater to the sensibilities of Chinese tourists. It was in the shadow of Taipei 101 and a shuttle bus ran between the hotel and the direct entrance to the tower's luxury shopping levels. Eastern Princess was also next to the National Sun Yat-sen Memorial Hall so the Chinese could pay tribute to the father of their nation and pray (or as close as Chinese people can come to praying) that Taiwan would be returned to the fold soon to complete the revolution Sun had sparked.

Silently observing both the Eastern Princess and Taipei 101 is the elegantly named Martial Law Era Political Victim Memorial Park. Set in a hillside to the south, and within shouting distance of the hotel, the "memorial park" is actually a graveyard of enemies, both perceived and real, of the Chiang Kai-shek regime. Frankie the Cat could have easily ended up in one of those cramped graves, marked with a brick-sized stone.

Eastern Princess was supposedly built on former execution grounds. Superstitious Taiwanese never wanted to build anything on the land out of fear of ghosts, and so the land sat neglected until a developer came along and proposed to build the hotel to accommodate Chinese tourists. The permits were issued and the building went up in record time, constructed mostly by foreign laborers who were ignorant of the area's ghoulish past.

THE TRAIN'S DOORS OPENED, springing me out of my thoughts. I could try to go to Eastern Princess myself and find out who was in charge of procuring entertainment for guests. I chuckled bitterly. What were they going to tell me? Not only was I not staying there, they would know right away I wasn't Chinese.

At best I would get a brush-off. At worst, a double-teamed beating in the trash-compactor room.

No wonder Mei-ling said she was in a place I couldn't go! You had to be a Chinese tourist to get in! At this point, I needed to call it in to a man with connections.

I remained on the platform as the train's closing-doors chime rang out. I watched the train leave the station before dialing Big Eye.

"Jing-nan," he said in a flat voice. I could already feel his eyes boring into me.

"Big Eye, I think I know where we can find Mei-ling."

It seemed an eternity before he spoke. "Where?"

"The Eastern Princess hotel. Someone I know saw her there."

"She's staying there?"

Oh, shit. I had to choose my words carefully. "She was performing there." That wasn't a lie. "She had a show."

"Singing her crappy songs for Chinese people," he murmured. "I hope they're paying her well."

"If you send someone there the front desk can probably locate her."

"Eastern Princess, huh?" It was rare to hear indecision in Big Eye's voice. "Are you sure?"

"Pretty sure."

His throat roared like a coffee roaster. "What do you mean 'pretty sure'? Yes or no, are you sure?"

"Okay! I'm sure!" Mr. Li, for the sake of my life please don't make a liar out of me.

"Hah," said Big Eye. "Out of all the fucking places. That's Black Sea turf. Wood Duck's faction. He's still sore about the money I took from him. I mean, won from him."

"I'm sure he'll help you get your daughter back."

Big Eye gave a falling grunt. "He's a bad guy."

"He's a human being."

"No, he's not. You don't know him at all, Jing-nan. He's the most ruthless bastard ever. One time the seat of his pants ripped and a top guy of his laughed. He threw that guy off a cliff."

I bit my lip. "Maybe if you give him his money back, he'll help you."

I heard him slap his table hard enough to rattle his glass. "What! You never give the money back! That's not an option! First of all, it's an insult to suggest that someone is sore over money, even if they really are. Secondly, there's no such thing as a refund in our culture. You know that! You run a business!"

I couldn't help but nod. My father taught me to think of the cash box as a black hole that a shiny penny's glint couldn't escape from. If the customer's mad about their food, give him three of something else in exchange.

"I called you as soon as I found out," I lied. "Now I'm going to get out of your way and let you handle it."

I heard his fingers typing on a keyboard. "Hold on, Jing-nan. Where are you right now?"

I began to walk to the down escalator. "I'm at work."

"No you're not. You're at a train station."

"I guess you could tell by the sound."

"You're walking south."

I stopped in my tracks. "What?"

"I'm following your location on my computer." I heard him take a satisfied swig of something before he swallowed with a grunt. "I'm glad you bring your phone everywhere. I had Gao stick a chip inside."

"Spying on your own family. Real classy, Big Eye."

"Don't give me this 'classy' shit. I won't stop at anything to find my daughter. I only wish I'd chipped her phone before letting her go to Taipei!"

"I'm hanging up."

"No you're not. You're gonna goddamn listen to me. Go to the Eastern Princess. Take pictures of the people working in the lobby and send them to me so I can see which specific jerks in Wood Duck's gang I'm dealing with. I'll figure out something after that." He sighed. "I know how hotel entertainment works. These naïve wannabes, of whom Mei-ling is one, sign on to contracts to perform for peanuts. It's practically a pimp-prostitute relationship."

You said it, not me, Big Eye. When I thought of pimps, I couldn't help but imagine drugs and guns.

"Big Eye, am I going to get shot?" I asked seriously.

"No one's getting shot, unless Gao's pulling the trigger. Anyway, someone tried to shoot you point-blank before and you came out of that just fine, right?"

"That was pure luck," I said.

"Hah!" said Big Eye. "You're a lucky guy! If I had your luck, I'd have so much money right now. Not that I don't. I'd have more."

"All you want me to do is take pictures of people working there? I don't have to leave the lobby or start asking where to find Mei-ling, right?"

"That's right. Just sit tight. Blend in. Read a paper. Eat a fucking cupcake. I don't know. Just go now."

"Yes, Big Eye."

"That's my boy!"

I'll admit that Big Eye's sincere praise felt good. I boarded the eastbound MRT and swayed as the train took off. One way or another Big Eye was going to get his daughter back and I was going to have a front-row seat to the action.

Not that there would be any action.

"Big Eye, I'm not going to be in any danger, am I?"

"You? In danger? You sound like you're wishing for it!"

"Because if I see a gun, I'm going to bolt out that door, you understand?"

"This is what's going to happen, Jing-nan. Money's going to do the talking. After you send me the pictures, maybe Whistle will come in and sit with you. Someone will drive up with Mei-ling. Whistle will give the handler some cash and the three of you are gonna walk out of the Eastern Princess into my car." To meet a fuming Big Eye.

Well, at that point, maybe I would make my excuses and head home instead of getting in the car. I sure as hell did not want to be there when Mei-ling detailed her show to her dad, as I'm sure the disaffected young girl would. She would throw it in his face.

Maybe I never should've called Big Eye, but Mei-ling was definitely in more trouble than I alone could handle. The girl needed help. Why else would she have dropped off a hint in her message to me? No, contacting Big Eye was definitely the right thing to do, if not the least-volatile option.

My hands began to sweat. The actual "rescue" of Mei-ling would pale in comparison with the reunion with her dad. *Gan!* Big Eye was going to explode like a year-old dental abscess and his daughter would wield the drill with a heavy hand.

I'VE ONLY SEEN THE Eastern Princess hotel in passing from the street. It was a shape-shifting trapezoid frozen between forms, and I hadn't realized that the entrance was set so far from the sidewalk, maybe to discourage members of the Taiwan branch of Falun Gong from walking in and harassing the Chinese. Falun Gong, of course, was banned in China as a seditious group and a cult. Members gather at the base of Taipei 101 with posters of graphic displays of victims of torture by the Chinese state. Falun Gong followers dodge the cops and force their pamphlets into the pockets of Chinese tourists. They might as well be stuffing dynamite. If the tourists returned to China with Falun Gong material they were bound for big trouble.

I walked up the curved drive to the entrance with my eyes on the hotel's illuminated sign. You knew it was a fancy establishment because the sign didn't have any Chinese characters and "Eastern Princess" was correctly spelled and capitalized.

No matter how much I walked, the sign remained as far away as the moon. It took forever to get around the towering circular fountain, which looked like the spindle of a roulette wheel that divine beings would bet on. Eight fire lanterns on the perimeter lit up corresponding water spouts. After fifteen minutes of walking, I found myself underneath a canopy of fragrant coniferous trees. After a turn, the path seemed to backtrack on itself before changing from asphalt to stone bricks. Finally, I was nearing the entrance.

My heart sank. A doorman in a Buckingham Palace knock-off uniform stood at the revolving door, making sure that all visitors swiped their card keys to enter. You couldn't simply walk up to the Eastern Princess and rent a room. This wasn't a love hotel. Everything was prearranged, pre-booked, and pretentious. Why did we treat the Chinese people so good? Two generations ago, you would have been shot on this very ground for even being suspected of being sympathetic to Communists. Now we scrounged and spread our legs for their tips.

I stayed out of the light and ducked behind a tall shrub. I'd have to call Big Eye and tell him I couldn't pull this off. Sorry. I can't help you get Mei-ling back.

I looked at the phone in my hand. I couldn't bring myself to cry uncle to my uncle. I twisted my mouth and crossed my arms. Just like a lull at the night market, when I thought we were going to end in the red, people would show up. Something would come up here. Something had to.

A light went on, just to my left. Two lights, actually. Headlights.

A tour bus with blacked-out windows rolled up to the entrance. The doorman got ready by swiping his own card and holding open the handicapped entrance.

This was it! I could sneak in with the Chinese tourists. I just had to hope it wasn't a solid demographic that I couldn't blend into. Please don't be all pensioners or only women.

The first person who stepped off was an older woman. She was dressed in a pantsuit and stood her ground like an aunt of Peggy Lee. The woman barked at the doorman that she had a number of shopping bags that needed to be brought in. He nodded obsequiously and spoke into his handset. The reply was shards of static.

Slowly the Chinese disembarked. It must have been a long trip. Everybody stepped off stiffly and looked disheveled. That first woman was an outlier.

Luckily for me there was a broad representation of Chinese elites. Parents with teens. Toddlers asleep in the arms of grandparents. By the number of aboriginal necklaces the women were wearing, the group had probably returned from a shop-and-destroy trip to Hualien, which is full of tribal tourist traps. I say "destroy" because Chinese tourists are notorious for littering, petty vandalism, and raising the noise-pollution index. Communities tolerate them because of the money they rain down.

I feel the same way. Each Chinese customer at Unknown Pleasures who buys more than NT$1,000 in food gets to scratch her initials into the chairs.

I spied a small group of grungy young men rummaging through their shoulder bags and comparing trinkets. They could have been Taiwanese. Everything they wore was Uniqlo. As they made their way to the entrance I slipped in a pair of earbuds, kept my head down and trailed them. We all jumped back as bellhops leading three brass-pole luggage carts charged out the door. The Uniqlo brigade bitched about the interruption and the spell was broken. They spoke clinically proper Mandarin; they were probably young recruits of the Communist Party touring the island for the first time. The liberal use of "*taibazi*" tipped me off that they hadn't been impressed by what they'd seen so far on this trip. When the way was clear the line began to move again. The first young man in the group held up a card key but the doorman waved it away. No need to show it. His comrades and I followed him in.

They didn't notice that I had infiltrated their group and neither did the middle-aged couple behind me.

"Everything is so pricey here," said the woman. "I can't find any bargains. No wonder the travel company had a Mid-Autumn Festival special. Everything else is a rip-off."

"We could go to Hong Kong again," the man offered.

She scoffed at him. "I don't like Cantonese people," said the woman. "They only want to eat animal feet."

I lost track of their conversation as the cavernous lobby revealed itself. It was brightly lit and the air smelled so sugary it was probably full of carbs. The ceilings were at least thirty feet high and from them two dozen crystal chandeliers pointed down like the sparkled tips of wizard staffs. The lobby furniture resembled swollen hawthorn fruit, blazingly red and rounded. People shuffled over and collapsed into chairs and chaise lounges. Available space was going fast. I glanced around and slid into an ottoman near the front desk. I was blending in beautifully.

I could really use a piss break. I was on a mission, however. A rescue mission. Craning my neck to try to get within earshot of the front desk, I edged down the ottoman and my butt scraped something that had been left in the folds of the cushion. It was a key card. I pocketed it. Could come in handy.

I continued to survey the room to see if my presence had attracted attention. I spied two of the men I had snuck in with. They were lingering over a rack of tourist-attractions pamphlets with strategically incomplete maps. One of the guys unbuttoned his linen shirt, revealing a T-shirt with the tomb image of Joy Division's *Closer* album. I had just worn my *Closer* shirt the other day!

I couldn't help but stare. Was this more than a coincidence? It had to be! This man and I were connected!

Did this mean that underneath China's calloused and colorless skin there was a heart, a facility to feel pain, an appreciation of beauty, and the need to be in love right now this second?

I was almost breathless. This Chinese guy loved Joy Division and he even had a bootleg shirt to prove it!

Of course it was a bootleg shirt. The version that Joy Division and New Order bassist Peter Hook sold at his shows featured "Manchester" underneath the album cover. The other official design sold by the continuing version of New Order featured Joy Division's name and the album title. The Chinese guy's shirt was the exact album cover, as originally issued. No words. Just the picture. Exactly as it should be.

Another Chinese guy joined them. He was now wearing a Flipper T-shirt. That was a punk band from San Francisco that I could never get into. Flipper had two bassists and the songs just never ended.

The dudes left the lobby and waited out front for a cab. Now that they had done the family-friendly tour, it was time for their night out at a club. Good for them and back to work for me.

Two concierges were behind the front desk, a woman and a man, both of medium height. They were wearing similar black jackets and bowties. Each was handling a line of three people. The woman was in her late thirties and had the insular-yet-friendly look down pat. I'll bet she didn't take any shit. The man was in his mid-fifties and had the beaten-down body language of the coach of a last-place high-school volleyball team. He nodded a lot. There was a deep-seated sorrow in his pudgy face but his eyes were dead and, even from where I was sitting, terrifying.

They looked like gangsters. Could that woman have been the one who escorted Mei-ling to The Perch? Maybe she was the one who'd driven the motorcycle.

I shot two close-ups of both employees and sent them to Big Eye. The doorman was the only other employee currently in view. I shot his face from the side.

Big Eye texted back, WHO ELSE IS THERE?

I wrote back, THERE ARE AT LEAST THREE BELLHOPS BUT THEY ARE BUSY NOW.

SEND THEIR PICTURES. WHATEVER HAPPENS, DON'T LEAVE THE LOBBY. STAY THERE UNTIL I TELL YOU TO GO.

ALL RIGHT.

I pulled out my earbuds. I needed to be fully alert so I could hear them the second they came back down the elevators.

I became aware of a burbling sound behind and beneath me. A koi pond. The sound came from a larger-than-life statue of a vaguely divine-looking woman. Water was pouring out of a magical vase she cradled. Her face was serene and too young for her exaggerated height.

It was also oddly familiar.

She bore a striking resemblance to Mei-ling, especially in the nose and ears. I looked over the figure's flowing multilayered robe and felt a chill.

A bell sounded and an elevator opened. Two of the bellhops emerged, strutting jauntily. I took each of their pictures, although honestly up close they looked nearly identical. Rounded jaws, jutting ears, freckles and light brown eyes. Must be brothers. As they crossed the lobby to the front desk, one of them slapped the other's ass. The woman at the desk reacted immediately.

"Act professionally!" she spat. The two shimmied to the side and stood with their backs against the wall. Where was that third guy? Maybe he was helping someone unpack.

I sent the two pictures to Big Eye.

ONE MORE LEFT, I typed.

HURRY UP. REMEMBER, DON'T GO UP INTO THE HOTEL. STAY IN THE LOBBY.

OF COURSE.

The lobby was never completely empty nor was it ever really quiet. When the human activity level seemed in danger of tapering down to an off-peak MRT platform, another busload of tourists would arrive. As people poured in, I understood how I'd missed the splashing fountain in the koi pool earlier. A group of five Chinese, yelling as if testing the lobby for echoes, easily blocked the statue and masked the sound.

A bell cut through the din and another elevator opened.

"Oh, shit!" I thought. I dove into a high-backed couch, hoping I had been quick enough.

CHAPTER SIXTEEN

I OPENED MY HANDS wide, held them in front of my face and examined my palms as if I were holding the most interesting book in the world.

When I felt somebody drop next to me on the couch I knew my efforts were in vain.

"Jing-nan?" asked Peggy. "What in the world are you doing? And why are you here?"

No sense in trying to ignore her. I had to try to get her to understand the situation and leave, or at least leave me alone.

"Listen, Peggy, I'm here because I'm trying to find my cousin."

"Your cousin!" she said. "Mei-ling! She's here?" If I hadn't already known that Peggy was from a mainlander family, I would have guessed it from the explosive way she was now yelling, surrounded by her ancestral brethren.

"Peggy," I said through my teeth, "please keep it down."

"I thought you had to be a tourist from China to stay here."

"I'm not staying here," I said, regretting it immediately.

"You're not staying here!" Peggy yelled. Aw, screw it.

"Yes! I'm just waiting in the lobby!" I yelled back.

"How are you going to find Mei-ling by sitting in the lobby?"

I lowered my head into my elbows, maintaining eye contact with her. "I've heard that she works here," I whispered.

Peggy seemed to get it. "She works here?" she whispered. "It's impossible to get a job here. You have to go through so many screenings. Supposedly, you have to be in good with Black Sea because they control where the tourists visit and all."

Of course Peggy would be aware of the criminal organizations and their territories, especially as many of them operated legitimate businesses. I was anxious to change the subject, as nothing would attract more attention from gangsters than discussing gangs. I clasped my hands and said, "Tell me something, Peggy. What are you doing here?"

"I was a keynote speaker at 'Modern Chinese Culture' in the main conference room. I made a lot of business connections. Looks like my family is going to be reconnecting with our now-less-distant relatives back on the mainland." She dropped her voice even lower. "I'm going to have to conduct some due diligence, though. Chinese people cook the books like they're raw meat."

"Don't tell me you don't trust your own people, Peggy."

"They're your people, too, Jing-nan." Here we go again. The starkest difference between mainlander people like Peggy's family and long-established Taiwanese families like mine is that the former still generally feel a close kinship with China and the latter, not really.

"My people left China centuries ago," I said.

"There are still lots of Chens in China!"

"Lots of Chens in America, and a bunch of them don't speak a word of Chinese."

Peggy put her head back and gave a Wookiee cry of exasperation. "It's utterly useless talking to you. How about a drink? The bar's still open upstairs."

"I have to wait here, Peggy."

"For what?"

"Too much to explain right now. You go ahead, all right?"

She swung herself to her feet. "At some point in the future," she warned me, "you're going to tell me everything."

I held up a noncommittal hand and she high-fived it hard. "Ouch!" I said. "You just knocked a few years from my life line!"

"Thought you didn't believe in that sort of thing, Jing-nan!"

As she walked away, I spied the third bellhop. I swung up my phone, changing the focal point between shots. When I had about a dozen pictures I paged through them, trying to find the clearest shot. The last one was a little hard to make out because the bellhop was standing over me and his shadow was messing with the auto-brightness setting of my phone's display.

"Why the fuck are you taking my picture, asshole?" he asked.

The bellhop wasn't a small man but he was smaller than me. He certainly shouldn't be talking to me in that way.

I ignored him and sent the last two pictures to Big Eye.

"Hey, jerk! I'm talking to you!"

I crossed a leg and turned away. My phone buzzed once. GOOD, SIT TIGHT.

Now he stuck a finger under my chin.

"You're not a guest here, are you?"

I looked up and met his narrowed eyes. "Is it any of your business?" I asked. "If you must know, I'm waiting for somebody."

"Who?" The lobby was in a state of emptying again. I saw the two other bellhops, arms crossed and looking at us with interest.

"Look, man, it doesn't matter," I said. "I just happened to

take your picture by accident. I'm doing a blog entry about this hotel."

His eyes flickered. "You're not supposed to be here if you're not a guest. If I report you, they'll escort you out."

I sighed. "How much do you want?"

He considered for a second and then flashed two fingers like a baseball catcher. NT$200. Annoying but cheap enough. I handed him the bills. He went away with a big smile.

Uh oh. He walked over to the other two bellhops and pointed me out. They came at me like I was a birthday cake and the candles were just blown out.

"You guys want money, too, huh?" I asked them. They nodded eagerly. This was all going to be worth it, in the end, after we had Mei-ling.

While I was paying them off, the woman at the front desk cocked her head and stared at us. She tapped the man and they both looked at me hard. The woman came around the desk and sailed right for me. The two bellhops saw her and beat it in the opposite direction.

"Why are you tipping the bellhops?" she asked point-blank. Mandarin, when spoken properly, makes everything sound like a reprimand. "You only have to tip them for bringing your luggage up or down."

As soon as I spoke she would be able to tell that I wasn't Chinese. "I was asking them where the bar was."

Her face soured immediately. "Who are you?"

"I'm here for the 'Modern Chinese Culture' event."

"What's your name?"

"I'm the plus-one of Peggy Lee, the keynote speaker."

She inhaled sharply. "Oh, Ms. Lee. Yes, we're very honored to have the Lee family attend a function here."

I rose. "Could you please tell me exactly how to get to the bar? She's been expecting me for quite a while now."

"Eighth floor R," said the woman. "It's right across from where the elevator doors open."

"Thank you." I walked slowly to the elevator. I figured I had a minute or two before the woman checked up on the guest list. I didn't know where I was going but I sure as hell wasn't going to go to the bar. Peggy and her loose lips could blow my cover.

I hit the up button and kept my back to the front desk.

"Excuse me!" I heard the woman yell out from across the room. The light on the button went out and the bell sounded. "Sir! Excuse me!"

The door slid open and I dodged a couple exiting. I jumped into the car and headed for the controls on the far side. I selected 33, the top floor, and tapped the "close door" button until it worked. Before the doors closed, a man squeezed through and completely disrespected my personal space by grabbing my wrists. He was the guy from the front desk. We swayed in sync as the car rose.

This guy was stronger than Dwayne. I wondered how he was with a butcher's knife. He twisted his hands, trying to make his grip more painful, but I compensated by jutting out my elbows. I saw crude bird tattoos just inside the cuffs of his long sleeves. It was the sort of tattoo you gave yourself in prison as you whiled the days away before your release.

"You're with that student protest group, aren't you?" he growled.

"What protest group?"

"You thought you could disrupt the 'Modern Chinese Culture' meeting, huh? Idiot. We moved it to an earlier time!"

"I have no idea what you're talking about." Nancy says I look like I'm lying when I am being honest. My widened eyes and open mouth look exaggerated. When I tell her that I didn't eat the last package of Pocky, she smirks. I don't even like Pocky that much. But the stakes right now were higher than chocolate-covered pretzel sticks. It was about exploring my pain threshold.

The man didn't believe I was telling the truth, either. As he looked at me, I could see that to him I represented every non-tipping hotel guest. "You stupid college students. Why don't you get real jobs and pay taxes? Then you can tell me you don't care about trade with China."

Correcting this guy wasn't going to help the situation. Instead, I thought about what I would do as soon as the doors opened. I moved my wrists and arms slightly to test his grip for weak points.

The elevator slowed prematurely and stopped at the twenty-fifth floor. The doors opened. A middle-aged couple stared at us, two men in the elevator in a tight embrace. The man was about to get in but the woman pulled him back.

"Sinful!" she chided.

The front-desk clerk, aware that he was in uniform, said, "Everything is under control." He nodded a few times but disgust remained on their faces. The doors closed without us or them saying another word. As the car began to lift I formulated a plan.

At the thirty-third floor, the doors opened and I threw my weight at the clerk. People usually pull away to try to break holds. In my years of grappling with Dwayne I'd learned a thing or two. Sometimes the best thing to do is bring your opponent even closer. As long as they hold on to you, their arms are effectively pinned.

The clerk's eyes blew up like airbags as he stumbled backwards. In quick succession, I headbanged his nose and brought my right knee into his balls. He fell away and hit the floor, twitching and bleeding. For a second I admired my victory, then I leapt out of the elevator car. I stood square in the hallway, feet directly under my shoulders, just in case he recovered and counterattacked.

"Gan!" the man on the floor cried long and loud. The doors closed and headed back down. I wondered if it would stop on twenty-five again, giving the same couple their second shock of the night.

I looked down the hallway. Ceiling cameras in both directions. I bolted for the stairs. A sign warned that opening the door would sound an alarm. I took a chance and rammed the push bar. The door swung open without a sound. Thank you, hasty construction practices and irregular safety inspections.

I jogged down two flights to the next floor. I should get out of the hotel. As long as I was in the building I was visible and vulnerable. As soon as that clerk recovered, he'd come after me hard.

I continued going down, pacing myself. I didn't see any cameras in the stairwell. They'd start looking for me on the thirty-third floor. They were probably on their way right now.

I had to believe that I would find a way out that didn't go through the lobby. Thirtieth floor. Twenty-ninth. Twenty-eight.

My phone buzzed.

DID YOU LEAVE THE GODDAMNED LOBBY? Big Eye had texted. How the hell did I get reception here?

STILL AT HOTEL.

I CAN SEE THAT!

STAIRWELL.

THAT'S WHY SHE CAN'T FIND YOU. I TOLD YOU TO STAY IN THE LOBBY!

WHO CAN'T FIND ME?

NANCY. SHE CAN'T TEXT YOU.

WHY IS NANCY HERE?

I NEED HER THERE.

I stopped and leaned against a wall and felt the cool tile through my shirt. Not again. I didn't want to involve her in another dangerous situation. I was here to rescue my cousin and Nancy had nothing to do with it.

HOW COME SHE CAN'T TEXT ME?

ASK THE PHONE COMPANY.

My NANCY, GET OUT OF HERE! text wouldn't go through.

I tried to call Big Eye but he didn't pick up.

DON'T CALL ME, he messaged back. TALKING WITH SOMEONE HERE.

TELL NANCY TO LEAVE! NOW! I'm sure Big Eye wouldn't take kindly to my demand, but for a minute he didn't respond at all.

YOU STUPID FUCK, he finally wrote. KICKED A CLERK IN THE BALLS?

He didn't mention the bloody nose? I was kinda proud of that. HOW DO YOU KNOW?

FORGET IT. JUST GO TO ROOM 1232.

I came off the wall and began walking down the stairs. I was in a stairwell and had no idea what was going on. I had to trust my uncle. HOW DO YOU KNOW ABOUT THE CLERK?

WOOD DUCK.

YOU'RE IN TOUCH WITH WOOD DUCK?

RIGHT NEXT TO ME.

YOU GAVE HIM THE MONEY BACK.

YEAH.

I couldn't suppress a laugh. MEI-LING IS IN 1232?

NANCY IS ON HER WAY THERE NOW. YOU TWO, GET MEI-LING AND WALK OUT. YOU'RE SAFE.

Safe. That was a relief to hear. Well, screw the stairs. I left the stairwell, headed to the elevator and hit the down button. I listened to voices of Chinese people reverberating in the hallway. It must be nice to be on a vacation. I ought to try one at some point.

The elevator opened. I rode down with other young people ready for a taste of Taipei's nightlife.

I got out at the twelfth floor and figured out which way to go. The room was near the middle of the hallway, next to a humming electrical closet. I pounded on her door with the fat of my fist.

"It's Jing-nan!"

"Come in!" I heard Mei-ling say.

I opened the door. Mei-ling and Nancy were sitting stiffly on the side of the bed closest to the door. I was so relieved to see my cousin again that I unleashed my suppressed anger. "Mei-ling, what the fuck is wrong with you!" I yelled.

"Jing-nan, don't worry about it," she said.

Nancy gave me the sternest look ever. "Please don't yell, Jing-nan," she said. I was annoyed by the restraint in her voice. I can't scream at Mei-ling after everything I went through? Who the hell can I take it out on, then?

"Why are you guys sitting like that?" I asked. "Let's get out of here."

Nancy raised an eyebrow and tilted her head at the bathroom.

I met her eyes. "I do have to go, but it can wait until we hit the lobby. Let's go. Now."

"No one's going anywhere!" someone said from behind the bathroom door.

I forgot all about minor annoyances like having to use the toilet and fighting a man on the elevator, and began to worry about the personal safety of my cousin, my girlfriend, and myself as two skinny guys emerged from the bathroom.

One was the third bellhop, still in uniform. The other, who was doing the talking, was also in his mid-twenties, dressed in an Adidas tracksuit. He looked vaguely familiar—I struggled for a moment to place him. His hair was a giveaway.

Ramen Head! The fanboy who saw Mei-ling perform at the night market and then followed us to the post-show snack. He didn't look so innocent now. Not with that gun he was holding to the side of his leg.

"Wood Duck isn't getting Mei-ling back," said Ramen Head. "She came to me, man."

The bellhop smiled, walked to the door, and locked and chained it. "Just relax and stay quiet. We're working on a plan here."

Dammit! Why did that guy have to have a gun? Big Eye had better have some contingency plan. As the two men put their heads together and whispered, I took a step back and forced myself to look away from the gun. I tried to give Mei-ling and Nancy a reassuring look but I think I only scared them more.

Maybe I could find something I could work with. I looked around the room. There was Mei-ling's handbag in the corner next to a desk. I recognized some of her clothes—what she was wearing when she split on me—hanging on the chair and her shoes neatly placed near the door. So this was where she was staying the entire time. It wasn't too bad a setup. The room was spacious and had a nice view of street traffic. I saw a maid outfit with a short skirt hanging on the closet's lever doorknob.

"Is that one of the sex outfits, Mei-ling?" I accused. Nancy gave me a stern look.

"No," said Mei-ling. "I clean rooms during the day. Early afternoons."

"Nancy," I said, "did you know that Mei-ling's been doing nudie shows here at night?"

"Is that true, Mei-ling?" she asked.

Mei-ling shifted on the bed. "There is no actual genital sex," she offered. "And it's only with other women. Tell him, Jimmy."

Ramen Head had a name. Jimmy brushed the handle of the gun against his waist. “It’s a classy act,” he said, “because I’m a classy guy.”

“I remember you, Jimmy,” I said.

He smiled. “I remember you, too.” He didn’t like me enough to put the gun down, though. “Mei-ling had a good show at the Shilin Night Market.”

The bellhop snapped and pointed a finger at me. “I saw you on TV! Aren’t you the guy at the night market who blocked the bullet with a pot?”

“That’s me,” I said. They both nodded and made knowing sounds.

Jimmy tapped the flat side of his gun against his thigh. “You don’t have a pot now, Jing-nan,” he said. “Can’t stop a bullet this time!” The bellhop chortled with delight. “Benson,” Jimmy said to the bellhop, “this is Mei-ling’s cousin.”

“No shit,” said Benson. “She’s related to the hero of Shilin Night Market!”

Jimmy lifted the gun to waist level and took an uncertain step toward me. If he pulled the trigger, the bullet would go into the floor, two feet in front of me. “He ain’t no hero,” said Jimmy. “He’s a chump. You should see him kissing all that tourist ass for money.”

“What’s wrong with making money?” I asked.

“You make money on your knees. I’m building an entertainment empire. Adult entertainment. Playboy 2.0. I’ve got girls. Talented ones who aren’t just pretty.” Jimmy tilted his head at Mei-ling. “Her first album isn’t going to have Hello Kitty crap on the cover!”

I kept my eyes on the gun and kept the conversation going. “If you’re so successful, then why does Mei-ling have to work cleaning rooms?”

He rubbed his nose with his empty hand. “Mei-ling’s been

making major money doing the nudie shows. Soon, she'll be able to afford her own apartment."

I turned to Mei-ling. "Can you see what's happening? Before long, he's going to turn you out as a prostitute."

"Jimmy's a legitimate producer, not a pimp!" said Mei-ling.

I nodded slowly. "Jimmy, why don't you let us go? Mei-ling can come back and record for you any time you want."

His face twitched. "Fuck that!" I saw that Benson was becoming uncomfortable with the situation. He didn't know what Jimmy had planned any more than we did. Maybe there wasn't any plan at all.

"What are you going to do with that gun, Jimmy?" I asked, careful to enunciate clearly. "You don't want anybody to get hurt."

He swallowed. "You've already hurt me, Jing-nan."

"*I* hurt *you*?"

"At the night market. You ignored me, just the same way everybody's always ignored me. Except for Mei-ling. She respects me." He was getting choked up.

I didn't want to contradict him. The guy with the gun always wins an argument, anyway. "I'm sorry, Jimmy. I was preoccupied with so many things that night. I should have introduced myself to you." Nancy's face was neutral when our eyes met. I knew that at some point one of us would spring something and the other would have to read the situation fast. "Are you all right, Nancy?" I asked.

"Stop talking to her!" Jimmy ordered as he swung the gun up and pointed it at my forehead.

There was an insistent knock at the door. Benson and Jimmy looked at each other.

"Get it, Benson," said Jimmy. "I'll cover you."

Benson snuck up to the door. "Yes?" he asked.

"What's the hold-up with the girl?" The deep voice must belong to a big man with little patience. Benson threw off the chain and opened the door, revealing exactly that, a broad-shouldered brute in a suit.

Jimmy stomped in anger. "Why did you open the door, asshole?"

Before Benson could reply the big man swept into the room. "You!" he declared, pointing to Mei-ling. "Come with me."

Jimmy stood his ground and waved his gun in the air like a winning racing ticket. "She's staying with me. Got that, cocksucker?" I had to admire the balls on Jimmy. Even if I had a gun I wouldn't be saying that to a man who was a foot taller and twice my weight. The man backed up, his eyes on fire. "Get out of here!" The man touched his tie and left.

Jimmy walked to the door and kicked it shut. He pounded on the door with his free hand, yelling, "Fuck off, fuck off!"

I noticed the maid uniform slip off the closet's lever knob. The door was now slightly ajar. I glanced at Nancy and Mei-ling to see if they had caught the movement but they remained fixated on the gun.

When Jimmy's tantrum was over, Benson tried to talk sense into him. "Jimmy, what the fuck are you doing? That was one of Wood Duck's bodyguards!"

Jimmy worked his jaw side-to-side. "Getting cold feet, bitch?"

"Look, we were just going to ask for more money and let Mei-ling go. Wood Duck is going to kill us if we delay this any more. Don't be stupid, Jimmy."

"Don't call me 'stupid'!" Jimmy clocked him in the right temple with the butt of the gun and the bellhop crumpled. I inhaled deeply. If Jimmy were willing to beat down his pal, what would he do to us? "Still worried about that old Wood Dick?" he pointlessly asked Benson.

Jimmy swung the gun to my head. "Don't move!"

"I didn't."

"Keep your hands where I can see them!"

I held up my hands and tried not to look at the closet door. "Jimmy, when are you going to record Mei-ling's album? I have some ideas."

Mei-ling spoke up. "We need some more money first."

"We could just ask your dad," I said.

The bed springs creaked as she flinched. "Fuck him! I wouldn't take his money if I was starving in the streets."

Nancy put her hands on her knees. "I agree with Mei-ling. Big Eye is despicable and all his money is bloodstained."

"I'm not going home!" Mei-ling added.

"You don't have to leave, Mei-ling," said Jimmy. "You always have a place with me."

"I want to get my own place," she said.

Jimmy glanced at me. "Mei-ling, let's talk about that later."

"I'm looking forward to Mei-ling's album," I cheerily added. "I'll admit that I didn't like the music at first but seeing her perform won me over."

"She did a great show," Jimmy said. His enthusiasm was genuine.

A crackling sound came from a walkie-talkie concealed by Benson's prone figure, then a voice that sounded familiar. "Benson? This is Daddy. Are you still with Jimmy?"

Jimmy took a deep breath. "Oh, shit."

I looked over at Nancy. Her legs were still and her arms were crossed. In fact, she seemed more impatient than scared. Mei-ling was a tougher read. She didn't want to go back to Big Eye but it seemed that she was fed up with Jimmy as well.

"Benson! Benson!" the walkie-talkie squawked.

"What am I going to do about his fucking dad?" Jimmy asked.

"Jimmy," I said soothingly. "Mei-ling, Nancy, and I are leaving."

"Nobody's leaving!"

"Okay, how about this. Why don't you just leave? Run away somewhere. Something bad is going to happen."

"I have to think!" Jimmy started to pace when another knock came at the door.

"Benson!" a man called out. "Open the door!"

Jimmy sprinted to closed door. "Benson's not here!"

"I'm going to kill you, Jimmy!" Keys jingled outside the door.

Jimmy tiptoed until he stood near the closet so that he had all of us and the front door covered.

The door blew open and the male desk clerk stomped in—the one I had just kneed in the balls.

Jimmy pointed the gun with both arms extended, the deadly prow of a ship. "You're going to kill me, huh?" he taunted the desk clerk.

He gave Jimmy a withering look. Benson himself began to stir but his father didn't bother to look him over. Instead, he focused on me as if he were a man dying of thirst and my throat was the plastic tab on a bottle of water. He raised a fist and I noted that his bruised-blue nose contrasted sharply with his red eyes.

"Fuck your mother!" he yelled at me.

"Sorry," I said, "but you started it."

The desk clerk sighed with the weight of a man accustomed to suppressing his feelings in a bureaucratic criminal enterprise. "Let these people go, Jimmy. Don't delay things." Benson's dad shook his head. "I can't believe you brought a gun here. It shames all of us."

Jimmy took the gun in his right hand and let it drop to his side. He remained on the offensive, however. "Mr. Chang," said Jimmy, "I'm not willing to put in twenty years with Wood Duck so I can end up wearing a bowtie, like some fucking rabbit like you." "Rabbit" in this usage also meant "faggot." The two words don't sound similar in Taiwanese, but the slur connects the bent paws of upright rabbits with the perceived limp wrists of gay men.

Mr. Chang, newly incensed, brought up an accusing finger. "You're still the same kid who wet the bed when you stayed over at our house!"

Mei-ling laughed out loud.

"Shut up, you slut!" said Jimmy.

Her eyes hardened and her mouth slid into the smallest smile. That expression may seem innocuous, but when an Asian makes it, she is done with you. My arms twitched.

"You're an asshole, Jimmy," said Nancy.

"I've got a bullet for you, bitch," he said. "I've got enough bullets for all of you."

I never have alpha-male impulses but after Jimmy insulted both my cousin and my girlfriend, I wanted to pound his face in.

Benson made a funny sound, like when a cartoon character swallows a bite that's too big, and rolled on his side.

Mr. Chang muttered, "This whole thing is your fault, Benson. You told me to vouch for your stupid friend."

"Don't call me 'stupid,' you rabbit!" said Jimmy.

Fearless, Mr. Chang raised a hand and walked to Jimmy to deliver a room-service slap. There was the sound of a sledgehammer on a steel plate as Jimmy shot Mr. Chang through his opened palm.

Mr. Chang stumbled but managed to smear his hand across the left side of Jimmy's face before folding to his knees. Jimmy wiped his face and was entranced by the sight of blood on his hand. He took a few steps before the closet door flew open. Because he slouched slightly, it caught him right in the face. Jimmy knelt against a wall as the gun dropped to the floor.

Frankie stepped from the closet and put his right foot on the gun. Now that the door was opened, I saw a large hole. There was only sheetrock between the closets of adjacent rooms. Cheap but appropriate for a hotel that catered to Chinese.

"Everyone all right?" he asked. "Thought I heard something." He glanced at us and then surveyed Jimmy, Mr. Chang, and Benson. "Reminds me of a poker game I was at, years ago."

Jimmy leaned back and looked up at Frankie. "Who the hell are you?" he demanded.

"I'm the guy who did this," said Frankie. He took a drag on his cigarette and blew smoke at the ceiling fire alarm.

Nothing happened.

Frankie shook his head and spat, "That cheap piece of . . ."

A piercing sound tore through the room. It was so loud it seemed to originate from my head. It was disorienting and we were all cringing and covering our ears, but Jimmy completely freaked out, writhing on the floor and crying. The alarm revived Benson and he helped his father up.

Frankie put the gun in his waistband, hopped on to the nightstand and removed the battery from the smoke alarm, killing the sound.

Frankie playfully leapt down and picked up Jimmy by the arm.

"We have to get out of here," he said. "This room's now in violation of the fire code." Jimmy stood up and lifted his head. A veil of snot covered his face. "You know what, kid? You have a lot of nerve for someone with a really shitty case of nerves."

CHAPTER SEVENTEEN

WE ALL CRAMMED INTO a single elevator car and quietly contemplated the immediate future.

Keeping with good Taiwanese conduct, Nancy and I didn't hold hands although we stood next to each other. I leaned my arm against hers to let her know that I was here and that everything would be all right. She pushed back in a silent reply.

Benson held his bellhop hat around his father's wounded hand. Fortunately the fabric was already red. Mr. Chang had his good hand on the back of his head. Both father and son were reaping some pretty bad karma tonight. They weren't exactly paying it forward, either, by being in Wood Duck's gang.

Jimmy had a big dark stain over his heart from where he had wiped his face with his track jacket. His eyes were red and he couldn't stop shaking. I didn't care that he had threatened my life, but I was still mad for what he'd said about Mei-ling and Nancy.

Frankie stood in the corner, lips pursed in a silent whistle, hands at his sides but open and ready.

Mei-ling stared at the bright lights in the elevator ceiling. Her eyes saw nothing. Some people might blame Mei-ling for everything that had happened tonight. I didn't feel that way at all. All she had wanted to do was get away from her family, but that's simply not possible.

THE DOORS OPENED AT the lobby. Three broad-shouldered men, Wood Duck's bodyguards, launched themselves at us from the couches. They were dressed in suits, just like the one who had barged into the hotel room, who could have been any of the three. Two of them grabbed Jimmy and hustled him out of the hotel. The third put his hands on the shoulders of Benson's dad and the two of them walked to the back office behind the front desk. Was poor Mr. Chang about to get his third assault of the night? Benson stood by himself and raked his hair.

Frankie, Nancy, Mei-ling, and I stuck together near a grotesquely large and twisty money tree in a massive glazed pot. I finally felt comfortable enough to have a semi-private conversation with my girlfriend. "Nancy, what did Big Eye say to you?"

"He called me and said you were in trouble, Jing-nan. I left the student meeting and Gao and Whistle picked me up and brought me to the hotel. It's funny. The students were originally planning to march on the Eastern Princess to disrupt the Modern Chinese Culture gathering, but we got word that the timing was changed." She touched my hands. "I'm glad we're both all right. That was a little scary back there."

"We're not out of here yet. What sort of trouble did Big Eye say I was in?"

"He said that Wood Duck wanted a woman to escort Mei-ling out of the hotel."

"I'm sorry I left the lobby, but I'm glad I met you in the room."

"Me, too. Right, Mei-ling?"

"I don't feel like talking," she said, turning her back to us.

"What should we do, Frankie?" I asked. "Should we play it cool and walk out the door?"

"Let's wait," he said, slightly widening his stance. "See how this situation plays out. There's no reason to do anything unless we face a direct encounter."

"Is that Taoist?"

"Naw, it's physics."

"How did you know what was going on in the hotel room?"

"Big Eye brought us to back up you and Nancy. His guys aren't allowed on Wood Duck's turf."

"Us?"

Frankie pointed to a figure three chandeliers away from the elevators, hiding behind a newspaper. Those were Dwayne's hands!

That raised an immediate red flag. "Who's watching Unknown Pleasures?"

"The guys who loaned us Big Eye's car. Whistle and Gao. They're not bad on the grill."

"They can't just jump in there and cook! Captain Huang's going to bust them for not being licensed."

"Gao's a cop, and cops never rat each other out. Anyway, at this point, all they need to do is warm things up. Any idiot can do that."

I took offense to that remark but before I could voice it, Mr. Chang, newly released, presented himself to us. His bandaged hand resembled an albino lobster claw.

"Looks like everything's all right now," said the bodyguard who accompanied Mr. Chang. His face was a steep stone cliff. He turned to Benson. "Listen to your dad, kid. Stay out of the shit." The big man headed outside.

"Put on your fucking hat, Benson," Mr. Chang said. "Be a goddamned professional!" He rubbed the wrist of his bad hand and eyed his son murderously.

The son complied. Confucius would have beamed in approval at Benson's supplicating shuffle as his father led the way to the front desk.

A bullet in the hand and back to work? Talk about work ethic. There were tasks to attend to. A new busload of tourists was ready to check in. The lone desk clerk was confronted with a group of Chinese who clung to the counter as if climbing out of the sea.

Benson's dad took his place behind his desk and put his mandatory military training to use. "Pay attention!" he called out. "You must form two lines to check in! Anybody not in a line will be sent to the end!"

The two other bellhops were already loaded down with bags and struggling to the elevators. Benson silently grabbed hold of the brass poles of a perilously overloaded luggage cart and put his weight against it to get it going.

Dwayne folded up his newspaper and approached us. "Just got the all-clear," he said. "We can exit the hotel but Big Eye wants to see us before we leave for the night."

I made a necessary bathroom detour so I was the last one to exit the revolving door and watch my ghost slide off the glass into the night.

DWAYNE GRABBED ME BEHIND by the shoulders as we headed down the drive.

"Oh, man," I said. "Not here, not now."

"Relax, Jing-nan. I'm glad to see you're all right. Nancy and Mei-ling, too. I was waiting in case things got ugly for you."

"It worked out."

"That punk kid, Jimmy. I've made sausages bigger than him."

We came upon a tour bus. It looked like all the others that the Chinese people rode in but its windows were tinted. A bodyguard stood by the door. "This way," he called to us.

The two other big men came around from the far side of the bus. One had his hands free. The other was brandishing Jimmy like a baton that he was about to throw into the air. Jimmy was shoeless and stripped down to his boxers, which were soaking wet. Long red scratches ran across his chest.

His handler noticed my stare and said, "This dumbass tried to escape. He got caught at the top of a fence and then fell into the fucking pool."

"No, I didn't!" Jimmy whined. "He's lying!"

"Yeah, let's see who Wood Duck believes."

Shit. We were all going to see Wood Duck.

I was the only one in our group who had met the old gangster so I followed the bodyguard inside first.

The aisle ended after the fifth row with an ornate black lacquer door that was obviously repurposed from a temple. The man knocked on the door as I stared at the carvings in the wood. Fantastic things squirmed beneath the dark finish: dragons, demons, endless rivers, and mountains shrouded in mists.

I still hadn't relaxed since that fateful elevator ride with Mr. Chang. And waiting outside this haunting door wasn't exactly putting me at ease. Did Wood Duck install this temple door because he thought of himself as a god?

The bodyguard must have heard something in the way of an invitation because he opened the door and stepped through. Mei-ling squeezed past me to go in next. The rest of us followed.

The bus interior beyond the doorway was remodeled into an oddly roomy walnut-paneled living room. Big Eye and Wood Duck were sitting next to each other on matching carved wooden chairs. The arms were dragon heads wearing stunned expressions.

Wood Duck raised his hand but remained seated.

"Please, be my guests." He gestured to an array of plain wooden chairs. There were more than enough for us. Mei-ling again took the lead, sitting directly across from her father, who couldn't help but raise an eyebrow at her boldness.

"You heard Wood Duck," said Big Eye. "Everybody, hurry up and take a seat." We did, with a collective grunt.

Wood Duck held up an opened palm as if checking for rain. "You've been through a lot. Would any of you like some oolong tea? Or maybe black tea?"

"Got any coffee?" asked Dwayne.

That appeared to be a trigger word. Wood Duck narrowed his eyes. "No," he said icily, adding, "Perhaps you'd like hot water instead?"

"Naw, I'll do oolong," said Dwayne, coughing and crossing his legs. He couldn't get comfortable. None of us could. I kept both feet flat on the floor in case I had to jump up and block fists or knives going in either direction between my cousin and my uncle. They had a lot of shit to deal with, but that would have to come later. There were still non-family in the room.

The big man who had brought us came out of the back with a tray of eight cups of tea—half oolong, half black. I went with black tea and admired the strong red color. When black tea leaves yield a red beverage, it's a sign that the tea is pretty damned expensive. I'm sure the yellow oolong tea wasn't much cheaper. My cup felt heavy for its size and had been spun on a potter's wheel.

There were just enough cups for all of us, including the big man. His two buddies were still outside doing who knew what to Jimmy.

Not even Mei-ling had the nerve to begin drinking before Wood Duck gave a toast. Instinctively we all knew to hold our cups below the level of Wood Duck's as the old boss spoke.

"Here's to a happy family reunion just in time for the Mid-Autumn Festival," he said. "We've reached the present circumstances under duress but at the same time, I'm glad for this time we have together."

He brought his cup to his lips and drank. We all followed suit. The bodyguard put his cup down on a cabinet shelf. He walked to the back area and returned with a tray that bore a single mooncake cut into eight pieces.

"I would be a terrible host if I didn't share one of my shabby pastries with my guests," he said. "It's not very good but I hope you find it acceptable."

I looked over the exposed jade-colored filling. Lotus-seed paste. The real thing, not the cheap bean mash that's often substituted. I also took note of the glitter in the crust.

"Is that gold dust?" I asked Wood Duck. He smiled slightly, pleased that I had noticed, but also bowed his head in a vain attempt to remain humble.

"It's very low-quality gold. I think it's barely twenty-four karat."

"It's too expensive to eat!" Nancy blurted out.

"It's very pretty," said Mei-ling.

Dwayne stared at the mooncake slices. I could hear what he was thinking. Fucking Han Chinese wasting money on this crap. You stole our lands but you don't care about wasting gold as long as the money doesn't flow back to aborigines.

Frankie reached in and grabbed a slice. He weighed it in his palm and then popped it into his mouth. As he chewed, Frankie made a generally contented murmur.

"You," said Wood Duck, shaking a finger at Frankie, "where do I know you from?" Like he had so many times before, Frankie answered the question with a small tilt of his head. Before Wood Duck could ask another question, Big Eye picked up a mooncake slice.

"This looks incredible!" he boomed. "This is the most singular mooncake I've ever seen, Wood Duck!"

The old man grunted. "Well, it was a limited edition. It's not terribly special because there are eighty-seven others just like it."

We all dug in after that. Mooncake doesn't necessarily have the best reputation. Based on what I've read about American fruitcakes, many people approach mooncake with the same dread, that "necessary evil" that haunts the year-end holidays.

For us, guys like Big Eye and Wood Duck were the necessary evils of Taiwan. I watched them put their heads together and alternate talking and nodding. Murderers, I thought, feeling more bewilderment than the recent disgust that I'd been harboring against Big Eye. I had just had a familial toast with murderers.

"It's really something, isn't it?" Nancy asked me.

"The mooncake is the best I've ever tasted, but I've only had cheap ones all my life," I said.

"No, I meant being here with two bosses. There's so much power in this room, you can feel it."

"I didn't think you'd find it to be a turn-on."

"It's not sexual. It's sort of a little-kid fascination I'm feeling."

I looked at Big Eye and focused on the grey outcrops in his mountain-shadow-black hair. "It'll pass," I said to Nancy.

Big Eye and Wood Duck broke away from each other, and the latter made a hand signal. The bodyguard left and closed the walnut door behind him.

Big Eye turned to Mei-ling. "I'm glad you're safe now," he said, unable to flush out the venom from his voice.

"I wasn't in danger," she said. She wasn't making anything easier.

Big Eye smiled. "Maybe you weren't in danger, but it wasn't where you should be."

Nancy took charge before the situation devolved into a brawl. "Well," she said, turning to Wood Duck, "your hotel is very nice."

"It is a beautiful hotel," I said.

The old boss nodded at our compliments. "I worked hard at it."

A knock came at the door.

"Yeah!" yelled Wood Duck.

The door swung open and Jimmy tripped in, managing to remain upright. Still only wearing boxers. Still wet. There were more scratches on his body.

"This idiot tried to run away again," said one of his handlers. "This time he tried to jump into the fountain!"

"I didn't!" cried Jimmy. "He pushed my head underwater!"

"Which one did it to you, Jimmy?" asked Wood Duck. Jimmy shuffled. Water was pooling at his feet and he was probably fearful past embarrassment.

"I don't know," said Jimmy.

Wood Duck stomped his foot and leveled a wickedly crooked finger at the young man's throat. "You're a liar and a coward! How dare you try to run away from your crimes! You hold dissolute performances in my hotel and drag my name through the mud! Still you don't apologize! I only let you work here because Mr. Chang vouched for you. You've betrayed us both!"

Jimmy cupped his hands over his crotch. "But you said it was all right as long as there wasn't penetration . . ."

Wood Duck's teacup bounced off Jimmy's nose and crashed on the floor. His head reeled.

"How dare you use such coarse language in my office! In front of my guests!" thundered Wood Duck. "At least have the decency to apologize to Big Eye and his daughter!"

Jimmy put his hands together, bowed, and apologized profusely to both. When he finally raised his head, a stream of blood was flowing from his right nostril and dripping on the floor. Wood Duck stood up and rolled his eyes.

"Oh, for fuck's sake," he said in English. He opened a cabinet door, pulled out a peach-colored bath towel and threw it to the floor. Jimmy picked it up and began to wipe his face. "No!" said Wood Duck. "Don't waste it on your face! Clean up the floor. In fact, I want you out of here now, so crawl backwards and wipe up behind you. I don't want my guests to suffer the sight of your blood or slip on all the water you dripped!"

Jimmy sat down in a daze. He was exhausted and his face had taken on a look of incredulity. The day had gone to shit in little more than an hour. If he had only let Mei-ling go. He shook his head, got down on his hands and knees and began to wipe the floor. Wood Duck stood up and barked at him.

"I'm leaving now. So wipe up after me!" Wood Duck made sure to step on each of Jimmy's calves. The old boss opened the door and looked back. "Say, Big Eye, about that other thing. No rush, but it would be nice if you could make it happen sooner."

Big Eye straightened up but didn't stand. "I will. Thank you for everything, uncle."

"I've been a terrible host," Wood Duck muttered and left.

Jimmy inched backwards as he wiped the floor. It was mostly water, not too much blood. He took a disciplined approach to it, rolling the towel as a section became too wet to properly absorb. Jimmy probably was once an up-and-coming kid under Wood Duck's faction. How else would he have been allowed to operate added entertainment at the Eastern Princess?

There wasn't a doubt in my mind that Wood Duck had

in fact laid down the ground rules to Jimmy, including that there would be no penetration. But Jimmy was an idiot for contradicting his boss in front of other people and causing the latter to lose face.

Reputation was all gangsters had, really. If people began to associate Wood Duck directly with sexual performances, he might be seen as a common pimp instead of a purveyor of high-end tourism and leisure. A common pimp who should be locked up.

I looked at poor Jimmy. The sneer was gone and now he seemed a decade younger. I didn't feel too badly for him. This exercise in humility may not have made Jimmy a good person, but it would give him pause for thought the next time he thought of disobeying a direct order to simply hand a girl over. In fact, why the hell didn't he just do it? It couldn't have been just for money. . .

"Mei-ling," Jimmy whispered, his face to the floor. "Mei-ling. You're very special to me."

She stood up, took three small steps to him and kicked him twice in the head. "Fuck you!" she yelled. Dwayne grabbed her and pulled her into the chair that Wood Duck had vacated.

Jimmy shook it off and continued his task. Big Eye rubbed the cake crumbs from his hands into the air.

"Ordinarily," Big Eye said to the air above Jimmy, "I'd be against kicking a man when he's down, but you—you're not a man."

Jimmy, contrary to Wood Duck's orders, stood up, opened the door and left the room.

When the door was shut, Big Eye moaned, cracked his knuckles and opened his legs wide. "That was so painful! I had to speak in Mandarin with that bastard for hours. It was like being back in school."

There were still non-family members present, so it wasn't

yet time for Mei-ling and Big Eye to have it out, but Mei-ling was in the mood to fight now. Big Eye had already let down most of his guard. “How would you know what it was like being in school, Big Eye? You hardly went!”

“I went enough to know that *you* should be in school! Do you think my kind of life is fair to women, now that you’ve lived it a little bit? Do you?”

Mei-ling sniffed. “It was really awful.” Big Eye closed a hand on her shoulder. “He said that he could help my singing career!”

Big Eye cleared his throat. “Could you all leave and give us some privacy for a few minutes? Everybody except for Jing-nan.”

Aw, shit.

Nancy and I shared a smile as she left. Dwayne and Frankie followed. Soon the temple door was closed again.

“Jing-nan, I don’t mean to keep you apart from Nancy,” said Big Eye. “She’s not family. Not yet, anyway.” He let that hang for a few seconds before turning to his daughter. “Your cousin is going to get married some day. Will you, Mei-ling? Considering everything that’s happened, when you’re a wife to a good man, I’ll be very happy for you.”

She slouched in her seat and stiffened her legs, unconsciously assuming the exact same pose as her father. “Isn’t it a little early for me to be thinking about marriage?”

“What I’m asking is, are you going to be eligible for marriage?”

“Why wouldn’t I be?”

He smacked his right fist into his open palm. Both Mei-ling and I jumped. “I think you like girls!” he accused.

Mei-ling curled up in her chair in a casual position that would still allow her to deliver a kick. “What’s wrong with liking girls? You sure do.”

He leaned toward her, both fists raised. "Do you want to . . . marry a girl?"

She shrugged. "I said it was too early to talk about marriage, but after I find the right girl, I will marry her."

Big Eye clenched his teeth and punched his armrests. He screamed and rubbed his face hard like a scratch-off lottery ticket. When he dropped his hands, his eyes were more red and raw than his face but there was calm.

"It's my fault," he said vacantly. "I didn't keep our family together. You didn't grow up seeing real, natural love between a man and a woman. That's why you're so sick."

Mei-ling lifted her chin. "I'm not sick, Big Eye! This is who I am."

Big Eye was beyond comforting. "I should have gotten you dolls of both sexes. You only had Barbies."

"None of that mattered!"

"Then what's the problem? Tell Daddy!"

Daddy. Big Eye never sounded more pained.

Mei-ling shook her hands at Big Eye's face. "There is no problem! Being gay is a part of human nature and so is being loved."

Big Eye snorted. "It's useless to talk about it," he said to his hands. "I'll ask the city god what to do."

"Yeah, that'll help," said Mei-ling. "Hey, if I asked you to stop being a fucking asshole, you wouldn't be able to change because you're intrinsically a fucking asshole!"

Big Eye nodded, not hearing what she was saying. "I'm not going to let you upset me anymore," he said. "You're young, not set in your ways yet. The important thing for now is that you're safe." He took a final sip of tea and swished before swallowing.

Mei-ling looked at me. "Jing-nan," she said, "I didn't think you would tell on me. When I saw Mr. Li at the show,

I thought it might get back to you that I was doing all right. Why did you tell Big Eye? You said I could trust you!" I knew she wouldn't gel with Big Eye again but she was slipping away from me, too.

I straightened up and looked into her face. "Mei-ling, you were in trouble. Jimmy was exploiting you! What if you ended up dead?"

Her eyes were brimming with tears. "I'm better off being dead! I hate you, Jing-nan!" she growled. "I'll never forgive you!" My cousin leapt to her feet and stomped out of the bus.

"He's your family and he cares about you," Big Eye mumbled after her. He turned to me and said, "You see what I have to deal with?"

I felt slightly numb. "No one's ever said they hated me before."

Big Eye laughed. "Lots of people have said it to me and I've heard it from her plenty of times. Just wait until you and Nancy have kids."

"Hey, Big Eye, about Nancy . . ."

"What, are you upset? C'mon, I'm just giving you shit. Hey, next week, you two come down to Taichung and have a barbecue with us for the holiday. Hell, bring Frankie and Dwayne, too. Mei-ling will be better by then, I promise. I'll find something to make her happy."

"Wait!" I shouted. "Tell me why you brought Nancy to the hotel!"

He flicked imaginary dust from his knees. "Wood Duck thought it would be a good idea. Jimmy was acting like a dick about giving up Mei-ling. If you walked into that room alone, he might've reacted badly. Why couldn't you simply have waited in the lobby until Nancy got there?"

"One of the bellhops was going to bust me for not being a guest!"

Big Eye laughed out loud. "A bellhop! You tell him to fuck off and he'd be too scared to do anything."

"So you and Wood Duck were planning things together this whole time. You gave me that bullshit assignment to take pictures of people."

He leaned over to me, earnest as a guidance counselor, and said, "Have you ever thought about pursuing photography? You have some ability."

I caught myself dismissing his words with a swipe of my right hand in the air. That was a gesture I'd picked up from Big Eye. I slid down in my chair. Now my uncle and I were slouching the same way. It was the only way to stay comfortable in these chairs.

"Are you still sore about Nancy being here?" asked Big Eye. "Come on! Everything turned out fine. I mean, who the hell could have guessed that that jerk would have a gun? Huh?"

"You lied to Nancy! You told her I was in trouble!"

Big Eye tapped his forehead. "Think about it, Jing-nan. That turned out to be the truth, didn't it?"

"We could have been killed! Nancy, me, and your daughter!"

He leaned into me, grabbed the inside thigh of my right leg and squeezed hard. "Nobody gets to hurt my family, Jing-nan. Nobody."

I noted the lack of compassion in his eyes and recognized my own mute face in them.

THE DAILY PINEAPPLE

SEPTEMBER 25 **Special to *The Daily Pineapple***

TAICHUNG CITY—Police have discovered the body of a young man in a ravine just outside the city.

Tung Yang-kang, 27, had been riding a stunt cycle on the little-used Wangxing Bridge when he apparently took a tumble below. Foul play has been ruled out.

"We get a lot of these kids who do tricks in dangerous places and upload videos so they can show off online," said Gao Ming-kung, Under Chief Superintendent, Taichung Police Department. Nearly every one of Tung's bones was broken in the fall. His phone, set up to record his tricks, was recovered on the bridge, but a heavy rain two days ago has rendered the device useless, and so his final dare—one that he risked his life for and lost—will go unseen.

Tung, who was also known as "Jimmy," had been working as a bellhop trainee at the Eastern Princess hotel in Taipei. It isn't clear why he had come down to Taichung although Gao noted that the deceased may have been trying to record stunts all over the island.

A man answering the phone at the Eastern Princess, an upscale business that caters to Chinese tourists, declined to provide his name but confirmed that Tung was on vacation leave.

Tung's private medical records obtained by *The Daily Pineapple* show the young man was taking medication for a "chronic nervous condition." It wasn't possible to contact his estranged parents for more details.

While recovering Tung's body, searchers stumbled upon an older set of remains that have not yet been identified. Gao noted the bridge was also a common site for suicides because of its desolate location. The Wangxing is a former railway bridge converted into a bike path but it hasn't been well-maintained since the longer Dongfeng Green Bike Corridor and connecting Houfeng Bike Path were built on the remnants of a more scenic rail line.

"Considering all that has happened recently," Gao added, "I hope the city council can expand the budget a bit and build a fence along the Wangxing Bridge to prevent people from falling over, whether they want to or not. It's really unfortunate and senseless that we've had to lose lives this way."

Calls for comment from Taichung's city council went unreturned. ■

ACKNOWLEDGMENTS

This book would not have been possible without the love and support of my incredible wife, Cindy Cheung. Major interference in a good way was caused by mischievous wunderkind Walter Lin.

Thank you to my parents and in-laws for your stories and other recollections about life in Taiwan.

Kenbo Liao keeps the spirit of Formosan pirates alive.

The Yilan crew's game is strong: Will Yang and Zheng Zhu-fu are awesome.

Liang Yiping and the faculty and students of National Taiwan Normal University were gracious enough to invite me in. Thank you.

A fistful of smoking joss sticks for the amazing agent Kirby Kim.

Juliet Grames is the best case yet for proving that editors are indeed divine. The rest of the pantheon at Soho reign as well: Bronwen Hruska, Paul Oliver, Meredith Barnes, Rudy Martinez, Amara Hoshijo, Rachel Kowal.

Epigraph from *Zhuangzi: Basic Writings*, translated by Burton Watson, published by Columbia University Press.